Duchess in Waiting

Of Noble Birth, Volume 1

Rebecca Lange

Published by Rebecca Lange Books, 2023.

Table of Contents

For all you ladies who think Colin Firth is the one and only Mr. Darcy

...and for those who rather be wrong

This is a work of fiction. Similarities to real people, places, or events are entirely coincidental.

DUCHESS IN WAITING

First edition, 2023.

Second edition. March, 2026

ISBN: 978-1-957089-32-4

Written by Rebecca Lange.

1
A Wild Spirit Unbound

"Make haste, Ellie. You are dreadfully slow today," Richard called over his shoulder, urging his horse forward with a laugh. The stallion's hooves struck the forest floor in a lively rhythm, scattering dry leaves and sending small woodland creatures darting for cover. The crisp air rushed past his face as the trees blurred on either side of the narrow lane. After a moment, he glanced back over his shoulder, expecting to see Ellie racing to close the distance between them. Instead, the winding path behind him lay empty. Richard slowed his horse, frowning slightly as he scanned the trail.

"Have you given up already?" he called, his teasing tone carrying easily through the quiet woods. A triumphant reply drifted toward him, though not from behind.

"I most certainly have not. How insulting of you even to suggest it."

Richard reined in sharply and turned toward the sound, his brows lifting in surprise. His gaze swept the clearing until it landed upon the wide branches of their favorite old oak. There, perched upon the lowest limb, sat Ellie. Her legs swung idly as though she had not a care in the world. For a moment, he could only stare.

With her chin tilted high, golden curls tumbling rebelliously from their loosened pins, and the faintest pout curving her lips, she looked every inch the picture of mischief and unrestrained beauty. Sunlight filtered through the leaves above, catching in the warm strands of her hair and setting them aglow like spun gold.

She met his astonished gaze with an impatient, knowing look, as though she had been waiting quite some time for him to notice her clever escape. Richard's grin spread slowly across his face.

How entirely typical of Ellie to outwit him yet again. Her cheeks were flushed from their swift ride, lending her an air of vibrant vitality no carefully composed lady of the ton could ever hope to imitate. While society prized pale delicacy and demure restraint, Ellie seemed made of something altogether different, sunlight, laughter, and daring. And Richard suspected the entire forest knew it.

Ellie watched as Richard slowed his horse to a halt and swung down with practiced ease. Dust clung to the hem of his riding coat, though the sparkle in his brown eyes made it plain he scarcely noticed. Tilting his head up toward her, amusement tugged at the corner of his mouth.

"And how, pray tell, have you managed to outmaneuver me again? I could have sworn I had left you far behind."

"That was your mistake, Lord Blackwood," she declared with smug delight. "You should never underestimate your oldest and dearest friend."

Her grin was infectious, and Richard felt the corners of his lips twitch despite himself.

"Indeed, I should not. You are by far the most accomplished young lady and deserving of every victory." He punctuated the compliment with a conspiratorial wink, which sent Ellie's cheeks into a betraying flush. She managed a retort, though her voice softened slightly.

"Accomplished in riding, hunting, and climbing trees, perhaps, but hardly in the duties my mother insists upon. My sisters are so much more graceful with their needlework, and far more skilled at the pianoforte. Mama despairs of me constantly, declaring that God must have blundered when He made me a girl. I ought, she says, to have been a boy."

Richard's expression softened, though the glimmer of humor never quite left his eyes.

"Your mother still rebukes your wild spirit, then?"

"Oh, worse than ever," Ellie sighed dramatically, brushing an unruly curl from her face. "She threatens me daily with more lessons, and even whispers of hiring yet another governess to tame me before my debut. Mama is determined to fashion me into a lady, no matter how hopeless I protest myself to be. I begged her to wait just one more year, until I am nine and ten, but she refuses, insisting it must be this year. I managed to delay it until late spring or early summer, but that is all the ground I could gain."

Richard leaned lightly against the tree, studying her with quiet attention as she continued.

"And mind you, Emilia is no happier about it. She insists I am selfish to delay, since Papa holds firm that I must be presented before her. She would have gladly made her debut earlier this year, but because I stood my ground, she is forced to wait as well. She has not forgiven me and is equally vexed with Papa for siding with me." Ellie's lips curved into a cheeky smile as she finished, her eyes flicking upward to meet Richard's warm gaze.

The sight of his strong jaw, the familiar kindness in his face, and the unguarded intensity of his brown eyes sent an unbidden shiver through her. She glanced away quickly, though not before her heart betrayed her with a sudden, unsteady flutter.

Richard was three years her senior, yet from Ellie's earliest memory he had always been part of her world. As children, they had been inseparable, partners in mischief, conspirators in games, and companions in every stolen hour of freedom. From dawn until dusk, they roamed the woods surrounding their homes, climbed trees that no proper young lady ought to scale, and invented endless adventures that seemed, to their young minds, as grand as any tale of knights and explorers.

Those carefree days had lasted until the inevitable moment when duty carried him away, first to Eton, and later to Cambridge.

Ellie had missed him fiercely. Letters arrived now and again, always witty and warm, filled with his easy humor and affectionate teasing. Yet ink on paper proved a poor substitute for the sound of his laughter or the steady comfort of his presence beside her. Holidays brought him home, of course, and those visits were treasures she hoarded in memory. But the weeks slipped away far too quickly, leaving her once more to watch the carriage disappear down the road while she counted the long months until his next return.

When his studies finally concluded, fate returned him to Darlington sooner than anyone had expected. His father's sudden passing left Richard heir to the title and the considerable responsibilities of a baron. The transformation from carefree student to Lord Blackwood had come swiftly and without warning. Though still young, he carried the burden with quiet determination. He was fortunate in one respect. His widowed mother possessed a sharp mind for estate matters, and the steward had served the Blackwood family faithfully for decades. Between them, much of the day-to-day management of the lands was well attended, sparing Richard from bearing every weight alone.

Still, expectations pressed upon him from every side. His mother, resolute in her sense of propriety and duty, had begun urging him to divide his time between his obligations in the House of Lords and appearances in London during the Season. There, among glittering ballrooms and watchful society matrons, he was expected to do what every eligible nobleman must eventually do, seek a wife suitable to his rank.

The very notion made Ellie's stomach twist with a strange and unspoken dread. Outwardly, she behaved exactly as she always had. She laughed, teased him about the parade of hopeful young ladies who would surely chase after the handsome young baron, and offered her cheerful congratulations whenever the subject arose. But in the quiet recesses of her heart, a far more fragile truth lingered. One day, he would indeed choose another.

The thought settled heavily within her chest, though she never allowed it to show. Her secret longing remained hers alone, guarded carefully behind bright smiles and playful words, locked safely away where no one, least of all Richard, might ever see.

Richard's smirk deepened when he caught the devilish curve of Ellie's lips. He knew that expression far too well. It was the very grin that had preceded every prank, every reckless adventure, and every scandalous escapade of their youth. How many times had that look been the beginning of trouble? Far too many to count.

His thoughts drifted, unbidden, to the Huntington sisters. Danielle—Ellie—was as different from her younger sister Emilia as night was from day. Emilia was everything society praised in a young lady. Proper. Composed. Meticulous in both manners and accomplishments. She moved through life with a quiet determination to be flawless, her posture perfect, her needlework delicate, her pianoforte playing faultless enough to draw approving murmurs from every matron who listened.

Ellie, by contrast, possessed little patience for such careful polish. Where Emilia sought perfection, Ellie sought freedom. Where Emilia followed rules, Ellie seemed almost compelled to test them. It had been that way for as long as Richard could remember. Emilia scolded her elder sister endlessly, as though Ellie's wild spirit was a disgrace to be corrected rather than something bright and wondrous that refused to dim. Richard had lost count of the number of times he had overheard Emilia lecturing her about proper conduct, suitable company, or the countless small expectations placed upon a young lady of their standing.

And yet, he realized with quiet amusement, very little had changed. Emilia's voice remained a constant note of reprimand in Ellie's life. But Ellie herself remained exactly as she had always been, untamed and irrepressible. Radiant. Unbowed. Entirely unwilling to bend herself into society's rigid mold simply to please those who demanded it. No drawing-room etiquette, no carefully rehearsed accomplishments, and certainly no husband's rule could ever truly cage her.

Richard suspected that any man foolish enough to attempt such a thing would quickly discover just how impossible the task would be. And yet... that very spirit, he realized, was what made her so utterly, and perilously, captivating.

Their gazes caught and lingered longer than either had intended. For a moment, neither spoke. The air between them seemed to hum with a strange, quiet energy, and Ellie felt warmth creep higher into her cheeks. To shake off the sudden awareness pressing upon her, she flashed him a cheeky smile.

"Let's see who can reach the treetop first," she challenged, her voice bright with daring. Richard chuckled, the sound warm and rich in the quiet of the woods.

"You know very well you are not supposed to climb trees anymore," he reminded her mildly. "I was there the last time your mother scolded you for it."

"Mama isn't here now, is she?" Ellie's eyes sparkled with mischief, the very sort that had always spelled trouble and delight in equal measure. Before Richard could argue further, she had already grasped the nearest branch and pulled herself upward.

With a resigned laugh, he stepped forward and grasped the trunk, beginning his ascent. But Ellie, nimble and determined, was already several branches above him. She climbed with the same fearless ease she had possessed as a child, moving with quick confidence that made the task appear effortless. Her skirts caught now and again upon the bark, and loose curls tumbled freely about her shoulders, but she seemed utterly unconcerned with such inconveniences. Decorous behavior had never been her chief concern.

Richard followed more cautiously, though with long limbs and steady strength he gained ground quickly. By the time he reached the upper branches, however, Ellie had already claimed the highest perch. She turned toward him with a triumphant smile. Her face flushed with victory and exhilaration. Sunlight filtered through the leaves above them, dappling her cheeks and catching in the golden strands of her hair. The sight struck him with such sudden force that his heart gave an involuntary jolt.

"Your climbing skills have not diminished one bit," he said, a note of genuine admiration threading through his voice.

"Or, in Mama's words," Ellie replied with a dramatic roll of her eyes, tugging at the edge of a torn sleeve, "I climb as well as any boy." She examined the rip with exaggerated dismay. "Another hole in my dress. I can only hope I can hide it from her or bribe my maid into silence." She sighed theatrically, though the laughter dancing in her eyes betrayed the performance entirely.

Richard merely watched her, thoroughly enchanted. Ellie leaned forward slightly, resting her hand against the branch as she gazed out over the countryside stretching beyond the trees. From their lofty perch, the view unfolded in gentle splendor, rolling green fields, sunlit woods, and the quiet beauty of Darlington's open land basking beneath the afternoon light. She breathed in deeply, savoring the freedom of the moment.

Yet Ellie remained blissfully unaware that the only sight capable of stealing Richard's breath away was not the countryside spread before them, but the radiant, untamed young woman seated beside him, defying every rule she had ever been expected to obey.

Ellie was so absorbed in the landscape unfolding before them, the patchwork of meadows gilded by the afternoon sun, the gentle hush of leaves stirred by the breeze, the distant call of a thrush, that she never noticed the longing glance Richard cast in her direction. His gaze lingered on the delicate curve of her profile, the way the light caught in her loosened curls, and the unconsciously contented smile resting upon her lips. For a moment he allowed himself the indulgence of simply watching her, committing the sight to memory as though it were something rare and fleeting.

A sudden flicker of movement across the field drew Ellie's attention. A stag burst from the copes of trees at the far edge of the meadow, followed closely by two young fawns bounding lightly behind him. She parted her lips, about to point them out, but before she could speak Richard cleared his throat.

"You could never be a boy, Ellie," he said quietly, his voice lower than before. "You are far too pretty for that."

The words lingered in the air between them, carrying a weight far greater than his usual teasing. Ellie felt them strike with unsettling force. Her eyes snapped back to his, and the intensity of his gaze sent a rush of heat flooding her cheeks. She shook her head quickly, trying to brush the moment aside with practiced defiance.

"You mustn't flatter me, Richard. I know I am not that pretty. Baroness Appleton makes certain to remind me of it every time she calls upon Mama. Her daughter, Felicity, is praised by all. She is prettier, more graceful, and quite the favorite among the older ladies of the ton. Many young men admire her."

"Is that so?" Richard asked, not looking away. There was skepticism in his tone, and a faint edge of irritation he made little effort to conceal. "If she is so universally admired, I cannot help but wonder why she is not yet married. Is she not two years your senior?"

Ellie gave a sharp little nod, annoyance flaring at once.

"Indeed, she is, and every inch her mother's daughter. Goodness, the two of them together could weary the patience of a saint." She exhaled in exasperation, barely suppressing an eye roll.

"I was the first victim of her visit upon their return from London this week. It is most unfortunate they chose to come home during the Spring Recess instead of remaining there. I tried to slip out the back door before they saw me, but I was too slow. Mama welcomed them with open arms and has praised Felicity without ceasing ever since, particularly whenever she wishes to remind me of my own deficiencies. It is maddening."

Richard's mouth quirked faintly. "And let me guess," he said dryly, "Miss Appleton recounted every glittering detail of the Season."

Ellie groaned. "Indeed she did. She boasted of every gentleman she danced with, how many admired her, and the endless proposals she claims to have received. Though, between us, I doubt the truth of half her tales. Still, she prattled on and on about the gentlemen she refused, for apparently her mother disapproved of them all."

Richard arched a brow. His voice laced with dry amusement.

"Her mother disapproved? Lady Appleton is but a baroness. Pray, how many suitors could she possibly find beneath her notice?"

"According to the baroness, very many indeed," Ellie replied tartly. "She even told Mama that Felicity is pretty enough to catch the eye of a marquess, or better still, the Duke of Wales himself. Imagine it! They have my poor mother quite envious, sighing over the gowns Felicity will wear for the remainder of the Season."

Richard shook his head slowly, his expression softening as his gaze returned to Ellie.

"Believe me, Ellie, Felicity Appleton is nothing compared to you. I have spoken with many gentlemen, and I have yet to hear one speak fondly of her. Some of the rakes perhaps gave her their attention, but such interest is shallow and fleeting, and more often than not, it ends in scandal. You, however..." His voice trailed off, though the meaning in his eyes was plain. "How did your sisters bear her endless tales?"

Ellie smirked. "Emilia was enchanted and praised her extravagantly. Felicity, in turn, fawned over my sister, and both she and the baroness left exceedingly pleased with themselves after staying far too long. I, on the other hand, was so desperately bored that I very nearly excused myself to the kitchen to fetch castor oil for their tea. But I decided against it, lest the servants be blamed, or worse, Mama suffer the consequences."

Richard laughed outright. "You let them leave without an antic? Forgive me, but I can scarcely believe that of you."

A wicked smile curved Ellie's lips. "Oh, I ought to have resisted temptation, but alas, I could not. When I could bear no more, I slipped into the garden, unearthed two fat worms, and tucked them neatly inside their lace parasols."

Richard's jaw dropped. "Ellie, no, you did not."

Her sheepish glance was all the confirmation he needed. His laughter rang through the trees.

"I heard their squeals before they even left the house," Ellie confessed, giggling herself. "But that was not all. Since I knew the baroness would not leave without criticizing my dress, I prepared myself. I dropped a spool of thread into my pocket and tied it to my sleeve. Sure enough, she spotted it and scolded me for being careless, insisting I would never become a proper lady. She tugged and tugged at the thread, expecting my sleeve to unravel before her very eyes. But of course, nothing happened. When I revealed the spool at last, her expression was priceless. Papa had just come home. He laughed so heartily he nearly choked, though Mama was rather less amused."

Richard could not take his eyes off her. The animation on her face, the sparkle in her eyes, the warmth with which she spoke of her father, all of it fascinated him. It struck him, not for the first time, that Ellie's admiration for her papa was the measure by which she would one day weigh her future husband.

"And did your mother make you apologize afterward?" he asked carefully. Ellie's expression hardened at once, her blue eyes flashing.

"She did. She even accompanied me to ensure I complied. The baroness, naturally, refused my request for a private word and demanded I apologize before her guests. Felicity stood smirking in the background the entire time, and I nearly lost my composure altogether." Her voice sharpened as she continued.

"The baroness scolded me mercilessly after my apology. She declared I would never make a good match, that her precious daughter would outshine me in every way. And then—" Ellie broke off, her face darkening. "...she said I was just like my father. Arrogant. Hard-headed. Destined to end as he did: disliked and forgotten. That was the moment Mama lost her temper."

Richard's brows shot upward. "Your mother told her off?"

Ellie's lips curved in sudden mischief, though her eyes gleamed with fierce pride.

"Oh, she did. Mama reminded the baroness of her humble birth and declared she had no right to belittle either Papa or me. And before the woman could even draw breath, Mama pointed out that I am the granddaughter of a duke, while Felicity should consider herself fortunate to catch the eye of a mere baronet. The baroness's face turned crimson, and Mama swept me out of the room before she could utter a word in reply."

Richard laughed, shaking his head. "Well said Lady Huntington. I imagine the baroness was left fuming."

"She was," Ellie said with relish. "And since then, she has vowed to see our family shunned unless we publicly beg forgiveness. Mama, of course, replied that no further apology would ever come from our house. If an apology is due, it must come from the baroness herself."

Richard studied her, waiting for her to continue. When she fell silent, her eyes drifting thoughtfully toward the forest floor, he caught the unmistakable glint of mischief returning.

"What did you do, Ellie?" he asked, narrowing his eyes in mock suspicion. She gasped, feigning innocence.

"Me? Why do you always assume I have done something?"

"Because I know you." His deep voice carried both humor and certainty. "You cannot keep a secret from me, not when your eyes betray you so easily."

Ellie's lips curved into a sly smile. "Well... I might have sent them chocolates. Anonymously, of course."

Richard straightened, anticipation gleaming in his eyes. "And?" He knew her too well. When Ellie set out to make a point, she did so with flair. Lady Danielle Huntington was not merely lovely, she was clever, daring, and entirely unpredictable. He leaned a little closer, his voice low with amused expectation.

"Ellie?"

2

Confessions in the Clearing

Danielle looked up, and his brown eyes caught her like a net. For a heartbeat, she could not breathe. There was a new depth in his gaze, serious, intent, with a flicker of worry, that made her falter. *Had Cambridge and London changed him so much?* Would he now disapprove of the mischief they had once delighted in together?

Richard had never been a stranger to pranks in their younger days. On the contrary, he had joined her in countless schemes, never cruel, always clever, and more often than not devised to humble the proud or deliver a lesson neatly wrapped in humor. Together they had turned dull afternoons into adventures and transformed small injustices into triumphs of wit. Yet this felt different. This time she had not acted merely out of playful mischief. There had been laughter, yes, but beneath it lay something sharper. This had been retaliation. A deliberate punishment for the arrogance and cruelty of Baroness Appleton and her daughter.

For the first time since the chocolates had been delivered, a sliver of doubt crept into Danielle's chest. Had she gone too far? The thought unsettled her more than she wished to admit. Richard's opinion had always mattered to her, far more than she would ever confess aloud. His approval had been as steady a presence in her life as the sun rising each morning, something she had come to rely upon without question. Now, with his gaze fixed so intently upon her, she felt suddenly uncertain.

Her fingers tightened slightly around the branch beside her, and she lifted her chin with an effort that was almost defiant. If Richard meant to scold her, she would endure it, but she would not pretend regret she did not yet feel. Still, the quiet concern in his eyes stirred something unexpectedly tender within her, and for the first time since he had asked, Danielle hesitated before speaking.

Ellie broke eye contact abruptly, her confidence faltering beneath the weight of his steady gaze. Without another word, she shifted on the branch and began her descent from the tree, gripping the rough bark and the lower limbs with uncharacteristic haste.

Richard blinked, momentarily stunned by the sudden retreat. Ellie, bold, fearless Ellie, was fleeing. The realization struck him almost at once. He knew her far too well to mistake the meaning behind her hurried escape. She was not merely climbing down. She was avoiding him... avoiding the confession she feared he might press her to give. He straightened instinctively, reaching for the trunk just as she dropped lightly to the ground. Leaves scattered beneath her boots as she straightened, brushing her hands quickly against her skirt as though eager to be rid of every trace of the moment. For an instant she kept her back to him.

Richard watched her quietly, the faintest crease forming between his brows. In all the years he had known her, Ellie had never shied away from his questions. If anything, she had often met them head-on with a daring grin and some outrageous explanation that left him laughing whether he wished to or not. But this was different. He could see the tension in the line of her shoulders, the way her fingers twisted briefly in the folds of her riding skirt before she stilled them again. Something about this prank troubled her, perhaps not the act itself, but the thought of what he might think of it.

That realization stirred something warm and unexpectedly protective in his chest. Without quite thinking, Richard moved after her, closing the short distance between them. He did not reach for her, yet his presence was unmistakably near as he stepped into her shadow.

"Ellie," he said softly. The single word held no reproach, only quiet curiosity and the gentle patience of someone who had known her long enough to wait for the truth to come on its own.

Her boots had barely touched the ground when she darted across the grass with the swiftness of a startled doe. Leaves scattered beneath her hurried steps as she reached her horse, her breath quick and uneven, as though distance alone might spare her from the conversation she feared. In one graceful motion she caught the saddle horn and swung herself upward, settling into the seat with the ease of long practice. Her fingers closed quickly around the reins, already gathering them, her heels shifting slightly as she prepared to urge the horse forward. But she never had the chance.

Before she could move, strong arms closed firmly around her waist. With effortless strength, Richard lifted her cleanly from the saddle. For a brief, breathless moment Ellie hovered in midair, the world tilting as the reins slipped from her grasp and her skirts rustled around her legs. Then her boots touched the ground once more, though this time she stood firmly within the circle of his arms.

Her heart leapt wildly in her chest. The suddenness of it stole the breath from her lungs, and for a moment she could do nothing but stare up at him in stunned disbelief. Richard had always been strong, but she had never quite realized just how easily he could halt her escape. His hands remained at her waist, steady and unyielding, as though he had no intention whatsoever of allowing her to bolt again.

"Running away?" he asked quietly, a hint of teasing threading through his voice. Yet beneath the lightness of the words lay something else entirely, an unmistakable determination that told her he would not be so easily evaded.

Her heart thundered wildly against her ribs, so violently she was certain he must feel it where she pressed against him. His face hovered dangerously close. Far too close for her peace of mind.

She could see the faint shadow of stubble along his jaw, darker than she remembered from the boy who had once climbed trees beside her. She caught the clean, warm spice of his cologne, something new, something decidedly masculine, and felt the soft brush of his breath against her cheek. The butterflies that had fluttered in her stomach only moments before transformed into an entire herd of elephants.

Her thoughts scattered like startled birds, leaving her strangely breathless and unsteady. She tried to avert her gaze, but he caught her chin with gentle insistence. His fingers were warm and steady as he tilted her face upward until her eyes were locked helplessly with his.

"You did not think you could escape so easily, did you?" he murmured, amusement curling low in his voice.

"It was worth the attempt," she managed, though the words emerged on an uneven breath. "Now, will you kindly release me?"

"Not until you tell me the truth." He shook his head slowly, his expression settling into mock sternness. "What mischief have you wrought this time?"

Ellie's shoulders drooped slightly as a sigh escaped her.

"Will you promise not to be angry with me?"

"Angry?" His lips curved into a faint smile, and his tone softened at once. "Ellie, when have I ever been angry with you?"

Her lashes lowered, uncertainty flickering briefly across her expression.

"You haven't..." she admitted quietly. "But I do not know how much Cambridge and London may have changed you. Perhaps you no longer find such things amusing."

Her lips curved into a small pout so endearing that Richard had to summon every ounce of discipline to drag his gaze back to her eyes. That particular expression of hers had undone him since childhood. Once, it had merely made him laugh and concede whatever point she wished to win. Now it carried a far more dangerous power. He had not expected that.

For a moment he said nothing, aware only of the warmth of her where she stood held against him, of the faint tremor in her breath, and of the way a single rebellious curl had slipped loose to brush against her cheek. His fingers tightened slightly at her waist before he forced them to relax again.

"Society," he said at last, his voice gentler now, "does not hold as much sway as you imagine."

His thumb brushed absentmindedly against the fabric of her riding habit, as though the motion helped anchor his thoughts.

"It is true," he continued, "I have grown more serious... more dutiful. Cambridge demanded it. And my father's barony demands it still." His gaze softened as it lingered on her face. "Responsibilities have a way of reminding a man he can no longer behave like a reckless boy forever." A faint smile touched his lips. "But do not mistake me, Ellie." His voice lowered slightly, the words meant only for her. "I am still your old friend."

Yet as he said it, the truth pressed quietly against his chest: something between them had shifted. Friendship alone had never made his pulse quicken like this. Never made him so acutely aware of the curve of her lips or the warmth of her breath against his skin. Never made him wonder what it might feel like to close the small distance between them and discover whether the softness of her mouth was as tempting as it appeared. His gaze flickered downward before he caught himself and returned it firmly to her eyes.

"Though," he added softly, a hint of teasing returning to his tone, "I confess I have become rather better at extracting the truth." The corner of his mouth lifted slightly. "So, I suggest you begin your confession, Ellie... before I am forced to resort to more desperate measures."

Ellie's brows lifted at once, curiosity sparkling through the lingering flush in her cheeks.

"Desperate measures?" she repeated slowly. Her eyes narrowed with playful suspicion as she studied him. "And what, pray tell, might those be, Lord Blackwood?"

Richard's smile deepened, though a glint of mischief flickered unmistakably in his eyes.

"You truly wish to know?" he murmured. Ellie lifted her chin, though the nearness of him made her pulse flutter traitorously.

"I do. Though I suspect you are merely attempting to frighten me into confession."

"Frighten you?" he said softly. "My dear Ellie, you have never been frightened of anything in your life."

"That is not entirely true," she replied quickly, though the teasing spark had returned to her eyes. "I am quite certain I ought to be frightened of whatever scheme you are plotting at this very moment."

Richard's low chuckle vibrated faintly through his chest where she still stood pressed against him.

"You wound me," he said. "To think you would suspect me of something so underhanded."

"I know you," she countered at once.

His brows lifted slightly. "Do you?"

Ellie hesitated then, suddenly aware again of how closely they stood. His hands still rested firmly at her waist, steady and warm through the fabric of her riding habit. The space between them felt far smaller than it had any right to be.

"Well," she said with forced brightness, "I know the boy who once filled the vicar's study with frogs."

Richard winced theatrically. "You promised never to mention that again."

"You promised not to blame it entirely upon me."

"It was your idea."

"You executed it brilliantly."

A smile tugged at the corner of his mouth despite himself. But his gaze remained intent.

"And yet," he said slowly, "you still have not answered my question."

Ellie's shoulders sank slightly in defeat. "Must I?"

"Yes."

"And if I refuse?"

His eyes darkened with unmistakable amusement. "Then," he said quietly, "I shall be forced to employ those desperate measures you were so curious about."

Ellie narrowed her eyes suspiciously. "You would not dare."

Richard's grin widened. "Oh, I most certainly would." Before she could protest, his fingers shifted lightly at her waist, and he gave the faintest warning squeeze. Ellie's eyes widened.

"Richard—"

But the word dissolved into startled laughter as he began to tickle her.

"Richard!" she gasped, twisting in his grasp as helpless giggles escaped her. "That is entirely unfair!"

"You leave me little choice," he replied calmly, though his eyes danced with wicked delight. "Confess your crime, Miss Huntington, and your torment shall end."

"I will not!" she protested between breaths. His fingers moved again. Ellie laughed harder, her protests dissolving into breathless laughter as she struggled to pull away. "Very well! Very well!"

Richard stilled at once, though he did not release her.

"Well?" he prompted. Ellie drew in a shaky breath, trying, and failing, to compose herself. Her cheeks were flushed, her curls hopelessly disordered, and her eyes sparkled with reluctant surrender.

"I sent the baroness and Felicity chocolates," she admitted. Richard's brows rose.

"Yes, you mentioned that part."

Ellie bit her lip, her heart thudding as she struggled to maintain her composure. For a moment, the words refused to come. Though she had braced herself to confess, hesitation seized her once more, leaving her lingering on the brink of speaking.

Richard noticed, and arched a brow again, suspicion gleaming in his gaze.

"And what did you hide in them? Castor oil, perhaps? A frog or two? A mouse to give them a fright?"

The images he conjured were so absurd that Ellie burst into helpless laughter. Her whole body shook against him, and she was suddenly grateful for the steady circle of his arms, without them she might very well have toppled over entirely. Her laughter rang bright and unrestrained through the quiet clearing, so infectious that Richard found himself grinning despite his curiosity.

"None of those things," she managed at last between breaths, dabbing lightly at the corner of her eyes. "Though I may consider them another time."

Richard groaned softly. "Heaven help us all."

Ellie's grin widened. "No, this time I took a more... artistic approach. I decorated the package, inside and out, with plants and leaves."

Richard's eyes narrowed slowly, suspicion sharpening. "Meaning...?"

Her mischievous smile returned, brilliant, unapologetic, and entirely triumphant.

"Meaning," she said sweetly, "that I laced the gift with poison ivy."

For a long moment Richard simply stared at her. The words seemed to hang between them as his mind caught up with the image she had so casually presented. Then the shock broke, and laughter erupted from him, deep and utterly unrestrained.

"Ellie!" He bent forward slightly, still laughing. "Good heavens, how did you avoid poisoning yourself?"

"I was not so foolish as to handle it barehanded," she replied with mock dignity. "I sent my chambermaid for gardening gloves."

Richard shook his head slowly, though the grin refused to leave his face.

"When did they receive this... thoughtful offering?"

"Yesterday."

"Which means," he mused aloud, a wicked gleam entering his eyes, "that tomorrow, at the town's picnic—"

"...they will likely be forced to remain at home," Ellie finished for him, her tone rich with satisfaction. Richard's laughter returned at once, full and hearty. At last, he set her down properly, though not without giving her waist a final playful squeeze before releasing her.

"Ellie," he said, still chuckling, "you do realize that if they discover it was you, they will declare a family war."

Ellie smoothed the folds of her riding skirt with exaggerated composure, though the sparkle in her eyes betrayed her complete lack of remorse.

"Let them," she said lightly. "Baroness Appleton never forgives, so the friendship was already dead the moment Mama told her off. She only sought our company for the chance to meet my grandfather. Wealth, titles, connections, that is all that matters to her."

Richard studied her quietly. Admiration stirred in him, along with something far more dangerous. She was bold, clever, and entirely fearless. A storm wrapped in laughter. A lady who climbed trees, plotted revenge with poison ivy, and faced the world with blazing blue eyes that dared anyone to challenge her. And in that moment, standing before him with her curls wind-tousled and her smile bright with triumph, she was almost unbearably enchanting.

Richard found himself torn between two impulses, one to scold her for the reckless brilliance of her scheme... and the other to admire the very mischief that made Ellie so irresistibly, unmistakably herself.

Everyone in the region knew that Baroness Appleton cared for no one but herself. Whispers of her selfishness had circulated for years, beginning with the scandalous truth that she had all but abandoned the children of her first marriage. Her late husband, a prosperous farmer, had left her widowed with four young children. Yet it was her brother and sister-in-law who stepped in to raise them. The brother inherited the farm and its land, while the young widow turned her sights elsewhere.

When Lord Appleton, a widowed nobleman of respectable means, expressed interest in her, she seized the opportunity with ruthless determination. Though the baron assured her that her children would be welcome in his household, she dismissed them coldly, insisting they were better off with her relatives. Within months, she ceased to visit them altogether. If she encountered them in town, or any member of her former family, she swept past as though they did not exist.

The townsfolk never forgot. It became a constant source of gossip, whispered in drawing rooms and repeated loudly in taverns, that a mother could so heartlessly turn her back on her own flesh and blood. For the baron, a kind man respected by many, it was a humiliation that clung to him. Though open scandal was narrowly avoided, the shame lingered, and his wife's complete indifference to the whispers only deepened his quiet despair.

When Felicity was born, the baroness poured all her ambition into the child. The infant was treated not as a daughter, but as a princess destined to elevate them all. The baron, with his steadier and more disciplined hand, attempted to temper the girl's upbringing, but his wife indulged Felicity in everything.

From her earliest years, the child was taught that she was exceptional, entitled, and destined to command the admiration of everyone she met. She grew into the very image of her mother's design, beautiful, willful, and utterly determined to be the center of every gathering. The baron did what he could, striving to guide both wife and daughter toward moderation. Yet his efforts met only resistance. Gentle and generous to a fault, he quietly provided support to his wife's estranged family, ashamed of the callousness she had shown them. She never suspected his charity, and perhaps it was better that way.

By the time he fully understood the depth of her selfishness, it was far too late. Divorce would have meant his ruin, a scandal that could have crippled his estate and damaged his title beyond repair. So, he endured. He governed his barony with quiet diligence and, whenever possible, removed himself from the company of his wife and daughter.

As the years passed, his worries only grew heavier. The baroness spent recklessly, pouring coin after coin into gowns, jewels, and lavish entertainments. Time and again, he warned her that such extravagance endangered their estate, that if she continued at this pace, Felicity might one day find herself with little or no dowry at all.

But his pleas only stirred her temper. She railed against him openly, accusing him of stinginess, of cruelty, of wishing his daughter to make a poor match. These outbursts, often delivered before guests or even in town, left him humiliated. At last, he ceased his arguments. He saw that reason would never sway her. Perhaps, he thought with weary resignation, only the hard lessons of consequence would one day teach her what his words never could.

"I should return home," Ellie said after a thoughtful pause, her tone softening as the laughter between them gradually faded. "I promised Mama I would be back in time for tea." She glanced up at Richard, and though her voice had grown quieter, the familiar spark of mischief still danced in her bright eyes. "Would you care to join us?"

Richard's smile warmed at once. The invitation was simple enough, yet something in the hopeful lift of her gaze stirred an unexpected tenderness in him.

"I would be delighted."

Ellie's answering smile was quick and bright, and for a moment neither of them moved. The quiet of the clearing settled gently around them, the soft rustle of leaves, the distant call of birds, the warm glow of the afternoon sun filtering through the branches above.

At last Richard stepped forward. With practiced ease, he placed his hands at her waist and lifted her back into the saddle. The motion was effortless, though far less casual than he pretended. His hand lingered at her waist for the briefest heartbeat longer than propriety strictly allowed. Ellie felt it.

A faint warmth crept into her cheeks as she gathered the reins, suddenly far too aware of his nearness. She told herself it was merely the lingering excitement of their conversation, yet her heart betrayed her with another quick flutter.

Richard stepped back reluctantly, though the small smile still playing at his lips remained. He swung easily into his own saddle a moment later, settling himself with the confidence of long practice. Side by side, they turned their horses toward the road leading to the Huntington estate. The pace they chose was unhurried, their horses moving easily beneath them as the path wound through the sunlit woods. From time to time their shoulders brushed lightly when the trail narrowed, each contact sending an oddly pleasant awareness through them both. Neither spoke for several moments.

The golden afternoon stretched quietly around them, the world softened by the mellow light of the lowering sun. It felt peaceful... yet somehow expectant, as though the day itself were holding its breath. Richard glanced sideways at Ellie once or twice, catching the wind tugging loose strands of her golden curls, watching the way the sunlight played across her face.

And Ellie, though she kept her eyes fixed resolutely on the path ahead, could not quite still the small smile that lingered on her lips. Together they rode toward the Huntington estate, the golden afternoon unfolding before them like a promise, one neither of them yet dared to name.

As soon as Richard helped Ellie down from the saddle, the crunch of hurried footsteps on the gravel drew their attention. Emilia and Lilian appeared at the front steps of the Huntington house. Emilia's brows were drawn tight in righteous indignation, while fourteen-year-old Lilian wore a grin she tried, and failed, to suppress. Without sparing Richard so much as a glance, Emilia stormed straight toward Ellie, her skirts swishing furiously with every determined step.

"Why would you do something so mean and awful?" she demanded, her voice sharp and trembling with outrage. "I am ashamed to be your sister." Her green eyes blazed like emerald fire as they fixed accusingly upon Ellie.

Ellie blinked, taken aback by the ferocity of the attack, while Richard stiffened beside her, his mouth parting slightly in disbelief.

"Oh, it isn't all that dreadful," Lilian piped up, barely managing to contain her giggles. "And you don't even know for certain that Ellie had anything to do with it."

"She was involved," Emilia snapped, her cheeks flushing red. "Who else would be? It has Danielle written all over it."

Lilian rolled her eyes with theatrical exasperation and folded her arms across her chest.

"Not everything in this world revolves around our sister's mischief, Emilia."

Richard felt his patience thinning. He took a step forward, ready to intervene, but Ellie touched his arm lightly. She shook her head, silently asking him to allow her to manage the situation herself.

"What, pray, are you talking about?" Ellie asked at last, her tone calm, though her eyes glimmered faintly with suppressed amusement.

"Oh, do not pretend ignorance," Emilia shot back, her voice rising. "Mama is quite beside herself with you."

Ellie lifted her chin, feigning innocence. "And what is it that I am supposed to have done that is so dreadful?"

"Baroness Appleton and her daughter are here," Emilia declared with relish, as though announcing the arrival of royalty. Ellie's stomach tightened. She already suspected where this was leading, but outwardly she merely arched a brow and waited.

"And?" she prompted smoothly.

"And they are accusing you of tampering with the package that was sent to them," Lilian cut in before Emilia could continue. Her eyes sparkled with irrepressible mischief as she went on. "They have dreadful blisters and a ghastly rash. Quite a sight, I assure you." She stifled a laugh and winked at Ellie. Emilia gasped in horror at her younger sister's levity.

"Lilian! This is no laughing matter. Danielle, you sent that package, didn't you? You put something vile in it just to make Felicity look hideous."

Richard's voice cut through Emilia's accusations, low and firm, edged with restrained anger.

"I suggest you stop speaking to your sister in that manner, Miss Emilia." His brown eyes locked onto hers, and for the first time, Emilia faltered. "Whether she is guilty of this thing," he continued evenly, "it is not your place to scold her as though you were her parent. Remember your manners and remember that you are the younger."

The rebuke was quiet but unmistakably sharp, and Emilia flushed crimson beneath his steady gaze. She opened her mouth as if to retort, then thought better of it.

"You have no right," Richard added, his tone softening only slightly, "to shame your own sister before guests."

Humiliated, Emilia spun on her heel. With a furious sweep of her skirts, she stormed toward the house and disappeared inside, slamming the door behind her.

"Oh, Sister," Lilian called after her sweetly, her voice laced with playful mockery. "Have you considered that Felicity and her mother may have deserved it? They have made a sport of belittling others for years. Perhaps justice has finally caught up with them."

Richard exhaled slowly, still displeased, though his expression softened as he turned back to Lilian. For her sake, he managed a smile.

"It is good to see you again, Miss Lilian. You have grown taller since last I visited and are lovelier too."

Lilian beamed at the compliment. "Thank you, Lord Blackwood. I am very well. When did you return from London?"

"A few days ago," he replied. "Business at the estate has kept me occupied, or I would have called sooner."

"Ellie," Lilian said, turning back to her eldest sister with a conspiratorial grin, "you ought to hurry inside. Mama and Papa are waiting for you, along with our illustrious guests." Her grin widened. "Lord Blackwood and I shall follow shortly. I will introduce him myself, which, I daresay, will make everything infinitely more amusing."

Her eyes danced with laughter, the same mischievous spark Ellie so often carried. It was little wonder the two sisters understood one another so well.

3
An Insult Too Far

"Baroness, Miss Appleton, how very good to see you again." Ellie's voice was calm, polite, and almost cordial.

"Lady Danielle, let us not waste time with false pleasantries," the baroness snapped at once, her tone sharp and imperious. "We did not come here for a social engagement. I demand to know whether you sent us a package. And do not dare deny it, we know it was you."

Ellie bit her lip, fighting the urge to roll her eyes. The woman's brazenness never ceased to amaze her. Out of the corner of her eye, she caught her father shifting tensely in his chair, his jaw tight with restraint. Even her mother, who so often endured such scenes in silence, looked distinctly irritated.

"Why would I deny sending you a package of chocolates?" Ellie asked, a sweet, deliberate smile curving her lips. "I thought you might enjoy them."

"And you added poison to it, didn't you?"

"Poison?" Ellie's eyes widened in exaggerated horror. Her hand fluttered to her chest in theatrical disbelief. "I would never poison anyone." Her expression was so convincingly aghast that her father coughed discreetly into his hand to hide a laugh. "Why would you even suggest such a dreadful thing?"

"Because no one else would do something so cruel," the baroness snarled, her cheeks blotched with fury. "It was nothing but a desperate cry for attention." With an angry tug she whipped off her hat. Felicity followed suit. Their veils fell back, revealing angry rashes and blistering across their faces.

Ellie's lips twitched. A snort threatened to escape until she hastily masked it with a cough. Her mother shot her a sharp, warning glance, but Ellie merely lifted her chin, entirely unrepentant.

"This did not happen on its own," the baroness shrieked. "Look at us, we are utterly ruined. Felicity cannot possibly attend the town picnic tomorrow. And do you know why that is such a calamity? Because a duke from Scotland is expected to attend." Her voice rose with every word.

"You did this deliberately, you wicked, selfish girl. You want all the attention for yourself. But mark my words, you will never secure a better match than my Felicity." The venom in her voice curdled the air and silenced the room.

At that moment the door opened and Lilian swept in with Richard at her side. She had intended to announce Lord Blackwood properly, but the baroness's insult froze her mid-step. The affront to her sister made her young blood boil. Feisty by nature, quick to temper and quicker still to defend those she loved, Lilian would never allow Ellie to be spoken of so shamefully.

"My sister is not evil or selfish, Baroness Appleton," Lilian burst out, her voice ringing with indignation. "How dare you slander her so? Perhaps it is you who ought to look into a mirror. You parade Felicity as if she were an angel, a saint, but she is nothing of the kind."

The baroness drew herself up stiffly, her eyes flashing, but Lilian pressed on, the words spilling out with fearless conviction.

"Only last Sunday, in church, Felicity bragged about how she ruined Miss Olivia's gown and hair at the last ball. She ordered a servant to strike a horse just as Olivia passed by, sending the poor creature leaping straight into a mud puddle and splattering her from head to toe."

Gasps rippled through the room. Even the baroness faltered, a flicker of embarrassment crossing her face.

"Miss Olivia is our cousin," Lilian continued fiercely, "and she wrote to us about it herself. Her evening was spoiled, her reputation mocked, and the servant lost his position because of your daughter's cruelty. That, Baroness, is nothing to boast of."

The silence that followed was sharp as broken glass. The baroness's cheeks burned crimson, but she lifted her chin defiantly.

"That incident is irrelevant. It does not excuse your sister's childish, spiteful behavior toward my Felicity and me." Her lip curled as she turned her fiery gaze upon Ellie's father. "Mr. Huntington, I demand that you punish your daughter severely."

"Baroness." Richard's deep voice cut cleanly through the tension, steady but edged with unmistakable steel. He stepped forward, his tall frame commanding the room with quiet authority. The shift in the air was immediate. Conversations stilled, and every pair of eyes turned toward him.

"I believe you are forgetting yourself," he continued evenly, "and forgetting whom you are addressing." His gaze did not waver from the baroness. "Have you forgotten that the Duke of

Durham saw fit, only Saturday last, to raise Lord Huntington to the rank of earl? He was honored for his tireless service to this community and his work in council." Richard paused deliberately. "I suggest you remember his rank before you presume to lecture him in his own home."

The baroness turned on him at once, her lips curling with open scorn.

"Forgive me if I do not take that title seriously." Her voice dripped with disdain. "The Duke of Durham received his own station through marriage, not by blood. My husband is far more deserving of an earldom than Mr. Huntington will ever be." She lifted her chin defiantly, her voice sharpening further.

"And let us not forget that his original title was reduced to viscount because of his selfish conduct and the dishonor he brought upon his family name."

Richard did not flinch. If anything, the insult seemed only to harden his resolve.

"Parliament restored his honor," he replied, his tone firm as tempered steel. "Restored it through the duke's influence, and, more importantly, through Lord Huntington's own merit. That—"

"Restored?" the baroness hissed, venom dripping from every word. "A man who disgraced his family name and was cast out by his own kin deserves no respect." Her gaze swept the room with theatrical contempt.

"And as for his marriage, he sank even lower by wedding beneath himself. A viscount marrying so far below his rank? That alone tells the world all it needs to know."

A deathly hush fell over the parlor. The insult struck like a slap, blatant, cruel, and utterly unforgivable. Gasps rippled through the room. Even Felicity shifted uncomfortably, though she said nothing. Ellie's mother sat very still, her hands tightening in her lap. Her father's expression hardened, though he remained silent, for the moment.

The baroness had overstepped before. Everyone in the room knew it. But this... this was beyond the pale. She had crossed a line no respectable guest would dare approach, emboldened by arrogance and the foolish belief that no one of true standing would call her to account. She was wrong.

Ellie stepped forward, her cheeks flushed crimson with outrage, though her eyes burned with an icy fire that cut sharper than any blade.

"How dare you speak of my father in such a way?" Her voice rang through the parlor, steady, clear, and utterly unyielding. "Who are you, Baroness Appleton, to cast stones at anyone? Because his title was renounced? Because his family turned their backs on him? That does not make him any less noble. He is twice the person you will ever be." She took another step closer, her hands trembling at her sides, not with fear, but with fury barely held in check.

"My mother was born of noble blood, even if her father was only a baronet. And as for marrying beneath one's station, was it not Lord Appleton who lowered himself? He chose you, a commoner, and a farmer's widow. A woman who has neither earned nor deserved the title she flaunts." Her words rang through the room with the cold clarity of steel. "The title you bear should be stripped from you this very instant."

The baroness's mouth opened in outrage, but Ellie did not allow her the chance to speak.

"You were fortunate that the baron took pity on you," she continued, her voice slicing the air. "He is a good man, a kind man, and he does not deserve such a wife. You, who abandoned your own children from your first marriage. You, who think only of yourself and your spoiled daughter."

Her gaze sharpened, blazing with righteous indignation.

"Your arrogance, your conceit, your cruelty, these will be your downfall. Why do you think your husband's steward is forever forced to hire new servants? Because no one can endure your tyranny. You may deceive London society for a season, Baroness, but sooner or later they will see you for what you truly are."

The baroness's eyes blazed with fury. She lifted her chin high, raising her voice so every servant within earshot could hear.

"Is that a threat, Danielle Huntington?"

Ellie's chin tilted proudly. "I need not threaten you, Baroness. The *ton* will expose you themselves. I pity only your husband, for he must endure the disgrace you drag upon his name." Her gaze held steady, her lips curving into a cold, deliberate smile. "And since you so arrogantly demanded earlier, yes, I sent the package. I laced it with poison ivy. Now, at least, your face matches the ugliness of your heart."

Gasps echoed throughout the parlor. The baroness staggered back, her face blotched with rage, then lunged forward again, her voice dropping to a venomous hiss.

"You conniving little vulture. I will ruin you. I will destroy your reputation, your family's name, everything you hold dear. And if it is the last thing I do—"

"It will certainly be the last thing you do, madam." The voice was deep, commanding, and resonant with such authority that the baroness froze mid-step. All eyes turned toward the doorway. Three distinguished gentlemen had entered the room, a maid trailing nervously behind them. Their very presence filled the chamber with the quiet weight of centuries, heritage, power, and rank woven into every measured stride. The eldest of the three stood slightly ahead of the others. His bearing was proud, his silver hair lending him an air of formidable dignity, and his gaze, cold and sharp as polished steel, rested upon the baroness with open disdain.

"You, madam, deserve to be publicly disgraced," he said coldly. "Clearly you were never taught the manners nor the respect owed to your betters." His voice did not rise, yet it carried effortlessly through the stunned room. "Leave this house at once, and do not return."

The baroness's face drained of color. "I will do no such thing," she sputtered, though the sharpness in her voice had begun to falter. "Who are you to order me so?"

Ellie's eyes darted toward the stranger. Her breath caught when she saw the shock etched across her parents' faces, the sudden pallor that washed over her father's features, the tremor in her mother's tightly folded hands.

The gentleman stepped forward slowly. As his gaze settled upon Ellie's father, something in it softened, only slightly, but enough to betray recognition long buried beneath pride and years of silence.

"Benedict," he said quietly, gravely. "It has been a long time."

Ellie's father's voice was low and unsteady when he answered. "Father."

Baroness Appleton turned as pale as a sheet, her outrage collapsing into raw horror. Never in her life had she been so publicly humiliated, so thoroughly undone. Only moments ago, she had stood in this very room with the smug certainty of victory, convinced that the Huntingtons had no witnesses of consequence, no allies of rank powerful enough to challenge her arrogance. She had believed herself clever. Untouchable. Now the illusion shattered before her eyes. She had been wrong. Utterly, fatally, wrong.

Then the maid, cheeks flushed with nervous urgency, stepped forward to complete the devastation. Her hands trembled as she gathered her apron, yet her training held firm. When she spoke, her voice quivered, but each name she announced struck the room like the blow of a hammer.

"Lord Henry Benedict Huntington, Duke of Essex. Lord Ezra Julius Woodworth, Duke of Northamptonshire. Lord Ezekiel Harry Beverton, Duke of Norfolk." The maid dropped into a hurried curtsy and all but fled the room, clearly unwilling to remain a moment longer beneath the suffocating weight of the silence she had left behind.

The baroness gasped aloud, the sound sharp and strangled. The color drained entirely from her face, leaving her skin an ashen gray. Felicity swayed beside her as though she might faint, clutching the back of a nearby chair with white-knuckled desperation. The rashes on her face stood out even more starkly against her sudden pallor. And Ellie—

Ellie stood perfectly still. For a moment, shock widened her eyes as the meaning of the names settled over her. Dukes. Not one... but three. But the surprise did not linger long. Slowly, deliberately, the astonishment on her face hardened into something far colder, an expression of unmasked disdain that she no longer bothered to conceal. From the doorway, Emilia appeared just as their grandfather's rebuke still echoed faintly through the air. She halted mid-step, her eyes widening in stunned disbelief. Her lips parted, ready, no doubt, to speak. But for once, wisely, she held her tongue.

The room fell utterly silent. No one dared move. The tension hung thick and suffocating, broken only by the thunder of Ellie's pulse beating in her ears. Baroness Appleton had been unmasked. Her arrogance, her cruelty, her venom, all of it now stood naked before men whose titles carried weight enough to crush reputations with a single word. At last, the poison she had hurled at others had recoiled upon her. And with that, her downfall had begun.

Everyone stared at the three dukes in stunned silence until Benedict at last stepped forward, his expression grave. His voice carried calm authority as he addressed the unwelcome guest.

"Baroness Appleton," he said, crisp and unyielding, "Gordon will show you and your daughter to the door." He lifted a hand toward the steward. Gordon bowed and, with quiet efficiency, crossed the room to stand at the baroness's side.

Realizing she was cornered, the baroness dropped into a deep curtsy before the dukes, her movements stiff and desperate. It was a pitiful attempt to repair the damage of her earlier arrogance. Not one of the men acknowledged her. Their stony silence cut sharper than words. The Earl of Darlington inclined his head toward the door with cold finality.

"Baroness."

The single word was command enough. Her lips thinned. Desperate to salvage some scrap of dignity, she straightened and turned back to Benedict.

"Shouldn't you ask Mr. Blackwood to leave as well, Lord Huntington?" Her tone was sharp, her eyes glittering with malice as she deliberately stripped Richard of his rightful rank. Everyone present understood what she was attempting, to provoke, to delay, to stage one last spectacle before she was forced to depart. Benedict had no intention of indulging her.

"It is *Lord* Blackwood to you, Baroness Appleton," he said, his voice like tempered steel. "Do not make me have you removed by force. You have been asked repeatedly to leave this house. Whether Lord Blackwood stays is no concern of yours. The door is there. Use it."

Her face flushed scarlet. She drew in a sharp breath, fury trembling on her lips.

"Mr. Huntington—" she began, rage boiling over.

"You will address my son by his title, and with respect!" thundered the Duke of Essex. His voice struck the room like a cannon blast. The sound reverberated through the chamber, and nearly everyone flinched, even the seasoned servants standing quietly along the walls. The duke stepped forward, his eyes blazing as the full weight of his authority bore down upon her.

"Never in all my years have I witnessed such insolence from a lesser noble. Mark my words, madam, your title will be stripped from you, and you will be shunned from decent society. Since you speak so freely, with such reckless arrogance, I can only conclude that your husband tolerates such behavior, perhaps even encourages it. If that is the case, then he too risks his standing."

The baroness gasped, the color draining from her face. For the first time, genuine fear fractured her defiance. But Benedict interjected at once, unwilling to see Lord Appleton condemned unjustly.

"Father," he said firmly, "Lord Appleton is a good man. He is well liked and widely respected. He has never shown discourtesy to anyone. His honor should not be tarnished for her behavior."

The duke regarded his son for a long moment before giving a brief, measured nod.

"Very well. He shall keep what is his. But this woman—", his gaze sliced back to the baroness like shards of glass, "...will lose what she has so carelessly abused. To insult me, to threaten my granddaughter, to demean my son..."

"Forgive me, Your Grace," the baroness broke in, her voice shrill with desperation. Her face was blotched red now, her composure unraveling entirely. "But it was your granddaughter who threatened *me*. And you cannot speak to me in such a manner, this is not your duchy and—"

"How dare you interrupt me?" the duke roared. His voice crashed through the chamber like a storm breaking over the sea. He took a menacing step toward her, his glare so fierce that she stumbled backward. "How dare you presume to dictate how I may or may not speak? It would take but a single letter from me to the Duke of Durham, and your conduct would be the ruin of you. By week's end, every salon and drawing room in London would whisper of your disgrace." He shook his head slowly, disgust evident in every line of his face.

"I have seen your kind before, haughty, venomous, forever grasping to elevate yourself by trampling others beneath your feet. Your insults and disrespect toward your betters tell me all I need to know. And no doubt those beneath you suffer worse." His voice lowered, though the authority within it only grew heavier.

"I will not abide a baroness who mistreats her servants, her staff, and the commoners placed in her care. Those who labor faithfully deserve dignity and gratitude. Even had you come from generations of nobility, you should have been taught as much." His eyes hardened further. "Clearly, you were not."

At that moment Richard stepped forward, his voice measured but cutting.

"If I may, Your Grace, the baroness does not descend from a noble line. She was a commoner before her marriage, a farmer's widow."

The duke gave a grim, knowing nod. "I suspected as much." He swept his gaze across the hushed room. "Let me be clear. I do not despise commoners. On the contrary, I have found among them hard work, loyalty, and honor. No, this woman is not scorned because she was once a commoner, but because she has forgotten humility. She has allowed a borrowed title to turn her head." His voice rang with quiet judgment.

"She is a disgrace to her husband's name, and she shall never again be welcome beneath this roof."

The baroness's face twisted with fury, but terror now flickered unmistakably in her eyes. She understood the cost of defying three dukes. Without another word, she seized Felicity's arm, snatched up their hats, and swept toward the door with what little dignity she could salvage. Gordon followed behind them in grim silence.

But just beyond the threshold, a small shadow shifted near the entryway. Lilian, who had slipped away moments earlier, crouched quietly beside the wall, her eyes gleaming with barely contained mischief. She had no intention of missing the baroness's parting words. For Lilian knew the woman too well. The instant she crossed the Huntington threshold, her venom would return in full force. And Lilian, being Lilian, was determined to hear every syllable.

Henry's deep, measured voice finally broke the suffocating silence that lingered after the baroness's departure.

"I am sure you are wondering why I am here, son."

Benedict's jaw tightened slightly, though he kept his composure. After a moment, he gestured toward the chairs arranged near the hearth.

"Indeed, I am. Please... be seated."

The three dukes took their places with unhurried dignity, their very presence filling the room with an almost crushing weight of authority. It was not merely their titles that commanded respect, it was the quiet certainty of men long accustomed to power. Benedict motioned for the rest of the family to follow suit. Chairs scraped softly against the floor as they settled, though the tension in the room remained thick. Ellie instinctively rose, intending to slip quietly away before whatever grave discussion was about to unfold began in earnest. But her father's voice stopped her.

"Danielle, stay."

She paused mid-step.

"You must hear this."

Her shoulders stiffened. Slowly, she turned back. Reluctantly, she crossed toward the window, the late afternoon light spilling across the floor at her feet. She rested her hand against the sill, her fingers tightening around the wood as unease stirred in her chest. Richard moved after her without hesitation, positioning himself quietly at her side. The gesture was subtle enough to escape notice from most of the room, but not from Benedict. The earl's gaze flickered briefly toward the young man. Yet he said nothing.

He had not asked Lord Blackwood to leave. And truthfully, he had no intention of doing so. For Benedict understood, perhaps better than anyone present, that his daughter might very well need the young man's steady presence for what was about to unfold. Drawing a slow breath, Benedict turned back toward the man he had not seen in years.

"Why are you here, Father?" he asked evenly. "You made your decision about me long ago."

Henry's lined face hardened slightly, shadowed by memories that clearly had not softened with time.

"You know it was not an easy decision to make, Benedict."

"And yet you still cast me out."

The duke's gaze did not waver. "I had no choice," he replied quietly. "But if you will hear me out, I will explain."

A heavy pause followed. Then Henry straightened slightly in his chair, his voice taking on a more solemn weight.

"For now, however, there is something you must know. Your brother passed away Saturday last."

4

The Heiress in Revolt

The words fell into the room like a stone dropped into still water. A stunned silence followed.

"And," the duke continued gravely, "His Majesty has expressed his wish to elevate me, to grant me the rank of Grand Duke."

Benedict went utterly still. Slowly, his eyes narrowed as the implications settled into place.

"Then... with the heir gone..."

Henry inclined his head. "Danielle," he said quietly, "is now next in line for the duchy."

The room erupted in startled gasps. Ellie spun around so quickly her skirts flared about her. Her face had gone pale as parchment.

"Me?" she whispered. Then her voice sharpened, indignation cutting through the shock. "Why am *I* next in line? What about Papa? Isn't it time you finally forgave your son? Isn't it time you accepted Mama as your daughter-in-law?" Her voice trembled with rising emotion. "Papa deserves the inheritance, not me."

The duke's gaze rested heavily upon her. "I *have* accepted your mother, Danielle," he replied steadily. "But this matter was not mine to decide. I had no voice in it."

Ellie gave a sharp scoff and turned her back on him, her anger radiating through the room. Her mother drew a breath, clearly preparing to scold her daughter's boldness, but Henry lifted a hand, stopping her.

"Do you have something to say, Danielle?" he asked, his voice deceptively calm. Ellie let out a tense breath.

"There are many things I want to say," she admitted, her tone wavering between restraint and fury. "But I know I shouldn't. If I did, Mama would only make me apologize later."

Lord Woodworth and Lord Beverton exchanged amused glances, quiet chuckles escaping them. There was fire in this girl. They saw it plainly. And perhaps, just perhaps, it was a courage London's *ton* sorely lacked.

"You may say whatever is on your mind," Henry said. "Speak freely. These are my oldest friends. We have no secrets between us."

Ellie hesitated. Her gaze moved from one duke to the next, her chest rising and falling as the weight of her family's history pressed down upon her. Would she regret this? Almost certainly. But she had never been one to remain silent. And her chance was here.

"Fine," she burst out, her eyes blazing. "Then I will say it all, Grandfather. Do you truly believe I would accept anything from you after the way you treated Papa?" Her voice rang through the room.

"You cannot expect us to welcome you with open arms and pretend nothing happened. Did you think you could ignore us for years, then stroll into this house and pluck an heir from among us whenever it suits you simply because you wear a ducal coronet?" Her chin lifted defiantly.

"What if I were to marry a man you deem beneath me? Would you cast *me* aside as you did my father?"

"Ellie, please," Benedict interjected quietly, almost pleading. "Let him explain. It is not as you think."

She rounded on him instantly, hurt blazing in her eyes.

"Why are you defending him now, Papa?"

"Because I was hurt once, just as you are now," Benedict admitted softly. His voice carried such quiet weight that the room fell completely silent. "I let pride and bitterness rule me," he continued. "And I should never have allowed you girls to carry the burden of my resentment. Your grandfather tried to reach out after *his* father passed away, but I refused to answer. I was too stubborn." He drew a slow breath.

"And now... your uncle is gone. That leaves you, Danielle. You must accept the obligation that has fallen upon you." His face remained unreadable, but his eyes pleaded with her. Ellie shook her head violently, tears burning in her eyes as she fought to keep them back. Before she could speak again, her grandfather's commanding voice cut through the tension.

"Danielle," Henry said gravely, "I know this shocks you. But you must listen to me." His gaze softened slightly, though his authority remained unmistakable. "You were born for this. Nothing you say can change it, you are the rightful heir. As the firstborn child of my eldest son, you are destined to become Duchess of Essex."

The words seemed to echo through the chamber.

"When Benedict was disinherited, your uncle stepped forward as heir. But now that he is gone, the right returns to you." He leaned forward slightly, his voice firm. "You will stand as Duchess-in-Waiting until the time comes. And yes, when the Season begins, I shall present you." A faint smile touched his lips.

"I have already found a most worthy young man for you. Of course, the Season will give you the opportunity to choose a husband for yourself, should you wish."

"No!" The word burst from Ellie like a cry of pain. "I will *not* be a duchess, not now, not ever!"

Her voice trembled with emotion. "I refuse to accept anything from you. I want to marry for love, not because I must shoulder the weight of a title. I will not be turned into some glittering prize for men to pursue." Her hands trembled as she spoke.

"Not for my fortune. Not for my name. And certainly not for a title that means nothing to me. You will not force me into marriage just to preserve the Huntington bloodline." Her voice cracked at last. "I do not want it, and you cannot make me." The tears she had fought so fiercely spilled over. Before anyone could stop her, she gathered her skirts and fled the room. Her footsteps pounded down the corridor, echoing through the house until the great front door slammed shut behind her.

A heavy silence settled over the parlor. Richard's gaze flicked briefly to Ellie's parents. Benedict gave a solemn nod. The countess's eyes shimmered with unshed tears. That was all the permission he needed. Without another word, Richard turned and strode quickly after Ellie, determined that she would not face the storm of emotions alone.

Baroness Appleton's face twisted with fury as the carriage waited at the Huntington steps. She gripped her daughter's hand so tightly that Felicity winced.

"What Danielle and her family did to us will never be forgotten," she hissed, her voice low and venomous. "Do not doubt it for a moment, Felicity. She set us up. She knew her grandfather was coming and orchestrated this entire charade to make us look like fools." Her eyes burned with bitter conviction.

"That girl timed the delivery of that wretched package perfectly, knowing full well we would confront her. She wanted me to expose her in front of witnesses, just so those dukes could see you in such a state. She meant for your rash to shame you, meant for them to dismiss you as unworthy of their sons or grandsons."

Felicity, her cheeks still blotched from the poison ivy, bit her lip uncertainly.

"But Mama—"

"You will still win them over," the baroness pressed on fiercely, her eyes gleaming with feverish determination. "You are prettier than Danielle ever will be, and she knows it. Oh yes, she will regret this. I will see to it that no suitor dares look at her twice. Whatever it takes, I will ruin her prospects." Her grip tightened again.

"You, my darling, will not remain a baroness's daughter forever. You will become a prince's wife, and I will drag us both to that station if it kills me."

At that moment the carriage driver opened the door and extended his hand to help them up the steps. The baroness swept

Felicity inside, already rehearsing her next cruel scheme. But before she could settle against the cushions, a clear young voice rang out.

"You seem very sure of yourself, Baroness." Lilian stepped boldly to the side of the carriage. Her eyes, so like Ellie's, fierce and bright, met the older woman's with steady contempt. "But your daughter is nothing compared to my sister. I suggest you cease your wicked manipulations and poisonous gossip while you still can." Her chin lifted proudly.

"Your behavior inside has already placed you on my grandfather's bad side. And when your title is stripped, what then? Do you truly wish to ruin your husband as well?"

The baroness's head snapped around, her face flushing with outrage.

"How dare you eavesdrop on our private conversation?" she spat. With surprising swiftness, she lunged forward, her hand darting out as if to seize the girl by the hair. But Lilian was quicker.

She stepped back sharply. Her chin still raised in defiance.

"You are still on our property, Baroness," she replied coolly. "That makes nothing private. I may listen to whatever I please."

The baroness's lips curled into a sneer. "What does it matter? Who will believe the words of a silly little girl of fourteen? Society respects me. They always will. No one would take your word over mine."

Lilian's eyes flashed, though her voice remained calm and cutting.

"Perhaps, for now. But respect built on fear and deceit cannot last." She folded her arms. "Once word spreads of how you lost your title, and of the tantrum you threw in front of three dukes, I doubt anyone will question my testimony. Not my grandfather. Not his friends. Not anyone." She dipped into a mocking curtsy. "Good day, Baroness."

With that she turned smartly on her heel and strode back toward the house, leaving Baroness Appleton to seethe in silence, her hands trembling with impotent rage as the carriage door slammed shut behind her.

"Ellie, stop, you cannot run away from this." Richard's voice carried after her, urgent yet steady. His long strides quickly closed the distance, but she pressed forward as though she might outrun the fate suddenly placed upon her shoulders. At last, he caught her arm, gently but firmly turning her toward him. Her cheeks were wet, tears streaming unchecked. In the next heartbeat she collapsed against him. Richard gathered her into his arms without hesitation, holding her close as though his embrace alone could shield her from the storm raging around them.

"Please," he murmured softly into her hair. "Tell me why this has shaken you so. I thought you were at least looking forward to your first Season."

She shook her head against his chest, her voice breaking.

"I was never truly excited," she admitted. "I only agreed to it because Emilia would never forgive me if I refused. But I had resigned myself to it... since I would be presented only as the daughter of the Earl of Darlington." Her voice softened, trembling.

"That title, *that* position, would have made me nearly invisible. I could have slipped quietly into society, unnoticed by most. Few men would have paid me any attention... and I would have been free." Her sobs gradually quieted as she leaned into him, her breathing steadying. "But now... now everything has changed."

Richard gently smoothed a hand over her hair, his voice tender yet certain.

"Ellie, you underestimate yourself. Even without a title, you would have drawn notice. You are far too beautiful to ever fade into the background."

She pulled back slightly to meet his gaze, her stormy blue eyes flashing with frustration.

"And yet we will never know, will we?" Her voice carried a bitter edge. "Because now, if I enter those ballrooms, it will not be *me* they see. It will be my title... my inheritance... the promise of wealth and power." She shook her head. "Not one of them will see Danielle Huntington, only the future Duchess of Essex."

Richard guided her gently toward a nearby bench and coaxed her to sit. He lowered himself beside her and carefully lifted her chin until their eyes met again.

"Why does that trouble you so deeply?" he asked quietly. Her lips trembled.

"Because I want to be loved for myself, for who I am, not for what I represent." Her voice softened. "If I marry, it should be because someone sees *me*... not the grandeur of my name."

"The right young man will come, Ellie," he assured her gently. "One who will sweep you off your feet and care nothing for wealth or rank."

Her laugh came out brittle. "And what if I fall in love with someone my grandfather deems unworthy?" Her eyes searched his face desperately. "He is already speaking of arranging my marriage as though I were a pawn. Do you think he would not disown me, just as he did Papa, if I chose a man with no fortune or title?" The anger returned, simmering beneath the tears.

"Must I also be cast out of Huntington pride because I chose love over duty?" Her tears had dried now, but defiance burned fiercely in her eyes. "If it came to that," she said quietly, "I would elope. I would run away... just as Papa did." Her chin lifted stubbornly. "And Grandfather would banish me as well."

"I will never do that to you, Danielle."

The voice was not Richard's. Ellie started, turning sharply. A few paces away stood Henry, her grandfather, his expression grave. Behind him, the Dukes of Northamptonshire and Norfolk lingered in respectful silence.

"You did it to Papa," Ellie retorted, her voice firm despite the tremor rising in her chest. "Why should I expect anything different?"

Henry sighed heavily, the sound laden with years of regret.

"The reason your father lost his place was not because of me, child," he said quietly. "My father still lived then, and his word was law." His gaze drifted briefly, shadowed by memory. "You must understand, your great-grandfather was Grand Duke, wed to a princess. Together they wielded immense influence, and he tolerated no disobedience. He demanded unquestioning submission." A faint bitterness edged his voice.

"I myself was forced into marriage by his command. Do not mistake me, I cared for your grandmother, and in time we found affection. But ours was not a match born of romantic love." He looked back at Ellie.

"When your father fell in love with your mother, my father forbade the match outright. A baronet's daughter, and her own mother a commoner? He would not hear of it. Benedict eloped in defiance, and my father was incensed." Henry's jaw tightened.

"He swore that unless Benedict was stripped of title and inheritance, he would renounce all Huntington claims and pass everything to my mother's youngest brother. He threatened to disinherit us all, even future generations, rather than see his will defied."

Ellie's breath caught. "He would have destroyed everything the Huntingtons built... simply out of spite?"

Henry nodded slowly, sorrow deepening the lines in his face.

"Yes. My father was a man who ruled by fear. My mother was much the same." He paused before continuing. "After their deaths, I swore I would never become like them. And yet..." His voice faltered.

"You did," Ellie said softly, though the sharpness in her tone had faded.

"I did," Henry admitted quietly. "But only because I weighed the cost. Cutting my son off seemed the lesser evil compared to losing everything forever." He sighed again. "Still, I tried. I visited your mother's parents and begged them to care for Benedict and his family, to shield them from my father's cruelty. I communicated through them, though my father forbade me from contacting Benedict directly." His gaze flickered briefly toward Benedict, visible through the open doorway behind them.

"And when my father finally passed, I reached out again. But your father, hurt and proud, would not hear me."

Ellie blinked rapidly, struggling to reconcile her anger with this new understanding.

"And my uncle?" she asked quietly. "Did he not have children to inherit?"

"They are but children still," Henry replied. "The eldest only twelve. Their mother has taken them to France to live among her family." His gaze returned to her. "That left you, Danielle."

"And if I refuse?" she pressed. Henry's expression grew grave.

"Then the title will pass to a nephew of my mother's youngest brother. He has coveted it his entire life, though he is nothing more than a viscount. He believes he will inherit upon my death, but he does not yet know that you exist in the line of succession." His voice darkened. "When he learns of it, I fear he will stop at nothing to see you ruined."

Ellie let out a sharp, humorless laugh. "Splendid. So, I am to be tormented not only by Felicity and her wretched mother, but now by a jealous viscount as well. What a delightful future awaits me."

Richard leaned slightly closer beside her, his smile gentle though his eyes remained solemn.

"I believe you are strong enough to face it," he said quietly. "And if nothing else, imagine how it will gall Felicity and her mother to see you succeed. You will look radiant, Ellie. No title could ever outshine you."

She shot him a fierce look, her blue eyes blazing. How could he jest when the weight of her future pressed so heavily upon her shoulders? Yet he only smiled faintly, unshaken.

"I need time to think," she muttered at last.

"What is there to think about?" Richard asked. "You will go to London early, receive instruction, and attend the rest of the Season as planned."

Ellie rounded on him, her temper flaring anew. "Easy for you to say. It is not your life being bartered. I have told you why I hesitate, and my reasons have not changed."

Richard spoke her name softly, warning in his tone.

"Ellie—"

"No." She cut him off, her voice sharp and trembling with hurt. "I will not discuss this with you." She turned back to her grandfather, lifting her chin with renewed defiance. "I will think about it and give you my answer soon," she said at last, her voice carefully controlled.

Then, narrowing her eyes with suspicion, she added, "But just out of curiosity... why are Lord Woodworth and Lord Beverton here? Surely, Grandfather, you could have made this journey on your own."

Henry's lips curved into a knowing smirk, and at once a low chuckle rumbled from the two dukes beside him.

"They wished to meet you," Henry replied easily. "Both gentlemen have grandsons of suitable age, and they were curious to see what my eldest granddaughter was like." His eyes twinkled faintly. "I daresay they approve."

Ellie's cheeks flushed crimson at the blunt revelation, but instead of lowering her gaze, she lifted her chin stubbornly.

"Forgive me, Your Graces," she said boldly, her voice trembling with both embarrassment and conviction, "but if either of you intends to press, manipulate, or trap me into a marriage, my answer is already no, Grandfather included." Her nose tilted higher, her eyes steely, though her deepening blush betrayed her turmoil.

For a heartbeat the air hung silent. Then all three men burst into hearty, booming laughter. Even Henry, usually the sternest among them, winked at his granddaughter with a sheepish grin.

"We wouldn't dare," he assured her.

"She certainly knows her own mind," Lord Beverton remarked dryly. "There will be no difficulty finding her a suitor. Outspoken, amusing, and refreshingly honest, that is a rare combination." He smiled faintly. "Most young ladies are either perfectly practiced and dreadfully dull, or so arrogant that their boldness becomes unpleasant."

Ellie's blush deepened to scarlet, but she held her ground, her lips tightening into a stubborn pout. Henry glanced toward the house before inclining his head.

"Perhaps we should give her space to decide without feeling pressed by a trio of old men." He rose slowly. "Come, gentlemen."

The three elder men withdrew toward the house, leaving Ellie behind, though not without casting her amused, approving glances as they went.

Danielle leapt to her feet the instant the dukes were gone.

"Where are you going?" Richard was at her side at once, concern edging his voice.

"I want to be alone." Her blue eyes flashed dangerously.

"But surely", his mouth curved into a teasing smile, "you'll allow me to join you?"

"No."

"Why not?"

"Because this decision is mine, not yours. You don't get a say." She turned sharply, her skirts swishing as she strode toward the park. Richard caught her arm and drew her back. Outrage flared instantly. "How dare you? Let me go this instant!" Her eyes blazed like blue fire. He smirked faintly, though frustration sharpened his tone.

"Ellie, why are you trying to shut me out? Have you not always shared everything with me?"

"That was when we were children," she shot back.

"You're still a child."

"And that is all I will ever be to you, isn't it?" Her voice quivered with hurt even as her chin lifted in defiance. Richard's brow furrowed.

"Why are you so stubborn today? What has gotten into you?"

"What has gotten into *me*?" she repeated bitterly, jerking her arm free. "Perhaps the realization that you don't understand at all. Perhaps you should leave."

"Danielle—"

Ignoring the warning in his tone, she spun on her heel and strode toward the stables. Richard overtook her easily, seizing both her arms and turning her to face him.

"Why are you being so unreasonable?" His brown eyes locked onto hers, fierce with both anger and worry. She blinked hard against the tears threatening to spill.

"You don't understand, Richard. Everyone expects something from me, every smile, every bow, every word judged. You know very well how ladies are supposed to behave. I am not like that."

"But the dukes said they approved of you," he countered. Ellie let out a short, humorless laugh.

"Now, yes, when no one else is watching. But what happens in a ballroom, in full view of society? What if a rake decides to make sport of me? What if I must put him in his place? Do you think they'll still approve then?"

"You worry too much," Richard insisted.

"Do I? London is full of rakes who delight in humiliating women. I will not stand idle while some arrogant fool attempts to shame me."

"You could always ask a gentleman to defend you," he offered lightly. Her glare could have frozen water.

"You expect me to make a spectacle of myself so some man may play the hero? Absolutely not."

"Ellie, men are meant to protect women—"

"I can protect myself."

"You should let a man defend you."

"And what then? So, he may throw it back in my face later? Remind me I owe him a favor?"

Richard shook his head in disbelief. "Not all men are like that. Do you think I would be?"

"No," she admitted quietly, her tone softening despite herself. "You are honest. But the rest?" She shook her head. "How am I supposed to know whether they want *me*... or my title and fortune?"

Richard's grip loosened slightly as he studied her face.

"You've always had a sharp eye for people," he said thoughtfully. "You'll see through them. You remind me of someone, actually, Lady Annabelle Elton. I met her last Season in London. She's much like you: wild-spirited, clever, worried that men might use her. A beautiful young woman, and such pleasant company—"

He was still speaking when Ellie's temper snapped. Her eyes widened, her lips parting in stunned disbelief as color rushed into her cheeks.

"How dare you compare me to another woman, and call her beautiful?"

Richard blinked, startled. "Ellie, I didn't mean—"

"Of course not. That must be why you added that she was such *pleasant company*."

He gaped at her, completely unprepared for the sudden storm erupting before him. For the first time, he saw something in her expression that was not merely anger, but something raw and wounded beneath it. Then he noticed the stubborn tremble on her lips. And despite himself, he grinned.

"You wouldn't happen to be jealous, would you?" he teased. Ellie scoffed, though the sound cracked under the weight of her emotions. Before he could say another word, she spun on her heel and stormed back toward the house, her skirts swirling as she disappeared inside.

Richard remained where she had left him, staring after her in bewilderment. After a long moment, he shook his head slowly. His best friend, he thought, had completely lost her mind.

5
Words Left Unspoken

"Grandfather, I have thought about your words, about everything you asked of me, but I cannot accept it. Forgive me." Ellie's voice cracked despite her effort to keep it steady. She forced the words out. Her chin lifted in stubborn defiance even as her eyes brimmed with tears she could no longer fully contain. The room fell silent.

For a moment no one moved, as though the finality of her refusal had stunned them all into stillness. Her father's expression tightened with concern, her mother's lips parted as if to speak, but Ellie did not wait to hear what they might say. If she lingered even a moment longer, she feared her resolve would crumble completely. Before anyone could respond, she turned swiftly and fled the room.

Her composure shattered the instant she crossed the threshold. Hot tears spilled freely down her cheeks as she hurried along the long corridor, her slippers whispering against the polished floor. The familiar walls blurred around her as she moved blindly forward, desperate to escape the weight of expectations pressing down upon her. The future they had spoken of, titles, obligations, London, marriage, swirled through her mind like a storm she could not outrun.

At last, she reached the sanctuary of her bedchamber. With trembling hands, she pushed the door shut behind her and leaned against it, as though the simple barrier of wood might keep the entire world at bay. Her chest heaved as she struggled for breath, the tears coming faster now, unchecked and relentless. For a moment she simply stood there, clutching the edge of the door as if it were the only thing holding her upright. Then her strength gave way.

She stumbled toward the bed and collapsed across the coverlet, burying her face in the soft fabric. Her sobs broke free in earnest, muffled against the quilt as her body shook with the weight of grief, anger, and helplessness tangled together inside her heart. Everything had changed. And for the first time since childhood, Danielle Huntington had no idea how to fight what lay ahead.

Downstairs, silence hung heavily over the room. No one had expected her refusal, certainly not with such stark finality. Henry sat rigid in his chair, his brows drawn together, his sharp gaze shifting first to his son and then to the two dukes seated beside him. The weight of the moment pressed upon them all. Benedict exchanged a helpless glance with Elizabeth. For a moment neither spoke. Years of pride, regret, and complicated family loyalties seemed to hover unspoken between them.

At the edge of the room, Emilia shifted uneasily. Her cheeks were flushed, her expression unsettled. Without a word she rose from her chair and quietly slipped out of the room, her departure so subdued that only a few noticed. Henry's jaw twitched slightly before he finally broke the oppressive stillness with a dry, almost weary remark.

"Well. She certainly has her great-great-grandmother's temper."

Lord Woodworth gave a quiet huff of amusement. Lord Beverton's lips curved faintly as well.

Benedict merely lifted his shoulders in a small, helpless gesture. It was not a claim he could deny.

Elizabeth rose slowly from her chair, her movements composed though concern clouded her gentle features.

"Your Grace," she said softly, inclining her head toward Henry, "forgive her display." Her hands folded neatly before her as she continued. "Benedict and I... we may have allowed our daughters too much liberty." Her gaze drifted briefly toward the doorway where Ellie had disappeared.

"After what happened when we eloped, we vowed our children would never feel trapped, nor ever doubt that our love was unconditional. We encouraged them to think for themselves... to speak their minds." A faint sigh escaped her. "Perhaps we gave them too much freedom." She inclined her head politely once more. "If you will excuse me, I shall fetch Danielle at once."

Henry lifted a hand at once, stopping her before she could move.

"Leave her be, Elizabeth." He shook his head slowly, his voice softer now. "This has been a shock for the girl. She needs time to consider. Not more pressure placed upon her shoulders." He leaned back slightly, the severity of his expression easing just a fraction. "Tomorrow will be soon enough to speak of it again."

Elizabeth hesitated. Then she inclined her head in quiet acceptance. Still, her troubled gaze lingered on the door through which her daughter had fled, the faint crease between her brows betraying a mother's worry that no title, no inheritance, and no family reconciliation could ever quite silence.

A sharp knock rattled Ellie's door sometime later. She buried her face deeper into the pillow, squeezing her eyes shut as if she could will the sound away. For a few blessed seconds the hallway fell silent. Then the knocking came again, firmer this time, insistent and unyielding. Ellie groaned softly into the bedding.

"Go away! I wish to be alone."

A familiar voice carried through the wood. "Danielle, it's me. Please, open the door."

Ellie let out a long, weary sigh. Recognizing Emilia, she pushed herself upright and dragged a hand across her damp cheeks. Her eyes still stung from crying, and her head throbbed from the storm of emotions she had tried, and failed, to outrun. With obvious reluctance she crossed the room and opened the door a narrow crack.

Emilia stood stiffly in the corridor. Arms folded tightly across her chest. Her posture alone announced disapproval, and the stern set of her expression suggested she had come prepared for a lecture. Ellie's patience frayed instantly.

"What is it, Emilia?" she asked, her tone edged with irritation.

"Why are you being so incredibly selfish?" Emilia demanded at once. "Grandfather needs you, and you refuse him? What are you hoping for, that he'll come and beg?"

Ellie's eyes flared with anger. "Selfish?" she repeated sharply. "Grandfather had no use for us all these years, and now suddenly *I* am the selfish one?" Her grip tightened on the edge of the door.

"And what does it matter to you? This is between him and me. Stay out of it."

"It has everything to do with me," Emilia shot back, her cheeks flushing with indignation. "Do you not realize that your behavior reflects on me as well? When I am introduced to society, everyone will compare us. Sisters are always compared." Her voice rose slightly with frustration.

"And if you persist in parading your wild ways, I will be judged for them too. You claim you are no lady, that you are hopeless, but you do not even try. You delight in misbehaving." Her gaze sharpened. "You are a terrible example for Lilian, and she already imitates you."

Ellie's teeth clenched. This—this was the version of Emilia she could not bear. Emilia the lecturer. Emilia the little moralist. Praised endlessly by adults for her grace and propriety, forever correcting others with an air of quiet superiority. Something inside Ellie snapped.

"I have had quite enough of your sanctimonious tongue, Emilia," she said coldly. "You make a sport of pointing out my flaws as though you yourself were perfect." Her eyes flashed with rising fury.

"You think yourself superior because Darlington society flatters you, because that dreadful baroness fawns all over you. But mark my words, you are not better than me... nor than Lilian." Her voice sharpened. "You are merely conceited."

Emilia's mouth fell open in protest, but Ellie did not give her the chance to reply.

"You lecture and preen, but your pride and vanity stink louder than any of my faults," Ellie continued, her voice rising, her blue eyes blazing dangerously. "You may impress the older ladies now, but people will see through you one day. They will grow tired of your judgment. They will resent that clever little tongue of yours." She stepped closer, her voice dropping to something colder.

"And when that day comes, Emilia, you will learn that being the perfect little lady is not enough to win love... or respect."

The words landed like blows. Emilia stood frozen in the corridor, stricken and speechless. Ellie did not wait to see whether she would recover. With a sharp turn she swept past her sister, her skirts swishing with angry force as she strode down the corridor. Within moments she had fled the house entirely.

The cool night air met her like a shock as she stepped into the garden. She drew in a deep breath, gulping the fresh air as though she had been drowning inside those walls. Yet the relief did not come. Fury and grief warred inside her chest, twisting together until she could scarcely tell one from the other.

"Ellie, what are you doing out here in the dark?" The familiar voice was gentle, though it carried a note of concern. Gordon Martin stepped closer, his lantern casting a warm, flickering glow across the garden path.

He had known Danielle all her life and loved her as though she were his own daughter. Of the three Huntington girls, she had always been the one who sought him out for comfort and counsel, treating him not merely as the estate steward but as a second father. Ellie sighed, her breath clouding faintly in the cool night air.

"I just needed time to myself, Gordon. I have too much on my mind." She hesitated, then asked quietly, "Is Lord Blackwood gone?"

"Yes, he just left." Gordon tilted his head, studying her troubled expression. "What's weighing on you, Princess?"

At the old nickname, a faint smile flickered across her lips. He had first called her that when she was only five years old, coaxing laughter from her after she had fallen and scraped both knees. Somehow it had remained ever since. But tonight, the word carried a bittersweet sting.

"Oh, you mustn't call me that anymore," she murmured. "I am no princess and never will be. A princess is elegant and ladylike, pretty and sweet... and I am none of those things."

Gordon's brows knit together. Hearing her speak so harshly of herself unsettled him deeply. Without hesitation he drew her into his arms and gently lifted her chin so she could not look away.

"Danielle Marianne Huntington," he said firmly, his green eyes steady upon hers, "I will not allow anyone to speak so poorly of you, least of all yourself." His voice softened. "Tell me, child, what has happened today to leave you so disheartened?"

Ellie blinked rapidly, fighting the tears gathering in her eyes.

"It is nothing of importance," she said weakly. "I don't even truly know."

"Ellie," Gordon coaxed gently, "you are close to tears, and that does not happen often. Please confide in your old friend. Let me help you shoulder the weight."

Those tender words shattered the last of her composure. The sobs came suddenly, and Gordon held her steady, strong arms around her as she wept against his chest. He said nothing, simply allowing her to cry until the storm of emotion began to subside. When at last her tears slowed, he pressed a fatherly kiss to the crown of her head.

"Tell me," he murmured softly, "was it Baroness Appleton? Has she finally managed to wound you with that poisonous tongue of hers? Shall I go give the woman a piece of my mind?" His mock severity had its intended effect. Ellie let out a weak but genuine giggle.

"It has nothing to do with the baroness," she said, brushing damp lashes with the back of her hand. "Though she is as unpleasant and hateful as ever."

"Then what is it?"

Ellie hesitated. Gordon's keen gaze left little room for evasion.

"Is it Lord Blackwood's return from London?" he asked quietly, a knowing smile tugging at his lips. Her eyes widened slightly. He knew her far too well.

"Yes... and no," she admitted at last. "I fear he has changed too much, Gordon. He does not understand me anymore. He pressed me today, pushed me, and I know he meant well, but he made me so angry."

"What happened?"

"He is not the same as he once was. Becoming a baron has made him grow up far too quickly, and now he sees me only as a child. He cannot comprehend why I do not wish to become the future Duchess of Essex... or why I hesitate about my first Season." She exhaled heavily, her lips pursing into a small pout.

"I know I am young, only eight and ten, and he is but three years older, but I am not a little girl anymore. I feel as though Grandfather is trying to mend what his father destroyed, but why must it be at my expense?" Her voice softened with frustration.

"Mama and Papa raised us to believe we might choose our own husbands, regardless of rank. I clung to that hope. I even begged Mama to allow me another year before my debut. I was content with the thought of being merely the daughter of an earl, ordinary, unremarkable, free of expectations." She shook her head slowly. "But now everything has changed." Her voice faltered.

"Lord Blackwood thinks it is a simple choice. But he does not understand. If I step into society as the Duke of Essex's granddaughter, I will lose my freedom, perhaps even my voice. I do not want to marry because I am told to. I want to marry for love." Her eyes shone with emotion. "I want what my parents have."

Gordon's expression softened with sympathy. He squeezed her hand reassuringly.

"Ellie, you could never have been ordinary. Even as the daughter of an earl, you were destined to stand out."

His lantern light flickered across her thoughtful face.

"And now, as your grandfather's heir, you cannot escape the truth of who you are. Your great-grandfather was a grand duke, and your great-grandmother a princess. For generations your bloodline has carried both nobility and royal ties." He spoke gently, yet the reality of his words carried weight.

"When you are presented, you will not simply be Lady Danielle, daughter of the Earl of Darlington. You will be announced as the granddaughter of Lord Henry Benedict Huntington, Duke of Essex. That alone sets you apart."

Her eyes widened in sudden realization. "You mean... men will never see me for who I truly am?" she whispered. "They will only see my bloodline, my heritage?"

"Not all men are selfish rakes," Gordon assured her kindly. "Do not allow that fear to take root in your heart. You are strong-willed, clever, and beautiful, and many will admire you for yourself."

He paused thoughtfully.

"Yes, some will covet your position more than your heart. That is the burden of nobility. But your grandfather and father know the pain of forced matches. They will not rob you of your choice, not after what they themselves endured."

Ellie bit her lip, uncertainty clouding her expression. "I still do not want this. Perhaps if I decline the duchy, no man will pursue me."

"You cannot deny what you are," Gordon said gently. "You were born to shine, Ellie, whether you desire it or not. Perhaps you will even change how others think, show them a new way. The *ton* could use someone like you."

She shook her head stubbornly. "All I see is endless strife. Jealous young ladies, envious whispers, women like Baroness Appleton making my life miserable. I do not wish to become a threat to everyone around me." Her mouth twisted slightly.

"And I am not dignified enough to spar with arrogant men as a proper lady should when they step out of line."

Gordon chuckled softly, his eyes twinkling. "Then let your suitors spar on your behalf. Let them prove their devotion. There is no shame in allowing a gentleman to demonstrate his chivalry."

"That is exactly what Lord Blackwood said," Ellie retorted, her pout deepening. "And I told him the same thing I will tell you, I do not want anyone fighting my battles. I can fight them myself." Her eyes sparkled again with fiery determination, though they still glistened faintly from her earlier tears. Gordon's chuckle grew warmer.

"Everyone who knows you already believes that." He squeezed her shoulder affectionately. "But Ellie, remember this: real men, honorable men, take joy in protecting those they love. It is not about your weakness. It is about their devotion."

Her shoulders sagged slightly, the weariness of the day settled upon her.

"Then why," she asked softly, "does Lord Blackwood treat me as though I am still a child?"

Her voice faltered. "Why does he try so hard to push me away?"

Richard had not gone home after all. He had led his horse away from the house with every intention of leaving, his jaw set with stubborn resolve. The night air had been cool against his face, the quiet road stretching ahead of him as though urging him onward. Yet something gnawed at him. An ache deep in his chest refused to be silenced. The farther he rode, the stronger it grew, an insistent pull that would not release him. At last, he reined in his horse with a quiet curse under his breath. He could not leave. Not like this.

With a weary sigh, Richard turned the animal and guided it back toward the Huntington estate. He told himself he only wished to circle the property once more, perhaps catch one last glimpse of Ellie before departing, perhaps even offer her a proper goodnight. But in truth, he knew the reason ran deeper than that. He needed to see her.

The house loomed softly in the moonlight as he approached from the far side of the gardens. The lanterns along the paths flickered faintly, casting pools of golden light against the darkness. And then he saw her.

Ellie stood in the garden near the path, Gordon Martin beside her, the steward's lantern casting a warm glow around them. The sight of her, her familiar posture, the way her hair caught the lantern light, made something in Richard's chest tighten painfully. He dismounted quietly and led his horse a little farther into the shadows, unseen. He had not meant to listen. But then her voice carried through the stillness of the night.

"Then why does Lord Blackwood treat me as though I am still a child? Why does he try so hard to push me away?"

The words drifted toward him like a dagger to the heart. Richard went utterly still. *Why would she think I wanted to be rid of her?*

6

The Secret She Could Not Bear

The thought struck him with painful force. He had never, not once, considered Ellie a burden. Quite the opposite. Every hour spent in her company felt far too brief, slipping away before he was ready to let it go. He cherished every laugh, every argument, every spark of defiance that lit her eyes. And yet... she truly believed he merely tolerated her. That he saw her as childish. His jaw tightened as the realization settled heavily upon him.

Nothing could have been further from the truth. If anything, it was he who had struggled to keep his distance, who had forced himself to speak sharply, to treat her as though she were still the stubborn girl who once climbed trees beside him. Because acknowledging the truth would mean facing something far more dangerous.

He wanted her. Not as a childhood companion. Not as a sisterly friend. But as the woman she had become. The admission burned within him like a slow, steady flame. For a fleeting moment he nearly stepped forward. The urge was almost overwhelming, to cross the garden, take her hands in his, and tell her everything that churned inside him. To wipe away the tears staining her cheeks and make her understand how fiercely he cared for her.

But then she turned slightly toward Gordon, and the lantern light revealed the damp tracks of tears on her face. The sight stopped him cold. Tonight was not the moment. She was too shaken... too wounded by everything that had happened. If he spoke now, his words would only add to the storm swirling in her heart. What she needed tonight was peace, not more turmoil.

Richard exhaled slowly, forcing himself to step back into the shadows. With a heaviness that nearly unmanned him, he mounted his horse once more. For a long moment he lingered there, watching her from afar, the girl he had known all his life, and the woman he was only just beginning to understand.

Then, at last, he turned his horse toward the dark line of the forest. Without a sound, he rode away into the night. Yet he carried something with him as he disappeared beneath the trees, words left unspoken, burning fiercely in his chest. Words he swore he would give her tomorrow.

"Why do you think Lord Blackwood is trying to rid himself of you?" Gordon asked at last, clearly baffled. He had watched Ellie and Richard grow up nearly inseparable, two children who had shared secrets, laughter, and a bond that once seemed unshakable. Ellie pressed her lips together, her voice trembling as frustration spilled out.

"Because he keeps pushing me to go to London. He insists I accept Grandfather's proposal and turn myself into a lady worthy of society. It feels as though I am no longer enough for him as I am, as though he cannot wait until I am married, so he no longer has to call on me." Her gaze dropped to the garden path.

"Today, I felt he only spent time with me out of pity. Perhaps he is eager to marry himself, and he wants me to find a suitor quickly, just to rid himself of the obligation."

Gordon gave a low chuckle and shook his head, though his heart ached at the doubt clouding her thoughts.

"Ellie, Richard Blackwood is your friend. He would never cast you aside so carelessly."

"You did not hear him," Ellie shot back, her blue eyes flashing indignantly. "He told me about a lady he met in London, beautiful and charming, and then said she reminded him of me. And if that were not insulting enough, he added that she was pleasant company." Her pout deepened. "I believe his meaning was clear enough."

Gordon's lips twitched despite himself. "So... he said he took a fancy to her?"

"Well, no," Ellie admitted reluctantly. "Not in those exact words. But it was implied."

"Ellie Huntington," Gordon said with a knowing grin, "I never thought I would live to see the day you grew jealous."

Ellie gasped, her cheeks flooding scarlet. "Jealous? That is ridiculous. I am not jealous. Gordon, you are misreading everything." She turned her face away, but her flustered tone betrayed her, and Gordon had known her far too long to be fooled.

"Do not deny it, child. I have known you since your very first steps. I can tell when your feelings have shifted." His voice softened kindly. "And they have. Your heart has changed where Lord Blackwood is concerned."

Ellie bit her lip, willing the heat in her cheeks to fade. For several long moments she said nothing. The quiet garden seemed to hold its breath around them. At last, she spoke again, her voice smaller now.

"That has nothing to do with how he treats me. Why must he speak as though I am still a child? Why would he tell me I ought to let men defend me if someone oversteps?"

Gordon studied her thoughtfully before answering. "Perhaps," he said gently, "because he wishes to be the one to defend you." He squeezed her hand affectionately. "Perhaps Lord Blackwood longs to protect you himself... just as I always would."

Ellie's breath caught. For a fleeting moment the possibility stirred in her mind, fragile and frightening all at once. But she shook her head fiercely, refusing to let the thought take root. Yet long after Gordon kissed her hand goodnight and left her to rest, his words lingered in her thoughts, echoing softly through the silence of the night like a whisper she could not quite silence.

Sleep did not come easily that night. Ellie tossed and turned beneath the soft coverlet, the quiet of her chamber doing little to soothe the turmoil in her mind. Moonlight slipped through the curtains in pale ribbons, stretching across the floor and climbing slowly along the bedposts as the hours crept by. Yet rest refused to come.

Every time she closed her eyes, the day replayed itself with merciless clarity. Her grandfather's grave voice. Her father's quiet plea. The stunned silence of the room when her name had been spoken as heir.

And Richard. His frustrated tone. His steady insistence that she must go to London. The teasing smile that had only angered her further, and the bewildered expression he wore when she stormed away. Ellie buried her face in the pillow with a frustrated groan.

Why had everything changed so suddenly? Only that morning she had believed her future was simple enough. A Season in London, perhaps a handful of tedious dances, and then, if she were fortunate, a quiet life with someone she truly loved. Nothing grand. Nothing burdensome. Just happiness.

But now the world seemed determined to transform her into something she had never wished to become. The Duke of Essex's heir. The thought made her stomach twist. She rolled onto her back, staring up at the canopy above her bed, her thoughts racing faster with every passing moment. Gordon's words returned to her unbidden, echoing through the quiet room.

Perhaps Lord Blackwood longs to protect you himself. Ellie squeezed her eyes shut. No. That could not be true. Richard had made it perfectly clear, he still saw her as a stubborn child in need of guidance. Nothing more. And yet...

Her thoughts drifted unwillingly to the way he had looked at her earlier that afternoon. The fierce concern in his eyes when she began to cry. The gentleness with which he had lifted her chin.

Her heart fluttered painfully in her chest.

Ellie turned again, tugging the blanket tighter around her shoulders. No matter how confusing Richard might be, one thing remained certain. She would not yield to her grandfather's will. The decision settled within her with quiet determination. She refused to be paraded before society as the duke's heir, as though she were some glittering prize to be inspected and claimed.

She would not allow London's salons and ballrooms to whisper about her fortune and her future duchy while strangers weighed her worth like merchants examining fine silk. If she must be introduced to society, then it would be on her own terms. She would ask, no, she would insist, that she be known simply as Lady Danielle, daughter of the Earl of Darlington. Nothing more. No mention of the duchy. No mention of inheritance. Only herself. And if the world could not accept that… then the world would simply have to learn.

Morning came far too soon. Ellie had scarcely closed her eyes when the faint creak of the door stirred her from the shallow sleep she had finally managed to find. Pale dawn light seeped through the curtains, casting a soft gray glow across the room. Her maid, Heather, slipped quietly inside, careful not to disturb her more than necessary. The young woman carried herself with the practiced gentleness of someone accustomed to tending her mistress's restless mornings.

"Lady Danielle," Heather said softly, drawing the curtains back just enough to brighten the chamber. "Your father and mother are waiting for you in your father's study. They wish to see you."

Ellie blinked, still heavy with exhaustion, and pushed herself upright against the pillows.

"Now?" she asked, her voice thick with sleep. "Before breakfast?"

Heather nodded apologetically. "Yes, My Lady. They asked that you come as soon as you are awake."

Ellie swung her legs over the side of the bed, the chill of the floor beneath her feet bringing her fully back to her senses. It was rare, very rare, for her father to summon her to his study. Such meetings were reserved for matters of real importance, discussions conducted with quiet gravity and careful words.

A chill of foreboding settled slowly over her. Though she already suspected the reason. *No doubt another attempt to persuade me into Grandfather's scheme.* Ellie drew a slow breath, smoothing her hair back with slightly trembling fingers. *I must remain calm,* she reminded herself firmly. *I must not yield, no matter how they plead.*

Heather moved about the room with quiet efficiency, laying out a simple morning dress and assisting Ellie as she dressed. Her hair was brushed and gathered neatly, though a few soft strands escaped despite the maid's careful efforts. When the last pin was set in place, Ellie rose from the dressing table and turned toward Heather. The maid's eyes lingered on her with gentle concern. Ellie offered her a faint, weary smile.

"Thank you, Heather." She straightened her shoulders slightly, summoning what composure she could. "Please tell Mama and Papa that I will come at once."

As soon as Ellie reached her father's study, she rapped sharply on the door. His voice answered at once, commanding her to enter.

"You wished to see me, Papa?" she asked, her gaze fixed on his face, though she had already registered the presence of her mother and grandfather. A knot tightened in her chest. This was no casual summons.

"Yes. Please, sit down, Ellie." Benedict gestured to the chair opposite his desk. He waited until she obeyed before continuing, his tone grave. "We understand that yesterday came as a shock. You were asked to absorb much in a short span of time, and I accept some of the blame for not preparing you sooner. But no matter how strongly you resist, we must speak of this again."

Her chin lifted defiantly. "I have not changed my mind, Papa."

"I expected as much." His expression hardened. "But your mother and I are united in this: you must accept it."

Ellie's stubbornness flared into indignation. "I am sorry, Papa, but I cannot. I will not. Is that all?"

Benedict rose slowly to his feet, his jaw tightening.

"No, Danielle. This is not all. The decision has already been made. We had hoped it would not come to compulsion, but you leave us no choice. You will leave with your grandfather at week's end."

Ellie shot to her feet, stunned. Never had she seen this side of her father, the man who had always listened, always reassured. Her voice shook, yet her words struck like steel.

"You cannot force me into this."

"Actually, we can," Benedict answered evenly. "You are the only heir of proper age, and the summer's lessons will give you the polish you lack. They will shape you into the lady you were born to be."

Ellie's breath caught, outrage flashing in her blue eyes.

"You want me to become someone I am not? To don a mask of refinement for society's sake? Then I must assume you have long been displeased with me." Her gaze did not waver, though her trembling voice betrayed the wound beneath her anger. Her father faltered at the accusation, but before he could answer, Elizabeth leaned forward urgently.

"Danielle, no. You are mistaken. We are not displeased. We love you dearly. This is not about changing you, only about guiding you into the young woman you were meant to become."

Ellie turned on her mother, her tone sharp. "Then why not wait for Emilia? She is already everything a lady ought to be, graceful, obedient, and perfect."

At that, Henry spoke for the first time. His voice was calm but firm.

"Emilia lacks what is required to lead. You do not. With my new title and your uncle's death, there is no time to delay. Danielle, I do not want you to surrender your spirit, it is precisely what sets you apart. But you must learn to temper it. Society will not be won by fire alone. They must be charmed as well as challenged."

Ellie's eyes narrowed as she turned back to her father.

"So, all the promises you made to me were lies, then? You vowed I could marry when I was ready, and to the man of my choosing. Yet the moment Grandfather appears, I am told to obey without question."

"Ellie—" her father began, his voice pained. But she cut him off with a bitter laugh.

"And let me guess, once I am reshaped into the duchess you envision, suddenly time will run out. You will remind me that I cannot inherit without a husband, and oh, how convenient, you will have one ready and waiting. Do not deny it. I know the ton's cruel rules. You want me softened, trained, and then wed like a prize horse, all under the guise of choice." Her voice shook with fury as she looked from father to grandfather. Henry leaned forward, his brow furrowed.

"Danielle, it is not as ruthless as you think. Yes, you must wed in order to take the duchy, but no one intends to rob you of choice. You will meet men of standing, and you will be free to select one worthy."

"Free?" Ellie's laugh was sharp and scornful. "And yet rushed, cornered, and under the eyes of the entire ton. You should have told me, Papa. You should have prepared me, instead of springing this upon me like a trap." She pressed her fists against her skirts, her breath trembling.

"Was this your plan all along? To feign sympathy for my dreams until duty called, and then marry me off at the first opportunity?"

"Danielle," her mother interjected, her tone stern with reproach. "That is unjust. We have never sought to barter you away. Watch your words. And I confess, I do not understand this sudden dread of marriage. You were never troubled by the notion before."

Ellie's eyes glistened, but her voice rang firmly. "Because you assured me it would be on my terms. That I could marry for love, like you did. But now everything is shifting beneath me. You already force me into Grandfather's custody, how can I trust you not to force me into matrimony next?"

The room grew tense, silence crackling like a storm. Then came a sharp knock. Benedict called for the intruder, and a maid stepped inside, curtseying.

"Forgive me, My Lord, but Lord Richard Blackwood waits in the parlor."

Ellie's temper broke like a dam. She rolled her eyes heavenward. "I cannot endure that right now." Rising swiftly, she dropped a hurried curtsy. "Forgive me. I require fresh air." Without giving anyone the chance to stop her, she swept out of the study.

Elizabeth stared after her, troubled. "Since when does Ellie avoid Richard?"

Benedict only sighed, rubbing the back of his neck. "They must have quarreled." He glanced toward the door. "I'll follow her. She needs to hear that we mean her no harm."

Benedict found his daughter in the stable, her hands busy with the bridle straps as she saddled her mare herself. Two stable boys lingered uneasily nearby, uncertain whether to intervene or risk her temper. At Benedict's curt nod, both lads scurried off, leaving father and daughter alone amid the scent of hay and horses.

"Ellie," Benedict began gently, though weariness edged his voice, "please try to understand. None of this is meant to ruin your life."

She turned toward him, fingers clenched tightly around the leather. Her eyes flashed with hurt and anger.

"Then why, Papa? Why did you never prepare me? Why did you not tell me Grandfather might one day come for me?"

Benedict stepped closer, his shoulders heavy, as though the truth itself weighed him down.

"Because I never believed it would come to this. After my grandfather disowned me, the duty passed to my brother. He was the heir, not I. We believed he would live to see his children grown and carry the title in his turn. No one imagined he would be taken so soon. And when he died before his son came of age..." His voice caught, and he exhaled slowly.

"Ellie, your mother and I never meant to deceive you. We tried, in small ways, to prepare you for life in London should you ever choose it. But we did not expect my father to outlive my brother."

Ellie's lips pressed into a thin line, her nose wrinkling in disbelief. Though she began to grasp the bare facts, her defiance had not softened.

"I don't know what you expect me to say," she muttered.

"I expect nothing but honesty," Benedict replied quietly. "I know this feels like chains upon your shoulders, but, my darling, you will see in time that it will not break you. You are meant to be a duchess." His smile was warm, tender even. Ellie scoffed, tossing her head like a spirited horse.

"Forgive me, Papa, but I cannot believe that. I am nothing like the girls who return from London polished and proper. And I am not speaking only of Felicity and her dreadful mother. I mean all of them." She folded her arms across her chest, pouting, and Benedict had to turn slightly away to keep from laughing at the sheer stubbornness painted across her face.

"You may be more outspoken than most," he admitted, "and your temper is quick. But you do not see what we see. You are already graceful, already poised in ways your mother never needed to teach you. It has always been in you, Ellie."

She blinked at him, incredulously. "Me? Graceful? Poised? Baroness Appleton would choke on her tea to hear such nonsense. She makes it her daily business to remind me how hopeless I am, how unworthy of society, how much of a disgrace to the family name." Ellie sighed, rolling her eyes with a flash of bitterness.

"Not that her opinion matters. I never sought her approval. Still, if she feels so strongly, I can only imagine how others must see me."

Benedict shook his head firmly. "Do not give that woman so much power over your thoughts. The baroness is no authority on character, despite her airs. Every lady in your mother's circle speaks poorly of her behind her back. The men tolerate her only out of respect for her husband. Lord Appleton is a good man, and society pities him for the misfortune of marrying such a vain creature."

"It hardly matters," Ellie said with a dismissive shrug. "London will be crawling with women who care only about marrying off their daughters to the highest bidder. And the men? They will scramble for the grandest prize of all, the wealthiest duchy in the kingdom." Her voice dripped with scorn.

He nodded slowly, not denying it. "You are right, it is the wealthiest. But Ellie—"

"I am not ready for this," she cut in sharply. "And what is more, I do not want to be ready for it."

"You are ready, Ellie," Benedict said softly, squeezing her hand. "You only underestimate yourself."

For a moment, her defiance faltered. Her gaze met his, searching his familiar green eyes, and something vulnerable flickered there. But the sound of footsteps broke the fragile silence. Their conversation had not gone unheard.

Henry and Elizabeth were entering the stable. At once Ellie's body stiffened, her expression hardening like ice.

"So, you are set on sending me away?" Her voice was flat and cold, her eyes suddenly distant.

Benedict inclined his head.

"Yes."

"Then hear me, Papa. I will go, but only if you swear that I may choose my husband, even if he does not wear the rank you prefer."

"I promise," he answered gravely, though hesitation lingered in his tone. "It would be best if you married a man worthy of a duke's mantle, but I will not interfere."

"Then promise me more," Ellie pressed, her voice trembling. "Promise you will not force me into marriage if I do not find a husband before Grandfather becomes Grand Duke. Surely, he can manage both titles until I am ready. Promise me I may marry for love, or not at all."

7

Before First Light

Benedict's breath caught. He looked at Elizabeth, then to Henry. Both had drawn closer, and in their silence, Ellie read her answer. Her heart clenched.

"I knew it," she whispered, her voice raw with betrayal. "I knew you would break your promise. The promise you gave me as a child meant nothing. Grandfather has been here scarcely a day, and already you strip me of every freedom you once swore I would have. How could I have been so wrong about you?" Tears stung her eyes, but she refused to let them fall. She turned, meaning to storm past, but Benedict caught her arm.

"Ellie, listen. You will find a husband quickly. I am certain of it."

"Then give me your word," she snapped, struggling against his grip.

"I cannot." His eyes were unyielding, his voice like iron. Ellie's lips curled into a bitter laugh.

"So, you admit it. If something unforeseen happens, you will bind me to a man of your choosing. You would force me into a loveless marriage for the sake of power and tradition. No, Papa. I will not go. I will not let you or Grandfather barter away my heart."

Henry's voice, deep and stern, broke in. "Danielle, an arranged marriage would only be a last resort."

"Last resort?" Ellie rounded on him, her words cutting like a blade. "Or whenever you decide you have waited long enough? Do you hear yourselves? You ask me, barely eight and ten, never even introduced to society, to shoulder a burden that belongs to older, wiser shoulders. You ask me to give up my freedom, my happiness, my very self, for a duchy I never asked for. I was invisible to tradition, to society, even to you, Grandfather, until the moment you needed me. And now you would control me as though my life were yours to command." Her voice rang through the stable, trembling with fury and grief.

"But you are wrong. None of you have the right. I will not do it. I will not be broken into the shape you desire."

Her parents gasped in unison, the sound sharp in the hushed stable, a sure sign their daughter had gone too far. Benedict's face darkened, and in one swift motion he seized Ellie by the arm. She froze, stunned by the storm in his eyes. Never in her life had she seen her father so furious.

"Danielle Marianne Huntington," he thundered, his voice cracking through the air like a whip, "that is enough. You will do as you are told, and you will apologize to your grandfather at once."

His tone was so stern, so absolute, that for the first time Ellie wondered if he struggled to keep from striking her. She pressed her lips together in a stubborn pout and gave the smallest, defiant shake of her head. Before Benedict could say more, Henry stepped forward, commanding, but far less harsh.

"I understand your anger, Danielle, even if you believe I do not. Your grandmother and I raged as well when our parents forced us into marriage. We, too, felt robbed of choice. But there are moments in life when choice is not afforded to us."

Ellie's eyes blazed, her chest rising and falling with indignation.

"We will always have a choice," she shot back hotly. "I would sooner lose everything and work as a governess than surrender my freedom and become a slave to a husband I did not choose."

Her words fell like a blade dropped between them.

For a heartbeat no one spoke. Her parents and grandfather stared, shocked into silence, as though she had uttered something indecent. Benedict found his voice at last, his anger spent, replaced with a raw edge of concern.

"Why would you think an arranged marriage would make you a slave to your husband?" His green eyes searched hers, desperate and imploring. Ellie's throat tightened. Tears pricked her eyes, but she blinked them back with fierce determination.

"Because it happens," she whispered. "Because I know."

Benedict's worry deepened. He reached out, lifting her chin so she could not look away.

"Know what, Ellie? How bad can it be? Please, help us understand where this anger comes from."

Her lips trembled, but she pressed them together and shook her head. "I can't." The single word, faint though it was, struck them like a blow. Elizabeth, moved by both fear and instinct, stepped forward and drew her daughter into her arms.

"Why can't you tell us?" she pleaded, her voice thick with emotion. "Sweetheart, please. From the first moment, I felt there was more troubling you than simply being named heiress. Let us share the burden."

"I can't tell you," Ellie sobbed, "because I promised I wouldn't. It isn't my secret to share." Tears streamed down her cheeks, and Elizabeth held her tighter, whispering into her hair.

"Darling, when a secret grows so heavy it makes us lash out at those who love us, it is too heavy to bear alone. Trust me. Let us help you. Why are you so afraid of an arranged marriage?"

For a long moment Ellie could not speak through her sobs. At last, she caught her breath and lifted her tear-streaked face to her mother's. Her voice cracked as she forced out the words.

"Because of Eleanor."

"Eleanor?" Henry echoed, his brow furrowing. Elizabeth searched her daughter's eyes.

"What does your cousin have to do with this?"

Ellie swallowed hard, her hands twisting together. "Because Eleanor is living the very fate you want for me. She is a slave to her husband."

Another ripple of shock passed through them. Benedict's heart sank, a gnawing dread taking shape.

"What are you saying, Ellie? Your cousin is happily married. Surely you must be mistaken."

Elizabeth shook her head. "Yes, Eleanor wrote of her wedding with joy. Perhaps you have misunderstood—"

But Ellie cut them off, her voice fierce with conviction. "No! You do not understand. I know because she told me." With trembling fingers, she drew a folded letter from her pocket, its edges worn from being read and reread. She held it out as though it burned her.

"You must read this. Eleanor is not happy, she never was. She was forced into that marriage. She lied, pretended it was the match she wanted, but it was all her father's doing. She had other offers, two suitors who would have treated her with kindness. But her father struck a bargain with Lord Ainsworth, and now she is paying the price." Her voice faltered, but she pressed on.

"She made me swear not to tell anyone, but she also made me swear something else, that I would never let myself be forced into an arranged marriage. That I would look out for other girls too, so they would not suffer as she does." Fresh tears streamed down her cheeks.

"I cannot break that promise, Mama. I must protect Emilia, Lilian, and every young woman who might share Eleanor's fate. Eleanor is already paying with her happiness, and if no one acts, she may soon pay with her life."

A heavy silence fell. Even Henry's stern face betrayed unease.

"Ellie..." Elizabeth's voice shook. "Do you know what you are saying? You are accusing Lord Ainsworth of dreadful things."

"You will know the truth if you read her words," Ellie said hoarsely. "We have exchanged letters since her wedding. At first, she only hinted, but in her last letter, three days ago, she finally confessed. I pressed her to tell me, and now I wish I had not, for I cannot bear the weight of it alone."

Benedict and Elizabeth exchanged a grave glance, and even Henry's eyes showed a flicker of alarm.

"Who is Eleanor?" he asked at last, his voice low. Elizabeth answered for her daughter.

"She is the eldest daughter of my sister. She was married several months ago." Her throat tightened as she looked back at Ellie's stricken face. Benedict exhaled heavily.

"Do you realize, Ellie, that Lord Ainsworth is heir to his uncle's duchy?"

"Yes," Ellie whispered, her eyes blazing through her tears. "And that is exactly why my uncle forced her into it. But title and wealth do not change what he is. Lord Ainsworth is evil, plain evil."

Elizabeth's composure cracked. "So, this is why you have lashed out, why you've struggled so to keep your composure?"

Ellie nodded, her voice trembling. "At times I could push it from my mind, but other times fury and horror raged inside me. And then you placed the burden of what I am meant to be upon my shoulders, and I simply could not bear it all."

Elizabeth glanced toward the stable hands and lowered her voice. "Come. Let us return to the house. We must read the letter in private."

Ellie recoiled, clutching the reins of her horse as if for protection. "No. I cannot stay to watch your faces when you learn the truth. I cannot bear it."

Before they could answer, she called for one of the boys. The lad hurried forward and helped her mount. In the next breath she was riding hard from the stable, the thunder of hooves fading into the forest.

Elizabeth pressed a trembling hand to her mouth, her eyes brimming with unshed tears. For a moment she could scarcely breathe. The words Ellie had spoken echoed through her mind, each one heavier than the last. Benedict and Henry stood equally stricken. The letter still lay in Benedict's hand, its worn folds a silent testament to how often their daughter had read and reread it alone.

"Good heavens," Benedict murmured hoarsely, running a hand through his hair. The weight of what they had just heard settled heavily upon him. His daughter had carried this fear in silence, this dread of marriage, this desperate vow to protect others, and he had mistaken it for childish defiance. Henry's jaw tightened, his expression grave. The proud duke who had weathered court, politics, and war now looked shaken in a way few had ever seen.

"We must read that letter," he said quietly. "At once."

Elizabeth nodded, though her gaze still lingered on the path Ellie had taken. They had not gone far when a tall figure approached them from the lane. Richard Blackwood came striding toward them, hat in hand, his expression respectful but alert.

"My Lords. Lady Huntington." He bowed with practiced courtesy. "Good morning." There was a brief pause before he continued, concern flickering in his brown eyes. "Have you seen Danielle? I have come to call upon her."

Elizabeth forced a faint smile, though the strain behind it was impossible to hide.

"You have just missed her," she said gently. "If you hurry, you might catch her. She went that way." She raised her hand and pointed toward the forest path. Richard followed the direction of her gesture, his expression sharpening with sudden focus. Without another word he inclined his head.

"Then I shall find her." He moved swiftly toward his horse, mounting in one smooth motion. The animal sprang forward at once beneath him, hooves striking the earth in a quick, determined rhythm as he rode after Ellie. For several minutes the Huntingtons remained where they stood, watching him disappear along the forest road. Elizabeth clasped her hands together, her voice barely more than a whisper.

"Perhaps he can calm her."

Benedict said nothing. His eyes remained fixed on the distant line of trees where the riders had vanished. At last Henry drew a slow breath.

"Come," he said quietly. "We must read that letter."

The three of them turned back toward the house, their steps heavy with worry, each carrying the uneasy knowledge that the truth waiting inside that folded paper might change far more than Ellie's future.

Ellie urged her horse into a brisk trot, forcing herself to focus on the steady rhythm of hooves rather than the turmoil raging in her mind. For days she had shed secret tears over Eleanor, lying awake through sleepless hours and wondering how she might possibly rescue the cousin she adored. Now, at last, a reckless idea had begun to take root, dangerous, chilling, yet impossible to dismiss. Eleanor had suffered long enough. Something had to be done. Ellie closed her eyes briefly, drawing in a deep breath as the cool forest air brushed her face.

Yes. Now that her parents knew the truth, there was hope. They would have to act. They would have to find some way to free Eleanor from that monstrous man.

"Ellie!" Her name cracked through the stillness, shattering her thoughts. Danielle stiffened in the saddle and glanced back. Richard was galloping hard after her, his horse devouring the distance between them.

A scowl tugged at her lips. She had nearly forgotten about him, and at the moment she had no wish whatsoever to speak with him. With a sharp tug on the reins, she urged her mare into a faster gait. The animal surged forward, breaking into a swift gallop that carried her down one of her favorite woodland trails. Sunlight flickered through the trees in shifting patches of gold, branches whipping past as the wind rushed against her face.

Then she felt it. The saddle shifted beneath her. Panic seized her chest. She had forgotten to tighten the girth.

"Ellie, wait!" Richard's voice rang out again behind her. But she ignored him, her mind racing as she struggled to steady herself before he noticed. If she slowed too abruptly, the saddle might slip entirely. She veered sharply onto a narrower path, hoping to regain control without drawing attention to the danger she was in. The crack of gunfire split the air. Her horse shied violently, leaping forward in terror.

Ellie's heart lurched into her throat. More shots followed, closer this time, echoing sharply through the forest. Somewhere nearby, hunters were firing, their shots ricocheting through the trees. To her frightened mount, it mattered little that the guns were not aimed at them. The mare bolted.

"Whoa, easy!" Ellie gasped, struggling to steady the reins. But the horse plunged forward in blind panic, crashing through the undergrowth and racing along the twisting path. Leaves scattered beneath pounding hooves, branches whipping past in a blur. The saddle slipped further. It tilted dangerously to one side. Ellie's stomach dropped. She was losing control.

Wild thoughts flooded her mind. If she fell now, at this speed, she might be crippled or killed outright. For one desperate instant a reckless thought flashed through her mind, perhaps an injury might free her from the crushing expectations of her family. But the grim shadow of death swept the thought away just as quickly. Clinging to the pommel with desperate strength, Ellie felt terror crash through her in a white-hot wave as the ground thundered beneath her.

Richard had seen everything, the slipping saddle, her panicked grip, the wild terror blazing in her eyes. His blood surged with adrenaline as he drove his own horse forward, steady even against the echo of gunfire ringing through the trees.

"Hold on, Ellie!" he shouted, urging his mount into a desperate burst of speed. Her horse thundered ahead, but his was swifter beneath his firm command. Inch by inch he closed the distance. Branches whipped past as he leaned forward, guiding his horse alongside the panicked mare. Then, in one practiced and utterly reckless motion, he reached across the gap, wrapped an arm tightly around Ellie's waist, and hauled her free from the failing saddle.

At that exact moment the loosened girth gave way entirely. The saddle slid from the mare's back and crashed to the forest floor. Freed of its burden, the horse bolted wildly into the trees. Richard tightened his hold around Ellie, steadying his own mount as it danced nervously beneath them. Only when he was certain they were safe did he rein in sharply and bring the horse to a halt.

Ellie trembled so violently he feared she might collapse.

Without a word he swung down from the saddle and lifted her gently to the ground, keeping one arm around her until her feet found their balance. Even then he did not release her completely.

Her breath came in ragged gasps, and she could not quite meet his gaze.

"Thank you," she whispered at last, the words barely audible. Her eyes flickered to his before darting quickly away.

"That was a close call," he said quietly, though a note of sternness edged his voice. "Why were you trying to outrun me?"

Her chin lifted at once, defiant. "Because I didn't feel like talking to you."

The coldness of the answer stung more than he cared to admit. Richard flinched inwardly but forced himself to keep his tone calm.

"Ellie, if this is about yesterday, please let me explain."

"There is nothing to explain. I heard you clearly." She turned away, but he caught her arm and gently pulled her back. "How dare you?" she snapped, her blue eyes blazing.

"I am tired of this stubbornness, Danielle Huntington," he said sharply, his patience fraying. "It is childish, and it must end."

Her mouth fell open in disbelief.

"I think," he continued firmly, "that time away from home will do you good. It will help you grow."

Her fury flared hotter. "I am not a child, Lord Blackwood, no matter how much you insist on treating me as one. You can hardly wait for me to be sent away, can you? Well, don't worry, I shall be gone soon enough. My departure is already arranged. Just do not be surprised if London changes me into someone you no longer recognize. After all, is that not what everyone desires?"

His expression softened instantly, the anger draining from his face.

"Ellie, nobody wants you to change," he said gently. "We love you exactly as you are."

But she was too wounded to hear the warmth in his voice.

"Of course you do," she muttered bitterly, turning aside. Before she could pull away completely, he stepped forward and drew her firmly back into his arms.

"Ellie, why would you think we do not love you?"

She pushed against his chest, but her strength was no match for his.

"It doesn't matter," she said, breathless with frustration. "I have other concerns, far more important than quarrels or London society. I must return to the house and speak with my parents. There is a change of plan."

Richard froze, studying her determined face. "A change of plan?" he repeated slowly. "What do you mean?"

Ellie lifted her chin. "I am not going to London. Not yet. My cousin needs me, and I must see to it."

His brows drew together in confusion. "Your cousin? What are you talking about?"

She hesitated for a moment, then exhaled sharply. "If you insist on staying near me, you may," she said stiffly, "but you will not interfere. Nor will you have a say in the matter. My mind is made up."

Richard's chest tightened as he looked at her, the fierce defiance blazing in her eyes, the tears she tried so hard to hide, the faint tremor still running through her frame after the ride. He knew that look. Danielle Huntington had decided. And when Ellie set her mind on something, nothing on earth could easily turn her aside.

For the first time, a troubling thought crossed his mind. If she truly meant to act on whatever reckless plan had taken hold of her... just how dangerous might it become, for her, and for them all?

Danielle and Richard reached the drawing room just as her father was moving past the pleasantries of Eleanor's letter and into the part Ellie dreaded most. Quietly, she slipped toward the tall window, standing half in shadow.

She could not bear to look at them, not when the truth was about to come crashing down. Her heart hammered as her father's voice filled the room. Benedict read aloud in a steady tone, though the deepening furrow in his brow betrayed his growing unease.

> *...You must promise me not to share any of this with your family. What I am about to confide must remain between us. I am in danger enough as it is, and I cannot bear the thought of you becoming a victim as well.*
>
> *Ellie, you have always been brave and outspoken, never letting anyone trample you. Please, never change that. You must protect yourself and others, especially your sisters and cousins. I beg this of you.*
>
> *The truth is this: my marriage is not what the world believes. I did not choose it, and I have never known happiness in it. My husband is harsh, with a temper that makes my days fearful and my nights worse still.*

He takes pleasure in reminding me that I belong to him, body and soul. I am treated with less kindness than even the servants. Often, I long for peace I may never know.

I have tried to escape, but I cannot. He has eyes everywhere, and those who once might have helped me now turn away in fear. I am isolated, trapped, and silenced. If ever he learns of this letter, it will be my ruin.

Promise me that you will never consent to such a fate. Promise me, Ellie, that you will fight for yourself and for others. My husband delights in breaking women, whether timid or strong. And worse, he has begun to cast his gaze upon Olivia. She is far too young to see the danger. I tremble for her future.

When you come to London, watch over her. I fear our father has already made his choice, just as he did with me. I can only pray he does not succeed a second time.

You are my only confidante. Burn this letter. Forget it was ever written. And above all, live free. Live safe.

With all my love,

Eleanor

The final words fell into silence, heavy as a death knell. Elizabeth lowered her hand slowly from her lips, her eyes brimming with tears. Benedict sat stiff and pale, the letter clenched in his fists as though it might burn him. Henry did not move at all, his face set like carved stone, every line deepened by horror.

Eleanor had left much unsaid, yet her silence spoke louder than ink. Every omission was a shadow, every careful restraint a cry. They needed no further confession to understand the truth. Behind her veiled words lay a torment darker than she had dared to write.

By the doorway, Richard found it difficult to draw breath. His gaze flicked instinctively toward Ellie. Though her back remained turned, the trembling of her shoulders betrayed her grief. In the window's reflection he caught the faint glimmer of tears streaking silently down her cheeks. His heart wrenched. Never had he felt so powerless. Anger and sorrow warred within him, not only for Eleanor, trapped in that nightmare, but for Ellie, who had borne the crushing weight of her cousin's suffering alone.

The room remained subdued, heavy as stone, as though even the walls themselves had absorbed the dreadful truth. No one dared speak. For to do so would shatter the fragile hush of shock and sorrow that bound them all.

Ellie straightened from the window. Her cheeks were damp, but her expression had hardened into something else, resolve.

"I cannot leave Eleanor to face this alone," she said, her voice steady though her heart raced. "She begged me not to tell anyone, but now that you know, I will not stand by while my cousin is harmed. I have a proposal. Please hear me out before you dismiss it."

Her parents and grandfather exchanged startled looks. Richard watched her, grave and intent.

"I will agree to become a duchess," she continued, "and do as you wish of me, if you first allow me to go to Eleanor instead of London. She can teach me what I must know for my Season. She was raised as a lady, and despite what she endures, she still carries herself with grace. She is a viscount's daughter, after all."

"Ellie, you will not go anywhere near Lord Ainsworth," Benedict broke in, shaking his head. "If he is half the man your cousin implies, I will not have him within reach of my daughters."

"I must be near Eleanor," Ellie insisted. "She needs hope. She needs someone to protect her. If no one acts, he will destroy her. Johnathon Ainsworth should be publicly disgraced, better still, arrested."

"Danielle," Henry said quietly, his voice heavy with solemn authority, "it is not so simple. No one can arrest the man without proof. The law binds a wife to her husband. Her testimony alone would be disregarded."

"Then disgrace him," Ellie shot back. "Tell the Duke of Devon the truth about his nephew. A man of honor would not permit this to continue. He might force a divorce."

Benedict shook his head again. "Do not be so certain. Exposing his nephew risks scandal for many families. Scandal ruins reputations. And divorce, divorce is ruin."

Ellie's eyes flashed. "What is a woman's life compared to reputation? What is a duchy worth if it rests on the silence of a ruined woman? I would rather see a duke shamed for exposing his kin than honored for turning away while his nephew proves himself a monster."

"There is still no evidence," Benedict said, his voice thick with strain. "Servants will not speak, they risk their livelihoods, perhaps even their lives. And Eleanor..." He faltered, unable to finish.

"That is why I must go," Ellie declared. "If I stay with her, he cannot hide his temper forever. I will earn the servants' trust and coax out the truth. Eventually, something will come to light."

"You cannot—", Benedict began.

"My mind is made up," she cut him off. "Forgive me, Papa, but I cannot sit idle."

"How would you gain entrance?" Benedict demanded. "Do you think Lord Ainsworth will welcome you if you write to him?"

"I would not write. I would arrive unannounced and claim I fled a dreadful match that Grandfather seeks to force upon me. If I appear helpless, Ainsworth may allow me to remain. He would not see me as a threat."

"No, Ellie. Absolutely not." Richard stepped forward, his voice firm. "That man has no scruples. Lord Huntington, you must forbid this."

"You have no say," Ellie snapped, her blue eyes blazing. "This is my choice. Stay out of it."

Richard did not flinch. "Then hear this: you are not going alone. I will not allow it. I will go with you."

Her head whipped toward him. "You cannot go. This is not your affair. If anything happens, who will care for your mother and brother?"

"My brother already manages much of the barony," Richard replied calmly. "He will see to everything in my absence."

Ellie flushed with frustration at his maddening composure. "Are you mad? I do not want you with me."

"I am not asking permission," Richard returned evenly. "The matter is decided."

A taut silence followed. At last Benedict broke it, his tone firm but edged with resignation.

"If this is to be done, it will be done under our terms. Gordon will accompany you, Ellie." His gaze shifted to the steward, who stood nearby, steady and resolute. "And Lord Blackwood will go as well."

Ellie threw up her hands in exasperation. "And what am I supposed to tell them when I arrive with two hulking men in tow?"

Her grandfather stepped forward, his gaze sharp as steel.

"Tell them I have reconciled with your father, and that I have resolved to marry you off to a man thrice your age. Your father, seeking to shield you, has sent you here under the guard of two loyal retainers, trusting your married cousin to provide sanctuary. It is a tale no one will question."

Ellie blinked, momentarily caught off guard. Then, despite herself, a faint smile touched her lips.

"Grandfather, I must admit, that is clever. Do you always conjure such tales so easily?"

The old duke's smile faded. "What I have heard tonight alarms me deeply. Your cousin must be rescued before it is too late." His voice hardened. "I will allow you one month under their roof. After that, if necessary, I shall write to the Duke of Devon myself. And if it comes to that, I will reveal what his nephew has done."

"But what if something happens to Ellie?" Elizabeth asked, her voice trembling.

"You will send word whenever you can," Henry replied, clasping Ellie's hand. "Gordon and Lord Blackwood will report regularly to my steward. And hear me well, Danielle: if at any moment we judge that you must be withdrawn, you will obey without protest. Do you understand? We are reckless even to consider this, but we will not risk your life."

Ellie looked at each of them in turn, her mother, resolute. Her father, pained. Her grandfather, stern. And finally, Richard, whose dark eyes promised unwavering protection. She drew a steady breath and nodded.

"I understand." Her whisper was quiet, but it carried iron. Beneath that calm assent burned a vow, one none of them could see. Nothing, neither fear nor caution, would stop her from saving Eleanor.

"We will not tell your sisters about this," Benedict said firmly, his tone brooking no argument. "You are leaving with your grandfather, and that is final. They need not know anything of this matter."

Before Ellie could respond, a sudden, urgent knock rattled the door. The sound cracked through the heavy silence like thunder. All heads turned. Benedict strode forward.

"Come in," he commanded. The maid entered quickly, cheeks flushed and breath unsteady.

"Forgive me, My Lord. An express has just arrived." She curtsied, stepped forward, and placed a sealed envelope into his hands before retreating with haste. Benedict broke the seal.

As his eyes raced over the page, his face blanched. The paper trembled faintly in his grip, his knuckles turning, bone white. When at last he lowered it, horror was etched into every line of his features.

"What is it, Benedict?" Elizabeth whispered, her voice frayed, her eyes wide with dread. His reply came hoarse, scarcely more than a breath.

"The express is from your sister. Olivia visited Eleanor for a few days... and was taken during the night. No one knows where she is."

A collective gasp tore through the room. Ellie turned as pale as linen, her knees giving way beneath her. Richard caught her before she could crumple, his arms steady as he drew her against him. His dark eyes locked on hers, burning with concern.

"Papa..." Ellie's voice cracked, raw with terror. "What does that mean? Do you think Uncle Magnus had a hand in this? Or—or is Lord Ainsworth behind it?" Her blue eyes brimmed with tears, her entire frame trembling. Elizabeth pressed a shaking hand to her lips.

"Benedict... what are we going to do?"

Benedict shook his head slowly. Helplessness carved deep into his face. But Henry surged forward with sudden, grim purpose. His voice cut like steel through the rising panic.

"Gordon, fetch Lord Woodworth and Lord Beverton. At once."

The steward bowed and vanished without hesitation.

8

Where Evil Wore a Smile

Ellie, still ashen, turned to her grandfather in confusion, her voice wavering.

"Why would you summon them? We did not want anyone else to know."

Henry clasped her hand, guiding her gently onto the settee beside him. Richard, unwilling to release her entirely, took the seat at her other side, his presence a quiet anchor of strength.

"Because, child," Henry said, his voice deep and unwavering, "this evil cannot be fought alone. Lord Woodworth and Lord Beverton wield influence beyond ours. Between them, they can move in places even most dukes cannot. If we are to uncover what has befallen your cousins, we will need every ally we can muster."

Ellie's lip trembled. "But Eleanor didn't want anyone to know..."

Henry's gaze softened, though sorrow darkened his eyes.

"Eleanor no longer has that choice. If Olivia is missing, your cousin will want help, desperately."

Before Ellie could answer, another sharp knock resounded. The door opened, and Gordon returned, two distinguished figures following in his wake.

"Come in, quickly," Henry urged, rising to greet them. His hand cut sharply through the air toward the steward. "Lock the door."

The heavy latch fell with a decisive click, sealing the chamber. The air in the room seemed to thicken, as though the very house itself understood the gravity of what was about to unfold.

The night air was cool, fragrant with damp earth and fresh grass. A pale ribbon of moonlight glimmered along the narrow creek as Ellie slipped quietly along its winding path. Her cloak brushed against the reeds, their soft rustle the only sound accompanying her hurried steps. She needed space, air that did not taste of fear, secrets, and the suffocating weight of duty. Inside the house the walls seemed to press inward, heavy with whispered plans, anxious glances, and the terrible knowledge of what Eleanor and Olivia might be enduring. Out here, beneath the open sky, the world felt wider. Freer.

Ellie slowed as the familiar shape of the old oak came into view. The tree had stood beside the creek longer than anyone could remember, its enormous trunk twisted with age, its gnarled branches stretching upward like ancient arms toward the stars. Moonlight shimmered across its leaves, and the breeze stirred them with a soft, comforting whisper. How many times had she climbed this tree as a child? When she was angry. When she was hurt. When she simply wished to disappear from the expectations of everyone around her. It had always been her refuge.

Without hesitation she grasped the lowest branch and pulled herself upward. Her movements were quick and practiced, the sort of skill learned over years of childhood mischief. Her skirts hindered her little as she climbed higher, finding the familiar footholds and bends in the bark until she reached her favorite perch.

At last, she settled onto a broad, sturdy branch high above the ground. The creek murmured quietly below. The stars glittered overhead, scattered across the velvet sky like shards of silver. Ellie drew a slow breath. For a fleeting moment she could almost believe she was a little girl again, hidden from the world, far from burdens she had never asked to carry. No dukedoms. No dangerous plans. No terrified cousins writing desperate letters in secret. Just a girl in a tree beneath the stars.

Her shoulders slowly relaxed as the quiet wrapped around her like a comforting blanket. Then a faint sound drifted upward from below. Footsteps. Ellie stiffened instantly, every sense sharpening. She leaned forward slightly and peered through the leaves toward the ground. A tall figure stood near the base of the tree, looking upward. Even in the dim light she recognized the familiar broad shoulders and dark hair. Ellie released a long sigh of exasperation.

"Richard," she muttered under her breath.

He climbed swiftly, sure-footed even in the darkness, the rough bark offering familiar holds beneath his hands. Within moments he reached her branch and settled beside her, balancing easily against the great trunk. His presence was steady, grounding in a way she had always known, even before either of them understood what it meant. Yet his eyes searched her face with quiet intensity, as though trying to read every unspoken thought she carried.

"What are you doing out here, Ellie?" he asked softly. "We leave at first light. You should be resting."

Ellie gave a faint nod, though it was clear she had not truly heard him. Her gaze remained fixed on the silver ribbon of moonlight shimmering across the creek below. The water moved gently over the stones, whispering through the quiet night. For a moment she simply watched it. Then she glanced at him. Only for a heartbeat. But it was enough.

In that brief turn of her face, Richard saw the glisten of tears she could no longer hide. His chest tightened painfully. Without a word he reached for her hand. His fingers closed around hers, warm and steady, as though anchoring her to the world when everything else threatened to pull her away.

"Are you certain you want to go through with this?" he asked quietly. His voice was low, but beneath it lay something deeper, fear. Not fear of the journey itself, nor of the man they meant to confront. Fear for her. Ellie drew a ragged breath, the sound trembling in the still air.

"I don't want to," she admitted at last. "But I must." Her voice faltered, and she looked away again toward the dark water. "If we stormed the estate with men, Ainsworth would see it as war. Eleanor warned us, he would kill her without hesitation." She paused, swallowing hard.

"And now, with Olivia gone..." Her voice broke. The words seemed to vanish into the quiet of the forest. "If we are not careful," she whispered, "I could lose them both."

Richard's grip tightened around her hand, fierce with sudden determination.

"I'm afraid for you, Ellie," he said softly. "More than I can say."

The admission hung between them, raw and honest. Ellie's throat tightened. She stared at their joined hands for a moment before speaking again.

"I know," she said quietly. "And I am frightened too."

For a moment the fierce, unyielding girl he knew seemed to fade, leaving only the young woman beneath, the one who carried far more weight than anyone her age should bear.

"But I love them," she continued, her voice growing steadier. "I will not turn my back while they suffer."

The words hung in the night air, solemn as an oath. Below them the creek murmured softly over the stones, and above them the stars burned bright and silent, witnesses to a promise Ellie knew she would never break.

Ellie was utterly spent as she stepped down from the carriage. Her limbs ached from the long journey, and her eyes burned with the heaviness of too little sleep. They had traveled nearly two days without pause, stopping only briefly to change horses and swallow a hurried meal before pressing onward again. The road had wound from Plymouth through miles of rugged countryside, rolling hills, narrow lanes bordered by stone walls, and forests that seemed to stretch endlessly toward the horizon.

At last, as the sun dipped low in the sky, the great estate had come into view. Now Ellie stood at the foot of the carriage steps, steadying herself as the stiffness in her legs protested the sudden movement. She drew a slow breath, lifting her gaze toward the imposing structure before her.

The secondary seat of the Duke of Devon rose proudly against the fading light, a vast stone manor perched upon gently sloping grounds. Its towering windows reflected the last golden glow of evening, while elegant terraces and carefully shaped gardens spread outward in orderly perfection. Gravel paths wound between sculpted hedges and ancient trees, their branches stirring softly in the breeze.

Even through the haze of exhaustion, Ellie could not help but feel a flicker of awe. The estate was magnificent. Its sheer size and quiet grandeur spoke of generations of wealth and power. Servants moved discreetly across the grounds, tending to the last tasks of the day, while the distant sound of horses and carriage wheels echoed faintly through the courtyard.

Yet Ellie forced her expression into calm composure, masking her amazement with the quiet dignity expected of a young lady. From what she had been told, only her own grandfather's duchy surpassed this one in scale and splendor. And yet, despite its beauty, a ripple of unease stirred within her. Something about the place felt... heavy. As though beneath its polished elegance lay shadows no amount of wealth could conceal.

Lord Errett Harold Ainsworth, the present Duke of Devon, had never declared which male heir would inherit the title and estate. According to her grandfather's acquaintances, the uncertainty had been quite intentional. Year after year, the duke had deferred the choice. Now Ellie understood why. Johnathon Ainsworth's reputation was already stained by whispers of cruelty, toward his servants, toward tenants, toward anyone who dared cross him. Stories had circulated quietly among those who knew the family well enough to speak in private.

Still, the old duke had hoped that marriage might temper his heir's darker nature. A wife, it was believed, might soften him. Might civilize him. Might force him into the responsibilities expected of a future duke.

Ellie's stomach tightened at the thought. Now she realized the bitter truth. This was not merely a residence for a young married couple. It was a test. A silent trial arranged by an aging duke desperate to believe his heir could still be redeemed. And Eleanor had become the unwilling instrument of that hope. The burden of proving whether Johnathon Ainsworth could be reformed... had fallen squarely upon the shoulders of the young woman forced to call herself his wife.

A solemn butler received her and, at her request, announced only that a visitor had arrived, concealing her identity. Ellie wished to surprise her cousin Eleanor and thought it best to remain discreet. The servant led her into the parlor, where tall windows spilled late-afternoon light across richly upholstered chairs and gleaming woodwork.

Moments later, the door opened and three figures entered. At the front stood a tall, broad-shouldered man with a stern, forbidding expression, Johnathon Ainsworth himself. Behind him came Eleanor, and with her another gentleman, strikingly handsome, though not so imposing as Lord Ainsworth. Eleanor gasped the instant she saw her.

"Ellie! What on earth are you doing here?"

Ellie had meant to feign distress, to play her part with carefully rehearsed tears. But the moment her gaze met her cousin's, and she saw the sorrow shadowing Eleanor's eyes, her composure crumbled. Real tears welled and spilled, born of exhaustion and aching empathy. Eleanor rushed forward and gathered her into a protective embrace.

"I apologize for coming unannounced," Ellie whispered, her voice trembling. "But I knew not where else to go." She clung tightly, as though afraid her cousin might vanish if she let go. "My uncle passed away, and now my grandfather insists I must assume his duchy. He appeared suddenly, demanding I go with him. He has already chosen a man he wishes me to marry."

Eleanor drew back, her face pale with alarm, and cast a fleeting glance at her husband before replying. Her fingers twisted tightly in Ellie's sleeve, a silent plea for restraint.

"Oh, Ellie... I am so very sorry. And your father?"

"Papa is doing all he can to shield me. He sent me away with two of his servants, hoping I might find sanctuary here, at least for a time."

At this, Eleanor's hand fell quickly from Ellie's arm, her shoulders stiffening as though she had suddenly remembered she was being watched. She lowered her gaze, her expression composed, though her lashes trembled faintly.

The marquess cleared his throat, his green eyes fixed on Ellie with a cold, assessing stare. Though outwardly stern, there was something in his expression that made her skin crawl. His gaze swept deliberately over her, lingering not only on her lips but on her figure, bold in its scrutiny, as though already measuring her for conquest. A prickle of dread raced up her spine.

"If you cannot remain here," Lord Ainsworth asked at last, his tone more businesslike than compassionate, "do you have another course to pursue?"

Ellie drew a steady breath. "We have kin in Ireland. Papa said I might go to them if all else failed, but I do not know them, and I have heard troubling accounts of their character. I fear I should not be safe there."

Johnathon remained unmoved, his silence heavy. Then the second gentleman stepped forward.

"Come now, Cousin," he said with an easy, confident smile. "Surely you will not ignore the plea of a beautiful lady in distress. It is our duty to protect such a one." His words carried a trace of smugness, yet his eyes held a warmth that seemed genuine.

Ellie studied him more closely. His charm felt somewhat rehearsed, yet there was kindness in his expression that eased her unease, at least where he was concerned. But when her gaze returned to Lord Ainsworth, she found his eyes fixed on her with a hunger that turned her blood cold. There was possession in that stare, an unspoken claim, as though he were already imagining her trapped beneath his roof, subject to his will.

She forced herself not to recoil, though every instinct within her screamed a warning. Eleanor had seen it too. Her lips pressed together so tightly they blanched white, her hands folding rigidly into her skirts. She lowered her eyes quickly, as though terrified to let her husband see even the smallest flicker of recognition. That tiny act of silence told Ellie everything.

"She could stay in the chamber next to mine," Eleanor suggested softly, her voice scarcely more than a whisper. Her chin dipped, as though even that small suggestion required courage. Lord Ainsworth inclined his head with a smile meant to appear gracious, though the darkness in his eyes betrayed it.

"But of course. Eleanor's family members are always welcome beneath this roof." His gaze returned to Ellie with unsettling intensity. "I presume we have not been formally introduced?"

Ellie shook her head silently.

"I shall be delighted to make your acquaintance," he said, flashing a grin that never reached his eyes. It was not warmth but a predator's amusement, and it sent a chill through her. Instinctively, she stepped closer to Eleanor, drawing strength from her cousin's presence.

"My wife can show you to your chamber," he added, straightening his cuffs as though already dismissing them from further thought. "I must beg to be excused. We have guests awaiting me, and I should not keep them waiting."

He was halfway to the door before noticing his cousin still lingering.

"Are you coming?" Johnathon asked impatiently.

"In a moment." The younger man did not look at him but instead fixed his gaze on Ellie. "Lady Ainsworth, will you not favor us with an introduction?"

Eleanor hesitated, her throat working as though the words caught before they could escape. At last, she inclined her head.

"Certainly, Your Grace. This is my cousin, Lady Danielle Huntington." She turned to Ellie, her voice softening though the flicker of fear remained. "Ellie, this is Lord Ainsworth's cousin, Lord Andrew Bennett, Duke of Somerset."

Lord Bennett gave a graceful bow, his dark eyes glinting with easy charm. Ellie dipped into a curtsy, forcing her composure firmly back into place.

"It is a pleasure to make your acquaintance, Lady Danielle," he said with a dashing smile before turning and following Lord Ainsworth from the room.

Ellie fell into step beside Eleanor, who paused briefly to instruct a servant to see her cousin's trunks delivered upstairs. The maid bobbed a quick curtsy and hurried away, while Eleanor gestured for Ellie to follow.

Together they ascended the grand staircase. Their footsteps echoed faintly against the polished marble, the sound hollow in the quiet hall. The wide stair curved gracefully toward the upper gallery. Its banister carved with intricate vines and gilded flourishes that caught the glow of the tall windows. Portraits of long-dead ancestors lined the walls, stern men in military coats, elegant ladies adorned with jewels, each gaze seeming to follow them as they climbed. Ellie might once have admired such splendor. Tonight, she felt only the weight of it.

Eleanor walked a step ahead, her posture perfectly composed, every movement measured and elegant in the manner expected of a lady of rank. Yet Ellie noticed the subtle tension in her shoulders, the way her fingers twisted briefly in the folds of her skirts before she forced them still again. Not a word passed between them.

At last, they reached the upper corridor, where thick carpets softened their steps and tall windows overlooked the sweeping gardens below. Eleanor led her down a long hallway until they reached a pair of carved double doors.

"This will be your chamber," Eleanor said quietly. She pushed the door open. The room beyond was vast and richly adorned. A grand canopied bed stood at its center, draped in layers of silk and velvet in deep cream and rose. Sunlight from the tall windows spilled across polished floors and delicate furnishings, gilded mirrors, embroidered chairs, and a writing desk set neatly beside the hearth. Fresh flowers stood arranged in crystal vases, their faint fragrance mingling with the soft scent of lavender and polished wood. It was a chamber fit for a duchess.

Yet for all its beauty, Ellie felt a shiver run through her. The room was luxurious, comforting even, but it could not dispel the unease that had settled deep within her chest. She could still see the way Eleanor had forced composure upon her face downstairs.

Still feel the lingering echo of Lord Ainsworth's gaze. Those cold, appraising eyes seemed almost to follow her into the room, as though the house itself were aware of his presence. Ellie wrapped her arms around herself briefly, pushing back the chill that had nothing to do with the evening air. Behind her, Eleanor quietly closed the door.

Only after Gordon and Richard had carried the trunks inside and quietly withdrawn did Eleanor clasp Ellie's hand and draw her down beside her on the settee. Her cousin's face was pale. Her eyes were shadowed with worry.

"Ellie," she whispered, "why have you come? Did your father truly send you here to hide from your grandfather?"

Ellie exhaled slowly, then tightened her hold on Eleanor's trembling fingers.

"Papa knows I am here, and so does Grandfather. I could no longer keep your suffering to myself. I told them, Eleanor. Forgive me, but I could not endure the thought of you left alone in such torment. I love you as dearly as a sister, and I refuse to sit idle while that monster destroys you."

At that, Eleanor's composure shattered. She buried her face against Ellie's shoulder, sobs breaking loose. Ellie wrapped her arms around her, stroking her back as though soothing a frightened child.

"I don't want you to be hurt, Ellie," Eleanor choked out. "Johnathon is dangerous, more dangerous than you realize. I am convinced he is behind Olivia's disappearance. She noticed things... things he did to me. She confronted him. I begged her to stay silent, but she would not. The next day she was gone. I fear she will be lost forever. I cannot bear the thought of him turning his malice upon you."

Ellie's jaw set, her spine straightening with resolve.

"Then even more reason I am here. I will find a way to free you, Eleanor. And I will uncover the truth of what happened to Olivia."

Her cousin caught her hand desperately. "Then promise me, at the very least, that you will not provoke him. No matter what he says, no matter what he does, do not answer him. Keep your distance. I beg you, promise me."

But Ellie shook her head, her eyes blazing. "I cannot. I will avoid him when I can, but if he dares lay a hand on you, I will not remain silent. That is why Papa insisted that Gordon and Richard accompany me. They will not let him harm us without consequence."

For a long moment the room was silent save for the faint crackle of the fire. Then Ellie spoke again, her voice low.

"What of Lord Bennett? Why is he here? What do you know of him?"

Eleanor lifted her head, brushing hastily at her tears.

"I cannot say for certain. I doubt even Johnathon knows his true purpose. But his presence unsettles my husband. He seems wary of him, perhaps unsure whether his cousin can be trusted. Because of it, Johnathon has kept his more dangerous companions away. While Lord Bennett has been here, no one has forced themselves upon me. For a fortnight I have been spared the worst of it. In that alone, his presence has been my safety."

Ellie's expression softened, though her brows remained knit with concern.

"Then I am grateful for it, though I still find the timing curious. I shall keep my eye on him."

Eleanor attempted a faint smile. "You must be weary from your travels. Shall I have supper sent up to you?"

Ellie shook her head. "No, thank you. Perhaps Richard and Gordon would welcome a tray, but I am well enough. I ate at our last stop."

Eleanor rose reluctantly, smoothing the folds of her gown.

"Then I must return to our guests. Rest, Ellie. Tomorrow will bring more than enough burdens of its own."

Ellie watched her cousin depart, her heart aching at the weight of sorrow that seemed to bow Eleanor's every step.

Nearly an hour passed before Ellie heard her cousin return to the adjoining chamber. She had not slept. Though exhaustion weighed heavily upon her limbs, her mind refused to quiet. She lay atop the bed in her nightgown, staring at the canopy overhead while the events of the day replayed relentlessly in her thoughts. At last, the faint creak of a door reached her. Moments later, muffled sobbing seeped through the adjoining wall. The sound pierced the stillness like a blade.

Ellie sat upright instantly, her heart tightening with dread. The quiet weeping continued, soft, broken, and utterly hopeless. Concern overcame her fatigue at once. She slipped quickly into her dressing gown and crossed the room. Just as she raised her hand to knock upon the connecting door, another voice reached her. Low. Venomous. Barely restrained. Ellie froze. Slowly, she leaned closer to the wall, her breath caught in her throat.

"You know my rules, Eleanor," Lord Ainsworth murmured coldly. "They've come to enjoy your company."

Ellie's stomach lurched violently.

"But my cousin is in the room next to mine," Eleanor whispered desperately, her voice taut with fear.

"That is your fault," Lord Ainsworth hissed. "I hesitated to let her stay for a reason."

A surge of dread flooded Ellie's chest. Heart hammering, she edged her door open a fraction. Through the narrow slit she glimpsed the scene within the adjoining chamber. Lord Ainsworth had Eleanor pinned against the wall. His hand was wrapped cruelly around her throat. Eleanor's fingers clawed weakly at his wrist, her face pale and strained as she struggled for breath.

"If Danielle learns even a whisper of what happens here," he snarled, leaning close to his trembling wife, "you will beg me for death before I am finished with you."

Ellie's nails dug into the doorframe.

"And if you dare tell her anything," he continued softly, his voice thick with menace, "I swear I will sell your precious cousin to a man who will tear her apart for sport."

Eleanor's body shook violently. "You cannot—" she gasped, clutching desperately at his wrist. "Ellie has nothing to do with you."

"She is in my house," he snapped. His grip tightened for a brutal moment longer. Then he shoved her away with savage force. Eleanor staggered backward, her head striking the carved bedframe with a sickening thud.

Ellie bit down on her hand to keep from crying out. Lord Ainsworth released her as though she were nothing more than refuse and strode toward the door. A moment later it slammed behind him with a violent crack that echoed down the corridor. Silence fell.

For a heartbeat Eleanor remained where she had collapsed. Then her strength gave way. She slid slowly to the floor, her shoulders shaking as the sobs she had held back burst free into the empty room.

Ellie rushed into the chamber and dropped to her knees beside her cousin.

"Eleanor!" she cried softly, gathering her into her arms. Her chest heaved with fury and dread as she held the trembling woman close. Eleanor clutched at her desperately.

"Ellie, go back to your room," she begged through her tears. "Please. It will be safer if you leave tomorrow."

"I am not leaving you," Ellie said firmly. "What did he mean earlier? What was he talking about?"

Eleanor's wide, glistening eyes lifted slowly to her. "You... you heard?"

Ellie nodded grimly.

"Then you understand why you must go," Eleanor pleaded, gripping her arm with shaking fingers. "He cannot know you overheard. I will endure whatever he does to me, I always have, but I cannot bear the thought of him selling you to some vile brute. For my sake, you must escape while you can."

Ellie's expression hardened with resolve. "Papa and Grandfather know I am here. If harm befalls me, Lord Ainsworth will face a reckoning from which he cannot hide. I will not leave. I will find a way to free you, and I will discover what happened to Olivia. But first, tell me what he meant."

Eleanor broke again, sobs shaking her frail body. "Two of his friends have arrived," she whispered hoarsely. "They only ever come for one reason."

Ellie gasped, horror twisting her features. "Those wretched swine."

Eleanor grasped her hands urgently. "You must go to your room," she urged, pale as death. "Better yet, I will have you moved to a guest chamber farther away. You cannot stay here tonight."

"No." Ellie's voice was fierce and unwavering. "I will remain. I will sleep on the settee if I must, but I will not abandon you to those fiends."

The last trace of color drained from Eleanor's face. "Ellie, I forbid it. I cannot let you risk yourself. Please, you mustn't stay."

"Forgive me, Eleanor," Ellie said gently but firmly. "But this is not your choice. I will not leave you defenseless. If your husband demands to know why I am here, I shall say I fell asleep waiting for you."

Eleanor's eyes filled with desperate tears. "Ellie, please—"

But Ellie had already risen. She crossed into her own chamber, fetched her pillow and blanket, and carried them back. With quiet dignity, she arranged them on the settee near the hearth, smoothing the folds with deliberate calm. When she finished, she turned back to her cousin.

"You are not alone tonight," she said softly, though her tone carried the weight of a promise. Eleanor pressed her trembling hands over her face, caught between gratitude and terror. For a long moment she simply wept. At last, she sank slowly onto the bed, too broken to argue further.

The cousins remained awake in the dim chamber, the fire casting faint shadows along the walls. Neither spoke. Their hearts seemed to beat in the same anxious rhythm, each listening for the sound they both feared. Half an hour crawled by. No footsteps approached. No knock disturbed the door. Gradually the dreadful silence softened, and exhaustion began to dull the sharp edge of their fear.

At last Ellie drifted into uneasy slumber upon the settee, one hand still curled tightly in the blanket as though ready to spring awake at the slightest sound. Across the room, Eleanor lay awake a while longer, tears soaking her pillow before fatigue finally claimed her as well.

9

A Storm Yet to Break

Ellie startled awake to the sound of muffled cries. For a heartbeat, disoriented, she could not remember where she was. Then memory struck, her arrival at Ainsworth Hall, Eleanor's tears, the horror she had overheard, and she was instantly alert.

A shadow loomed in the darkness. As her eyes adjusted, her blood ran cold. A man bent over Eleanor's bed, one hand clamped over her cousin's mouth, the other bracing himself as he tried to climb atop her. Eleanor thrashed beneath him, muffled sobs sharp and desperate.

Rage ignited in Ellie's veins. With a surge of fury, she leapt from the settee, seized the intruder by the arm, and wrenched him back with all her strength. He stumbled, crashed against the wardrobe, and crumpled heavily to the floor. Eleanor gasped for air, trembling violently, as Ellie planted herself before her like a shield.

"Stay away from her!" she cried, fists clenched.

The man lurched upright, swaying unsteadily, the heavy reek of liquor rolling from his breath. Before he could lunge again, the chamber door burst open. Light flooded the room as Lord Ainsworth strode in, flanked by his steward and butler, each bearing a lamp. The flickering glow fell across the intruder's face, and Ellie's breath caught. It was not some nameless scoundrel. It was Lord Bennett, the Duke of Somerset.

"What is the meaning of this?" Lord Ainsworth thundered, his eyes darting from his cousin to his wife's terror-stricken form. Ellie drew herself up, chin high, her eyes blazing.

"What it means, My Lord," she snapped, "is that your cousin attacked your wife. I woke up to find him forcing himself upon her. He was climbing into her bed when I dragged him off."

"I—" Lord Bennett swayed, his words slurred. "I beg your forgiveness, Cousin. I wandered into the wrong chamber. I... I had promised a maid a visit, you see." He gave a leering grin, his eyes glassy with drink, and even dared to wink at Ellie. Her stomach turned with revulsion.

"You are vile, sir," she spat before she could stop herself. "One would think a duke possessed better command of his manners."

The room stilled. The butler and steward exchanged startled glances, while Lord Ainsworth's face darkened at her audacity.

"What are you doing in this room?" he demanded sharply, too quickly, too defensively. Ellie nearly rolled her eyes. Instead, her voice turned cold as ice.

"That is your first question, My Lord? Not why your cousin was assaulting your wife in the dead of night? Curious priorities indeed."

Lord Ainsworth's mouth snapped shut. His silence was not that of a man caught off guard, but of one calculating, measuring how much she had seen, how much she might reveal. A flicker of cold fury crossed his eyes, gone in an instant, yet enough to chill Ellie's blood. This was not embarrassment. It was a warning.

"I fell asleep on the settee while waiting for Eleanor," Ellie continued, her voice steady though her pulse thundered. "A noise woke me. I saw Lord Bennett, drunk and disgraceful, forcing himself upon her. You may feign ignorance, but I know what I saw." Her gaze flicked to Bennett with open disdain before returning to the marquess.

"You would do well to keep a closer watch on your cousin, or better still, curb the drink that robs him of what little decency he possesses."

The steward coughed, suspiciously close to laughter. Even the butler struggled to conceal the twitch of a smile. Ellie's gaze sharpened.

"If I were mistress here, I would demand your cousin's departure at first light. No household is safe with such a man inside its walls."

Lord Ainsworth stiffened. His smile was thin and reptilian, his voice clipped.

"You forget yourself. My cousin is my guest, not yours."

"Oh, I am well aware," Ellie shot back coolly. "Which is precisely why, for my cousin's protection, my retainers will stand watch through the night. My father was wise to send them with me. We had heard whispers that you entertained men of questionable character. I dismissed them, for Eleanor's sake. Yet tonight proves otherwise. Your cousin is no gentleman, and certainly no man of honor."

Silence thickened, heavy and dangerous. The men stood stunned, struck momentarily speechless by the young woman's audacity. But it was Ainsworth's eyes, flat, assessing, predatory, that warned Ellie, she had not humiliated him. She had provoked him. And he would remember this moment.

"It is late," Ellie said at last, her tone calm and commanding. "We require rest. Lord Bennett, I suggest you find your chamber, sober yourself, and prepare to beg forgiveness, from Lady Ainsworth, and from the maid you so crudely maligned." She inclined her head toward the door, every inch the future duchess she refused to be.

One by one, and without a word, the men withdrew. The door shut heavily behind them. For a long moment the chamber remained silent. Then Eleanor clutched Ellie's hand, still trembling. But in her eyes flickered something new. Something fragile and dangerous. Hope.

Eleanor gazed at her cousin as though she were some marvelous, impossible creature, her eyes wide with awe and disbelief.

"How can you be so confident, so fearless, Ellie?" she whispered, her voice trembling. Ellie sighed softly. She pulled a chair close to the bedside and sat down so she could meet her cousin's gaze.

"Because I was raised differently." Her voice softened. "Eleanor... your father tormented you your entire life, didn't he?"

The silence that followed was heavy. Eleanor's lips quivered, and her eyes fell helplessly to her lap. At last, she gave a small, broken nod. Ellie reached across and laid her hand gently over hers. When she spoke again, her voice was quiet, but it carried both warmth and steel.

"Papa never harmed us. Not once. Mama would sometimes sigh that I was too wild, too unladylike, too disinterested in the accomplishments expected of a proper young lady. Emilia absorbed those lessons like a sponge. She is the very picture of refinement." A faint, fond smile touched Ellie's lips. "But Papa allowed me to be myself. I could climb trees, speak my mind, laugh too loudly, even argue with him, and he encouraged it." She paused, her brow furrowing slightly as she considered her next words.

"I know I do not have much in common with the young ladies of the ton. Perhaps that will be a disadvantage when the time comes for me to marry." She lifted one shoulder in a small shrug. "But even so, I will never allow any man to treat me as though I were a child, nor will I allow anyone to silence my voice." Her gaze sharpened, the quiet fire returning to her eyes.

"Women are not foolish creatures to be managed like disobedient children. And any man who expects respect ought to grant us the same dignity in return."

Eleanor stared at her for a long moment, tears glimmering faintly in her eyes, yet this time they were not born solely of sorrow. For the first time in a very long while, they held the faintest spark of admiration.

Ellie's words, spoken with quiet conviction, sank deep into Eleanor's heart, steadying her like a balm against years of fear. For a moment, the tight knot that had lived in her chest for so long seemed to loosen. And yet, beneath that fragile comfort, a darker truth pressed insistently against her thoughts. Johnathon would not forgive Ellie's boldness tonight. His silence during Bennett's disgrace had not been shame. It had been calculation. Eleanor knew that look too well, the cold stillness behind his eyes when he was already deciding how, and when, to make someone pay.

She sat very still beside Ellie. Her hands folded tightly in her lap as her mind drifted backward through the years. What might her life have been, she wondered, if her father had allowed her to laugh... to question... to simply be?

She remembered the rare visits with her cousins during childhood. Those fleeting days had been filled with sunlight, laughter, and freedom so intoxicating it had almost frightened her. Ellie climbing trees with reckless delight, Emilia reciting poems beside the garden fountain, their aunt smiling warmly as though joy were the most natural thing in the world.

Those moments had felt like stolen treasure. But the moment Eleanor returned home, the illusion shattered. If she dared to answer back... if she showed even the smallest glimmer of spirit her cousins had awakened in her... her father would notice. And he would crush it. The punishments had been swift and merciless. He would beat the defiance from her until her body trembled and her voice broke into sobs. Then came the colder cruelties, the long days locked away in silence, meals withheld, kindness denied, until the fire within her dimmed and obedience replaced the courage she had once glimpsed in herself.

Little by little, her voice had been ground down into trembling submission. But Olivia had been different. Olivia had always been braver. She had seen things, things Johnathon had done to Eleanor after the marriage, and she had not remained silent. Eleanor had tried desperately to shield her sister. More than once she had stepped forward to take punishments meant for Olivia, begging her to keep quiet, to stay safe, to let the storm pass. But Olivia had refused to bow.

And then, one day, she was simply gone. No explanation. No farewell. Only absence. The memory tightened around Eleanor's heart like a vice, the pain as sharp now as it had been the day she realized Olivia would not return. Deep within her soul she knew the truth. Johnathon's cruelty had never ended with her.

Ellie squeezed her cousin's trembling hand. "We will get you away from this man," she said gently. "And perhaps one day a good man, one who is protective and kind, will come along for you. You are of age now, Eleanor. If we can find a way for you to obtain a divorce, your father will have no claim over you."

"My father would never forgive such a scandal," Eleanor whispered, her eyes brimming with tears. "He would cast me out of the family forever."

"Your father is a tyrant," Ellie replied firmly. "He bartered you away to this demon of a man. If he disowns you, so be it. You would be free, and you would not be alone. My family would welcome you. They know what it means to suffer rejection. Do you not remember?"

"What of your grandfather?" Eleanor asked hesitantly. Ellie leaned back slightly, her expression softening.

"It was his father's doing that led to Papa's disownment," she explained. "He forced a loveless marriage upon my grandfather and grandmother, and he tried the same with Papa. But Papa resisted. He eloped with Mama instead. For years I was furious with my grandfather, but now..." She paused, her gaze lowering thoughtfully.

"Now that I know what has been done to you, I see things differently. His story, and Papa's, make more sense. We cannot always know the battles fought in silence." She exhaled slowly, then rose from her chair. "But for now, we both need rest. I suggest you lock your door."

Eleanor winced and shook her head. "I am not allowed to do that," she murmured, shame coloring her cheeks. "Johnathon took the key long ago. He insists on access at all times."

Ellie drew in a sharp breath through her teeth, her entire body tensing. Rage flickered in her eyes, but she forced herself to remain calm. She had already provoked Lord Ainsworth more than enough for one night, and she knew he was the sort of man who bided his vengeance. To push further now might invite disaster.

"Then we will go to my room," she said at last, her voice steady with resolve. "We can lock the door there."

Eleanor's face went pale. She glanced nervously toward the chamber door.

"He will be furious if I do such a thing."

"Let him be furious," Ellie said firmly. "I doubt anyone will dare come here again tonight. But if Lord Ainsworth storms in, I will take the blame."

Eleanor stared at her in disbelief. "How would you take the blame? He will only turn his anger on you."

"I will tell him," Ellie replied without hesitation, "that I was too unsettled by his cousin's drunken intrusion to sleep in an unlocked chamber. I will say I insisted you remain with me. If he must be angry, let him be angry with me."

For the first time that night, Eleanor let out a soft, genuine giggle. For a fleeting moment she could almost imagine Ellie standing boldly before her husband, meeting his fury with fearless defiance and demanding obedience rather than yielding it. The thought warmed her heart and frightened her all the same. For she knew Johnathon would not forget the insult Ellie had delivered tonight. His fury was merely waiting. A storm yet to break.

Just as Ellie had predicted, no one disturbed Eleanor's chamber again that night. The corridors remained quiet, the oppressive silence of Ainsworth Hall settling heavily over the sleeping house. No footsteps approached their door. No knock shattered the fragile peace. Perhaps Ellie's bold defiance had rattled them more than they wished to admit.

Yet even as exhaustion slowly dulled the sharp edge of their fear, Eleanor could not find rest.

She lay awake long after Ellie's breathing softened into the steady rhythm of sleep on the settee. The fire had burned low, its fading embers casting faint shadows across the walls, while the distant creak of old timbers echoed through the vast manor like uneasy whispers.

Eleanor stared into the darkness, her hands clasped tightly against the coverlet. She knew her husband too well. Johnathon Ainsworth was not a man who forgot humiliation. Nor was he one to lash out blindly in anger. His cruelty was colder than that, measured, patient, deliberate. His silence tonight had not been the restraint of a chastened man. It had been calculation.

Somewhere within the house, Eleanor knew, he was already deciding how to repay the insult Ellie had dealt him before his servants... before his cousin. The thought chilled her more deeply than the cold night air slipping through the window. She turned her head slightly and glanced toward the dim outline of Ellie sleeping across the room. Her brave, reckless cousin.

Even in sleep Ellie looked stubborn, one arm flung loosely across the blanket as though she had fallen asleep ready to rise again at the slightest alarm. A faint ache tightened Eleanor's chest. Ellie believed she could protect her. Perhaps she even believed she could defeat Johnathon. But Eleanor knew the truth. Johnathon never forgot. And he never forgave.

Outside, the wind stirred softly through the trees, rustling the leaves like a quiet warning. Eleanor closed her eyes at last, though sleep came only in restless fragments, haunted by the certainty that her husband's silence was not surrender. It was only the beginning.

Ellie woke at sunrise, her mind already restless. The events of the previous night echoed relentlessly, yet the stillness of morning offered her a fragile breath of peace. Eleanor had slipped back to her own chamber before dawn, leaving Ellie alone.

Determined not to linger under Lord Ainsworth's roof longer than necessary, she dressed quickly, braided her hair, and slipped outside before the household stirred. The air was cool and fresh, touched with the warmth of the rising sun. Mist hovered over the fields, while shafts of gold pierced the trees at the wood's edge. Birds trilled overhead, and the distant bark of dogs carried across the land. For a fleeting moment, Ellie felt free, alive, unshackled from the suffocating air of Ainsworth Hall.

She smiled when a duck suddenly appeared on the path, her tiny ducklings scurrying comically behind her before vanishing into the reeds. The tender sight softened her heart. But the moment shattered at the thunder of hooves on packed earth.

Ellie stiffened. Someone was coming. Too late to slip away, she froze as a tall black horse emerged from the trees. Lord Bennett.

Her heart leapt, half dread, half indignation. He swung down with practiced ease, that polished smile already in place.

"Lady Danielle," he greeted warmly. Ellie curtsied stiffly, her pulse quickening.

"Your Grace. Forgive me, I was just returning to the house."

He lifted a hand, halting her retreat. "Stay. It is too fine a morning to hurry away. I should like to know you better." His eyes lingered with unearned confidence. Ellie lifted her chin.

"If you wish conversation, Your Grace, do so at the estate, in the presence of others."

For a moment, surprise flickered across his face. Then he grinned.

"You don't trust me?"

Her reply cut clean as steel. "No. Your conduct last night proved you a rake at best."

His mask slipped. Shock rippled across his features, unguarded, affronted. For a man accustomed to admiration, her words struck like a slap.

"Last night was not what it seemed. I was not—"

"Drunk?" Ellie cut him off mercilessly. His mouth fell open. "I know you were not," she continued coolly. "You attacked my cousin on purpose."

Color flared in his cheeks. "If you knew that, why accuse me before the others?"

Ellie's eyes narrowed. "To spare Eleanor further terror. She suffers enough without believing your vileness is deliberate. I will not add to her misery."

His arrogance bristled. "You are being quite judgmental. Do you realize who I am?"

"Oh, I realize it well, Your Grace," Ellie snapped. "Yes, you are a duke. But rank does not excuse cruelty, least of all against a woman already imprisoned in her own home."

He smirked faintly. "Careful. It is unwise to challenge me."

"Then let me remind you of my rank," Ellie replied steadily. "You are a duke, but I am the granddaughter of one. That makes us equals. And one day I will be a duchess in my own right." The words burned her tongue, she despised wielding her birth as a shield, but he had forced her hand. Before he could respond, another voice cut through the morning air, low and cruel.

"You will only be a duchess if you find a husband first." Lord Ainsworth rode into view, his steward beside him. His grin widened at Ellie's visible indignation. "Are you letting her speak to you like this, Bennett?" he sneered. "I'd have used my crop until she begged forgiveness."

Disgust churned in Ellie's stomach. But before she could reply, Bennett's expression hardened.

His voice turned to ice.

"I do not need to beat a woman to prove my point."

Before Ellie could comprehend what was happening, he seized her by the waist and slung her over his shoulder.

"Put me down!" she cried, pounding her fists against his back. "You arrogant brute!"

He ignored her protests and carried her with effortless strength down the grassy bank toward the lake. Then, without warning, he tossed her straight into the water.

Cold shock swallowed her whole. Ellie plunged beneath the surface with a startled cry, the icy water closing over her head before she could draw breath. For one disorienting instant the world became nothing but chill darkness and muffled sound. Then she kicked desperately and burst back to the surface with a gasp, sputtering as strands of wet hair clung to her face. Her gown dragged heavily about her, soaked skirts tugging at her legs as she struggled toward the shallows.

From the bank, Ainsworth and his steward roared with laughter. The sound rang across the lake, loud and cruel, carrying their mockery with it as they wheeled their horses and rode away without a backward glance.

Ellie's fury blazed hotter than the rising sun. She waded to the shore and hauled herself onto the grass, water streaming from her sleeves and hem. Her whole body trembled, not from the cold alone, but from sheer indignation. Droplets fell steadily from her hair as she straightened, fists clenched at her sides. Bennett stepped closer and extended his hand, his expression maddeningly pleased with himself.

"There now," he said with a grin. "That should have brought you to your senses."

Ellie stared at him, disbelief flashing into open fury.

"Yes," she snapped, her voice sharp as a whip. "What a gallant display, using your strength against a woman. You must be very proud." Without waiting for a reply, she turned and marched toward the path, dripping water with every step. But Bennett moved quickly, placing himself squarely in her way.

"Allow me to take you back to the estate," he said smoothly. "You're soaked to the bone, and my horse can carry us both."

Ellie's spine stiffened. "I have no intention of going anywhere with you, Your Grace." Her eyes flashed with cold disdain. "If anything, you have confirmed what I already believed, you are rude, arrogant, and certainly no gentleman. I want nothing from you. Not your horse. Not your hand. Not your presence." She moved to brush past him. But a rustle of movement behind her made her half-turn, distracted for only an instant.

That was all he needed. His arm swept around her waist, dragging her flush against him before she could react. His other hand seized her wrists, pinning them firmly against her.

"Let go—!" The protest barely left her lips before his mouth crashed down on hers. It was not a gentle kiss, nor even a teasing one. It was fierce. Claiming. Utterly uninvited. Ellie stiffened in shock, fury flaring through her as she struggled against his hold, her heart hammering wildly in her chest.

10

Moonlight in the Marquess's Study

Ellie's world tilted. Shock, outrage, and disbelief collided all at once. She pushed against him with all her strength, her fists straining against his grip, but he held her fast, inexorably driving her backward toward the trees. His kiss, rough and domineering at first, slowed, turning disturbingly tender, as though he meant to coax instead of claim.

The change unsettled her. A storm of butterflies burst through her stomach, confusing and deeply unwelcome. Fury sharpened her resolve. She wrenched herself against his chest until, at last, he released her. Ellie staggered back, breathless, her chest heaving. For a moment she simply stared at him, then her fury erupted. Her voice shook with the force of it.

"How dare you?" she demanded. "What gives you the right to take such liberties, to lay claim where none exists? From the very beginning, you have offered me nothing but contempt, arrogance, and mockery, not a single breath of respect. I have crossed paths with rakes before, but you—", her voice rose, fierce and unyielding, ringing with judgment.

"You are no rake. You are a scoundrel... and a coward." Her eyes blazed like blue fire. Though she had stepped back, the movement was not retreat but challenge, an unflinching line drawn in the ground that no man could cross unscathed. He glared at her, his voice low and sharp.

"Would you have preferred I do as Ainsworth suggested? You've shown me no respect either. Perhaps a good spanking would suffice."

Ellie's lip curled in disdain. "I have only ever defended myself against you. Respect is not granted by rank, it is earned. And you, My Lord, have earned nothing but my contempt."

His mouth twisted with venom. "Perhaps you should be more like your cousin. She seems to know her place as a woman."

The words pierced her like a blade. Tears stung her eyes at the thought of Eleanor, beaten into silence by a cruel husband. Ellie blinked furiously, unwilling to let him see her break. But his gaze sharpened. He had noticed. Her voice trembled with restrained fury.

"Do not dare speak of Eleanor. She is the way she is because of men like you, because of cruelty paraded as authority. And those who forced her into silence have nothing to be proud of."

Something flickered in his expression. His arrogance faltered... softened. His dark eyes, suddenly intense, seemed almost gentle.

"I know," he murmured, his voice unexpectedly low. For a fleeting moment he looked almost human. He reached out, as though to take her hand. Ellie slapped the gesture away with a sharp crack.

"Do not touch me." Her voice shook with fury. "You know nothing. Nothing of what she endured. Or what countless women endure. And you—", her words broke, though her anger surged stronger than ever, "... you see me as some fiery creature who must be humiliated and broken into submission." She drew in a trembling breath.

"But hear me now, Your Grace: I will not break. Not for you, not for your cousin, not for any man. And I will never allow anyone to harm Eleanor, or any woman I can protect." Tears spilled at last, hot and fierce. She swiped them away quickly, but he had already seen.

Lord Bennett stepped closer, his expression softened by something that might almost have been sincerity.

"Is that why you've come?" he asked quietly. "To protect her?"

But Ellie was not fooled. Her heart was not so easily swayed. She drew herself up tall, her expression hard as granite.

"That is none of your concern, Your Grace."

"Danielle..." His voice had changed, lower now, smooth, and dangerously gentle. Her name fell from his lips like a caress, tugging faintly at her heart despite herself. But Ellie knew better. She recognized the trap. The moment his hands moved again, she shoved him with all her strength.

Caught off guard, he stumbled backward. His heel struck a fallen tree trunk, and he pitched over it with a startled grunt.

Ellie did not wait. Lifting her sodden skirts, she darted past him, seized the reins of his horse, and with one swift motion hauled herself into the saddle. Before he could recover, she dug her heels into the animal's sides. The horse surged forward. Without a backward glance, Ellie galloped down the path, the wind whipping through her wet hair as she thundered toward Ainsworth Hall, leaving Lord Bennett sprawled among the roots and shadows behind her.

Ellie had barely swung one leg over to dismount when two strong arms caught her, lifting her down and pulling her into a firm embrace. She gasped, startled, but the scent and warmth were unmistakable. Richard. Relief and dread collided in her chest. He held her tightly, his brow furrowed, his dark eyes searching her face with anxious intensity. Ellie tried to blink away the tears clinging to her lashes, but his sharp gaze had already caught them.

"Ellie, where were you?" he demanded softly. "How on earth did you come by Lord Bennett's horse? Gordon and I have been half-mad with worry. You should never wander off alone. And why are you soaking wet?" His voice darkened with sudden alarm. "Did someone hurt you?" The questions tumbled over one another, each sharper than the last. Despite herself, Ellie's lips curved into a fleeting smile. His protectiveness, though overwhelming, warmed her aching heart.

"I am fine," she whispered. "Truly. I am not hurt." She forced her voice steady. "I... tripped during my walk and fell into the lake, that is all. As for the horse, it must have gotten loose from the stables. I found it wandering and thought I ought to bring it back." The lie pricked at her conscience, but she held firm.

Richard could never know the truth, not without risking his cover. If he confronted Bennett or Ainsworth, Eleanor would pay the price. And what could a baron do against a duke and his ruthless cousin? Still, she added quickly, hoping to ease his concern.

"But you are right. I ought not to have gone out alone. Next time I will wait for you and Gordon."

The reassurance softened his expression. He exhaled slowly, the tension leaving his shoulders, and Ellie felt her own tight nerves loosen in response. Just then Gordon appeared, striding toward them across the courtyard, worry etched into every line of his face. The moment he reached her, he pulled her into a fierce, fatherly embrace.

The unexpected tenderness broke what little composure Ellie had managed to maintain. Tears welled anew as she clung to him, burying her face briefly against his shoulder. Between shaky breaths she told them of the horrors of the previous evening, that Lord Ainsworth had permitted men into his wife's chamber. Her voice faltered as she described Eleanor's terror, though she carefully veiled her cousin's humiliation at Bennett's hands. Instead, she pleaded only that one of them stand guard at Eleanor's door through the night.

Gordon's keen eyes searched her face. He seemed to sense there was more she had not said.

But he did not press. Instead, he laid a steady, reassuring hand upon her shoulder and turned to Richard.

"You will return to your room," he instructed quietly, "so you can keep watch tonight."

Richard hesitated, clearly reluctant, but one look from Gordon convinced him. With a final worried glance toward Ellie, he nodded.

Once Richard departed, Gordon turned back to Ellie, his voice firm but gentle.

"You must change at once. If you remain in wet clothes, you will fall ill."

Ellie nodded obediently. The chill from the lake had begun to seep into her bones, and she realized how heavily the damp fabric clung to her skin. The simple instruction gave her something practical to focus on, something that steadied her racing thoughts.

"I will only be a moment," she said quietly. She withdrew to her chamber and changed quickly into a dry gown. As she brushed out her damp hair and braided it anew, she welcomed the brief solitude. For several precious minutes she could breathe without Richard's anxious gaze or the oppressive presence of Ainsworth's household pressing upon her.

By the time she returned, Gordon was waiting in the corridor exactly where she had left him.

He offered his arm with quiet dignity. Ellie accepted gratefully, slipping her hand through his as though she were once again the young girl who had run to him for comfort in childhood. Without a word he guided her outside, leading her away from the main house and its curious eyes. The estate's park stretched wide beyond the manor, rolling lawns bordered by ancient oaks and winding paths that disappeared into groves of trees.

From the distant terrace came the faint murmur of voices. Eleanor, it seemed, was entertaining neighbors, her gentle laughter drifting across the gardens like a carefully rehearsed illusion. The sound made Ellie's heart ache. It also granted them a rare pocket of privacy.

Gordon led her toward the pond, where a weathered wooden bench rested beneath the shade of a great willow. The water shimmered softly in the sunlight as ducks glided across its surface and two elegant swans drifted near the reeds, their long necks arching with quiet grace. For a time, they simply sat together in silence. The calm scene seemed almost unreal after the chaos of the previous night. The steady movement of the water, the distant rustle of leaves, and the soft calls of birds slowly eased the tight knot in Ellie's chest.

At last, she drew a deep breath. Then she began to speak. She told him everything, everything that had happened since her arrival. She described Ainsworth's cruel threats to Eleanor, the terror she had witnessed in her cousin's eyes, the drunken intrusion in the night, and the confrontation that had followed. Only one truth she kept hidden. She did not speak of Bennett's violation.

Gordon listened in grave silence, his steady green eyes never leaving her face. He did not interrupt. Yet Ellie saw the tension build in him all the same. His jaw tightened each time she spoke of Ainsworth's cruelty, and his hands curled slowly into fists upon his knees when she described the terror Eleanor endured beneath her husband's roof.

Still, he remained composed. Ellie knew him well enough to recognize the discipline behind that stillness. He was angry. Furious, even. But he would not allow that anger to erupt recklessly. Like her, Gordon understood the danger they faced. To challenge the Duke of Somerset openly, or even to accuse his cousin without proof, would bring ruin down upon them all.

In the days that followed, Ellie avoided both Bennett and Ainsworth whenever she could. Their polished smiles and hollow civility unsettled her more than open hostility might have done. There was something deeply disturbing in the way they greeted her at table or in the corridors, voices smooth, expressions courteous, as though nothing improper had ever occurred. It was a performance. And Ellie trusted it no more than she trusted the men themselves.

Whenever she caught Bennett's gaze lingering across the room, she felt a prickle of unease along her spine. Ainsworth, meanwhile, watched with colder calculation, his eyes weighing every movement she made, every word she spoke.

So, Ellie kept her distance. Instead, she devoted herself almost entirely to Eleanor. She rarely left her cousin's side, accompanying her through the gardens, sitting with her in the drawing room, or walking beside her through the estate's winding paths. Wherever Ellie went, Richard or Gordon remained near, never intrusive, yet always within sight. Silent, watchful sentinels. Their presence alone seemed to restrain the darker impulses lurking within Ainsworth's household. The servants, too, appeared more cautious when the two men were nearby, as though sensing that this time Eleanor was not quite so defenseless.

Still, the tension within the house never fully lifted. More than once, Ellie attempted to speak of Olivia. At first, she tried gently, weaving the subject into quiet conversations while they embroidered together or walked beside the pond. Later, when that failed, she spoke more directly, hoping that Eleanor might reveal some small clue, anything that could lead them closer to the truth.

Each time the result was the same. Eleanor's fragile composure shattered. Her voice faltered, her hands trembled, and soon grief overwhelmed her entirely. Tears would come in uncontrollable waves, her body shaking with sobs as the name alone reopened wounds that had never begun to heal. Ellie would gather her into her arms then, whispering soft reassurances, though she felt painfully inadequate to the task. More than once she found herself blinking back tears of her own, anger and helplessness twisting together in her chest.

After the third such attempt, Ellie could bear it no longer. It became painfully clear that Eleanor could not speak of Olivia, not yet. The grief was too raw, the fear too deeply rooted. If answers were to be found... Ellie would have to seek them herself.

A few nights after the unsettling incident with the Duke of Somerset, Ellie lay wide awake. Sleep would not come, no matter how tightly she closed her eyes. The house was silent, wrapped in the deep stillness of night. Every creak of timber, every whisper of wind along the eaves seemed unnaturally loud, magnified by the restlessness of her thoughts. Olivia. The name haunted her.

Again, and again her mind circled the same relentless questions. What had truly become of her cousin? Where had she been taken, and why? Had she been carried away in secret? Hidden somewhere on the estate? Or worse... sent far beyond reach?

The uncertainty gnawed at Ellie's mind until it became unbearable. At last, she threw back the covers with quiet determination and reached for her dressing gown. Pulling it around her shoulders, she moved carefully across the chamber and eased her door open with the lightest possible touch.

The corridor beyond lay dimly lit by a single dying lamp. Just outside, Gordon sat slumped in a cushioned armchair.

Eleanor had insisted the chair be placed there so the two men might keep watch in comfort, but its softness seemed only to hasten their slumber. Gordon's chin had fallen to his chest, his broad shoulders rising and falling with the slow, steady rhythm of deep sleep.

Ellie hesitated in the doorway. For a moment guilt tugged painfully at her heart. Gordon had sacrificed his rest to guard them, and yet she was about to slip past him like a thief in the night. Still... she could not turn back. This might be her only chance. Holding her breath, she stepped quietly into the corridor and tiptoed past him. Her slippered feet made scarcely a sound upon the carpet as she crept toward the staircase. Only when she reached the first step did she dare breathe again.

Slowly she descended, her fingers trailing lightly along the polished banister for balance. The grand hall below lay drenched in silver moonlight that poured through the tall windows, casting long, eerie shadows across the marble floor. The hush of the sleeping house pressed heavily against her ears. Every step seemed to echo like thunder. She paused more than once, listening carefully for movement, any sign that a servant or guard had heard her. Nothing stirred.

Ellie continued forward, her heart pounding. She knew, or at least strongly suspected, where Lord Ainsworth kept his study. During the past few days, she had watched him disappear into one particular room often enough to form a quiet certainty. At last, she reached the heavy oak door. She paused. Leaning closer, she pressed her ear lightly against the wood. Silence. No voices. No movement within. Drawing a steady breath, Ellie gathered her courage. Then she slowly turned the handle, slipped inside, and closed the door behind her with careful, deliberate quiet.

The room smelled faintly of smoke and ink. Luck was with her, the moon was full, its pale glow spilling through the tall windows and striking the great desk where Ainsworth no doubt conducted his business. The shelves and cabinets lining the walls loomed in the silvery light like silent sentinels.

Ellie's hands trembled as she began her search. She opened drawers with painstaking care, lifting each one slowly so it would not creak. Inside lay stacks of correspondence, ledgers, and official documents tied neatly with ribbon. She sifted through them quickly but methodically, lifting page after page into the wash of moonlight, scanning each line for Olivia's name, anything that might explain her disappearance.

Minutes stretched on. The quiet room seemed to grow heavier with each passing moment. The distant ticking of a clock somewhere in the house echoed faintly through the silence. Nearly an hour passed. With every drawer she emptied, Ellie felt her hope slipping further away. At last, exhausted and disheartened, she almost abandoned the search altogether. Perhaps there was nothing here. Perhaps she had been foolish to believe the truth would lie waiting in plain sight. But then, her eye caught something.

A small corner of folded parchment peeked out from beneath a thick leather-bound book at the edge of the desk. Her pulse quickened. Ellie slid the book aside and drew the letter free, her fingers shaking as she unfolded it. The handwriting was unmistakable, Eleanor and Olivia's father. She lifted the page toward the moonlight and read.

Ainsworth,

I hope this letter finds you well. I write in response to your inquiry about Olivia. Just as you suspected, my younger daughter is not nearly as submissive and obedient as Eleanor. She flatly refuses even to court your friend. Lord Thatcher has been patient, but his understanding wears thin. No matter how harshly I punish her, she will not yield, and she has already attempted to run away several times.

If your offer still stands, I will be sending her to you and Eleanor. Perhaps you can instill some sense in her. The arrangement with Lord Thatcher is concluded, and I cannot afford Olivia's defiance. Do whatever you must do to make her bend.

Ellie's stomach turned. Her grip slackened so suddenly she nearly dropped the page. Fury burned hot in her chest, mingling with a cold thread of dread. Olivia had not been abducted, not outright. She had been sent here. Her own father had delivered her into Ainsworth's hands to break her. But where was she now?

The question struck Ellie like a blow. Her thoughts shattered when voices suddenly sounded in the corridor. Men's voices. Drawing nearer. Ellie's heart lurched violently. She glanced wildly around the room. There was no time to escape, not without being seen. In desperation she folded the letter quickly and dropped to her knees, wriggling beneath the massive desk just as the door handle turned. She pressed herself into the shadows, scarcely daring to breathe. The door creaked open.

"I don't understand why this cannot wait," Lord Ainsworth grumbled, his voice thick with irritation. He carried a candle, its wavering light spilling across the floor and making Ellie's hiding place feel perilously exposed. "It is the middle of the night, for heaven's sake."

A dry, mocking scoff answered him. Ellie stilled, her teeth gritting. Of course, it was Lord Bennett.

"Our uncle has pressed you for weeks about your finances," Bennett said smoothly. "This is his estate, his land. If you continue to withhold matters from him, he will not hesitate to cast you out. Best you hand over the documents now."

"Why send you?" Ainsworth sneered. "I can manage my own affairs without interference. Uncle's steward would have sufficed."

"But you ignored him." Bennett's tone sharpened, clipped and impatient. "He has tried repeatedly to reach you, and you refused. What are you hiding, Cousin?"

"I hide nothing. And even if I did, it would be none of your concern."

"It becomes my concern if your incompetence ruins our family's prospects." Bennett paused, his voice dropping into a colder register. "Our uncle has made no secret of his intentions. He will not leave the Devon duchy to just anyone, and your reputation is... shall we say, less than spotless."

A brief silence followed. Then Bennett spoke again, his voice edged with deliberate challenge.

"That reminds me, what did you do with your wife's sister? Where is she?"

Ellie's breath caught. She leaned forward slightly beneath the desk, straining to hear.

"I have done nothing with Olivia," Ainsworth spat, irritation seeping through every word. "I am not hiding her, and even if I were, what is it to you?"

"I met her in London last season," Bennett replied coolly. "I intended to court her."

"Her father already found a match for her."

"Did he?" Bennett's voice dropped lower, dangerous now. "And does she agree?"

Despite the peril of her position, Ellie almost smiled. For once, the arrogant duke's words pressed exactly where they should, forcing Ainsworth to squirm.

"It is her father's decision," Ainsworth snapped. "Olivia has no say in the matter."

"Then I take it your wife had no choice either?"

"I am done talking to you," Ainsworth growled. "If it is documents you want, I will fetch them."

Ellie's blood froze. His footsteps moved toward the desk. She scurried silently to the far side beneath it, curling herself into the smallest space she could manage. Her skirts rustled softly as she pressed herself tight against the wood.

The hem of Ainsworth's coat brushed the edge of the desk as he passed. Then Bennett followed. His boots stopped so close that the tip of one nearly grazed her arm. Ellie clamped both hands over her mouth, forcing herself to breathe slowly through her nose, praying he would not hear the frantic pounding of her heart. One glance downward, one careless lean, and she would be discovered. In the darkness beneath the desk, she closed her eyes and prayed for a miracle.

11

The Pain Behind His Embrace

"How will you send this to our uncle?" Ainsworth's voice snapped like a whip.

"I shall dispatch a footman at first light," Bennett replied evenly.

"Then perhaps it is time for you to leave."

Ellie silently echoed him: *Yes, leave.* Every moment he lingered, sharpened the danger of discovery. But, of course, Bennett had other intentions.

"I will remain as long as necessary," he said firmly. "Our uncle entrusted me with this task, and I intend to see it through."

Ainsworth scoffed. "He doesn't even trust you, does he?"

"Can you blame him?" Bennett's tone darkened. "After what your father did, distrust is only sensible."

Ellie stiffened beneath the desk, her breath catching. *What was this?*

"My father?" Ainsworth demanded, his voice suddenly tight.

"Yes. Your father." Bennett's words dropped like stones, heavy and cold. "It was your father who murdered my family. He would have killed Uncle Errett as well, had he not been caught in the act. Do not feign ignorance. The gallows claimed him, and rightly so."

Ellie's hand flew to her mouth, stifling the gasp clawing up her throat. Could this be the root of Ainsworth's cruelty, the shadow of a father's crimes staining the son?

"There was no proof," Ainsworth spat, his voice rising with fury. "No proof my father was behind any of it."

"There was plenty," Bennett countered, his voice taut with barely restrained rage. "Uncle's steward caught him with the vial in hand, ready to pour poison into Uncle's tea, the same poison that killed my mother and father." His voice cracked for just a moment, and in that brief fracture Ellie heard it clearly, grief, raw and real.

"Your father wanted everything," Bennett continued hoarsely. "He eliminated anyone who stood in his way. First my parents, his own kin. Then your aunt and uncle, so they could never contest him. And he would have murdered me and my sister as well, had he not been stopped."

Ainsworth growled low in his throat. "My father had nothing to do with your family's deaths."

"Lies!" Bennett's voice thundered, stripped now of its usual polish. "It was your father's steward they found at the ruins of my home. Do not insult me by claiming he acted alone. A servant does not burn down an entire estate of his own accord. He followed orders, your father's orders."

Silence fell, thick, suffocating. Fury crackled between the two men, so palpable that Ellie trembled where she crouched beneath the desk.

"The only reason my sister and I survived," Bennett said at last, his voice low and bitter, "was because we happened to be in France. Otherwise, his hatred would have consumed us as well."

Ainsworth's tone sharpened. "Where is your sister now?"

"That," Bennett replied icily, "is none of your concern. After what your father did, I would not trust you with her safety if you offered me ten thousand pounds."

A brief pause followed. Then came the sound of papers shifting.

"Here," Ainsworth said at last, his voice dripping venom. "The documents our uncle demands. Take them and be gone from my sight."

A stack of papers landed heavily upon the desk above Ellie's head. She closed her eyes as relief flooded through her chest.

Perhaps now they would leave. If they did, she could slip back to her chamber unseen, the stolen letter hidden safely in her hand, and pray Gordon never discovered she had been gone. But the men did not move. They lingered. And Ellie felt her fragile relief teeter on the brink of shattering at the faintest sound.

"That should be enough. Now, let us both get a few more hours of sleep." Lord Ainsworth inclined his head toward the door, dismissing his cousin. Ellie held her breath, frozen beneath the desk. The scrape of boots, the creak of the door, and at last the fading murmur of their voices made her pulse slow, though only slightly. She remained crouched in the cramped darkness until silence truly reigned once more. Only then did she dare to move.

Her limbs stiff and her heart still racing, she slipped from her hiding place. The letter trembled faintly in her hands. She smoothed the crumpled parchment and stared at it one last time before folding it neatly and sliding it back beneath the heavy book. If it were discovered missing, her presence here would be undeniable.

She had just turned toward the door when arms shot out of the shadows and seized her from behind. A hand clamped brutally over her mouth, cutting off her gasp. She nearly screamed against it, her blood icing, her mind already whispering *Ainsworth.* Terror crashed through her, so sudden and violent she thought she might faint. *No one came back. How did I not hear?*

"What are you doing in Ainsworth's study?" The furious whisper scorched her ear. "Who gave you leave to rifle through his papers?"

Relief and dread collided as recognition struck. It was not the marquess. It was his cousin. Lord Bennett. He pinned her in place, his arms like iron bands, his breath hot against her temple. Even in his anger he kept his voice low, careful not to rouse the household. Ellie writhed, struggling against him, but his grip did not loosen. At last, he lifted his hand from her mouth, though he held her firmly.

"It is none of your concern what I am doing here," she hissed, her voice sharp despite the thunder of her pulse. "I do not answer to you, Your Grace."

He spun her around, his grip tightening on her shoulders. She gasped to find his face so close, his dark eyes stormy and fixed on hers.

"What you are doing is dangerous and reckless," he snapped. "My cousin is not a man to be trifled with. If he caught you here, he would not hesitate to punish you, and he would not care who you are."

Ellie gave a bitter laugh. "Oh, I am well aware of his monstrous temper. But someone must stand against him. Someone must stop him before he ruins more lives."

A humorless chuckle escaped Bennett. "And you believe that someone is you?"

Her gaze hardened into scorn. "I will do what I must. Who else will? Not her father, who abandoned her. If I do nothing, Eleanor remains his prisoner, and Olivia's fate may already be sealed." Her chest rose sharply with indignation.

"Tell me, why do you always target me? What crime have I committed against you that makes you so eager to belittle and insult me, as though I were some foolish child?"

For once, Bennett faltered. His grip loosened slightly, his expression unsettled.

"Let me go at once," Ellie demanded, seizing the moment. "I will return to my bedchamber."

"No." His voice was firm. "I will return you to your room myself. You have proven you cannot be trusted."

Her eyes flashed. "Oh, and you are trustworthy? You, who sneer and scold, who thinks your title grants you the right to command? Unhand me."

Instead of obeying, Bennett's mouth curved into a faint, infuriating smirk. Without warning, he swept her up and slung her across his shoulder like a wayward child. Ellie's outrage erupted.

"Put me down this instant, Lord Bennett! I am not a child."

"You certainly behave like one," he shot back, his tone laced with mocking amusement. "And I advise you to hold your tongue, especially as we walk through this house. Ainsworth is already close to breaking. You would not wish to provoke him further."

Ellie seethed, rolling her eyes heavenward but swallowing her fury. She had never met anyone as vexing as the Duke of

Somerset. On the one hand, he was the most insufferable man of her acquaintance. On the other hand, disconcertingly protective. It made no sense. He might easily have betrayed her to his cousin. Instead, he had warned her to remain silent and taken it upon himself to return her safely to her chamber.

Thinking back to the moment he had thrown her into the lake, it now seemed as though he had chosen the lesser of two evils. He could have beaten her, as Ainsworth had suggested, yet he had plainly decided against it. Why? Was it because he was not a violent man, one who would not raise his hand against a woman? Or had he chosen the cold water so he would not have to strike her, yet remain in the marquess's good graces? He confounded her.

When they reached her chamber, Gordon startled awake at once, springing from the chair outside the door. His hand instinctively moved to his side as though searching for a weapon that was not there. For a heartbeat he looked ready to confront an intruder, until his gaze fell upon the duke striding down the corridor with Ellie slung over his shoulder. His brows shot upward. Without a word, he stepped aside and followed them into the chamber.

Bennett carried Ellie straight inside and set her down upon the settee with little ceremony, as though depositing a troublesome parcel. Ellie's skirts rustled indignantly as she righted herself, shooting him a glare that could have withered stone. Bennett ignored it. Instead, he turned to Gordon, his expression cool and clipped.

"I found this young lady in Lord Ainsworth's study," he said curtly. "She was fortunate the marquess did not discover her."

Gordon's face darkened at once, the color draining from his cheeks as understanding struck. His eyes flicked briefly toward Ellie, searching her face, but she avoided his gaze. Bennett continued, his tone edged with warning.

"Keep a sharper watch, Gordon. She is playing with fire, and next time she may not be so fortunate."

For a moment the two men regarded one another in silence. Gordon's jaw tightened, but he inclined his head stiffly.

"I understand, Your Grace."

Bennett gave a short bow, more acknowledgment than courtesy. As he straightened, his eyes shifted to Ellie. For a brief instant something unreadable flickered in his gaze, annoyance, perhaps... or reluctant concern. Then the mask returned. Without another word, he turned and strode from the room. The door closed softly behind him, leaving a heavy silence in his wake.

Gordon's expression was stern as he turned back toward her. Ellie dropped her gaze, suddenly aware of the weight of his disapproval.

"What have you to say for yourself, child?" he asked quietly. Ellie lifted her chin, defiance flickering in her blue eyes.

"I was only trying to find information about Olivia. We have nothing—nothing at all."

Gordon's brow furrowed more deeply. His arms folded across his chest. His steady gaze fixed upon her.

"And why, pray, did the Duke of Somerset have to carry you back upstairs?"

Color rushed to her cheeks. "He did not *have* to," she snapped. "He only believes far too highly of himself, being a duke and all. He takes a particular pleasure in vexing me at every opportunity. He is arrogant, rude, and forever quick to judge." She crossed her arms tightly, her irritation rising again at the memory. "If it were not for Eleanor and Olivia, I would leave this place at once simply to be rid of him."

The fire in her eyes made Gordon suppress a laugh with a discreet cough. He turned slightly aside, hiding the twitch of a grin behind his hand before schooling his expression once more. When he faced her again, his voice was grave.

"You must take care, Ellie. Whatever his faults, Lord Bennett spoke truth tonight. You are playing with fire. Do not underestimate Ainsworth. If he uncovers your purpose here, or finds you prying where you ought not, he will show no mercy."

Ellie exhaled slowly, some of the defiance draining from her shoulders. She nodded wearily.

"I know. Believe me, I know. But what choice do we have?" Her voice softened, heavy with sorrow. "If we remain idle, Eleanor remains his captive, and Olivia..." She faltered, swallowing hard. "We do not even know what fate awaits her. I cannot stand by and do nothing." She hesitated, then continued more quietly.

"I found a letter tonight. It was written by my uncle." Her fingers curled tightly together in her lap. "He encouraged Ainsworth, practically urged him, to do whatever was necessary to break Olivia's will. Her father intends to force her into marriage."

Gordon's face darkened. Ellie looked up at him, anguish flickering through her eyes.

"If we do not act soon, Gordon," she whispered, "it may already be too late."

Ellie was quietly relieved when Lord Ainsworth and Lord Bennett spent the following days hunting. Though they returned each evening to dine and prowl the corridors long after nightfall, their absence during daylight hours brought a blessed calm to the house.

Eleanor seemed less tense. The rigid line of her shoulders eased, and the constant flicker of dread in her eyes softened, if only slightly. Ellie treasured those hours with her cousin, guarding them fiercely. In those brief moments, laughter, fragile and uncertain though it was, sometimes returned.

Richard and Gordon rarely left their side. Whether strolling through the gardens or sitting in the morning room with embroidery that neither of them touched, the two men remained nearby. Their steady presence lent the cousins a sense of protection they would otherwise have been denied.

With the marquess occupied elsewhere, Ellie seized the opportunity to make discreet inquiries among the servants about Olivia's disappearance. It did not take long to realize how deeply fear had taken root within the household. Maids avoided her gaze, trembling at the simplest questions. Footmen stammered awkward excuses before retreating at the earliest opportunity. Conversations fell abruptly silent whenever she entered a room, and the few servants who dared meet her eyes did so with a look that bordered on pleading, silent warnings not to ask further. The house was steeped in unease.

One morning Ellie noticed that her chambermaid, a timid girl named Ireen, had not come to assist her as usual. When she asked after the girl, the housekeeper muttered something about illness, but her clipped tone and darting eyes, only sharpened Ellie's suspicions. Ireen had not seemed ill the day before. Nor the day before that.

Unwilling to accept the explanation, Ellie waited patiently until preparations for that evening's dinner party drew most of the staff away to the kitchens and great hall. When the corridors at last grew quiet, she slipped silently toward the servants' wing.

The air there felt different, closer, heavier, burdened by the constant labor of those who lived below stairs. She moved carefully through the narrow passageways until she reached the small row of servants' chambers. At the far end, behind a half-closed door, she found Ireen.

The girl lay in a narrow bed, bruised and battered, her face swollen and her breathing shallow.

Shock tore through Ellie's chest. For a moment she could not move. Then she dragged a chair close and sat, her hand hovering uncertainly before she finally brushed the limp fingers resting on the coverlet. Ireen's eyes fluttered open, wide and fearful.

"You... you shouldn't be here, Lady Danielle," she whispered, her voice raw with pain.

"I will not bring trouble upon you," Ellie said softly. "I'll leave before anyone knows I came."

"That is not it." Ireen's lips trembled as tears gathered in her eyes. "If the master finds out you were here, you will be in danger."

Ellie leaned forward, her own eyes stinging. "I need answers, Ireen. I promise I will see you safely away from Lord Ainsworth and from anyone else who torments you. But I beg you, tell me the truth."

The maid hesitated, fear flickering across her bruised face. At last, she gave the smallest nod.

"Does your family live here?" Ellie asked gently.

"No... my family is in London, ma'am."

"Was it Lord Ainsworth who did this to you?" Ellie gestured to the dark bruises and angry welts lining the girl's arms. Ireen shook her head. "Then who?"

For a long moment she said nothing, fear and despair warring in her expression. At last, she forced out the name in a trembling whisper.

"Mr. Darwin."

Ellie gasped. "The butler?"

A tear slid slowly down Ireen's cheek as she nodded. Ellie clasped the girl's hand gently.

"Has he done this before?"

"Once."

"When? And why?"

"Shortly before Miss Olivia disappeared." Her voice faltered. "She asked questions. I... I didn't want to lie to her."

Ellie's heart lurched.

"Do you know what happened to Olivia?"

"No." The girl's voice broke. "After he beat me, I couldn't work for days. He had me whipped. By the time I returned to my duties... Miss Olivia was gone." She covered her face with shaking hands, sobbing softly. "He swore he would do worse if I ever spoke of it."

Ellie fought her own tears, fury and grief colliding inside her chest. How could anyone inflict such cruelty?

"Does this happen to all who displease him?" she pressed quietly.

"Only the women," Ireen whispered. Ellie's stomach twisted.

"And the men?"

The girl's answer came in a thread of dread. "The men... end up dead."

Ellie drew back in horror. "And no one has gone to the authorities?"

"We cannot. They threaten our families." Her voice faltered again. "And some of the women..." Her words broke apart. "Some have been sold, Lady Danielle. Sold to men Lord Ainsworth knows."

Ellie's fists clenched until her nails bit painfully into her palms.

"Monsters," she breathed.

"You must not concern yourself with me," Ireen pleaded weakly. "I am only a maid. I will heal. I will continue my work."

"No," Ellie said firmly, lifting the girl's chin until their eyes met. "No one deserves to be treated as less than human. I gave you my word, I will get you out of this house, and I intend to keep it." She leaned closer, lowering her voice. "Tell me, is there a way out unseen by the butler?"

Ireen hesitated, then gave a faint nod. Relief flickered through Ellie.

"Good," she said softly. "Can you walk if I help you?"

Slowly, Ireen pushed herself upright, biting back a cry of pain. Ellie slipped an arm around her shoulders, steadying her while she dressed the girl in plain clothes that would draw no notice. Together they slipped quietly through the servants' wing, guided by Ireen's whispered directions.

Above them the house bustled with noise, footsteps, clattering trays, voices preparing for the evening's grand dinner, but down here the shadows protected them.

At last, they reached a narrow passage and a hidden side door. Beyond it lay the gardens, silent in the fading light. Ellie led Ireen to a grove of trees at the far edge of the park and pressed the maid's trembling hands in her own.

"Stay here until I return," she said gently. "You will not be abandoned. I promise you."

Leaving the girl hidden among the sheltering branches, Ellie gathered her skirts and hurried back toward the main house, her heart pounding with urgency. She needed help. And only Richard and Gordon could give it. She found them in the parlor with Eleanor, her cousin still blissfully unaware of the danger festering within the walls of her own home.

Both men greeted her with sharp, disapproving glances, and Ellie's stomach sank with guilt. She had excused herself to visit the washroom, yet more than an hour had passed. The last thing she wanted was to alarm Eleanor. Lowering her voice, she stepped closer.

"Richard, Gordon. May I have a word with you?"

Without protest, they rose and followed her outside. The afternoon air was crisp, and Ellie led them far enough from the house to ensure that no servant, or worse, Lord Ainsworth, could overhear. She drew a steadying breath, preparing to speak. But Richard's temper broke first.

"Where have you been?" he demanded, his voice low but seething. "You cannot keep wandering off whenever it pleases you. Do you have any idea of the danger you place yourself in?"

Ellie lifted her chin. "I cannot have you shadowing me at every moment, Richard. People would grow suspicious, Ainsworth most of all. I am already walking a narrow line with you standing guard outside my door each night. If I am to play my part convincingly, he must believe I trust him... at least in some measure."

Her fierce tone silenced him. Richard muttered something beneath his breath, clearly conceding her point, though unwillingly. Ellie seized the moment and quickly explained where she had been, what she had discovered, and the desperate need for action.

"I believe Grandfather and Lord Beverton have positioned, or at the very least contacted, men here who can aid us. Is that true?"

Richard and Gordon exchanged a glance before nodding.

"Yes," Richard admitted. "I have spoken with several since our arrival. Both dukes are kept informed of what happens within these walls."

"Then you must see Ireen to safety," Ellie pressed, urgency breaking through her voice. "Her family lives in London. If Lord Beverton can secure her a position, she might be near them again. But first she must see a physician. She is badly hurt."

Richard did not hesitate. "I will leave tonight. She can ride with me as far as Plymouth. From there, I'll arrange a carriage to London and ensure she travels under protection. I will not allow her to make the journey alone."

Relief washed over Ellie. "Thank you, Richard." Her smile was weary but warm. He squeezed her arm briefly in reassurance before turning and striding toward the stables to ready his horse. Ellie watched him go, then turned to Gordon. Together they slipped into the shadows and made their way toward the grove where Ireen waited.

The poor girl was pale and weak, each step clearly an agony, yet her eyes shone with gratitude that someone, anyone, cared enough to help her escape. Ellie's throat tightened at the sight.

That evening, when the dinner party commenced, Lord Ainsworth entered the dining room wearing an expression of thinly veiled fury. At first glance, his manners appeared perfectly composed. He greeted his guests with practiced courtesy, offering polite smiles and measured conversation, every movement controlled and deliberate. To anyone unfamiliar with him, he might have seemed the picture of aristocratic refinement. But Ellie saw the truth beneath the mask.

The rigid set of his jaw betrayed him. A dark tension flickered behind his eyes, and there was a sharpness in his movements that suggested restraint rather than calm. Something had angered him. As the guests gathered around the long dining table, Ellie watched him carefully from her seat beside Eleanor. The marquess moved through the room with calculated ease, pausing to exchange pleasantries with one nobleman, then another.

Then his gaze shifted. It settled across the room on Mr. Darwin. The butler stood near the sideboard, overseeing the servants as they carried in the first course. His posture remained perfectly straight, his expression dutiful and composed. But for a single, fleeting moment, his eyes lifted to meet his master's. The look that passed between them was brief, almost imperceptible. Yet it chilled Ellie to the bone.

No words were spoken, but an unmistakable understanding flickered between them. A silent message. Darwin inclined his head ever so slightly before returning to his duties. Ellie's stomach tightened. Had her efforts with Ireen already been discovered?

Her fingers curled beneath the tablecloth as dread crept through her chest. She forced herself to keep her expression calm, to smile politely when spoken to, to lift her fork and pretend interest in the meal set before her. But inside, her thoughts raced. If Darwin had noticed Ireen's absence...

If he had already reported it... Ainsworth would know. And if he knew, there was only one conclusion he might draw. Ellie's heart turned cold. In trying to help, had she only placed Eleanor in even greater danger?

Sometime in the middle of the night, Ellie woke to someone shaking her shoulder. At first, she thought it was part of a dream, until the acrid sting of smoke filled her nostrils. Her eyes flew open.

"Quickly." Richard's urgent voice cut through the haze of sleep. He pulled her upright, already dragging her toward the door. "Fire."

The word sent a bolt of cold terror through her chest. Ellie snatched up her dressing gown and long overcoat, fumbling them over her nightdress as Richard urged her into the corridor.

The moment the door opened, a thick cloud of smoke rolled toward them, stinging her eyes and burning her throat. Coughing, she pressed a sleeve to her mouth and stumbled after him down the hall.

Doors were opening all along the corridor now. Servants and guests poured into the passage in various states of dress, some clutching candles, others shouting confused questions into the growing chaos. The air was already choking with smoke, making it nearly impossible to see where the fire had begun.

"Outside!" someone shouted. "Everyone outside!"

Richard guided her through the confusion and down the staircase, his hand firm at her back. By the time they burst into the courtyard, a large crowd had already gathered, guests wrapped in cloaks, servants rushing back and forth, grooms running toward the well with buckets. Confusion reigned. Smoke poured from the house in thick black coils, yet no one seemed certain where the flames had started.

Ellie's gaze darted frantically across the courtyard. Faces blurred past her, maids, footmen, frightened ladies, disoriented gentlemen. But the one face she searched for was nowhere to be found. Eleanor. Her heart lurched violently. Panic seized her chest like a vice. She turned sharply toward the entrance, ready to rush back inside. Strong arms wrapped around her waist and pulled her back.

"You cannot go in there." The command came low and firm. Startled, Ellie twisted in his grip and found herself staring straight into Lord Bennett's face. His hold was iron-strong, his dark eyes blazing with urgency. Smoke curled around them, casting shifting shadows across his features, yet beneath the severity of his expression lay unmistakable concern. Tears stung her eyes as the smoke scorched her throat.

"Eleanor," she gasped, coughing violently. "I—I cannot find her. Please, I must go to her."

His expression softened, though his grip did not loosen.

"I will find her," he said steadily. "But you must promise me you will not run inside. If you do, you will both be lost."

Ellie struggled instinctively, torn between desperation and reason. Her gaze fixed on the dark smoke pouring from the house, her heart hammering wildly. Bennett reached up and tilted her chin, forcing her to meet his eyes.

"Danielle," he said quietly. His voice carried both command and gentleness. "Promise me you will not endanger yourself."

Her breath caught. For a moment the world seemed to narrow to the intensity of his gaze, steady, unwavering, impossible to ignore. At last, she nodded, trembling. He squeezed her hand briefly before releasing her. Then he turned and strode back toward the house, already barking sharp orders at the servants as he went. Within seconds he disappeared into the thick smoke.

Ellie stood frozen in the courtyard, her heart pounding like a drum in her chest. Around her, chaos continued, shouting, rushing footsteps, the clatter of buckets. But she barely heard any of it. Her eyes remained fixed on the burning house.

Please, she prayed silently. *Please let him find her. Let Eleanor be safe.* Every passing moment stretched into eternity as dread tightened its grip around her heart.

12

An Apology Without Repentance

Lord Bennett emerged suddenly through the haze, striding toward her with urgent purpose. Smoke curled around him as he approached, his hair slightly disordered from the chaos within. Ellie's breath caught. Her eyes searched his face desperately, dreading the news he might carry. Fear flickered openly in her gaze, her hands trembling at her sides as she waited for him to speak.

"She is safe," he said at once, his tone steady and reassuring. The words reached her almost before she could draw breath. "Ainsworth and Eleanor came out together. She's by the fountain." He inclined his head toward the far side of the courtyard.

Ellie's gaze darted past him. And there, dimly lit by lanterns and moonlight, stood the pale, shaken figure of her cousin beside the stone fountain. Eleanor's shoulders were wrapped in a hastily thrown cloak, her face ghostly in the glow of the flames behind the house. Relief crashed over Ellie so violently that her knees nearly gave way. For a moment she could only stare, scarcely trusting her eyes. Then she turned back to Bennett, gratitude flooding her expression.

"Thank you," she whispered, her voice breaking with emotion. The smile that followed, radiant, unguarded, and wholly sincere, could have melted ice. For an instant he seemed almost startled by it. But before he could respond, Ellie had already turned and fled across the courtyard, her skirts flying as she ran toward Eleanor.

She fell into Eleanor's arms, clutching her tightly, only for her cousin to flinch in sudden agony and collapse into sobs.

"What's wrong? Are you hurt?" Ellie cried, instantly loosening her hold and dropping to her knees before her. Her wide eyes brimmed with worry as she searched Eleanor's face.

"It's nothing... I'm fine," Eleanor wept, though the tremor in her voice betrayed her. The raw pain etched across her features told another story entirely. Ellie's heart twisted. Lord Ainsworth stepped forward then, his expression carefully arranged into an imitation of concern. Without hesitation, he reached for Eleanor and drew her to her feet, pulling her into his arms in what appeared to be a tender embrace. To any onlooker, the gesture might have seemed protective, even loving. But Ellie saw the truth.

Eleanor stiffened at once, her face contorting in silent agony as his arms tightened around her. Her body strained against the iron grip, though she dared not struggle openly before the guests around them.

"Let her go!" Ellie cried, rushing forward to pull her cousin free. She tugged at Eleanor's arm desperately, but Ainsworth shoved her back with effortless strength. "You're hurting her!"

"You mustn't concern yourself, Danielle," he replied through clenched teeth, his voice coated in false gentleness. "She was injured escaping the house, but she will recover. She only needs a moment to cry it out."

Ellie's stomach turned. His performance might deceive the gathered guests, many of whom were already whispering among themselves, watching the scene with sympathetic expressions, but she could not ignore the silent anguish burning in Eleanor's eyes. Her cousin would never reveal the truth while her husband held her captive like that. And Ellie could not bear to watch her suffer.

Biting her tongue to avoid causing scandal before the assembled company, Ellie spun on her heel and strode away, her composure cracking with every step. She barely noticed the startled looks that followed her as she crossed the courtyard.

Once she reached the shelter of the park, far from the lanterns and the murmuring crowd, she broke into a run. Her breath tore in her chest as she clutched her nightgown, dressing gown, and overcoat in her fists, sprinting through the darkened paths without a thought for dignity or propriety. Branches whipped past her. Gravel crunched beneath her hurried steps. She did not stop until she reached the lake. The same quiet place where Lord Bennett had once thrown her into the cold water.

The moon shimmered across the still surface, casting silver light over the dark shoreline. Only there, far from the house, far from Ainsworth's cruel charade, did Ellie finally slow. Her chest heaved as she stood by the water's edge, fighting for breath.

The lake shimmered faintly beneath the moonlight, its surface rippling with the steady fall of water from the nearby cascade. Ellie's eyes sought out the great oak whose branches stretched toward the heavens. Without hesitation, she ran to it, grasped the low boughs, and began to climb.

The bark scraped her palms, and her overcoat tore in several places as it snagged against the rough wood, but she paid it no mind.

Higher and higher she climbed until she reached a broad perch against the sturdy trunk. There, at last, she drew a deep breath. The crisp air filled her lungs, rich with the scent of damp earth, leaves, and water. She closed her eyes, trying to shut out the memory of Eleanor's anguished face, of Ainsworth's false display of tenderness before the gathered guests.

For a fleeting moment, peace enveloped her. Nightingales trilled softly in the distance. The waterfall splashed in a soothing rhythm. Two foxes darted playfully along the far bank, their sleek bodies flashing silver in the moonlight, and an owl swept silently past, its wings cutting the night with effortless grace. The serenity was almost intoxicating.

For one reckless instant, she considered diving into the cool waters below, but she restrained herself. She had already strayed far beyond what any young lady, let alone one destined to be a duchess, ought to display. A bitter laugh nearly escaped her.

Perhaps I should climb a tree in front of Grandfather, she thought wryly. *Then he would see, once and for all, that I am hardly fit to be a duchess.* With a sigh, she began her descent. That was when she noticed it.

Tucked between thick leaves rested a small nest. Inside lay several delicate, speckled eggs, glistening faintly in the moonlight. Curiosity tugged at her, and she leaned closer for a better look.

She had scarcely moved nearer when a furious cry split the silence. Two nightingales swooped down, their wings beating furiously, shrill cries piercing the stillness of the night.

Ellie jerked back in surprise, nearly losing her footing. She raised her arms to shield her face, ducking as sharp beaks darted toward her. The enraged birds circled her head, striking again and again, relentless in their defense of the nest.

"Stop—please!" she gasped, scrambling backward along the branch. Panic seized her as she tried to retreat, but the birds only grew more aggressive. Her hand slipped. She gave a horrified gasp as her grip failed, her foot skidding on the rough bark. For one terrifying instant she was weightless, the ground rushing up to meet her, but instead of earth, she fell into strong arms.

Ellie blinked up at the young man holding her, still dizzy from the sudden fall. If she had expected anyone to catch her, it certainly would not have been him. The firm arms that steadied her belonged to Lord Bennett, and the slow, knowing grin curving his lips deepened as her wide, startled eyes met his.

For a breathless moment, the world seemed to still. The warmth of his chest pressed against her, the faint scent of spice and leather enveloping her senses. Her cheeks flamed, and she quickly dropped her gaze, mortified by the way her heart stumbled in its rhythm.

"Forgive me," she whispered, her voice trembling like a secret.

"Have your parents never taught you," he murmured with a low chuckle, "to stay clear of nests this time of year? The little creatures are most... protective." His eyes twinkled with mischief, the husky undertone of his voice far more dangerous than his words. To Ellie's ears, it sounded less like teasing and more like a mockery or challenge.

"Of course they did," she snapped, trying to smother the flutter rising in her chest. She lifted her chin in defiance. "But I suppose this will only give you yet another excuse to treat me like a child."

His brows rose, surprised by her sharpness. Then something softened in his expression, and instead of releasing her as she struggled, he drew her ever so slightly closer. His gaze lingered on her lips before rising again to meet her eyes.

"What are you doing? Let me go," she demanded, glancing up, only to falter. There was no scorn in his eyes this time. Only warmth. And something far more unsettling, desire, quiet and restrained, yet undeniably present.

"I've no intention of treating you like a child for climbing a tree," he said gently, his voice pitched low enough that it brushed against her skin like a caress. "I was teasing, nothing more. Perhaps we might even make a sport of it, have a climbing competition someday."

The corners of Ellie's lips betrayed her, twitching before she could stop them. Her blue eyes brightened with reluctant amusement.

"You know how to climb a tree?" she asked, incredulous.

"Of course," he replied, feigning offense. "Isn't that the business of every boy?"

"Yes," she admitted slowly, her cheeks warming all the more. "But you are no boy anymore."

He chuckled softly, the sound rich and intimate. "No, I confess I am not. Still, once a skill is learned, it is not so easily forgotten."

Ellie arched a brow, though her heartbeat raced. "Perhaps. Yet I should boldly declare that most dukes would sooner be found dead than caught scrambling about the branches of an oak."

"Is that so?" His grin widened, though his eyes held hers with unnerving intensity. "You believe all dukes are dull creatures, even in their youth?"

Her gaze faltered beneath the weight of his. She lowered her eyes, her voice softer now.

"I have not had much interaction with dukes, young or old. So, I could not say for certain."

At last, he set her gently on her feet. Yet even when she stepped back, her body still hummed with the memory of his nearness. She hated to admit it, but she liked this playful side of him. It softened his arrogance and made his striking features even more difficult to ignore.

"And what of young ladies?" he pressed, his voice dipping lower, almost testing her. "Do you suppose many of them know how to climb a tree?"

Ellie giggled, despite herself, the sound light and unguarded. "I believe not. It is hardly proper, or ladylike, to do such a thing."

"And yet," he said, eyes glinting as he winked, his tone rich with suggestion, "you do it anyway."

Her laughter faded into a wistful smile. "I am not a lady, or so my mother insists. She calls it one of my greatest shortcomings and has tried all her life to make me into something I am not."

Lord Bennett tilted his head, his gaze lingering on her face. When he spoke again, his voice carried an unexpected sincerity.

"Then your mother is mistaken. It is no shortcoming. It suits you." He paused, studying her thoughtfully. "Perhaps the world could do with more young women unafraid to climb trees."

Ellie blinked, startled. A compliment. From him. The very man who had scolded and provoked her now spoke with a tenderness that unraveled her defenses. Confusion swirled through her chest, her pulse quickening. Afraid he might read too much in her expression, she turned away before she revealed more of her feelings than she dared.

Thirst woke Ellie once more. With a weary sigh, she slipped from the bed and glanced toward the small table beside it. The maid had forgotten, again, to leave water for the night. She rubbed her eyes, her throat dry and aching. Pulling on her dressing gown, she padded quietly into the corridor.

The house lay wrapped in a heavy silence. Long hallways stretched before her, drowned in shadow. Only the pale glow of dying lamps guided her steps as she made her way toward the staircase. At night, the old manor felt different, larger, darker, almost alive with creaks and faint whispers that vanished with the morning light.

Ellie moved slowly, careful not to disturb anyone. The boards beneath her bare feet were cool, the silence pressing in around her like a held breath. A faint trace of smoke still lingered in the air, though it had nearly faded by now. The scent clung stubbornly to the wood and stone of the house, a ghost of the chaos from earlier that night. There had never truly been a fire. At least, not the sort that consumed walls and beams.

Two chimneys that had not been used since the end of winter, and had also gone uncleaned far too long, had caught fire when large birds' nests lodged inside them ignited. The blaze had been discovered early enough to extinguish before it could spread, but the thick smoke had billowed through the house, creeping along the corridors and filling the chambers with choking haze. For hours afterward the entire household had been thrown into confusion. Forcing the servants to air out every single room.

Now the danger had passed, yet the smell remained, a stubborn reminder of how quickly peace could dissolve into panic. Ellie descended the staircase, her hand trailing lightly along the polished banister, the quiet house watching her descent in silence.

She reached the kitchen and pushed the door open. The room was dimly lit by the dull red embers of the hearth. Pots hung motionless above the stove, and the scent of smoke and bread lingered faintly in the air. Ellie found a jug on the counter and poured herself a glass of water. She raised it to her lips with relief.

The first sip had barely touched her tongue when the faint creak of a door made her freeze. The sound was soft. Too soft. The hairs along her arms prickled. Slowly, she lowered the glass. A figure stepped into the kitchen doorway. Ellie's breath caught.

Lord Ainsworth. The look in his eyes told her at once that his presence was no accident. He had been waiting. Watching.

"Lord Ainsworth," she said quickly, forcing her voice to remain steady while suspicion coiled tight in her chest. "The kitchen is yours. I was just leaving." She set the glass down and moved to pass him. But in an instant, he stepped forward, blocking her path.

Before she could react, his arm snaked around her waist and shoved her backward against the cupboard. The impact rattled the dishes behind her. His body pressed against hers, trapping her completely. His shirt hung partly open, the cravat discarded, exposing the hard line of his chest. The scent of wine clung faintly to him. Heat rushed to her face, yet with it came a rising tremor of dread.

"What are you doing? Unhand me at once," she demanded, her voice sharp though her courage faltered. His nearness chilled her.

"You are a beautiful woman, Danielle," he murmured, leaning closer. His breath brushed hot against her cheek. She shoved at his chest, but he barely moved.

"You are married, sir," she snapped. "Married to my cousin. Let me go."

He laughed. The sound was cold. Mocking.

"You have much to learn about marriage," he said softly. "Most men are not content with one woman. And you, my dear, walked willingly into my house." His fingers tightened around her waist. "Did you truly believe I would not notice?" His hand rose, gripping her chin and forcing her face upward. The intent in his eyes made her stomach turn. Panic surged through her.

Was nothing sacred to this man, not even vows made before God? "If you do not release me this instant," she hissed, her voice shaking with fury, "I will scream."

His lips brushed the edge of her ear as he chuckled. "And if you do," he whispered, "I will tell everyone you came to me, that you tempted me." His fingers tightened painfully. "Who will they believe?" he continued softly. "The marquess, nephew of the Duke of Devon... or the wayward granddaughter of a duke?"

Revulsion coursed through her. As he leaned forward to claim her lips, Ellie's hand groped blindly along the counter. Her fingers struck wood. A board. With all her strength she swung. The crack echoed through the kitchen as the board struck his temple. Ainsworth cursed and staggered backward, then shoved her violently. Ellie crashed onto the tile floor.

Pain shot through her hip and elbow. The breath knocked from her lungs. But she did not hesitate. Before he could seize her again, she lashed out with her foot, driving her heel into his shin. He swore viciously. Ellie scrambled upright and darted behind the kitchen table, trying to put space between them.

"You little beast!" he snarled. His hand tore his belt from his waist in one swift motion, the leather snapping sharply in the air. "I will teach you what happens when a woman defies a man." His eyes glinted with fury. "You will not escape me."

Horror seized her. Ellie spun toward the door, but he was faster. His hand clamped around her arm, jerking her backward. The belt lifted. For a split second she thought this might be the moment her luck failed.

The door burst open. Lord Bennett and Ainsworth's steward stormed into the kitchen. In a blur of motion, Bennett seized the belt from his cousin's hand and flung it across the room before shoving Ainsworth hard against the counter. Wood cracked beneath the force. The steward rushed forward, bracing himself between the two men, ready to prevent the violence from erupting further.

Ellie trembled, shaken to her core, and instinct urged her to slip away unnoticed. But Bennett caught her hand, holding her fast. His face was thunderous, though his fury seemed directed as much at her as at his cousin.

"You simply cannot stop courting danger, can you?" he bit out. "Do you enjoy playing with fire? Have you not learned that it is unwise to tempt a man? What possessed you to wander the halls in nothing but a nightgown and dressing gown at this hour?"

Ellie stared at him, stunned. He had saved her, yet now he scolded her as though she had invited the assault. Her throat tightened. Ainsworth's cruelty she had expected. With him, at least, she always knew where she stood. But Bennett? His shifting judgment was worse, for she never knew whether she would find defense or condemnation.

"So?" he pressed, his anger still burning hot. "Nothing to say? You dislike being called out for your folly, Danielle?"

Her silence only seemed to provoke him further.

"Perhaps we should have allowed Ainsworth to finish what he began," he continued harshly. "A sound punishment might have beaten some sense into you."

The words cut deeper than any lash. Ellie's lips trembled, but before she could answer, the steward's deep voice rang out across the room.

"Your Grace. That is enough." The tone carried unmistakable steel. "Remember who you are, and who she is."

Bennett scoffed and released Ellie's arm, though not before his gaze faltered. For the briefest instant, something broke through the storm in his eyes. Regret. A flicker of awareness, as though even he heard the cruelty in his own words and despised himself for them. But the moment vanished almost as quickly as it appeared, buried beneath pride and anger. The damage, however, was done. His hesitation only deepened the wound, leaving Ellie reeling with hurt and confusion.

She drew herself up, blinking back tears.

"Always so quick to judge," she said quietly, though her voice trembled. "So quick to scold. Always so certain of your own superiority." Her chin lifted. "I do not know what I have done to earn your disdain, Your Grace, but it no longer matters. Stay away from me. Do not ever come near me again."

Her words seemed only to amuse Ainsworth, who now wore a smug grin, clearly delighted to see his cousin rebuked. The sight fueled Ellie's resolve.

"You are a horrible man, Lord Bennett," she continued, her voice trembling with anger and hurt. "Do you take pleasure in saving me only so you may lecture me, belittle me, and remind me of every failing? If so, you needn't trouble yourself. I already have people in my life who ensure I never forget how unworthy I am." Her chest rose sharply as she drew a breath.

"And another thing. My name is *Lady Danielle.* Not Ellie. Not Danielle. Lady Danielle." Her gaze locked with his, bright with wounded pride. "I am the granddaughter of a duke, and I will be treated with the respect due to me. My great-grandfather was a grand duke, my great-grandmother a princess." She swallowed hard. "I despise wielding titles like weapons. But if it is the only language you understand, then so be it."

With that, she turned on her heel and strode toward the door, her head held high despite the tears burning fiercely in her eyes. Behind her, the kitchen fell silent. She could feel the weight of three stunned gazes upon her as she left.

Only when she reached the night air and the solitude of the park did her composure finally collapse. Her steps faltered as she reached a bench beside the pond. She sank onto it, buried her face in her hands, and wept. Tears of fury. Of humiliation. Of aching loneliness. They fell freely into the stillness of the night.

"Ellie." The deep, steady voice of her father's steward reached her just as she sat trembling on the bench by the pond.

She lifted her head, tears still coursing down her cheeks. When she saw him standing there, her composure crumbled entirely. Rising unsteadily, she crossed the short distance between them and flung herself into his arms, burying her face against his chest like a child seeking shelter from a storm.

He said nothing at first. He simply wrapped his arms around her and held her close. One large hand settled firmly between her shoulders, rubbing slow, reassuring circles as though he meant to anchor her there. The familiar scent of leather, pipe tobacco, and horse clung to him, a scent of the outdoors. When her sobs finally began to quiet, she drew back slightly and looked up into his weathered face. His kind eyes brimmed with concern.

"How did you know where I was?" she whispered.

"I saw you," he answered gently. "I was coming down the stairs just as you fled the kitchen. You were in such a state that

I feared something terrible had happened, so I followed." He studied her face carefully. "Tell me, child, what was it?"

Ellie's throat tightened. Still, she forced herself to speak. In halting words, she recounted everything, the way Lord Ainsworth had cornered her in the kitchen, the terror of being trapped against the cupboard, his threats, her desperate strike with the wooden board. And finally, Lord Bennett's scathing rebukes. Those words had cut nearly as deeply as his cousin's violence.

By the time she finished, her voice trembled with a mixture of anger, humiliation, and lingering fear. The steward's jaw tightened as she spoke. When she fell silent, he drew her close once more, his embrace firm and protective.

"I have lived long enough to see men at their worst," he said quietly, his voice rough with restrained fury, "but rarely have I witnessed cruelty so vile." His gaze darkened. "Ainsworth is wicked, yes, but at least with him, the evil lies plain upon his face. The Duke of Somerset..." He paused, his expression hardening.

"He cloaks himself in honor yet strikes with the tongue of a snake. Two-faced and sharp as venom. A man like that cannot fathom loyalty or sacrifice. He believes you are here for leisure, when in truth you would risk everything for your cousin's freedom."

Ellie closed her eyes briefly, his words echoing the thoughts that had been circling in her own mind.

"Yes," she whispered. "I would do anything to free Eleanor."

For a moment she fell silent, caught between bitterness and honesty. At last, she sighed softly.

"And yet... my heart aches for him, if only a little."

The steward looked down at her in surprise.

"Before Lord Bennett found me in Ainsworth's study," she continued slowly, "I overheard them quarreling. It seems the marquess's father was the one who murdered Lord Bennett's family."

She paused, her gaze drifting across the moonlit water.

"I do not know when it happened," she murmured, "but I think perhaps those wounds left scars no one can see. Perhaps they made him so harsh... so bitter." She shook her head slowly. "It does not excuse him. Nothing can excuse the cruelty he has shown me." Her voice softened. "But it must be dreadful, living without the love of a family to soften a man's heart."

The steward studied her quietly. Pride softened his expression.

"You have your father's compassion," he said at last. "Even in your pain, you can feel pity for the one who wounded you." He rested a hand gently on her shoulder. "That is no weakness, Ellie. It is your strength."

Her lips trembled at his words. But she nodded.

13

Beneath Silk and Malice

In the days that followed, Ellie withdrew almost entirely from the household. She kept to her chambers, venturing out only when she was certain both the marquess and the duke had gone hunting or departed for town. To the rest of the house, it appeared that she merely lingered at Eleanor's bedside.

Her cousin still slept for long stretches, recovering from whatever ordeal had been forced upon her, and that provided a convenient reason for Ellie to take her meals privately. In truth, she much preferred the company of Gordon and Richard. Their presence was a balm, two steadfast protectors who neither scolded nor belittled her. Yet her mind refused to rest.

Determined to uncover what fate had befallen Olivia, she returned again and again to Lord Ainsworth's study whenever the halls fell silent. With painstaking care, she sifted through his papers, searching for even the faintest clue. But always, in the back of her mind, loomed the butler.

Mr. Darwin seemed to glide through the house like a shadow, soundless and watchful.

More than once she caught him lingering in doorways, his cold eyes calculating. His silence was more chilling than words. Servants stiffened in his presence, their chatter dying mid-sentence whenever he approached. His loyalty to Ainsworth was absolute. And Ellie suspected it ran far deeper than mere duty.

After what the maid had confessed, she trusted him least of all. He moved too quietly, appeared too suddenly, his gaze lingering as though weighing her every breath. He was the sort of man who might know every secret before it was spoken aloud and bury it without leaving a trace. Ellie never forgot the bruises that had marred Ireen's body, nor the whispered truth that some who crossed him had vanished altogether. Each time his measured footsteps echoed down the corridor, she felt the air grow heavier, as though the house itself held its breath in dread of him.

Still, she pressed on, for Eleanor's sake, and for Olivia's. Yet she could not shake the uneasy feeling that Mr. Darwin knew far more than he revealed... and that one day soon, his shadow would fall directly across her path.

When Eleanor at last regained enough strength to leave her chamber and resume dining with the household, Ellie could no longer excuse herself from joining the others at table. The fragile peace she had carved out for herself in the quiet of Eleanor's rooms ended abruptly. Now she was once again forced to sit beneath the same roof, at the same table, with the very men she most wished to avoid.

Ellie carried herself with perfect composure. Her manners were faultless, her voice polite, her posture graceful. Anyone observing her might have believed she had fully recovered from the distress of the smoke without fire and the chaos that had followed. But the calm was only a mask.

In truth, she had no desire to exchange so much as a single word with either Lord Ainsworth or the Duke of Somerset. Every smile she offered, every courteous response she gave, was carefully measured, and reserved entirely for the sake of appearance.

The servants were always watching. And in a house like Ainsworth Hall, servants' whispers traveled faster than the wind. So, Ellie smiled. She thanked the footmen who served the courses. She asked after Eleanor's comfort. She responded when addressed by the guests who occasionally visited the estate. But whenever either of the two men spoke, she answered with the barest civility required by decorum. Nothing more.

One afternoon, Lord Ainsworth had even approached her in the drawing room and offered an apology. His tone had been soft. His expression solemn, almost remorseful. Anyone overhearing might have believed him sincerely contrite.

"Lady Danielle," he had said quietly, "I regret the unpleasantness of the other evening. My conduct was... inexcusable."

For a moment, Ellie had studied him in silence. His words were smooth. His manner almost convincing. But sincerity? She doubted he even understood the meaning of the word. So, she had inclined her head politely, offered a cool acknowledgment of his apology, and withdrawn before he could attempt anything further. The performance had been flawless. But deep in her bones, Ellie knew one truth with absolute certainty. A man like Johnathon Ainsworth did not repent. He merely waited.

Ellie stood before her mirror fastening a ribbon in her hair when her cousin entered her chamber without warning. Eleanor rarely came to her. Usually, it was Ellie who sought her out. Her sudden appearance could only mean something was wrong.

"Ellie," she said in a hushed, uneasy tone, "I just spoke with Richard. He warned me that he must keep his distance for a time. My husband has received guests, guests from Darlington."

Ellie froze. Her hands slipped from the ribbon as she turned wide eyes toward her cousin.

"Darlington? Your husband knows someone from my little town?"

Eleanor nodded gravely. "Yes. Apparently, they are distant kin, at least the baron is."

Ellie's stomach tightened, the very air in the room seeming to grow heavier. Surely it could not be true. Of all the people in England, the last she wished to see were those who bore her no greater malice than the Appletons. She would almost have preferred to face Lord Ainsworth alone in a locked room.

"Baroness Appleton and her daughter are here for a visit," Eleanor confirmed quietly. "And they intend to stay for some time."

Ellie let out a sharp, incredulous laugh and rolled her eyes heavenward.

"Of course they are. They will fit seamlessly into your husband's household, pretension, cruelty, and venom appear to be the family creed."

Eleanor blinked in surprise. "Whatever do you mean?"

"Did Olivia never tell you?" Ellie asked softly. At the mention of her younger sister, Eleanor flinched, but this time grief did not overwhelm her. She steadied herself and shook her head. So, Ellie told her.

She spoke of the ball in London, of Felicity Appleton's jealousy and spite, of the humiliation she had deliberately orchestrated for poor Olivia. As Ellie spoke, her voice grew heated, trembling with indignation at the memory. Eleanor's hands slowly curled into fists.

"That wretched brat," she whispered fiercely. "She was the one who tormented my sister?"

Ellie nodded solemnly. "Yes. And now fate has brought her here." A faint, grim smile touched her lips. "It will be... amusing, in its own dreadful way. Her mother despises me with passion. She will not rest until she has insulted, slandered, or outright lied about me before every ear willing to listen." Her lip curled in disdain.

"She still calls herself Baroness, though she has no right to the title. She disgraced herself before my grandfather, lost her standing in society, and yet clings to the remnants of rank like a drowning woman clings to driftwood. Her bitterness only sharpens with time, and naturally, she directs it toward me." Ellie sighed, though a wry smile followed.

"Still, perhaps Lord Bennett's presence will prove a convenient distraction." Her eyes glinted faintly. "I imagine Lady Appleton will waste no time parading her daughter before him like a prize mare at auction. If they spend their energy pursuing him as Felicity's prospective husband, perhaps they will leave me blessedly alone."

Mrs. Appleton had not yet entered the dining room, so Ellie forced herself to exchange pleasantries with Felicity.

"I am surprised to see you here," she said lightly. "Why are you not in London, enjoying the Season?"

Felicity gave a careless shrug. "There was nothing amusing to keep us there. This year's Season feels dreadfully dull, so Mother suggested we spend a little time visiting Father's distant cousin instead."

Before Ellie could reply, Mrs. Agatha Appleton swept into the dining hall, her chin lifted in practiced hauteur.

"Danielle Huntington. Of course you would be skulking here, away from decent society."

The party was just settling when Mrs. Appleton dropped into her seat directly opposite Ellie, her eyes gleaming with malice.

"My word, Mrs. Appleton," Ellie replied, her gaze flashing like ice, "I know you take pleasure in insulting me, but why malign your hosts in the process? Are you suggesting Lord and Lady Ainsworth are not decent society? How appalling."

Mrs. Appleton gasped, her face blotching red with humiliation and fury. The hateful glance she leveled at Ellie spoke volumes. Lord Ainsworth and Lord Bennett both coughed discreetly to mask their amusement, while even Eleanor lifted her napkin to hide a smile.

"That is not what I meant, and you know it," Mrs. Appleton hissed, her eyes narrowing to slits. Then, as though Ellie's jab had never landed, she composed herself, smoothing her skirts and painting on a brittle smile.

"I heard whispers you've been hiding from your grandfather," she said sweetly. "Afraid of facing him, are you?"

Ellie ignored her, calmly unfolding her napkin as though she had not heard. Mrs. Appleton's cheeks flushed deeper with indignation.

"You insolent girl," she snapped. "Still too arrogant to answer your betters."

At last Ellie turned toward her, her smile honeyed but edged with steel.

"Betters? Forgive me, Mrs. Appleton, but I am Lady Danielle Huntington, the granddaughter of a duke, the great-granddaughter of a grand duke and a princess. You, on the other hand, were once a commoner and lost your title and standing through your own disgrace. If anyone here sits beneath a shadow of shame, it is not I."

The woman gasped. "You will address me properly. I am Baroness Appleton to you."

Ellie's voice cut like glass. "No, you are not. You forfeited that claim when you disgraced yourself before my grandfather. Yet here you sit, clinging to a title that no longer belongs to you, as though repeating it might make it true."

Mrs. Appleton's eyes narrowed. "And do you imagine styling yourself 'Lady Danielle' will make you anything more than a troublesome girl your own family cannot manage?"

Ellie's chin lifted. "Lady Danielle is not a style I imagine. It is my birthright. Nothing you say will strip it from me."

Mrs. Appleton leaned forward, her smile poisonous.

"We shall see what your grandfather thinks when I write to him. Perhaps he will be less indulgent of your impertinence once reminded how you disgrace his name."

Ellie's answering smile remained cool and unshaken. "By all means, write. I am certain he will treasure your letter, though I doubt he recalls your last meeting with the fondness you hope."

Mrs. Appleton stiffened. Out of the corner of her eye, Ellie saw Lord Ainsworth smirk and Lord Bennett suppress a laugh, while Felicity fluttered her lashes in vain at the duke.

"Lady Ainsworth," Mrs. Appleton suddenly turned, her sharp voice slicing across the table toward Eleanor, "has your sister been found?"

Eleanor froze, the effort to compose herself painfully clear. Before Ellie could intervene, Mrs. Appleton pressed on, her tone dripping with false pity.

"There are whispers in London about that unfortunate girl. After what Felicity confided, I fear they may be true. Some insist she ran away with a man, quite the scandal. Lord Blackwood, perhaps? Felicity swears she saw... familiarity between them."

At Richard's name, Ellie's stomach twisted. Eleanor broke, rising abruptly and fleeing the table. Ellie shoved her chair back, ready to follow, but Mrs. Appleton's gloating voice stopped her cold.

"How humiliating for your poor cousin," she purred, "to have a sister so wild, so wanton. A blot upon your family name and—"

Ellie's hand slammed onto the table with a crack that silenced the room. Her voice cut through the air like a blade.

"You venomous hag. Eleanor has endured enough, her sister missing, her health hanging by a thread, and still, you dare to pour filth upon her name? You call yourself a lady, yet you gorge yourself on lies and cruelty like a common gossipmonger in the streets." Her eyes blazed, daring anyone to look away.

"Do not speak of Olivia again. Do not dare breathe her name with your poison tongue. Every word you spew only proves what we have all long known, that you are petty, bitter, and desperate to wound others because you cannot endure the misery of your own disgrace."

Gasps rippled down the table, but Ellie's fury only sharpened. She leaned forward, her voice rising, clear and unshakable.

"You lost your title, your standing, and your honor through your own actions. And now you skulk about like a carrion crow, picking at the sorrows of others to make yourself feel grand. You are no baroness, no gentlewoman, you are a disgrace, an embarrassment to every decent soul forced to endure your company."

Mrs. Appleton's lips trembled, her face blotching red as she fumbled for words, but Ellie pressed on, relentless.

"So, mark me well, Agatha Appleton: if you ever again slander Eleanor or Olivia in my hearing, I will not merely silence you with words. I will drag your name through every drawing room in London until even your so-called friends spit you out. Cross me again, and you will learn just how merciless I can be."

The hall fell deathly still. Even Lord Ainsworth leaned back in his chair, his eyes widened with something between astonishment and dark amusement. Felicity stared in open horror, her face gone pale, while Lord Bennett's lips twitched as though he were struggling not to smile. Ellie swept from the hall like a storm unleashed, her skirts snapping in her wake, leaving Mrs. Appleton stricken and the entire company stunned into silence.

Outside, Gordon intercepted her before she had gone more than a few steps into the corridor. His grave expression betrayed a concern far deeper than the calm composure he attempted to maintain. Without a word, he inclined his head toward the garden path and quietly guided her away from the house.

"The greenhouse, Ellie," he murmured softly. "Your cousin went there."

Ellie did not hesitate. Gathering her skirts, she hurried across the damp gravel path, the cool evening air brushing her flushed cheeks. The glass panes of the greenhouse glowed faintly in the dim light, lanterns inside casting soft reflections against the night. She pushed open the door at once.

Warm, humid air wrapped around her, thick with the scent of soil and blooming flowers. Beneath the arching vines and rows of potted plants, Eleanor sat slumped on a narrow wooden bench. Her shoulders shook with quiet, helpless sobs, her hands covering her face as though she wished to disappear entirely.

Ellie's heart clenched painfully at the sight. She crossed the room in quick strides and sank beside her cousin, immediately drawing Eleanor into her arms. Cradling her close, she rocked her gently, just as one might comfort a frightened child.

"Hush now," Ellie murmured softly, one hand stroking Eleanor's hair. "Do not listen to that vile woman." Her voice sharpened slightly, though it remained low and steady. "She thrives on cruelty. It is the only thing that gives her satisfaction. She and Felicity cannot bear the thought of other women being loved, admired, or cherished. Anyone who threatens their petty vanity becomes their enemy." Ellie's jaw tightened.

"She has done the same to me for years, scheming, whispering slander, always seeking some new way to wound. Unless you bow to her pride and flatter her vanity, she will stop at nothing to tear you down."

Eleanor's sobs slowly began to subside, fading into trembling breaths. Her fingers loosened their grip on her face, though tears still glistened along her lashes. Ellie waited patiently, continuing to hold her until the worst of the storm had passed. Then she gently lifted Eleanor's chin, urging her to meet her gaze.

"Listen to me," Ellie said quietly but firmly. "None of what she said about Olivia is true." She brushed a stray tear from Eleanor's cheek. "Rumors spread because women like Agatha cannot bear uncertainty. They demand explanations for everything, and when none are given, they invent lies to satisfy their own vanity. It feeds their pride to believe they know secrets no one else does."

Her voice softened slightly.

"But Olivia is not what they claim. I know it in my heart." Ellie's expression grew resolute, a quiet fire settled behind her eyes. "We will find her," she vowed. "I swear it. I will not stop searching until we do." Her gaze darkened, the warmth in her voice turning to something colder. "And if your husband has had any hand in her disappearance..." she said slowly, her words edged like steel, "...then he will answer for it."

The greenhouse fell silent around them, the soft rustle of leaves the only sound as Ellie held her cousin close, her promise hanging heavy in the warm night air.

Just as Ellie had expected, both Felicity and Mrs. Appleton devoted every ounce of their energy to convincing Lord Bennett that Felicity would make him the perfect match. Their efforts, however, fell utterly flat. The duke's cool indifference made it abundantly clear that he had no interest in the young woman. Before long, his irritation with their relentless maneuvering became impossible to ignore. He began avoiding them altogether, vanishing on long rides across the countryside or retreating to the hunt, leaving Felicity fuming and Mrs. Appleton quietly seething.

One morning, as the household lingered over the last sips of tea and toast, Mrs. Appleton unveiled a new scheme. Turning toward Lord Ainsworth, her voice syrupy sweet, she presented her proposal.

"With so many distinguished guests in your home, would it not be splendid to host a ball? May is such a beautiful month, and Plymouth's finest could gather here. Felicity, of course, is longing for proper companionship. Such an event would give her the opportunity to meet all the eligible gentlemen in the district who have not gone up to London for the Season."

Lord Ainsworth brightened at once, clearly pleased. "A splendid idea indeed. Nothing enlivens a house more than a ball. And I am convinced it would do you good as well, Lady Danielle." He turned a dazzling smile in Ellie's direction. Ellie, quietly buttering her bread, raised her brows.

"Oh, do not trouble yourself with me. I have not yet been formally introduced to society, and my parents always wished to be present for my first ball. There is no need to hurry such a thing."

"But surely you enjoy dancing, Lady Danielle?" Felicity pressed, her voice eager, bright with hope. Ellie inclined her head, though her reply remained reluctant.

"Yes, I do enjoy it. But what good would a ball do me here? Lord Blackwood cannot attend, and aside from His Grace, I know none of the gentlemen in this county. Besides," her voice softened slightly, "as I said, my parents wished to be present at my debut. To step into society without them would feel improper... even disloyal."

Lord Ainsworth waved away her concerns with a careless gesture.

"This will hardly be an official ball, my dear. Not like the grand affairs of the London Season. There will be no rigid protocol, only music, laughter, and good company."

Ellie hesitated, her thoughts racing. Perhaps he was right. A gathering like this might offer her the perfect opportunity to discreetly question the local nobility. Someone might know what had become of Olivia. She gave a small shrug, concealing her deeper motives.

"Shall we begin planning the ball, Mother?" Felicity asked eagerly. Her bold words caused several heads to turn, forks pausing in midair. Ellie cleared her throat and fixed Felicity with a firm look.

"That duty belongs to Lady Ainsworth, not you. She is mistress of the house, and together with her husband, she alone has the right to issue invitations."

A flicker of satisfaction crossed Eleanor's face, though she quickly lowered her gaze. Mrs. Appleton's lips thinned, her eyes narrowing at Ellie.

"Lady Ainsworth is already married. It does her little good to stand in the spotlight. It would be far better for Felicity to take the reins. She would shine even more as a prospective bride."

Ellie's patience snapped. "Then perhaps, Mrs. Appleton, you should host a ball at your own estate. That is, if you had not forfeited your standing in society."

The older woman's face turned crimson. Her hands trembled, as though she could scarcely restrain herself from striking Danielle across the table. Ellie rose smoothly to her feet, her chin held high.

"Cease your tantrums, Mrs. Appleton. The reason you lost your title and respect was your own disgrace, not mine. Yet you persist in blaming me for your downfall. Resent me if you must, but the truth remains: it would be unseemly for a marquess to host a ball under the direction of a distant relation rather than his wife."

Mrs. Appleton's mouth opened, fury blazing in her eyes, but before she could unleash it, Lord Bennett's voice cut through the tension.

"Lady Danielle is correct." His tone was smooth yet commanding. His dark gaze settled coolly on the furious woman. "It is always the master and mistress of a house who host such gatherings, unless the lady is indisposed through illness or childbearing. In such a case, a close relation may step in."

"I am a relation, Your Grace," Mrs. Appleton snapped, her voice tight with desperation.

"A distant relation," Bennett corrected coldly, his eyes narrowing. "And only through marriage, not blood. If Lady Ainsworth were unable to fulfill her duties, then Lady Danielle, her cousin and the granddaughter of a duke, would assume that role long before you."

The pronouncement struck like a slap. Mrs. Appleton stiffened, her lips trembling with rage. With a dramatic sweep of her skirts, she stormed from the room, Felicity scrambling after her. Ellie exhaled slowly, her hands trembling beneath the table. Dealing with Agatha Appleton was like fighting an endless war. No matter how many defeats the woman suffered, she always returned, brimming with fresh malice and ready for the next battle.

The very next day, invitations for the ball were dispatched. Eleanor, aided by the housekeeper and a small retinue of maids, soon became wholly absorbed in the planning. Yet Mrs. Appleton managed to interfere at every turn, forever suggesting alterations, forever maneuvering to thrust Felicity into prominence.

As the date drew nearer, preparations consumed the entire household. Determined that her daughter should outshine every other young lady present, Mrs. Appleton whisked Felicity into town to order a gown fashioned from the finest silks. Lord Ainsworth, claiming urgent business, departed for the day, taking both his steward and his butler with him. Eleanor had wished to remain at home to rest and oversee the household, but Mrs. Appleton would hear none of it. She insisted Eleanor accompany them, arguing that the mistress of the house ought to ensure Felicity's gown eclipsed every rival. Lord Bennett, as ever, had his own pursuits to occupy him.

And so, for the first time in days, Ellie found herself effectively mistress of the estate. She did not waste the opportunity. With the house eerily quiet and the servants mostly tucked away in their quarters, she slipped into Lord Ainsworth's study. Once again, she searched through drawers and cabinets, carefully rifling through letters and ledgers. Yet she uncovered nothing more than she had before. Frustration gnawed at her. Perhaps the truth lay hidden elsewhere.

Grasping a candlestick, she lit the taper. Its frail flame flickered uncertainly, casting long, restless shadows across the paneled walls. Quiet as a breath, she crossed to the cellar door. Her hand hovered over the latch, her pulse pounding in her throat. Then, drawing a steady breath, she pushed the door open and descended into the darkness below.

14

When Trust Became a Weapon

It was cold and damp in the cellar, the kind of chill that clung to the skin and seeped slowly into the bones. Ellie descended the narrow stone steps with care, her shoes echoing faintly against the worn surface. The air reeked of mildew and earth, laced with the acrid tang of candle smoke. The flame sputtered and hissed in protest, casting a frail glow into the suffocating darkness.

At first the gloom seemed impenetrable, but as her eyes adjusted, shapes gradually emerged. To the left stretched a vast storage area: shelves lined with jars of preserves, barrels of salted meat stacked against the walls, and a hulking icebox in the corner, its iron handle dull in the flickering light. Beyond that, however, the cellar changed in character. The walls grew rougher, the floors uneven, the air heavier. The space looked less like a storehouse and more like a dungeon.

A shiver coursed down Ellie's spine. She set the candle carefully upon an old chest of drawers so her hands would be free to search. The wavering glow fell across iron hooks set into the wall, and faint outlines that looked disturbingly like chains. Her stomach tightened.

She had just begun to step forward when a high-pitched squeak pierced the silence. Rats. Their claws skittered across the stone, and her blood froze. Of all creatures, she despised rats most. Her heart lurched violently when a firm hand suddenly seized her arm from behind. A muffled cry escaped her as she whirled in terror, only to find herself staring into Richard's familiar face.

"Richard!" she gasped, clutching her chest. "What on earth are you doing here?"

He gave her a crooked, mischievous smile that did nothing to calm the frantic beating of her heart.

"I saw Eleanor, Mrs. Appleton, and Felicity parading through town," he said lightly. "That told me you'd been left behind. When I reached the estate, I noticed you slipping into the cellar. I thought you might need an ally."

Her breathing was still uneven. "I am searching for answers about Olivia," Ellie said quietly. "With Lord Ainsworth gone, I thought this the perfect moment to look deeper."

Richard's expression sobered at once, though his hand remained resting warmly on her arm.

"A carriage from your grandfather is waiting in town," he said in a low voice. "It will be ready whenever we need it."

"That is good to know." Ellie lowered her voice further. "I wish I could spirit Eleanor away at once. But if she leaves, I must leave as well... and I cannot yet."

Together they pressed deeper into the cellar. The brick walls, slick with condensation, seemed to close in around them. Shadows clung stubbornly to every corner, and the occasional skittering of rats sent Ellie jumping sideways more than once.

Richard chuckled softly at her alarm. She shot him a sharp glare that only made his grin widen.

Then Ellie's foot caught on something. She stumbled with a startled gasp, nearly pitching forward, but Richard's arms shot out instantly to catch her. He pulled her against him. Closer than he ever had before. Her breath caught. Not only from the near fall, but from the sudden, unsettling awareness of his strength, his warmth, the steady beat of his heart beneath her hands. His arm circled her waist instinctively, holding her upright, and the heat of his body seeped through the thin fabric of her gown.

For a moment she forgot entirely where they were. Her gaze lifted slowly to meet his. The candlelight flickered across his features, leaving his eyes shadowed and intense. For one suspended heartbeat neither of them moved. His grip tightened slightly at her waist. Her pulse thundered in her ears. His face lowered a fraction, close enough that she could feel the warmth of his breath brush across her cheek. Close enough that the air between them felt charged, fragile, as though the slightest movement might shatter the moment, or seal it.

Ellie's cheeks flamed. The world seemed to narrow to the quiet space between them. His lips parted slightly. So close. So very close... when suddenly her skirt snagged. The sharp tug of fabric shattered the moment like glass. Ellie glanced down to find the hem caught on a small iron lever jutting from the wall. Flustered, she tugged at the cloth. The mechanism groaned. Stone grated against stone. Both of them froze.

Slowly, impossibly, the wall beside them began to shift. Heavy blocks slid inward with a deep grinding sound, revealing a narrow, black passageway yawning open before them. For a long moment neither spoke. Their hearts were still racing, though not entirely from the discovery.

"A secret passage," Richard whispered at last, his voice hushed with awe... and something else that still lingered from the closeness between them. Ellie stared into the darkness.

"Perhaps," she breathed softly, "the very place where Olivia has been hidden."

Richard stepped through first, holding the candle aloft, and Ellie followed close behind. The passage twisted sharply, damp and narrow, before finally opening into a small chamber. At its center stood an iron-barred cell. From within came the faint sound of movement, hesitant, wary.

"Olivia?" Ellie called softly, hope and fear warring in her voice. A rasping reply answered her, trembling.

"Who... who are you?"

Richard lifted the candle higher, and the glow revealed a young woman chained to the wall. Her hair hung in tangled strands, her dress in tatters. She lay half-reclined on a filthy old settee, the chains so short she could scarcely move. Her eyes, dull and hollow, yet blazing with shock, fixed upon them.

"My name is Miranda," she whispered hoarsely. "Miranda Ainsworth."

Ellie's breath caught. Richard's jaw tightened.

"I am Lord Ainsworth's wife."

Both of them gasped.

"That cannot be," Richard growled. "We were told his first wife had died."

Miranda gave a bitter, humorless laugh. "That is the lie he told the world. He spun a tale of my death to clear his path, then locked me here. His schemes required no wife who opposed him. He demanded I support his vile trade, his plan to sell women like cattle. When I refused, he beat me. When I tried to escape, he chained me here and told the world I was gone."

Ellie's stomach twisted in horror. "But... how did he convince everyone?" she asked weakly.

"He deceived them all," Miranda spat. "He told my family I was buried here. Told others I was buried with them. He even built a false family cemetery behind the estate so my kin could mourn there, then tore it down once they had gone. Lies upon lies, and no one dared question him."

Tears welled in Ellie's eyes. "Why does he keep you here still?"

Miranda's voice broke, her body trembling. "Because he enjoys it. He delights in suffering. He uses me when it pleases him, when Eleanor is too ill, when guests arrive, when his cruelty nearly kills her. Next to this cell is another chamber... a place he calls his punishment room. It was mine once. Now it is hers."

Ellie's hand flew to her mouth. Richard's face darkened with fury.

"He is a demon," Miranda whispered.

"How long?" Ellie managed.

"Over a year. Months spent here in the dark."

"Does Eleanor know?"

Miranda shook her head, sobbing openly now. "No. She believes I am dead, as does everyone. He brings her through another entrance. The room is soundproof. Even if I screamed, he would kill her to silence me."

Ellie knelt beside the bars, gripping the cold iron. "Then we must get you out."

"You should not be here," Miranda pleaded desperately. "If the butler, or Jonathon himself, finds you, he will make you pay."

"He is gone today," Ellie said firmly. "And the butler with him. Where are the keys?"

"There, behind the wall mechanism. He hides them there."

Richard moved swiftly, retrieving the keys. But before unlocking the chains, he caught Ellie's gaze.

"If we take her, Ainsworth will know you were involved."

Ellie's chin lifted. "Then let him suspect. He cannot expose me without condemning himself. And if I must, I will tell him I have already informed his uncle."

Miranda reached through the bars, her eyes wide with gratitude and fear.

"Please... do not risk yourselves. He is dangerous beyond measure."

"We risk it anyway," Ellie said firmly. "My cousin is still missing. I cannot stop until I find her. But you will not suffer here any longer."

Within moments the chains fell away. Miranda staggered forward into freedom, collapsing against Ellie as though her strength might fail entirely.

"There is another way out," she whispered urgently. "A hidden door beyond the cellar that leads into the woods."

"Perfect," Richard said. "We will take you there now. I will escort you to safety, then fetch the carriage. You must vanish from this place before he returns."

Miranda nodded weakly, hope flickering in her hollow eyes. She embraced Ellie fiercely before allowing Richard to guide her into the passage that led toward the trees. Ellie remained behind for a moment, the echo of chains still ringing in her ears. She turned back toward the shifting wall, preparing to close it again.

Footsteps startled her. Her heart leapt, but it was Richard, returning. Without a word, he stepped forward and pulled her tightly into his arms.

"Be careful, Ellie," he murmured, his voice rough with urgency.

Ellie had carefully restored everything to its place, the chains fastened as she had found them, the keys rehung behind the secret panel, when the faint creak of footsteps reached her from above.

Her pulse quickened.

Was it so late already? Had the servants begun preparations for supper? She extinguished the candle at once, plunging herself into darkness so complete, it felt like a suffocating cloak. Shivering, she steadied her breath and crept toward the door. Her fingers had just brushed the cellar latch when the handle turned sharply from the other side.

Startled, Ellie recoiled. Her heel caught on a wicker basket of potatoes left on the steps. With no time to recover, she tumbled backward down the stairs. Pain exploded through her ankle and back as she struck the stone floor. A gasp tore from her lips. The door flew open. Light flared as someone hurried inside, carrying a lamp.

Not him. Please, not him. Her dread hardened when Lord Bennett rushed to her side, dropping to one knee with an urgency that betrayed genuine concern.

"Danielle," he murmured, his voice unexpectedly soft. Ellie squeezed her eyes shut. Hot tears burned against her lashes. She could not bear to look at him. "Are you hurt? Did you break anything?" he asked, leaning closer.

She shook her head weakly. "I think... only my ankle. My back pains me as well."

Without hesitation he slipped his arms beneath her and lifted her from the cold stone as though she weighed nothing. His scent, sandalwood and smoke, closed around her, unsettling in a way that had nothing to do with the fall. She forced her eyes open and met his steady gaze. Something inside her frayed and unraveled. Words spilled out before she could stop them.

"Listen, before you begin lecturing me about recklessness and playing with fire, I did not do this on purpose. I would not have fallen if I hadn't heard you. And I am not sneaking about for amusement. I am trying to find my cousin Olivia. The night you found me in the kitchen, I wasn't seeking Lord Ainsworth's attention. You think poorly of me, but I am here because I love my cousins. I will not stand idle while your cousin destroys them both." Her voice rose with every sentence, trembling with pent-up fury. His lips curved in a faint half-smile, but he said nothing, allowing her to continue.

"I found someone today, someone believed long dead. I don't know what game you are playing, but I am not imagining these things. And I will not allow you to belittle me with your disdain. I have had enough."

"Danielle—"

"And another thing," she pressed on, cheeks flushed with heat. "It is *Lady Danielle* to you. I am not the foolish girl you imagine. Eleanor does not deserve this fate. Olivia does not deserve to be bartered away like cattle. Lord Ainsworth is a monster, and I will fight him however I must. If you wish to tell him of my doings, then do it, but I will not stop."

"Danielle, if you would only—"

She cut him off again, her voice shaking with equal parts anger and pain.

"I know you do not think me a lady. Perhaps I am not, by your measure. But I will not bow to men who think women exist only to suffer. Why must we be broken and silenced? Shouldn't men protect us rather than destroy us? If only you—"

Her tirade ended abruptly when his lips pressed against hers. The kiss was not harsh or demanding, but gentle, lingering, stealing the breath from her before she even realized what was happening. Ellie froze, utterly stunned. When he finally drew back, her entire body trembled. A rush of heat and vertigo fluttered through her stomach.

"Why... why did you kiss me?" she stammered, eyes wide, cheeks blazing. His grin softened.

"Because you would not let me answer with words. I thought a kiss might succeed where speech could not."

For a moment she almost laughed, almost smiled. Warmth crept into her chest despite herself. The kiss had silenced the torrent of words she so often used as a shield when he was near.

"I am not here to chastise you," he said quietly. "I know you are not reckless for the sake of it. You are fighting for what matters to you. I see that now."

Her eyes searched his face. "But all these weeks you have done nothing but attack me. You scolded me in front of your cousin. You made me feel like a child."

His smile faded. "I know. And I regret it. Just as you are not the girl I first believed you to be... I am not the man you imagine."

Ellie's voice wavered. "I do not know what to think of you. At times you are the perfect gentleman. Then, in the next moment, you cut me with your words. Who are you truly? Why are you even here? Shouldn't you be at your duchy? How can a duke linger here so long?"

He chuckled softly. "So many questions. Very well. I am here because my uncle has long distrusted Ainsworth. He knows the man betrayed both our families. And when Ainsworth's first wife... supposedly died, we suspected murder."

Ellie shook her head. "She did not die. She is the one I found today, Miranda Ainsworth. He kept her hidden, chained in a secret chamber for more than a year. Richard is taking her to safety now."

Lord Bennett's expression shifted to pure shock. "Your servant? How is he to protect her?"

"Richard is no servant," Ellie said firmly. "He is Baron Blackwood, my dearest friend since childhood. He only pretends to serve so that he might protect me. The Appletons know him too. His identity could not remain hidden if he stayed under this roof." The confession tumbled out before she could stop herself. Her heart hammered with sudden apprehension, but it was too late to retract.

"Have you uncovered anything else?" he asked quietly, his eyes intent upon hers. Ellie hesitated, then nodded.

"The night you caught me in the study, I found a letter from Eleanor's father. He sent her to Ainsworth, and together they tried to force Olivia into a match. She was sent here to be 'broken.' She vanished not long after."

His jaw tightened. He shifted her slightly in his arms, but his hand brushed her injured foot. Pain lanced through her ankle and she gasped, tears springing to her eyes.

"My apologies," he said quickly. "I will take you upstairs. You need ice for that ankle, and a physician."

"No! Not a doctor," Ellie blurted, panic flashing across her face. His grin returned, softer now.

"Afraid of a physician, are you?"

"Of course not," she snapped, though her voice trembled. "But I do not want Lord Ainsworth to learn I am injured."

He arched a brow. "He will discover it regardless. Such a fall cannot easily be hidden."

He carried her back to her chamber with surprising gentleness, moving with a care that seemed at odds with the blunt, commanding man she had come to expect. Ellie kept her eyes fixed anywhere but his face, painfully aware of the steady strength of his arms and the warmth of his chest beneath her cheek.

Once inside her room, he laid her carefully upon the bed, arranging the pillows behind her so she would not have to shift her injured ankle. Then his expression hardened with quiet authority. A maid was summoned to fetch ice, and another servant was sent at once for the physician. Ellie tried to protest, but one look from Lord Bennett silenced the attempt before it left her lips.

Within the hour, the doctor arrived and examined her ankle with practiced hands. After several careful movements and questions that made Ellie wince more than once, he finally pronounced it badly sprained but not broken.

"Rest is essential," the physician declared firmly. "You must not place weight upon it for several days. Keep it elevated and cold compresses applied frequently. With care, you should recover fully."

Ellie murmured her thanks, enduring the examination in silence. Her cheeks burned, not from the pain, but from humiliation. Being fussed over, prodded, and discussed as though she were some fragile invalid, made her want to vanish beneath the blankets.

Yet what unsettled her far more than the injury itself was Lord Bennett's constant presence. He had not left the room. Even while the doctor worked, the duke stood a few paces away, arms folded loosely behind his back, his tall figure unmoving beside the window. His steady gaze never strayed far from her, watchful and intent. Every time she dared glance up, she found his eyes upon her. Not mocking. Not scolding. Something else, something quieter, heavier. It made her pulse flutter in a way she could not quite explain.

When the physician finally gathered his instruments and took his leave, Ellie exhaled softly in relief. But Lord Bennett remained exactly where he was.

When the physician finally departed, Lord Ainsworth returned to the house. The moment he learned that it was Lady Danielle who had required medical attention, his composure fractured.

His eyes widened in alarm, and he demanded at once to know what had happened.

Andrew, Duke of Somerset, observed his cousin with narrowed eyes. From the upper gallery he watched Ainsworth pace in and out of his study, restless energy vibrating through every movement. The marquess ran a hand through his hair, barked orders at passing servants, then abruptly disappeared down the corridor that led toward the cellar.

Andrew remained where he was, leaning lightly against the carved railing, his expression thoughtful. Several minutes passed. Then Ainsworth reemerged. The change in him was unmistakable. His face had gone rigid, every line sharpened with fury barely contained beneath a veneer of civility. His mouth was drawn tight, his eyes dark with a dangerous intensity that set Andrew instantly on guard.

Without a word, Ainsworth strode toward the staircase. His steps were heavy. His jaw clenched so tightly the muscles flickered beneath the skin. Andrew pushed away from the railing and followed at a measured pace. He intercepted his cousin just as Ainsworth's hand closed around the latch of Ellie's chamber door.

"What is the matter, cousin?" Andrew asked smoothly, stepping into his path. Ainsworth halted, his glare sharp and immediate.

"None of your concern."

Andrew tilted his head slightly, his expression one of mild curiosity.

"You seem rather upset."

"Upset?" Ainsworth repeated, his voice cracking like a whip. His eyes gleamed with barely concealed malice. "I am furious."

He gestured sharply toward the corridor. "Ever since Eleanor's cousin arrived, nothing but misfortune has followed. And I cannot shake the suspicion that Lady Danielle is behind it all. I intend to question her at once."

Andrew raised a brow. "Question her about what, precisely?" he asked, his tone calm, almost amused.

"About her sneaking about. About her meddling. About the chaos she has brought into this house."

Andrew studied him for a long moment before giving a low, quiet laugh. He shook his head.

"Sneaking?" he said lightly. "Of course she has been sneaking."

Ainsworth blinked in surprise.

"Did you truly believe her tale when she first arrived?" Andrew continued. "She has made no secret of her determination to find her missing cousin, or to free Eleanor from your... rather firm grasp." He folded his arms loosely. "Honestly, Ainsworth," he added with a faint, mocking smile, "you cannot be that blind."

From behind her closed chamber door, Ellie stiffened. The voices in the corridor carried clearly through the heavy wood. Every word, every measured tone, every pause reached her ears with cruel precision.

Andrew. Lord Bennett. She had trusted him. Each syllable twisted the knot in her chest tighter.

Fool. She had confided in him only hours before, shared truths she had guarded carefully from everyone else in that house. She had opened her heart in a moment of exhaustion and fear, believing, if only for a moment, that he understood her. And now he was using her confession as a weapon.

Her fingers tightened in the bedclothes. Heat stung behind her eyes, though she refused to let the tears fall. How could she have been so naive? She had known he was dangerous. Had reminded herself of it countless times. A duke, a man of power and calculation, cousin to the very monster she sought to expose. And yet he had looked at her with such quiet understanding. Had spoken with such gentleness. He had kissed her.

The memory burned now like a cruel mockery. Her chest rose and fell unevenly as she listened to his voice outside the door, smooth, controlled, almost amused. As though revealing her secrets were nothing more than a clever move in some private game between men.

Her stomach churned. She pressed a trembling hand to her lips, forcing herself to remain silent, to remain still. If Ainsworth entered that room... if he knew what she had discovered... the consequences would be far worse than a wounded heart.

"You knew this all along?" Ainsworth demanded, his nostrils flaring. "Why did you not tell me sooner?"

Andrew smirked. "And spoil all my entertainment? Where is the joy in that?" He leaned lazily against the banister, his grin infuriatingly smug. "I have rather enjoyed watching her make a fool of you." He paused, studying his cousin with open amusement.

"Besides, she is beautiful. You are not the only man capable of appreciating a lovely woman. Having her here has allowed me certain... opportunities."

Ainsworth's eyes narrowed. "Opportunities?"

Andrew's grin widened. "I kissed her. Twice. What harm is there in that?"

The fury that ignited across Ainsworth's face was nearly incandescent.

"She is not yours to kiss."

"Oh, forgive me." Andrew's tone dripped with mockery. "I did not realize a kiss might offend you. I would have thought your long history of... indiscretions would place such a trifle well beneath your notice. Surely the great Jonathon Ainsworth does not blush at so small a sin?"

"Cease your nonsense," Ainsworth growled. "Nothing shocks me. But heed this once, stay away from her. Lady Danielle is not for you."

Andrew chuckled darkly. "You are married, cousin. Do not pretend to play the gallant now. Or are you so desperate to replace your wife with another pretty captive?"

"Lady Danielle is my wife's cousin," Ainsworth spat. "I look out for her."

Andrew's eyes hardened. "You look out for no one but yourself. Tell me, were you looking out for your first wife when you locked her in your cellar and spread the tale of her death?"

For a moment, silence fell between them. Then Ainsworth paled.

"How do you know?"

Andrew's grin turned razor-sharp. "Danielle told me. She trusts me. She found Miranda alive, chained like an animal behind your secret passage."

Ainsworth gasped, his hand curling into a fist. "I'll kill her."

Andrew stepped closer, his voice low and cold.

"And how exactly do you plan to accomplish that? She is clever, always one step ahead of you. Do you imagine her family does not know where she is? It was Danielle who secured Miranda's escape, and she is well protected now. If you harm her, you will answer to far more than our uncle." His gaze sharpened. "The Duke of Essex himself will see to it. And he has friends in very high places."

Ainsworth's lips slowly curled into a sinister smile. A low laugh escaped him, cold enough to chill the air.

"You are bold, cousin... but foolish." He straightened his coat with deliberate calm. "I have done nothing anyone could call evil. No crime you can prove. Even if Miranda opens her mouth, who will believe her? The world believes her dead."

Andrew arched a brow. "And when a woman long buried suddenly walks among the living?"

His voice softened dangerously. "Do you truly think society will dismiss her testimony so easily?"

The violent string of curses that followed sent a shiver through Ellie's body. Behind her chamber door, her nails dug deep into her palms, fury burning hotter than the pain in her injured ankle. Each word from the corridor struck her like a lash. So, this was Lord Bennett's grand strategy. Throw her name into the fire. Bait his cousin. Gamble with lives that were not his to risk.

Eleanor. Olivia. Miranda. Did he truly care so little for their safety?

Ellie's throat tightened painfully. Her breath came shallow as the realization settled over her like ice. She had been a fool. A fool to trust him. A fool to confide in him. A fool to mistake stolen kindness, even a kiss, for something deeper. For loyalty. For understanding. But now she saw the truth with brutal clarity. Andrew Bennett was not playing the same game she was. She fought to save the innocent. He hunted his enemy. And if that hunt required using her as bait, so be it.

Her stomach twisted. He had listened to her fears, her plans, her hopes, and then carried them straight to Ainsworth, tossing them between them like pieces on a chessboard. The quiet gentleness she had glimpsed in him earlier now felt like a cruel illusion. He was no ally. He was a weapon. And like any weapon, he would strike wherever it served him best.

Ellie drew a slow, trembling breath, forcing the sting from her eyes. Never again, she vowed.

Never again would she mistake him for a decent man. Never again would she allow herself to be swayed by his charm, his teasing smile, or the warmth of his voice. Andrew Bennett had betrayed her. And as far as Ellie was concerned, he had done so for the last time.

15
The Hidden Chamber

The long-anticipated day of the ball finally arrived, and the Ainsworth estate hummed with frenetic energy from the moment the sun rose. Servants hurried through the corridors carrying trays, flowers, and linens. Footmen polished silver until it gleamed like mirrors, while maids rushed from chamber to chamber preparing guest rooms and arranging fresh bouquets. The scent of beeswax, roses, and newly polished wood lingered throughout the house.

Eleanor moved quietly among them, doing her best to oversee the last-minute arrangements. Though mistress of the house in name, she seemed almost like a guest within her own walls, soft-spoken and careful, offering gentle instructions where she could.

In truth, it was Mrs. Appleton who appeared to preside over everything. Agatha strode about the estate as though it belonged to her, barking orders at servants and family alike. Her sharp, shrill voice echoed endlessly through the halls.

"No, no, those flowers belong in the ballroom, not the corridor!"

"Felicity must have the eastern chamber. The light is far better there!"

"And mind that the musicians are placed properly. My daughter cannot dance in darkness!" The woman swept through the house like a storm, scattering irritation wherever she passed.

By midday, Ellie felt thoroughly exhausted. Weary of the noise and constant demands, she quietly slipped away for a walk in the gardens. Gordon, ever her steadfast shadow, joined her without a word.

Outside, the world felt mercifully different. The air was warm and fragrant with blooming roses and lavender. Bees drifted lazily between flowerbeds, and a soft breeze stirred the leaves of the tall lindens that bordered the paths. Above them stretched a brilliant May sky, clear and bright, promising a fair, glittering evening.

For several precious minutes Ellie allowed herself to breathe freely. Here, beyond the walls of the manor, Mrs. Appleton's suffocating presence seemed almost unreal. Gordon walked beside her in companionable silence, his hands clasped loosely behind his back. Now and then he cast her a quiet, watchful glance, but he asked no questions. He knew she needed the peace.

Eventually, however, duty called her back. When Ellie returned to the house, the familiar weight of expectation settled over her once more. She must prepare for the ball. Though her heart resisted the thought. Richard would not be there. And for the past two weeks she had managed, through sheer stubborn determination, to avoid both Lord Ainsworth and the Duke of Somerset entirely.

The prospect of an evening filled with forced smiles and hollow pleasantries held little appeal. Still, Gordon had mentioned that several grandsons of Lord Beverton and Lord

Woodworth were expected to attend. Perhaps their company would prove tolerable. At the very least, it might distract attention from Felicity's inevitable attempts to monopolize the duke and parade herself before him like the prize Mrs. Appleton so desperately wished her to be.

She was about to ring for her maid when a muffled sound reached her, faint at first, then sharper. Weeping. Alarm clenched her chest. The crying came from Eleanor's chamber. Without a thought for propriety, Ellie pushed the door open. What she saw stole the breath from her lungs.

Two maids hovered anxiously over Eleanor, who lay face-down upon the bed, her shift drawn low across her back. Angry welts, bloody, raw, and cruel, scored her cousin's skin from shoulder to waist. The sight was so barbarous Ellie nearly collapsed where she stood.

"Eleanor..." Her voice broke. She hurried to the bedside. Horror etched across her face. Eleanor gasped and snatched at the sheet, dragging it upward as though she could hide the damage, and her shame.

"Ellie, please... leave."

"Did your husband do this to you?" Ellie's voice trembled, though steel ran through it. Eleanor turned her face away. Silent tears slipped down her cheeks.

"Please, Ellie... go."

"No." Ellie dropped to her knees beside the bed, her hand gripping the coverlet. "Tell me. Did Lord Ainsworth do this?" Her voice cracked under the weight of fury and grief. Eleanor hesitated.

Then, with a broken sob, she gave the smallest nod. Ellie's chest burned. Her own tears spilled freely as she clenched her jaw.

"He is going to pay for this," she whispered fiercely. "Why would he hurt you so brutally?"

One of the maids, seeing her mistress too shaken to answer, stepped forward with downcast eyes.

"His lordship accused Lady Ainsworth of inviting his uncle to stay. His Grace is expected to arrive in a few days."

Ellie stared at her in disbelief. "That is absurd. Eleanor would never summon his uncle. The man invents excuses merely to vent his cruelty." Swallowing hard, she turned toward the other maid. "Carla, fetch Gordon at once. Tell him to wait in my chamber."

The maid bobbed a quick curtsy and hurried away. Eleanor lifted her head weakly, her face pale and wet with tears.

"Why are you calling Gordon?"

"Because he will fetch the doctor."

"No!" Eleanor's cry was desperate. "Ellie, leave it be. It will only make everything worse."

"I will not ignore this." Ellie's voice was unyielding. "You need a physician. If these wounds fester, your life could be in danger."

"The doctor, he cannot see me like this. He will think—"

"That your husband is a monster?" Ellie cut her off, her eyes flashing. "That you are the victim of his savagery?" Her voice softened slightly, but the resolve in it did not waver. "That is the truth, Eleanor. And I will not allow it to remain hidden."

Her cousin shook her head weakly, trembling. But Ellie pressed on, her voice low and urgent.

"If this is not stopped now, he will kill you. I swear it. We need witnesses, people who will speak when the time comes. Especially with his uncle arriving soon." A new thought struck her. "Tell me... was this what happened the night of the smoke? When you were so weak?"

Eleanor did not answer. Her silence said enough. At that moment Gordon entered Ellie's adjoining chamber. She hurried to him and whispered a swift account of what she had discovered.

His face blanched with horror. But without hesitation he turned and left to summon the physician.

Ellie closed her eyes for a moment, gathering every scrap of courage she possessed. Whatever came of this, she would not allow Eleanor to face her torment alone.

Ellie had only just returned to Eleanor's side when a sharp rap sounded at the door, followed by Lord Ainsworth's cold, commanding voice. The sound made Ellie stiffen like a cornered cat. One look at her face warned anyone nearby that she was ready to bite a man's head off. She half rose, prepared to fling the door open herself, but Eleanor caught her wrist and held it fast.

"Ellie," she said urgently, her voice firm despite the tears streaking her cheeks. She forced her cousin to meet her eyes. "Promise me you will say nothing that betrays what you know. Promise me you will not provoke him."

Ellie's chest heaved. "Eleanor, I cannot. I cannot pretend ignorance after what I've seen. He tortured you. He beat you as though you were a slave—" Her voice cracked. "He is a demon, and the only one who deserves a beating is him."

Her cousin's grip tightened. "Please," Eleanor whispered. "Promise me. Do not risk yourself. Bite your tongue if you must."

The pleading in Eleanor's eyes pierced Ellie's righteous fury. Every instinct within her screamed to refuse, to confront Ainsworth and expose him then and there. But at last, she gave a stiff nod.

"I will try," she whispered. Another knock, sharper and more demanding, rattled the door. One maid hurried to open it while the other hastily draped a blanket across Eleanor's wounded back.

Lord Ainsworth entered with Lord Bennett at his side. His eyes went instantly to his wife. Irritation darkened his expression.

"Why are you not dressed?" he barked. "The ball is about to begin, and you are not ready."

Before Eleanor could answer, Ellie stepped forward, planting herself firmly between the bed and her cousin.

"Eleanor is gravely injured and can scarcely move," she said, her voice controlled though her heart thundered. "She will not be attending the ball this evening. I have already sent for a physician."

The words struck like powder meeting a spark. Ainsworth's face darkened instantly.

"You did what?" His eyes burned with a murderous glare. "You had no right—"

"I had every right," Ellie cut in, her voice rising with conviction. "I have never witnessed such barbarity, and I will not stand by while infection takes her life."

He turned sharply toward Eleanor, his hand twitching as though he meant to seize her. Ellie stepped directly into his path. Any promise she had made of restraint vanished in that instant.

"I suggest you leave, My Lord," she said, her eyes blazing. "I will not allow you to lay hands upon her again. The marks on her back testify to your cruelty. The physician will see them, and so will others. Your uncle will know exactly what you are."

"Get out of my house!" he roared.

"No!" Ellie's voice rang through the chamber like a bell. She shoved him with all her strength.

"Eleanor is my cousin, my blood, and I will not allow you to torture her any longer. I will not." Tears streamed down her cheeks, but she did not falter.

For one dangerous heartbeat, Ainsworth looked ready to strike her. His face twisted, his eyes blazing with barely restrained violence. Then he forced himself still. They were not alone. Slowly, deliberately, he drew himself upright and smoothed his coat, reclaiming his composure.

"We are hosting a ball," he said at last, his voice sharp as steel. "If Eleanor cannot attend, then you will take her place."

Ellie stared at him, stunned. He could not possibly mean... but one look at his expression told her he did.

"No," she said, shaking her head. "I will remain with Eleanor. I will not play hostess for you, nor pretend you are anything other than the brute you are. Let Mrs. Appleton or Felicity take your arm. They are as false as you." She turned slightly, shielding her cousin.

Ainsworth seized her arms in a brutal grip. Pain shot up her shoulders, but she refused to cry out.

"You will host this ball with me," he hissed, leaning so close she could feel his breath against her cheek, "or I will drag Eleanor downstairs myself and force her to smile through her pain. The choice, Lady Danielle, is yours."

Lord Bennett shifted as though to intervene. Ainsworth snapped a warning glance at him, his grip on Ellie unyielding. Fury surged through her, hot and fierce, then a cold, sick realization struck her. One more act of defiance, and he would turn his rage upon Eleanor. The terror in her cousin's eyes confirmed it. Ellie swallowed hard, forcing down the fire burning in her chest. Slowly she lowered her head in what must have appeared to be submission and pushed the words past her trembling lips.

"Forgive me for losing my temper," she murmured, feigning humility. "I will do it."

Ainsworth's expression smoothed into a grotesque imitation of warmth. A triumphant smile curved his mouth.

"Splendid." He released her, straightened his coat, cast a satisfied glance toward Bennett, and strode from the room. Bennett followed. Just before leaving, however, he paused long enough to cast Ellie a final, unreadable look. Then the door closed behind them.

Ellie's knees nearly gave way. She pressed her hands over her face, trembling. She had bought Eleanor a reprieve. But the question now clawed at her heart. At what cost?

"Ellie, why did you do that? What if he makes you disappear next?" Eleanor's voice broke, and fresh sobs shook her fragile frame. Ellie sank onto the edge of the bed and took her cousin's trembling hand, squeezing it with quiet strength.

"I'm sorry," she whispered, her throat thick with emotion. "I never meant to place you in greater danger. But I could not stand by in silence any longer. Watching him hurt you was unbearable."

"You need not worry about me, Ellie." Eleanor turned toward her, tearstained and fearful. "It is you who are in danger now."

Ellie nodded slowly, her jaw tightening. She knew Eleanor was right. Her temper had flared, and in her righteous fury she had provoked the monster who ruled this house. They would all pay for it now. Then, as if struck by lightning, a cold thought seized her. Her heart began to pound.

"Eleanor... is that what happened when Olivia disappeared?"

Eleanor's brow furrowed faintly. "What do you mean?"

"Were you and your husband supposed to host a ball that day?" Ellie pressed, her voice urgent. "And you could not attend because he had beaten you?"

Eleanor's face drained of color. Her lips trembled, and after a long moment she gave the smallest nod. Ellie's stomach twisted.

"So that's it," she breathed, her voice low and shaking with fury. "He plans these entertainments, ensures you are too battered to appear, and then uses the distraction to do his devil's work." Her fists clenched until her nails bit deep into her palms. "We are running out of time."

She rose abruptly, determination igniting within her like a flame. Instead of returning to her chamber, Ellie slipped quietly from Eleanor's room and hurried down the grand staircase. Servants bustled through the corridors, balancing garlands, trays, and candelabras. The chaos of preparation provided the perfect cover.

Moving silently, Ellie slipped along the corridor toward the marquess's study. Her steps were light despite the pounding of her heart, every sense sharpened by urgency. If there was any truth left to uncover, any clue she had overlooked, it would be there. She reached for the door. Then froze. Voices. Low, muffled, and far too close.

The door stood slightly ajar. Ellie's breath caught. With the utmost care, she eased it open a fraction more and pressed herself against the wall, retreating into the deep shadows of the corridor. She scarcely dared to breathe as she peered through the narrow gap. From that hidden vantage, she saw the figures gathered within. The Appletons stood near the center of the room, Mrs. Appleton rigid with self-importance, Felicity hovering beside her like an eager shadow. Their expressions carried the smug confidence of people who believed themselves entirely in control.

But Ellie's gaze darted past them, and her breath caught in her throat. The great bookcase behind the desk had swung wide. It gaped open like a dark mouth, revealing the outline of a hidden chamber beyond. Ellie's pulse hammered so violently she feared they might hear it. The realization struck her with such force she nearly swooned. A secret room. Someone was inside. Someone they had hidden away.

She leaned closer to the crack in the door, straining to see past the shifting candlelight and the figures blocking her view.

And then she saw her. Olivia. Pale and drawn, her dress wrinkled and her hair disheveled, but unmistakably alive.

Relief and fury collided in Ellie's chest so fiercely it left her dizzy. For a moment the world seemed to tilt around her. Olivia stood within the hidden chamber. Her shoulders squared with stubborn defiance despite the exhaustion etched into her face. Alive. But very clearly a prisoner.

"What a pleasant sight this is," Felicity drawled, malice thick in every syllable. "It was about time someone taught you a lesson."

Olivia lifted her chin. Her voice was steady, though weakened by exhaustion.

"What are you doing here, Felicity?"

"I am here as a guest of your brother-in-law," Felicity sneered. "We are having a ball tonight. Too bad you cannot attend."

Ellie's nails dug into the wood of the doorframe. Every word fanned the flames of her anger.

"You will pay for what you did to my daughter," Mrs. Appleton snapped, her voice sharp with venom. "This will be the last time you ever come near her."

Olivia gave a dry, scornful laugh. "I have no desire to be near your insufferable child."

A slap rang out like a pistol shot, Mrs. Appleton's hand striking Olivia's face. Ellie flinched, fighting the overwhelming urge to burst into the room and tear the woman apart. Lord Ainsworth's voice cut through the tension, cool and commanding.

"Enough. Your soon-to-be husband will arrive at midnight, and you will go with him. Your father made a bargain with Lord Thatcher, and you will not escape it."

Before Olivia could respond, Felicity spoke again, her voice dripping with spite.

"A shame you did not know, Lord Ainsworth, but Olivia is already engaged, to Lord Richard Blackwood. A secret engagement, perhaps, but one cannot simply drag her away from her rightful betrothed."

Ellie's breath stalled. *Richard? Engaged to Olivia?* Her world lurched. Had he not stood with her in the cellar, his eyes lingering, his voice warm with something that had felt dangerously close to tenderness? Had he not drawn her into his arms when she stumbled? Had he not nearly kissed her? And all the while he had carried this secret.

Tears blurred her vision. Betrayal crashed over her, sharp and merciless. He had scolded her for guarding her heart, for keeping secrets... yet he had kept the largest secret of all. Ellie pressed her fist against her mouth, stifling the sob that rose in her throat before it could betray her hiding place.

"We must prepare for the ball now," Lord Ainsworth said curtly, his voice strained and edged with suppressed fury. "You can thank your cousin for our haste. She has been snooping where she ought not. Rest assured, she will pay for it."

A chill ran through Ellie at the cold promise in his tone. The heavy creak of the bookcase closing filled the room, stone grinding against hidden hinges as the secret chamber vanished once more behind polished wood. Ellie sprang back from the door at once, retreating deeper into the shadows. Her heart pounded so violently she feared the sound might betray her. She scarcely dared breathe as footsteps shifted within the study.

A moment later, the voices moved away. Only then did she slip silently down the corridor. Her breath caught tight in her throat as she hurried toward her chamber, every nerve alive with urgency. The sounds of preparation drifted through the house, servants rushing past with flowers, trays of crystal, armfuls of candles, yet the bustle barely registered in her mind. Her thoughts raced too fast to grasp.

She had seen enough. Olivia was alive. Alive, and in mortal danger. The Appletons and Ainsworth had woven their trap with care and cruelty, and by midnight the snare would close around her cousin like a tightening noose. Ellie slowed only when she reached the safety of her chamber, pressing a trembling hand against the door as she gathered herself.

Not if she could stop it. She straightened, determination hardening within her chest. Tonight, she would watch Felicity and her mother like a hawk. And when the moment came, she would tear Olivia free from their clutches, whatever the cost.

As Carla fastened the final hooks of her gown and arranged her hair, Ellie's thoughts churned with purpose. For the first time, the ball felt less like a dreadful obligation and more like an opportunity. The glittering distraction would provide the perfect cover, to smuggle Eleanor to safety and, if courage held, to free Olivia before Lord Thatcher's arrival.

The risks were immense. Ellie knew she was placing herself in even greater danger. But if her cousins were spared further torment, she would gladly pay the price. She called for Gordon and, in a hushed but steady voice, outlined her plan. His face darkened as she laid everything before him.

"You are asking me to leave you behind," he said at last, his jaw tightening. "I cannot say I find that agreeable."

"I know," Ellie admitted, her eyes softening. "But you understand why it must be done. Eleanor cannot endure another night in this house, and Olivia has already suffered enough."

Gordon exhaled slowly and gave a reluctant nod. "The doctor is with Eleanor now. I asked him to report to me when he had finished. I am certain he will aid us. He treated Lady Miranda after you and Lord Blackwood freed her."

Ellie's heart leapt. "Have you heard from her? Has she returned to her family?"

"Yes." Gordon's expression softened. "She has been safely restored to them. Before she left, she went to the Duke of Devon and told him everything. Only afterward did she travel home."

Ellie's throat tightened with relief. "They must have rejoiced to see her again, even through the shock. To believe a daughter dead, only to have her restored—"

Gordon offered a small, sad smile. "Indeed. And I will come back for you, Ellie. What you intend is brave, but it may cost you dearly. Perhaps Lord Bennett might keep an eye on you while I'm away."

Ellie scoffed. "I would not count on that. He pretends to be his uncle's spy, but his treatment of me leaves no room for trust. He is too changeable, too careless with his words. He would sell me out if it amused him."

Before Gordon could reply, a knock sounded at the door. He opened it to admit the physician, pale and shaken, yet with a fire burning beneath his composure.

"Was that his lordship's doing?" the doctor asked grimly. Gordon and Ellie exchanged a glance before nodding. The doctor's mouth set into a hard line. "She cannot remain here. We must move her at once. Lord Ainsworth lingered while I treated her and threatened harsher punishment once the ball concludes."

Ellie's stomach twisted, but her voice remained steady. "We intend to move her tonight, under cover of the festivities. And I have discovered where he is keeping Eleanor's sister. Once Eleanor is safe, someone must return to rescue Olivia."

The physician frowned. "And what of you, Lady Danielle? Do you intend to remain behind in this viper's nest?"

Her smile was brave, though she did not feel it. "I want my cousins to be freed before anything else. They have suffered long enough, first under their father, and now beneath Lord Ainsworth's cruelty. Once they are safe, I will follow."

Gordon's glance told her he saw straight through the bravado. Fear gnawed at her, cold and relentless. She knew what Ainsworth was capable of and dreaded what might happen if his fury turned upon her. Yet the thought of Eleanor enduring another beating hardened her resolve. If no one acted, Eleanor would not survive.

"I will wait with my carriage near the back entrance," the doctor said suddenly, his voice firm. "Once Lord Ainsworth is occupied with his guests, we shall spirit her away. I will take her to my clinic in town. When she is strong enough, she will be sent to the Duke of Devon himself. He must see what his nephew has done."

Ellie's eyes widened. "You believe His Grace already suspects?"

The doctor gave a short nod. "He has long harbored doubts about his nephew's conduct. I believe he has simply been waiting for proof."

Ellie met his gaze and found the same determination burning there that she felt in her own heart. It gave her strength.

"Then perhaps," she said quietly, "this nightmare will finally come to an end."

16

The Ball of Reckoning

When Ellie stepped from her chamber clad in a gown of pale silk, her pulse quickened. The fabric shimmered softly in the lamplight, its delicate folds falling with effortless grace. To any observer she might have appeared the perfect vision of a young lady preparing for an elegant evening. Yet Ellie felt nothing like a lady. She felt like a prisoner disguised as a guest.

Every breath came tight with tension. Beneath the calm mask she had practiced before the mirror, her mind raced with plans and dangers. One misstep tonight could destroy everything. Lord Ainsworth stood waiting at the foot of the corridor. The moment he saw her, his lips curved into a smooth, practiced smile, one that gleamed with false charm.

"You look radiant, Lady Danielle," he said, his voice honeyed and warm to any listening ear.

He extended his arm. Reluctantly, Ellie slipped her hand through it. The instant their sleeves brushed, she felt the truth beneath the polished courtesy. His grip tightened just slightly, an iron pressure hidden beneath velvet manners. It was a silent reminder of the power he held within these walls. The sensation sent a chill down her spine.

Together they descended the grand staircase into the glittering chaos of the ball. Light burst from the chandeliers in dazzling cascades. Hundreds of candles burned in golden tiers. Their flames reflected in polished mirrors and crystal glass. Music drifted down from the gallery where the musicians played, violins weaving bright melodies above the steady rhythm of the cello. The marble floor gleamed beneath the swirl of silk skirts and the measured steps of polished boots. Laughter rose and fell like the tide. Perfume mingled with candle wax and the faint scent of fresh flowers.

To the gathered guests, the evening was nothing less than splendid. To Ellie, it felt like walking into a gilded cage. Lord Ainsworth wasted no time displaying his prize. With exaggerated flourish he guided her from group to group, introducing her again and again to the assembled company. Each introduction was delivered with theatrical warmth.

"Allow me to present Lady Danielle Huntington," he declared repeatedly. "My wife's cousin, who graciously stands beside me this evening in place of Lady Ainsworth, who has unfortunately taken ill."

Each repetition scraped against Ellie's nerves like the edge of a blade. She longed, desperately, to cry out the truth. To tell them Eleanor lay upstairs, broken and bleeding from his cruelty. But she forced a gracious smile instead, dipping her head politely, murmuring the proper greetings expected of her. Silence, she reminded herself, was the safer weapon tonight.

Her gaze drifted across the room until it found the Appletons. Mrs. Appleton stood rigidly near the far wall, her mouth tight with indignation. Felicity hovered beside her, her carefully arranged smile strained to the breaking point. Both women watched Ainsworth's attentions with growing displeasure.

So intent was he on parading his borrowed 'hostess' before the company that he scarcely acknowledged them at all. Not once did he present Mrs. Appleton or Felicity as mistresses of the evening, though both had clearly expected to occupy that role. The slight was unmistakable. Their outrage simmered visibly beneath their composed expressions.

The sight offered Ellie a small, bitter consolation. She kept her expression serene, but beneath the calm her thoughts burned with equal parts fury and determination. Tonight, would not end as Ainsworth expected. Tonight, Eleanor would escape. And if courage and fortune, held, Olivia would be free as well.

"How do you do that, you little temptress?" Mrs. Appleton hissed through gritted teeth the moment Lord Ainsworth turned away. Her eyes narrowed with venom. "This ball was meant to be Felicity's triumph, and yet every gaze lingers on you."

Ellie stiffened. Her patience had reached its limit.

"Perhaps you should ask Lord Ainsworth that question," she snapped, her voice low and cutting. "I did not seek this attention, nor do I desire it. I would rather be anywhere than here, paraded about like some prize mare."

Mrs. Appleton's lips parted in fury, but before she could retort, Lord Ainsworth returned, his smile gleaming like polished steel.

"It is time to open the ball," he announced. Extending his hand, he left her no room for refusal.

Reluctantly, Ellie placed her fingers in his and allowed him to lead her to the center of the floor. The musicians raised their bows, and the strains of a waltz filled the hall. Guests stepped aside, leaving a wide circle for the hosts.

Ainsworth swept her into the dance with practiced ease, but his hand at her waist was far too tight, his body pressed indecently close. Ellie tried to pull back, her voice calm though her pulse thundered.

"Lord Ainsworth, release me. This is not proper."

He bent closer, his breath hot against her ear, a slow, sinister grin curving his lips.

"And why is it not proper? Let them all see, my sweet Danielle, that you came here not to support your cousin, but to seduce me. I intend to let the whole of London believe it."

Her eyes flew wide. "What?"

He chuckled softly, the sound cold and cruel. "Did you truly think your meddling would go unpunished? You sought to ruin me. Now I shall return the favor."

His arm tightened around her as she tried to push away.

"Do you know what I will tell them?" His voice dropped, poisonous. "That you, desperate for me, ordered your servant to whip your cousin so you could slip into my chamber undisturbed. That you begged me to take you in ways that would make even hardened men blush."

Revulsion swept through her. Ellie shoved him, tears burning in her eyes.

"Stop this at once! You are vile, vulgar and loathsome."

"Oh, but my dear Danielle," he murmured, lifting her chin so she could not look away, "this is only the beginning. When the ball concludes, I shall prove every word true. We cannot have me exposed as a liar, can we?"

Terror spiked through her as his lips descended, so near she could feel the whisper of his breath.

She twisted her head aside, struggling against his iron hold. He meant to force a scandal here, before every guest, and then build his lies upon it.

"Let me go," she hissed, her voice trembling with fury. "Or I will scream."

His smile widened. "And what good would that do? Who here would believe you? You may have freed my first wife, meddled with that servant girl, but you are mine now to destroy. If I must drag you from this house and hide you away, I shall." He leaned in again, his grip bruising, but before his lips could touch hers, a firm hand seized Ellie's arm and yanked her free.

A tall figure stepped between them, blocking Ainsworth's advance. His presence filled the space like a wall of steel.

"What is the meaning of this?" Lord Bennett's voice rang out, deep and commanding. His eyes blazed as they locked on his cousin. "What are you doing with my bride?"

The words fell like thunder. A collective gasp rippled through the hall. Fans snapped shut. Whispers darted through the crowd like wildfire.

My bride. Ellie's breath caught. Her heart slammed against her ribs so violently she thought it might break. For one wild instant, she longed to deny him. To declare she was no man's possession. Yet the heat in his voice, the raw edge of fury and protectiveness, left her trembling. Did he mean it as a shield, a ruse before the crowd... or something more?

Ainsworth's face darkened with rage. "Your bride? Do not be absurd."

Bennett did not flinch. He stood taller, his frame rigid, his voice resonant enough to fill the ballroom.

"You heard me. Lady Danielle Huntington is under my protection, my claim, my vow. And if you dare lay another hand on her, cousin, you will answer to me." His hand moved back instinctively, steady and protective, guiding Ellie behind him without ever looking away from Ainsworth. To the onlookers it appeared he shielded his betrothed with every breath in his body. And Ellie, caught in the motion, felt a warmth rush through her veins that she could not quell. The marquess gave a short, mirthless laugh, though it wavered slightly.

"A claim spoken in jest. She despises you."

Bennett's lip curled. "Perhaps. But despised or adored, she is mine to defend. And I would sooner die here and now than watch you degrade her further."

A murmur swept through the guests. The Duke of Somerset, so often whispered about as cold and untouchable, stood aflame before them, staking his honor, perhaps even his life, upon a young woman's dignity. Ellie's knees nearly buckled. Every nerve in her body screamed to protest. To tell him he had no right. And yet... some fragile, treacherous part of her longed to believe him. Longed to believe he spoke not for convenience, but for truth.

Lord Ainsworth's eyes narrowed, his jaw flexing as though barely restraining himself. With a sudden lunge he reached for Ellie again. Bennett moved faster. He stepped squarely in front of her, blocking the grasp with such force that Ainsworth's hand never brushed her sleeve.

"She agreed to open the ball with you only because your wife could not," Bennett declared, his voice carrying clearly through the stunned silence. "And because she is your wife's relation. But this display, this filth, is sick and devilish."

Ainsworth gave a harsh laugh, his face twisting with fury.

"Can you not see what she's about? She threw herself at me. She plots to seduce me, to make me abandon my wife. She wants me for herself, wants me stolen from her cousin—"

"Do you take us for fools?" Bennett cut in, scorn dripping from every word. He gestured sharply toward Ellie. "Look at her. She is a slight young lady, and you tower over her. You would have us believe she cornered you? The absurdity insults every man's intelligence here."

"You know nothing of the power of a seductive woman," Ainsworth spat, lunging again. But Bennett caught him by the cravat, twisting the fine silk until his cousin choked before thrusting him hard against the paneled wall. The crowd gasped.

"You will keep your filthy hands off her, and off any woman you are not bound to by honorable vows," Bennett thundered. "You have no decency, no restraint. You are a coward who preys upon the weak. And the greatest disgrace of all, you do this while your wife lies upstairs, broken from your cruelty. You disgust me."

Ainsworth snarled, hatred blazing. "Danielle is not your bride. You have no claim to her. You have not even sought her father's consent."

"How do you know that?" Bennett roared, his fury unleashed. "How would you know whose blessing I have sought?

You are nothing but a demon and a scoundrel. Worse than your father ever was. Yes, he murdered men, but you—", his voice cut through the room like steel, "...you torture women with relish, which makes you more monstrous still."

"You know nothing!" Ainsworth barked, his face slick with sweat. "You will regret this. I opened my house to you—"

"Your house?" Bennett barked a laugh of pure contempt. "This house belongs to our uncle, the Duke of Devon. He allowed you to remain here out of mercy, hoping you might prove better than your father. Instead, you have proven yourself worse. You deserve no respect, no courtesy, and no title, nothing."

"Get out," Ainsworth hissed. "Get out before I have you dragged out."

"The hell I will." Lord Bennett released him with a shove, his voice deadly calm. "You insulted and threatened Lady Danielle. I demand satisfaction."

Ellie gasped, her hand flying to her lips. Until that moment she had stood frozen in shock, but now she saw another side of the Duke of Somerset. No careless rake. No idle aristocrat. His eyes blazed with righteous fury. He was defending her, her name, her dignity, as though it mattered more than his own life. Her heart lurched.

Without thinking, she stepped to his side and grasped his arm, her fingers trembling against the firm line of his sleeve. When he glanced down, she met his gaze, pleading.

"Do not do this, Your Grace. Do not fight him. Please."

From behind them Ainsworth barked a cruel laugh. "Listen to her beg, Bennett! She pleads for you to save yourself. You will die before the night is out, and she knows it. Who is the coward now?"

A murmur swept through the crowd, shock, scandal, fascination. The insult left no room for retreat. Ellie's eyes flashed. Before Bennett could respond, she stepped boldly in front of him. Dwarfed by the two men, her voice rang clear across the silent ballroom.

"You boast loudly, Lord Ainsworth, yet it is plain you know nothing of a woman's heart." Her tone struck sharp as steel. "I did not plead with His Grace because I feared he might fall to you. I pleaded because I feared he might kill you. And truly, you are not worth the bullet. A gentleman's hands should not be sullied with the blood of a brute."

The silence that followed was broken by muffled coughs as several gentlemen disguised their smirks behind gloved hands. A few exchanged impressed glances. The little lady had struck harder than any fist. Lord Bennett's voice rumbled low, steady as stone.

"Lady Danielle speaks with mercy. But I will not be so forgiving. Your insults cannot be overlooked. You have crossed every line of decency tonight. And as the Duke of Somerset, I will not retreat from the challenge."

The ballroom fell utterly still. The music had long since ceased. Every eye fixed upon the two men, waiting to see whether violence would spill forth. For the first time, Ainsworth faltered. His mouth opened, but no words came. He had not expected his cousin to stand so firm. Nor had he expected the lady to strike him with such fearless contempt. His gaze flicked toward Ellie. Her chin remained high, her eyes bright with defiance. Even cornered, she had somehow prevailed.

At last, fists clenched and voice dripping with disdain, he muttered, "I have no intention of fighting you, Bennett. It is beneath me. And this woman is hardly worth the effort."

Lord Bennett gave a derisive laugh. "Yet moments ago, you lusted after her like a starving wolf. Which is it, cousin? Is she beneath you, or the one prize you cannot resist?" His scorn rang clearly. "No one here will forget what you revealed tonight: a coward and a predator."

Ainsworth's face darkened. He turned sharply on his heel and stalked toward a knot of his dubious companions. His voice rang hollow as he barked for the musicians to play again, urging the guests back to dancing.

But the spell of the evening had shattered. The air itself had shifted. Men who only minutes earlier admired the marquess now regarded him with thinly veiled disgust. Ladies whispered behind their fans. Respect had fled the room. Only disdain remained. And though Lord Ainsworth feigned indifference, every soul present understood the truth. He had been utterly humiliated.

Ellie turned sharply and hurried out of the ballroom, desperate for air. Her body was rigid, her pulse pounding so fiercely she feared it might burst from her chest. As she pushed through the crowd, she caught sight of Lord Bennett scanning the room, his gaze searching with unmistakable urgency. But before he could move toward her, Mrs. Appleton swept forward and intercepted him with practiced eagerness. A moment later, Felicity was twirling across the dance floor in his arms.

Ellie rolled her eyes. How could they not see that shamelessly thrusting themselves at every opportunity was the height of impropriety? She slipped through the terrace doors and stepped into the garden. The cool night air wrapped around her like a blessing. She drew in a deep, unsteady breath, pressing a hand against her racing heart. Her hands still trembled as she tried to steady herself. How could she ever free herself from that dreadful man without endangering everyone else?

The door behind her creaked open. Ellie spun around, alarm knotting her chest. For a moment relief flickered when she saw Mrs. Appleton step onto the terrace. But the relief vanished just as quickly.

"You always seem to be in the way, Lady Danielle," Mrs. Appleton sneered, striding forward. Without warning, she seized Ellie by the arms and shoved her off the terrace into the shrubs below.

Ellie landed hard among the branches, leaves scratching against her gown. She scrambled to her feet, fury blazing in her eyes.

"How ever did you manage to secure the Duke of Somerset?" Mrs. Appleton continued with bitter scorn. "I thought at least he would see through you."

Ellie brushed dirt from her sleeves, her voice sharp as ice.

"Just because your daughter cannot secure a husband does not make it my fault. Perhaps it isn't Felicity's failing at all. Perhaps no one wishes for a mother-in-law who is a shrew."

Mrs. Appleton gasped, her face mottling with rage. Instead of replying, she gave a small, deliberate nod. Ellie turned and froze. Lord Ainsworth's butler loomed behind her like a shadow.

Before she could react, his hand clamped around her arm, dragging her back toward the back of the house. She tried to scream, but his palm crushed over her mouth. She thrashed, kicking and clawing, but his strength easily overpowered her. Mrs. Appleton watched the struggle with a cruel, satisfied smile.

"This will be the last time you meddle," the butler hissed into Ellie's ear, careful to keep his voice low enough that Mrs. Appleton would not hear. "You'll spend the night in the cellar's dungeon, and tomorrow My Lord will send you somewhere no one will ever find you."

Terror flooded through her. Then Lord Ainsworth emerged from behind the trees, his eyes blazing. Ellie's stomach dropped. The butler shoved her toward him. Ainsworth seized her at once, hurling her onto a nearby bench. Before she could rise, his hands closed around her throat.

"Where is my wife, Danielle?" he roared. "How did you spirit her out of this house without anyone seeing?"

Ellie clawed desperately for air. "She is safe from you now," she rasped. "I promised her I would get her away."

His palm cracked across her cheek. Stars exploded behind her eyes as his grip tightened around her throat. The world tilted. Darkness crept in at the edges of her vision.

Hands suddenly wrenched Ainsworth backward. The violent grip on Ellie's throat vanished as he was dragged away from her. She collapsed forward on the bench, gasping desperately for air, her lungs burning. Across from her, the steward stood rigid and unmoving, a pistol leveled steadily at his master. Several footmen had thrown themselves upon the butler. They wrestled

Darwin to the ground, struggling to pin his arms as he fought like a cornered animal. The marquess staggered backward, his face gone pale with shock.

"You—Gray," Ainsworth spat, fury breaking through his disbelief. "You are my steward. How dare you betray me?"

Gray's eyes were hard as iron. "Your trust?" he replied coldly. "You never trusted me." He gestured toward the struggling butler. "Darwin ruled this household and brutalized the staff with your full blessing. Did you never wonder why your last steward resigned so abruptly? I was placed here by the Duke of Devon himself, to watch you, to document your cruelty." His lip curled with undisguised contempt.

"It was nearly impossible not to intervene when you beat your wife. I would have exposed you long ago, but when Miss Olivia disappeared, I had no choice but to hold my ground. Lord Bennett came to aid me, hoping together we might uncover her whereabouts. Yet nothing moved forward, nothing, until Lady Danielle arrived."

Ainsworth's gaze snapped toward Ellie. Gray continued, his voice grim.

"Your secrets began unraveling the moment she set foot in this house."

"That is right." Lord Bennett stepped forward from the shadows of the terrace, his expression carved from fury. Without hesitation, he seized his cousin by the collar and shoved him violently to the ground. His voice rang out with fierce conviction.

"It was her courage, and her persistence, that uncovered the truth. Do you know why she was always a step ahead of you?" He gestured toward Ellie, who still struggled to steady her breathing.

"Because she cared for nothing but saving her cousins. That was her only aim, to see them safe."

Ainsworth stared at him, stunned. Then he gave a hollow, incredulous laugh and shook his head.

"I cannot fathom you, Bennett. You hate her. You undermined her at every turn. You mocked her openly." His eyes glittered with bitter triumph. "You treated her with nothing but contempt."

Ellie's throat burned as she still fought to draw breath. Each inhalation scraped painfully against the bruised skin Ainsworth's grip had left, and the world still swayed faintly around her. But his words struck deeper than his hands ever had. They echoed the doubts that had haunted her for weeks, the fear that she had misjudged everything, that she had been naïve enough to trust the wrong man.

Her knees buckled. The strength drained from her legs as the weight of the night, terror, fury, betrayal, crashed down upon her all at once. She stumbled. Before she could collapse to the ground, Lord Bennett caught her. His arms closed around her with surprising gentleness, steadying her against the solid strength of his chest. One hand came up instinctively to support her back, the other braced her shoulders as though he would not allow her to fall again.

Ellie's breath shuddered. The composure she had clung to all evening shattered. Her chest heaved, and the sobs she had fought so desperately to contain broke free at last. If Gordon had been there, she might have turned to him instead, might have buried her face against the familiar comfort of the man who had protected her since childhood.

But Gordon was not here. And for this one fragile moment, it was Bennett's arms that held her upright. The warmth of him surrounded her, steady and unyielding, like a wall placed between her and the chaos of the world. In that disastrous, dazzling moment, when she should have felt only anger and mistrust, Ellie felt something else. Something dangerously close to shelter.

The Duke of Somerset could feel Ellie trembling in his arms, her body taut with fear, her breath ragged, as though she stood on the brink of breaking into sobs. He tightened his hold, drawing her closer against his chest, silently vowing that nothing and no one would ever touch her again.

"Ainsworth, you are a fool," Bennett said coldly, though his thumb brushed reassuringly against Ellie's arm. His voice rang through the garden, but his gaze lingered on her pale face, a protective fire burning in his eyes.

"I never hated her. Every cruel word, every calculated slight was not born of malice, but necessity. I needed you to believe I disdained her, to keep your suspicions at bay. With your eyes, and your footmen, always upon me, I had no choice but to play the villain. Yes, it wounded her, but it spared her worse from you."

Ellie's heart stuttered. His admission, raw and unvarnished, struck deeper than she expected. Ainsworth's mouth opened in protest, but Bennett silenced him with a raised hand.

"Of course, you believed those footmen were yours. That was your greatest mistake. Three of them were mine, men taken in by our uncle after your father burned my family's estate to the ground. He placed them in your household to serve me. And now—" Bennett's voice hardened, flashing with grim triumph, "now you shall learn of the cousin you never knew. A man ready to take your place."

Even as he spoke, he shifted slightly, angling his body so Ellie remained shielded behind him. Every line of his stance declared the same unmistakable truth: She is under my protection. Ainsworth laughed harshly, though the color had drained from his face.

"Impossible. There is no other cousin."

"There is," Bennett replied, steady as stone. He gestured toward a tall footman standing at the edge of the gathered crowd.

"Lord Wallace."

The man stepped forward and cast aside his hat, coat, and false beard. Ainsworth staggered back, stunned.

"I have never seen this man before in my life," he snapped. "How could he be my cousin?"

Lord Wallace's eyes burned with contempt as he began to reveal the truth, of his mother's stolen birth, of the secret that had hidden him from the family for years. His voice shook with restrained fury.

But Ellie barely heard the details. Her awareness had narrowed to the steady presence beside her, to Lord Bennett's hand firm at her back, to the silent reassurance in his touch, as if he knew she needed something solid to anchor her.

"This is absurd, a fairy tale," Ainsworth scoffed.

"You may call it what you wish," Wallace said bitterly. "But the truth remains."

Bennett allowed himself a grim smile. "And here he is," he said quietly. "Your replacement."

Ainsworth spat accusations, but Bennett cut him down with scorn as sharp as steel.

"Our uncle gave you every chance to prove you were not the wretch your father was. But you squandered it. From the beginning he suspected the truth, that you were nothing but a cowardly, vile shadow of the man who sired you."

"Watch your tongue when speaking of me or my father!" Ainsworth bellowed, lunging forward. At once the steward and several footmen seized him, restraining him before he could move another step.

"You are in no position to threaten anyone," Bennett said with icy finality. His voice dropped, dangerous and steady, as his arm brushed Ellie's again, as though reminding her she was not alone.

"Your evil game is finished. Lord Wallace and I will see your sham of a marriage to Lady Eleanor dissolved, and free the women you bound in misery. You should never have been wed to her at all, not while Lady Miranda still lived. You are a foul creature, fit only for a cell or the gallows."

Ainsworth's face twisted with rage, but Bennett's command rang out like a sword drawn from its sheath.

"Take him," he ordered. "And Darwin as well. Lock them in the dungeon where they belong."

The footmen dragged the struggling marquess away.

Ellie sagged against Lord Bennett's side, the last of her strength leaving her. His arm closed firmly around her, steady and unyielding. The world swam with the weight of everything that had been revealed. But one truth cut through it like sunlight breaking through storm clouds: Andrew Bennett had fought not only to expose his cousin, but he had also fought to protect her. And though his words had been meant for Ainsworth, Ellie knew they had been meant for her as well. He would not let her be broken. Not while he lived to stand before her.

17
The Arms of Her Family

Ellie had listened to the entire exchange in silence, her pulse still racing, her body taut with the lingering remnants of fear. Only then did she realize Lord Bennett's arm remained firmly around her shoulders. Gently, almost reluctantly, she eased herself free and took a small step back. When she lifted her gaze, his eyes were already fixed upon her. He offered a smile, warm, sincere, and utterly unlike the cold sneers he had worn before.

"So," she whispered, her voice trembling between disbelief and hope, "you did not truly despise me? The disdain, the contempt, it was all for show?"

He inclined his head, and the smile deepened, transforming his entire countenance. Ellie had always known him to be handsome, but the warmth behind that expression disarmed her in a way that unsettled her. She quickly lowered her eyes, lest he see how deeply it affected her.

"I hated every moment of it," he admitted quietly. "When you first arrived, it was unplanned and ill-timed. We had to act swiftly, or Ainsworth would have grown suspicious. At first, I thought if I pretended to take liberties with your cousin, and treated you harshly enough, you might choose to leave of your own accord. I wanted you far from this place, away from the danger." He paused, his voice softening.

"But Gray and I soon realized you had not come idly. You were here for your cousins, and you would not rest until they were safe."

Her eyes flickered back to his. "And yet you betrayed me," she said, her voice tightening with hurt. "After I opened my heart to you in the cellar, you turned and handed my words to your cousin."

He nodded gravely. "I know. And I regret it more than I can say. It was my last desperate attempt to drive you away, to frighten you into abandoning this peril before it consumed you. But your determination... your fire... proved stronger than anything I imagined." His gaze lingered on hers, filled with quiet admiration.

"I saw how deeply you loved your cousins, how you would risk everything to find Miss Olivia and free Eleanor from her tyrant of a husband. That resolve humbled me."

Heat crept into Ellie's cheeks despite herself. She quickly turned the conversation aside.

"We should free Olivia from her prison chamber at once."

The steward stepped forward and gave her hand a reassuring squeeze.

"Already done, My Lady. That is why we could not intervene more swiftly when Ainsworth attacked you. We were moving her to safety."

Ellie's breath caught. "Where is she?" She glanced around the garden, searching anxiously.

"She is freshening up," the steward answered gently. Her brows furrowed.

"But the bookcase—how did you know how to open it?"

"We persuaded Felicity and her mother to reveal its secrets," the steward said grimly. "They are secured now, locked away until it is decided how best to deal with them."

Lord Bennett's voice broke through, steady and assured.

"Tomorrow both dukes will arrive. The Duke of Devon will be pleased beyond measure to know Miss Olivia is safe and that Eleanor is free at last." His eyes met hers again, unguarded.

"My grandfather will come as well?" she asked hesitantly.

"Yes. He has been restless with worry ever since word of your arrival reached him."

Ellie exhaled slowly. That could mean only one thing. London awaited her, with the remainder of the Season and all its endless expectations. But before she could dwell on the thought, movement near the house caught her attention. Olivia stepped into the garden, her face radiant with relief. Ellie's heart leapt. She was just about to run to her cousin when a sudden cry shattered the moment.

"Richard!" Olivia's voice rang out across the garden. Ellie turned just in time to see her dearest friend racing past her. In the next instant he swept Olivia into his arms. His mouth found hers without hesitation, his kiss fervent, certain, and utterly unashamed.

For Ellie, the world tilted. The blood drained from her face, and the ground seemed to sway beneath her feet. The pain in her chest was sharp, cruel, too much after everything she had endured that night. Lord Bennett reached for her, but she warded him off with a trembling hand.

Without a word, she turned and fled down the familiar path toward her refuge by the pond. Hidden among the reeds and willows, she finally surrendered to the storm raging inside her. Tears came hot and relentless. Each sob tore through the fragile composure she had clung to for so long.

Richard's kiss had only deepened the ache already consuming her heart. It was no longer fear or exhaustion. It was loss. Raw, undeniable, and devastating.

She collapsed onto the bench, burying her face in her hands as sobs tore free. Her whole body shook beneath the weight of grief and exhaustion. Everything had come crashing down at once, too much sorrow, too many revelations. She wept until her breath came in ragged gasps, the release as painful as the emotions she had kept caged for far too long. There was, of course, much to be grateful for. Eleanor no longer had to live in fear of her monstrous husband. Soon she would be free, once the divorce was secured. And Olivia, precious Olivia, had been found alive, spared from a forced marriage.

Yet even as Ellie gave silent thanks for those blessings, her heart splintered anew. Olivia's secret engagement to Richard, her dearest friend, the man Ellie had quietly loved for two long Seasons, was a betrayal so sharp it felt like a blade twisting in her chest.

Why had he nearly kissed her? Why had he allowed her, even for a fleeting instant, to believe his heart might belong to her? She had built so many hopes upon those small glimmers of affection, those moments when she had been certain she glimpsed tenderness in his eyes. Yet how could he have cared for her when, all along, he had been in love with Olivia?

A bitter clarity struck her. Richard had not joined her and Gordon solely out of loyalty or protection. He had hoped they would lead him to Olivia. The realization stole her breath. But shame followed quickly. That was not entirely fair. Richard had cared for her safety as well, in his own way. Still, the truth remained cruel: his heart had never been hers.

Her sobs grew harsher. She gasped for air, trembling, drowning in the ache of it all. Then, without warning, strong arms lifted her from the bench. She collapsed against a familiar chest, clinging as though it were the only anchor left in the storm.

"It's over, Ellie," came Gordon's steady voice, low and soothing. He said nothing more at first, simply holding her while the worst of her tears poured out. After a moment he gently tilted her chin upward. Through the blur of tears she found his eyes, compassionate, steady, and unwavering.

A weak but grateful smile tugged at her lips.

"I know," she whispered, her voice raw. "And I am glad you are here with me."

"I would never leave you behind, Princess," he murmured, drawing her closer and letting her lean fully into him. She let her gaze drift toward the pond, its dark surface rippling softly beneath the moonlight. The water blurred through her tears. Gordon's embrace tightened slightly, as though he could shield her from the hurt inside her heart.

"I know your heart is broken now," he continued gently, "but it will mend. One day someone will sweep you off your feet and love you in a way Lord Blackwood never could."

Fresh tears sprang to her eyes at his words. They spilled faster, but she did not turn away.

"How did you know?" she asked softly. He sighed.

"I returned from town just as Miss Olivia stepped outside. I saw everything. I saw the joy in her eyes... and the pain in yours." With a tenderness that made her throat ache, he brushed her tears away with his thumbs.

"I do not understand why he chose her," Gordon admitted quietly. "I always believed his heart leaned toward you. I even thought he was torn after last Season, when he returned from London. But tonight... tonight he made his choice."

Ellie nodded faintly, though more tears slipped free despite her efforts to contain them. Gordon lifted her chin again, urging her to meet his gaze.

"It is all right to be heartbroken, Ellie," he said gently. "It is all right to cry. Do not swallow it down, let it out. It is the only way your heart will heal. Take the time you need." He paused before adding softly, "But remember this: Miss Olivia is looking for you. She longs to thank you for everything you have done for her, and for her sister."

Ellie hesitated. Of course she longed to see Olivia, to embrace her, to reassure herself that her cousin was truly safe. But the thought of facing her beside Richard was unbearable. The wound was too raw. The sight of them together too cruel. Gordon seemed to read the fear she could not voice. His hand brushed lightly against her arm, a quiet promise.

"I will see to it that Lord Blackwood is kept far from you," he assured her. "When you return to London, you will have time to mend, to breathe, to rediscover yourself." His voice softened. "And when the time is right, someone worthy will sweep you off your feet... the way you deserve."

Olivia and Richard were approaching just as Gordon and Ellie made their way back toward the house. Ellie's body tensed at once, but Gordon lengthened his stride.

"Lord Blackwood, might I have a word with you?"

Richard blinked in surprise but gave a polite nod. The two men stepped aside, leaving Ellie face to face with her cousin. Olivia wasted no time. She rushed forward and threw her arms around her.

"I can never thank you enough, Ellie. What you did for my sister and me will never be forgotten."

Ellie shook her head quickly. "It wasn't only me, Olivia. Lord Bennett and Mr. Gray did their part as well."

"But it was your stubbornness that brought it all to an end tonight," Olivia insisted softly. Tears sprang to Ellie's eyes.

"I failed Eleanor."

Olivia pulled back, startled. "How can you say that? You rescued her and freed her from that awful man."

"But he still beat and tortured her while I was here." Ellie's voice trembled. "I should have been faster, cleverer, done more to stop him."

"Did you know he was harming her in such a way?"

Ellie's lips trembled as she shook her head.

"Then how could you have prevented it?" Olivia's voice gentled, though her words were firm. "Lord Ainsworth is a despicable vermin who delighted in cruelty. There was nothing you could have done differently. You risked enough simply by being here."

Ellie swallowed hard. "But what happens now? Your father is still free. He could still do whatever he wishes."

Olivia clasped her hand tightly. "His Grace and Mr. Gray promised that neither Eleanor nor I would ever be forced back to Father. They will even help Mama if she chooses to leave him."

Relief flickered across Ellie's face. "My parents will take you in. They'll help you start over."

Olivia's smile was small but bright. "I shall begin again very soon. Lord Blackwood and I are engaged. And if Father dares to interfere, Richard has already vowed we will elope."

The words cut like a blade. A sharp, stabbing pain seized Ellie's chest. She gasped, tears spilling before she could stop them. Turning away, she tried to flee, but Olivia caught her hand.

"What is it, Ellie?" Concern filled her voice. She moved to embrace her cousin, but Ellie pulled back, shaking her head.

"I just... I need a little time. It has all been too much."

A puzzled look crossed Olivia's face. Then realization dawned. Her expression softened with sorrow.

"Oh. I didn't know you cared for him. Ellie, I swear, I am not trying to steal Richard away from you."

Ellie winced, her sobs breaking harder at the very mention of it. After a moment she sank onto a nearby bench, gently tugging Olivia down beside her.

"I know you're not. He isn't mine, Olivia. He never was."

"I don't believe that," Olivia whispered. "I think he did have feelings for you... until he and I met last Season. We spent time together, as much as propriety allowed. He proposed the night before he left, but I could see he was torn."

Ellie's throat tightened. "Did he tell you about... me?"

Olivia shook her head slowly. "No. But I could tell. He's known you all his life. You've always been his dearest friend. I wasn't sure if your heart leaned toward him, we had been apart so long. When did friendship become something more for you?"

Ellie hesitated before whispering, "Two Seasons ago. He seemed... different. More grown, more serious. I couldn't help myself. I fell."

Olivia nodded thoughtfully. "When I realized he was divided, I refused to pressure him. I told him in my letters that if he ever doubted us, if his heart leaned toward someone else, I would release him. I love him, but I would never hold him through selfishness or society's rules."

Ellie forced a trembling smile. "He deserves you, Olivia."

"Did he never tell you about us?" Olivia asked gently. Ellie shook her head, hurt flashing in her eyes.

"Not a word. That is what feels like betrayal. He confided everything to me, except that."

Olivia looked stricken. "I was certain he would tell you. We chose to keep it quiet, yes, but you... you are his best friend. How did you find out?"

"By accident. I overheard Felicity before the ball. She spoke of it while visiting you in the secret room. That's how I knew where you were." Ellie sighed, her shoulders sagging beneath the weight of it all. Olivia frowned.

"But how on earth would Felicity know?"

Ellie shrugged. "Perhaps she spied on you. She's always listening where she shouldn't. Or she guessed, seeing how much time you and Richard spent together."

Olivia nodded reluctantly. "That would explain it."

Ellie drew in a shaky breath and forced the conversation forward. "I'm surprised Lord Thatcher hasn't arrived yet. Ainsworth made it sound as though he would be here at midnight."

Olivia's lips curved in a wry smile. "Lord Thatcher never intended to marry me. It was all for show. He encouraged me to be firm with Father, that I wanted no part in such a match, though he is actually a good man."

Ellie blinked in astonishment. "But I thought he was Ainsworth's friend."

"He only pretended. What the marquess never knew is that Lord Thatcher is a second cousin to Ainsworth's first wife. He befriended him after her supposed death."

Ellie scoffed, fire flashing in her eyes. "Supposed? She isn't dead."

Olivia stiffened. "What?"

"That vile creature lied. He locked her in the cellar, chained like an animal in a dungeon." Ellie clenched her fists, fury trembling through her. "I found her while searching for you."

Olivia gasped, horror draining the color from her face. "I cannot believe it."

Ellie's voice was low, trembling with loathing. "Believe it. He is the devil himself."

Ellie woke later than usual the next morning, the heaviness of exhaustion at last giving way to the quiet relief of knowing Eleanor was safe. Her cousin was free from her husband's cruelty, and though the path to healing would be long, Ellie drew strength from the certainty that Eleanor would no longer have to walk it alone. That thought steadied her as she rose.

Two maids slipped quietly into her chamber, their arms laden with gowns and ribbons. They spoke in hushed tones as they drew back the curtains to admit the pale morning light, then moved softly about the room, smoothing her gown and arranging her hair into neat coils. Ellie sat before the looking glass, her mind still weighted with memories of the night before, allowing them to work in silence.

A gentle knock sounded before the door opened to admit Olivia. Her cousin stepped inside, her cheeks still rosy from sleep, her eyes brighter than Ellie had ever seen them.

"Good morning, Ellie," Olivia greeted warmly, her voice touched with quiet contentment. Ellie managed a small but genuine smile.

"Good morning. Did you sleep well?"

Olivia nodded, her lips curving with hope. "Better than I have in a very long time, certainly not since before I came to Eleanor's house. Last night, I slept without fear." She moved closer, her gaze soft. "Come, we must go down to breakfast. The Duke of Devon and your grandfather have just arrived."

Ellie's heart gave a sudden leap. Her grandfather was here. The weight of the past days lifted slightly, replaced by a flutter of nervous anticipation. Whatever awaited her, questions, decisions, even confrontations, she would no longer face them alone.

As soon as Ellie was properly dressed and presentable, she thanked the two maids with quiet sincerity and hurried after

Olivia. Her heart beat quickly as they made their way down the corridor toward the breakfast room. The moment they entered, every gentleman present rose at once. The solemn dignity of the scene struck Ellie. So many distinguished faces were gathered together, united by the revelations of the night before.

Her gaze caught on Lord Wallace, whose resemblance to his grandfather was so striking it startled her. It was like beholding the Duke of Devon in his youth, sharpened by years of secrecy and survival.

Before Ellie could even cross the room to greet her grandfather, a pair of strong arms swept her close. She looked up, stunned, and found herself face to face with her father. She had not noticed him among the company, and her breath caught.

"Papa?" she whispered, scarcely believing it. "What are you doing here?"

His eyes warmed with relief as he smiled down at her.

"Your mother and I were going mad with worry, knowing you were here and not knowing how it would end. When Father sent word that all would be concluded after the ball, we left at once for London. There I met your grandfather, and we traveled together to be with you."

Ellie's eyes darted anxiously about the room. "Mama is here too?"

Her father shook his head gently. "No, my dear. She is waiting in London, at your grandfather's townhouse. Mr. Gray was thoughtful enough to send an express as soon as Ainsworth was overpowered and Olivia was freed." He pressed a tender kiss to her brow before turning her toward her grandfather.

The Duke of Essex opened his arms, sweeping her into an embrace she had never known before, firm, protective, and unreserved.

"Danielle," he murmured, his voice unexpectedly thick with emotion, "just like your parents, I have been worried sick over you."

For a moment Ellie froze, startled by such tenderness. Then, hesitantly, she wrapped her arms around him.

"I can imagine, Grandfather," she said softly. "But it had to be done."

He drew back to study her, his proud gaze steady. "And done it was. I am proud of you, child. You are strong, and you will make a fine duchess one day."

Ellie flushed and shook her head with a faint smile. "I somehow doubt that, but thank you, Grandfather."

Before he could reply, the Duke of Devon stepped forward. He clasped her hand and gave it a gentle squeeze. Gratitude shone in his eyes, though pain lingered there as well. This ordeal had cut deeply into his family's honor. Ellie felt her cheeks warm further when she caught Lord Bennett's gaze upon her, intense and unwavering. Quickly she lowered her eyes, though she could not hide the rush of color betraying her.

"Lady Danielle," the Duke of Devon said, his dignity softened by warmth, "thank you, for all you did. Not only for freeing your cousins, but for bringing my nephew to justice."

"You are too kind, Your Grace," Ellie replied with a curtsy and modest smile. "But Lord Bennett and Mr. Gray accomplished far more than I."

"That is not what I have been told," he countered gently but firmly. "Lord Bennett praised you in every letter he sent me. According to him, my nephew never stood a chance."

"Oh, Your Grace," Ellie murmured, her smile tinged with embarrassment. "He greatly exaggerated. I fear I caused more trouble by being here than I did good."

Before the older duke could protest, Lord Bennett himself stepped forward, his voice quieter, almost contrite.

"Please do not remember only my harsh words and cold manner, Lady Danielle. I know I made you feel unwanted, perhaps even despised. But the truth is, your presence was precisely what was needed to end this."

Ellie studied him, her relief mingled with lingering hurt.

"Forgive me, Your Grace, but I fear there was truth in some of your words. I let my temper rule me and provoked your cousin too far."

"Not too far," Bennett countered swiftly, sincerity sharpening his tone. "Far enough. Without your spirit, much would have remained hidden. If there is fault, it lies with me, not you."

Mr. Gray stepped closer, inclining his head gravely. "His Grace speaks the truth. We realized too late that our very presence threatened Ainsworth. Had you not arrived, he would have rid himself of us one way or another. You unsettled him, yes, but because you were a woman, he never considered you a true threat. He believed he could overpower you if it came to it. Last night, he nearly did."

Bennett's jaw tightened. "And that was my failure. When I saw how he treated you, his words, his impropriety, I could not remain silent. I stepped in, and in doing so, I forced his hand."

Ellie shivered at the memory. "Then I am glad you did. His behavior terrified me, and I had no control over the moment." Her voice faltered, but she lifted her eyes to his, allowing him to see her gratitude. The Duke of Devon raised a hand, gently bringing the conversation to a close.

"It is over. That is what matters now."

Ellie nodded before asking the question, pressing most urgently on her heart. "What will happen next?"

"My nephew will answer for all he has done," the Duke of Devon declared gravely. "I will ensure both his wives are freed from him forever. And his crimes, every one of them, will be made known. His name shall be stained beyond repair."

Ellie's eyes softened. "And Lady Miranda? Have you heard from her since she returned to her family?"

The duke inclined his head. "Yes. She is safe and well, and she sends her gratitude. Though still shaken, she has agreed to testify, to stand before a judge and speak of the beatings, the imprisonment, and his vile deceit in faking her death."

A shudder ran through Ellie as she recalled the ghastly sight of Miranda chained to the cellar wall. She closed her eyes briefly to banish the image.

"And the Appletons?" she asked quietly. "What will become of them?"

At this, her grandfather's face darkened, but the Duke of Devon answered.

"I have already sent an express to Baron Appleton, urging him to come to Plymouth at once. Though scandal may follow, I will persuade him that divorce is the only course left to him. That woman will destroy him if she remains at his side. She must be cast out of society altogether."

Ellie breathed a quiet sigh of relief before turning back to her father and grandfather.

"When shall we leave?"

Her father smoothed her hair with a tender smile. "As soon as breakfast is finished, my dear. Once the servants have packed your trunks, we will travel to London. Your mother is waiting."

18

She Would Not Be Cowed

Ellie slipped away from the bustle of servants and family preparing for departure. Her steps carried her swiftly through the gardens and across the manicured lawns, her heart urging her to visit the lake one last time before being confined to a carriage for the long journey ahead.

The morning air was warm and fragrant, threaded with birdsong from the hedgerows. Sunlight danced across the rippling water, scattering sparks of gold until the surface glittered like a field of jewels. Spring still lingered over the land, yet Ellie felt in her bones that its hold was fading. Already the heat of summer pressed in during the day, whispering of what was to come. She closed her eyes, determined to drink in the sun's gentle warmth before it grew too heavy to bear.

London would be different. No quiet lakes, no endless fields where she could walk unseen. Still, her grandfather owned not only a townhouse in the city but also a country estate beyond its crowded streets. Perhaps there she might find some patch of green, some place to breathe, to think, to belong.

Ellie rested her back against the sturdy trunk of an oak, its bark rough but steady beneath her palms. She watched a pair of ducks' glide serenely across the pond, their feathers glinting in the light. For a fleeting moment, peace touched her. Then a ripple of girlish laughter broke the stillness.

She turned, and her breath caught. Olivia and Richard were strolling along the path that wound back toward the house, their heads bent close together. Richard's arm curved easily around Olivia's waist, and with careless affection he drew her nearer, pressing a kiss to her lips.

Ellie's heart lurched as if struck. She turned sharply back toward the lake, pressing her fingers hard against the oak as though its strength might steady her. Tears sprang hot and unbidden, but she forced them back. She would not let them see her break. The ache gripping her chest was not merely jealousy, it was loss. Loss of the friend who had been her anchor for as long as she could remember.

Richard had scarcely spoken to her since Olivia's rescue, as though their easy companionship had already been swept aside to make room for the woman he intended to marry. Soon he would be her cousin's husband, and nothing between them would ever be the same. Her thoughts drifted uneasily toward the future awaiting her in London. She tried to picture herself in glittering drawing rooms, surrounded by unfamiliar faces, young men who would bow politely, young ladies who would smile with practiced grace.

Yet no new acquaintance could ever replace what she had shared with Richard. Their friendship had been effortless, rooted in years of laughter, secrets, and trust. Nothing new could ever measure against it. A cold certainty settled in her heart. Wherever she went, she would not quite belong. No matter how fine the house, how splendid the company, she would carry with her this hollow ache, the sense of being an outsider, longing for what was lost, and for the one man who had never truly been hers to lose.

Ellie heard footsteps drawing near and hastily brushed the tears from her cheeks. By the time she turned, Lord Bennett was only a few paces away. His features, usually so stern, were softened by a warm, disarming smile, and when their eyes met, his gaze lingered with startling intensity.

"Lady Danielle," he said in a low, steady voice, "everyone is preparing to depart. But before we travel to London, might I have a word with you?"

Her heart gave a nervous flutter, curiosity stirring, but before another word could pass between them, strong arms suddenly swept her off her feet. Ellie gasped, nearly crying out, only to realize with a jolt that it was Richard. He held her tightly, his unexpected embrace stealing her breath and sending her pulse racing.

"I must finally tell you, Ellie," he declared, his voice brimming with excitement, "that Olivia and I are engaged. She makes me so happy, and I love her dearly. I hope you, too, will find that special someone who makes your heart glad."

The words pierced her like a blade. Her vision blurred, and she fought desperately not to sob in his arms. When Richard set her down, she swayed slightly, pale as parchment. A deliberate clearing of the throat sounded behind them. Lord Bennett stepped forward, his expression calm but edged with quiet amusement.

"Lord Blackwood," he said, a faint smile touching his lips, "is it your habit to interrupt others so boldly, or only when a lady is already engaged in conversation?"

Richard faltered, the confidence draining from his face. Color rose on his cheeks.

"Forgive me, Your Grace. I did not mean to intrude. But Lady Danielle and I... we have been friends since childhood. I only wished to share my happy news with her." He gave Ellie a fleeting glance before adding, "Now, I must return to Olivia." He turned and strode away, but after several steps he pivoted back, his voice carrying boldly across the lawn.

"As soon as we arrive in London, I will seek her father's blessing. And if he refuses, Olivia and I shall elope at once. Nothing will keep us from returning to Darlington as husband and wife."

With that, he hurried off, vanishing toward the house.

Lord Bennett shifted, placing himself fully before Ellie, as though to shield her from the sting of Richard's parting words. She kept her gaze fixed firmly on the ground, unwilling to let him see the storm in her eyes.

"Forgive me, Your Grace," she whispered, her voice trembling. "But I must beg to be excused." She turned to flee, but his hand came gently to her arm.

"Are you well, Lady Danielle?" His tone was quiet, full of compassion. That tenderness undid her. Her composure shattered, and tears spilled freely down her cheeks. She averted her face, ashamed of her weakness, though the tremor in her slender frame betrayed her grief. "Please," he murmured, reaching as though to take her hand. But she shook her head, desperate to escape before she utterly broke. With a sharp breath she slipped free of his grasp.

"Forgive me," she whispered again, then gathered her skirts and fled toward the house without once daring to look back.

Lord Bennett remained where he stood, watching her retreat. Every instinct urged him to follow, to comfort her, to tell her she need not bear her pain alone. Yet he held himself still. Some grief, he knew, could not be eased with words. She needed space. But his heart ached for her all the same.

Ellie remained quiet for most of the journey to London, her gaze fixed on the shifting landscape beyond the carriage window. The rhythmic beat of hooves and the steady rattle of wheels did little to soothe her aching heart. Fields rolled past in endless shades of green, dotted with cottages and hedgerows glowing beneath the afternoon sun. Normally she would have delighted in such sights, but now they passed before her eyes like a painted backdrop she could scarcely see.

She folded her hands tightly in her lap, willing her composure to hold. She was silently grateful that Richard had chosen to ride on horseback alongside the carriage rather than sit within. His absence spared her the torment of meeting his eyes, or of enduring the tender tones in which he spoke of Olivia whenever the conversation turned to her.

Across from her, Olivia leaned now and then toward her uncle, speaking with quiet excitement about wedding preparations and the life that lay ahead. Her voice carried an airy happiness that was impossible to mistake. Each word pressed heavily against Ellie's chest. She kept her expression composed, nodding when spoken to and offering an occasionally polite reply, but her silence did not go unnoticed. From time to time, she felt the weight of watchful glances, concern etched across her grandfather's face, sympathy lingering in Lord Bennett's steady eyes.

More than once she sensed his gaze resting on her longer than propriety required, as though he wished to speak yet restrained himself. No one pressed her to join the conversation. For that mercy, she was deeply grateful. She had no strength for words.

As the hours passed, the countryside slowly gave way to the outskirts of the great city. Villages thickened into crowded streets, and the steady quiet of rural life dissolved into the bustling clamor of London. Carriages rattled over cobbled roads. Vendors called out from crowded corners. Elegant townhouses stood shoulder to shoulder along wide avenues lined with plane trees.

At last, the carriage rolled into one of the grander districts and slowed before her grandfather's imposing townhouse. Its stone façade rose tall and dignified, its wide steps and towering windows proclaiming both wealth and long-standing influence. Freshly polished brass gleamed beside the front door, and liveried servants hurried forward the moment the carriage came to a halt. The household had clearly been warned of their arrival. Footmen quickly opened the carriage door while a maid appeared with a shawl, and the bustle of arrival filled the air.

Olivia and Ellie's father were the first to step down, already speaking in earnest about arrangements for the coming days and the precautions that must be taken to ensure Olivia and Eleanor's continued safety. Ellie followed more slowly, her skirts brushing the stone steps as she descended. For a moment she paused at the foot of the carriage and lifted her eyes to the tall townhouse before her.

London. The word echoed quietly in her mind. This was to be her new world now, one of glittering ballrooms, whispered gossip, and expectations she had never truly desired. Behind her she felt movement as Lord Bennett stepped down from the carriage as well, his presence calm and steady, though he said nothing.

Ellie gathered herself, straightened her shoulders, and crossed the threshold into the house, unaware that the life awaiting her inside would prove far more complicated than anything she had imagined.

The moment Ellie had entered the house, her mother appeared. Lady Huntington let out a cry of joy and hurried forward, gathering her daughter into a fierce embrace.

"My dearest child. Oh, how I have missed you." She kissed Ellie's cheek again and again, her eyes shining with tears of relief as she held her close, as though unwilling to let her go. "You must tell me everything. Everything you have endured, all that has happened."

Ellie managed a weary smile, though exhaustion and sorrow still clung to her like a heavy cloak. Seeing it, her mother's joyful urgency softened at once into tender understanding. Lord Huntington stepped forward as well, placing a protective hand upon his daughter's shoulder. His gaze lingered on her pale face, and he exchanged a quiet, knowing look with his wife, one that spoke of shared concern and silent resolve.

"You need not speak of it now, darling," her mother said gently, brushing back a loose curl from Ellie's temple. "You are safe, and that is enough for us tonight."

Ellie swallowed hard, grateful beyond words for the mercy of their restraint. They promised to return the following afternoon for tea, when she might feel stronger and more ready to recount everything that had transpired. For now, her father explained, he must meet with her uncle and several trusted men of influence to ensure Olivia's protection and see that every precaution was taken to keep both her and Eleanor forever beyond Lord Ainsworth's reach. Lady Huntington kissed her daughter once more before reluctantly stepping away.

"Rest, my love," she whispered. "Tomorrow will come soon enough."

Ellie watched quietly as her parents departed, the door closing softly behind them. Silence settled over the vast entrance hall of her grandfather's townhouse. The marble floor gleamed beneath the tall windows, and portraits of long-departed ancestors gazed down from gilded frames. The grandeur of the house surrounded her, rich carpets, polished wood, and the faint scent of beeswax and lavender lingering in the air.

Yet instead of comfort, Ellie felt a strange emptiness pressing in around her. She stood motionless in the middle of the hall, her hands clasped before her, her heart heavy. Surrounded by family and safety, she felt more adrift than ever, unsure where her place truly lay in a world that seemed determined to shift beneath her feet.

19

The First Two Dances

Ellie felt considerably better after a long, unbroken night's sleep. The peace and safety of her grandfather's estate outside London soothed her spirit, and the morning sunlight streaming through the tall windows made the house feel almost welcoming. The gardens beyond were charming, with neatly trimmed hedges and blossoming roses, and for the first time in weeks she felt a flicker of excitement for what lay ahead, particularly the thought of seeing her grandfather's larger estate in Colchester.

She had only just taken her seat at the breakfast table opposite her grandfather, a steaming cup of chocolate warming her hands, when the butler entered with a solemn expression. Bowing slightly, he made his announcement.

"Your Grace, the Viscount of Bromley is here to see you."

Her grandfather looked up from his plate, his brows knitting together.

"A little early for a visit, don't you think?" he muttered, his voice tinged with irritation. The butler hesitated, as if weighing his words, before continuing.

"With him is His Royal Highness, Prince Carsten."

Ellie froze, her eyes flying to her grandfather in astonishment. *A prince?* Her breath caught, but if she expected Lord Huntington to share her shock, she was mistaken. He did not look impressed in the slightest. In fact, his expression darkened with annoyance, and he released a long sigh, as though some tedious chore had just been thrust upon him.

"Don't let this interrupt your meal, my dear," he said with a measured nod. "This will probably take a while."

But the butler, still standing stiffly by the door, cleared his throat again.

"Actually, Your Grace... both gentlemen insist on meeting Lady Danielle."

Ellie set her cup down with trembling fingers. "Meeting me?" she repeated, bewildered. "Why on earth would they wish to meet me? And who, exactly, is the Viscount of Bromley?"

At this, her grandfather and the butler exchanged one of those wordless, weighted glances that seemed to carry far more meaning than Ellie could yet decipher. At last, Lord Huntington turned his attention fully back to her.

"Lord Alastair Maughan," he said with deliberate calm, "is the nephew of my late wife's youngest brother."

Ellie's eyes widened. "So, he is the one who would inherit everything if I were to refuse the duchy?"

Her grandfather inclined his head. "Precisely."

Ellie arched a brow, curiosity sharpening. "Do you know him well?"

Lord Huntington shook his head. "Not well at all. We met in passing a few times, years ago, but nothing more. I was somewhat acquainted with his father before he died, though truthfully, the family was never pleasant company." His expression hardened slightly.

"The late Lord Maughan was a bitter man. He could not abide that his sister married a duke while he was 'only' made a viscount." His tone sharpened on the final words, as though the memory itself left an unpleasant taste. Ellie frowned.

"But what does that have to do with you, or with me? They are connected only through marriage, not blood. Why should they believe the duchy is theirs to claim?"

Her grandfather's mouth curved into a grim smile.

"Because, my dear, the Maughans have always been greedy vultures. They grasp at whatever they can, whether it belongs to them by right or not." He paused before adding with clear disdain, "and they pride themselves on being distantly related to the House of Windsor, which has only made them more arrogant."

Ellie sat back slightly, her heart quickening. "Then I assume this will not be a good, or friendly, visit?"

Lord Huntington's eyes held hers for a long moment before he gave a slow shake of his head.

"Most likely not." He rose with deliberate composure, his presence instantly commanding the room. "But," he added evenly, straightening his coat, "let us hear what they want before we decide how to respond."

Two strapping young men rose when Ellie and her grandfather entered the parlor. Though both wore polite smiles, their expressions were too practiced, and too smug, for Ellie to feel at ease. Something in her spirit recoiled.

"Lord Maughan. Your Highness," Lord Huntington greeted curtly. He inclined his head, and the two men bowed in return. "May I present my granddaughter, Lady Danielle Huntington."

Ellie sank into a graceful curtsy, careful to keep her distance as her grandfather gestured toward the chairs. Once all were seated, Lord Huntington wasted no time.

"To what do we owe the pleasure of your visit?"

The Viscount of Bromley cleared his throat, his dark eyes sweeping over Ellie in a way that made her skin prickle.

"I received word that you are hosting a ball in honor of your granddaughter, to introduce her to society. Tell me, why is that necessary? She is only the daughter of a man stripped of his title after his most disgraceful behavior."

Ellie's fists tightened in her lap, but she held her tongue. Her grandfather, however, bristled with fury.

"It is none of your concern whether I hold a ball for my granddaughter. Whatever my son's failures, his children remain innocent, and unblemished heirs to the Huntington line."

The viscount's expression darkened. "And yet you did not think to invite me to so important an occasion?"

"I did not see the need," Lord Huntington shot back. "We share no bond save a tenuous marriage connection, and we have never sought each other's company before. Why begin now?"

The viscount's mouth curled into a sly grin. "Because it would have been polite. Besides, I should quite like the chance to become... better acquainted with such a beautiful young lady."

Ellie suppressed a shudder. The man was not handsome. His gaze was predatory. Every instinct urged her to flee, but she remained seated for her grandfather's sake, and to avoid offending the prince beside him. It was Prince Carsten who spoke next, his tone deceptively smooth.

"Tell me, Your Grace, is Lady Danielle intended to be your heiress?"

"She is indeed, Your Highness," Lord Huntington replied without hesitation. "As the eldest of my grandchildren, she is next in line."

The prince's brows lifted in mock surprise. "But surely you know that only males may inherit titles and estates?"

"That is incorrect," Lord Huntington countered, his voice hardening. "I discussed the matter at length with your elder brother, Prince Edward. He assured me my granddaughter's claim is sound."

"Perhaps," Prince Carsten said, tilting his head, "but surely you realize that a young woman must be married to assume such responsibility?"

"I am well aware," the duke said dryly, "but my granddaughter will not be of age for nearly three years. Until then, my duties as Grand Duke will not prevent me from safeguarding my estate."

A smug smile crept across the prince's face. "You must think us fools, Your Grace. Leaving your duchy under an unmarried girl's care is no solution. The rules are clear: land and title must pass to a male relation unless a suitable marriage is secured before he reaches his majority. That, as I understand, is in but a few weeks' time."

Ellie's breath caught. The veiled threat was unmistakable. Her grandfather's hands clenched upon the armrests, his anger barely contained.

"The Viscount of Bromley is not my nearest relation," Lord Huntington growled. "He is connected only by marriage. The Huntington estate has been in my family's bloodline for centuries. No vulture may swoop in and claim it."

"The duchy remains part of the kingdom, does it not?" Carsten asked sweetly.

"Are you threatening me, Your Highness?"

"Threat is such a harsh word," the prince murmured, feigning innocence. "I am merely informing you of... consequences."

"That is not how your brother conducts himself," Lord Huntington snapped. "I have a clear understanding with him."

"My brother is abroad," Carsten said with disdain. "He left me to govern in his absence. And yes, should I choose, I may support Viscount Maughan's rightful claim."

"Then let me be plain, you mean to help him steal from my granddaughter what is rightfully hers."

Ellie's eyes widened. She had not expected her grandfather to be so blunt, so openly defiant. Both prince and viscount faltered at his boldness. Yet before they could answer, Lord Huntington pressed on, his voice sharp as a blade.

"You spoke of deadlines. When, Viscount, do you come of age?"

The young man grinned. "Six weeks hence. Prince Carsten has graciously promised a ball in my honor, held at his castle just outside London. You are, of course, invited."

Ellie gasped. Her grandfather leapt to his feet, his chair scraping back.

"This is preposterous! You have no right to bind my granddaughter with such schemes. I will write to His Majesty himself and inform him how his cousin's son abuses his station."

The prince's smile turned to ice. His voice dropped to a chilling whisper.

"Careful, Your Grace. You would not want to lose everything, or rot in a dungeon for insolence. Remember to whom you speak."

Lord Huntington straightened to his full height. "I, too, am of royal birth. As is my granddaughter. We will not—"

"If you think we are cowed by threats, Your Highness," Ellie cut in, her voice steady and fierce, "you are mistaken." She rose, chin lifted proudly, her eyes flashing. "Like Grandfather said, our bloodline is royal, and it deserves respect. The Huntingtons worked for everything they possess—we did not have privilege handed to us. My great-grandmother was Princess Isadora, and she outranked you. Do not think a prince's title makes you untouchable." Turning, she fixed her gaze on the viscount.

"And you, Lord Maughan, will not take what belongs to us. I know your kind. Too lazy to better yourself, too proud to labor, always scheming to take what others have earned. Do you believe you can leap from viscount to duke without merit? No doubt you are drowning in debt, squandering your fortune, and now seek to buy influence by bribing a prince."

The room fell silent. Both men stared at her, visibly stunned. Even her grandfather blinked in astonishment at her boldness, and at the uncanny accuracy of her accusations. Ellie drew a steady breath.

"Before I see the Huntington name disgraced, I will marry. And rest assured, I will find a husband if I must." Her tone sharpened, commanding. "Now, you have interrupted our morning meal long enough. Mr. Matthews will show you out."

The butler stepped forward at once, bowing. "This way, gentlemen."

With stiff bows, the prince and viscount withdrew, their pride wounded. Ellie remained standing tall, her heart still racing, as the parlor doors closed firmly behind them.

Ellie trailed her grandfather into the breakfast room, her steps heavy after the tense encounter. The moment she sank into her chair, she released the breath she had been holding, her shoulders slumping with relief. Lord Huntington gave her a sideways glance, then chuckled softly, his stern features easing into a grin.

"You are more than ready to be a duchess, Danielle. Mark my words, you will keep even the loftiest nobility in their place when the moment demands it. Tell me, how on earth did you manage to remain so calm?"

Ellie shook her head faintly, still astonished by her own boldness.

"I honestly have no idea. Forgive me for interrupting you, and for speaking so forwardly before a prince of the realm. I fear I must have embarrassed you terribly. But something within me... I simply could not sit silent while they insulted us. My tongue acted before my thoughts could catch up."

Her grandfather's eyes softened, his smile filled with pride rather than reproach.

"Embarrassed? Not in the least. You made me proud, fiercely proud. Your defense of our family name proved you to be every inch the heir I have always known you were meant to be." He leaned back in his chair, his gaze growing distant, almost wistful.

"Perhaps you did not realize such fire slept within you, but your parents and I have long suspected it would reveal itself in time." He studied her for a moment, his expression thoughtful.

"For a moment, as you stood there, I thought I was watching my grandmother reborn. She possessed that same unyielding spirit. None dared belittle our family while she still drew breath."

Ellie tilted her head curiously. "Was she like your mother and father?"

He shook his head slowly, the corners of his mouth tightening.

"No. She was my father's mother. A remarkable woman, sweet in temper, yet fierce as a lioness when protecting those she loved." His voice softened as the memory returned.

"She had been a princess before her marriage to my grandfather. Forced into the match, truth be told. There was no love between them. My grandfather was not a kind man, and she endured much unhappiness. But she never allowed him to disrespect her or her children. With every breath she drew, she shielded them as best she could."

Ellie's eyes widened with admiration. "She sounds extraordinary."

"She was," he agreed, his voice filled with quiet reverence. "She tried with all her might to teach her sons compassion and honor, to mold them into men unlike their father." His expression darkened slightly.

"But my grandfather ruled with an iron fist. His word was law, and despite her efforts, my father and his brothers idolized him. That is why my father grew into such a tyrant." He paused, his gaze meeting Ellie's, filled with something deeper, grief, perhaps, or gratitude.

"Still, my grandmother never ceased her quiet resistance." He folded his hands thoughtfully on the table. "I was closest to her of all. Before she died, she made me promise I would never become like my father or grandfather. It was a heavy vow for a boy to carry."

Ellie's heart tightened. "That must have been terribly difficult."

His smile returned, though it was tinged with sadness. "It was. I had to tread carefully, masking my convictions so as not to draw my father's suspicion. To him, kindness was weakness, and weakness intolerable." He shook his head slightly.

"He never understood that true strength lies not in cruelty, but in restraint, in honor, in the ability to protect without oppression." He gave a quiet, almost rueful breath. "My mother, his wife, believed as he did. In that regard, they were well matched."

For a moment he fell silent, as though shaking off the long shadows of memory. Then his eyes returned to Ellie, warm and steady.

"But you, Danielle, you carry your great-great-grandmother's spirit. And hers was not easily subdued." A faint smile touched his lips. "Today you proved you are her descendant in every way that matters."

Her grandfather guided Ellie through the winding corridors of the house, pausing now and then before portraits of their ancestors to share fragments of family history. From there, they passed into the gardens, where roses spilled over trellises and neatly trimmed hedges framed the gravel walks. Beyond the formal beds stretched the parkland, broad, green, and dotted with ancient oaks whose branches arched like protective arms overhead.

At last, they reached a weathered bench beneath a great chestnut tree, its leaves rustling softly in the breeze. Before them lay a wide pond, its surface glimmering in the morning light. Ducks glided lazily across the water, while swans arched their long necks with effortless grace. For a few moments, neither spoke, content to sit in silence and let the peace of the place settle around them.

Then Lord Huntington broke the quiet, his tone unusually grave.

"Danielle," he said, turning to meet her gaze. "You do not have to do this. I know I once told you that an arranged marriage might become necessary should you reach your twenty-first birthday unwed, but the time frame they have thrust upon us is outrageous. Prince Carsten has no right to press us so cruelly."

Ellie's brow furrowed. "Is there no one we can appeal to? What of his parents? Surely, they would not condone such intimidation."

Her grandfather exhaled heavily, his eyes fixed on the rippling water.

"His parents are abroad. They sailed for the colonies on a royal tour, and their absence may stretch for weeks yet. I knew of their travels, but I had not realized their elder son, Edward, had gone with them. He, at least, is a fair-minded man. Still, I do not expect their return until the very end of the Season, just before the last great ball."

Ellie lifted her chin, her expression resolute. "It matters little, Grandfather. Lord Maughan will not gain a single acre of what is yours. This family has endured enough at the hands of domineering men, and I will not see us made victims again."

He studied her face, his own lined with both pride and concern.

"You speak with courage, but, Danielle, you must not sacrifice your happiness out of duty to me. I know you have always opposed the notion of an arranged marriage. I would never have you bound to a man you could not respect, or love. I did not realize Maughan's ties to the royals were so close. It complicates matters."

Ellie's eyes softened, though her voice remained steady. "I am still against an arranged marriage, Grandfather. That will not change. And yes, six weeks is little time to decide the course of one's life." She paused, drawing a quiet breath.

"But even so, the choice will remain mine. No prince, no viscount, no man alive, will dictate whom I marry. If I must wed, I will do so by my own hand… and my own heart." Her gaze did not waver. "That is a promise."

Lord Huntington's expression eased into a faint smile, though worry lingered in his eyes. He reached over and clasped her hand, giving it a gentle squeeze.

"You remind me more of your great-great-grandmother with each conversation we share."

As the silver tray of tea was brought in and cups were poured, a quiet murmur of voices filled the drawing room. Moments later, Ellie's parents and Olivia were announced, and a maid guided them inside with practiced grace.

They were received warmly by the duke himself, who rose to greet them with quiet dignity. Yet Ellie noticed a flicker of curiosity in his eyes, as though he had already guessed the purpose of their visit. Ellie smoothed her gown as she took her seat.

"So," she asked, her voice steady though her gaze searched their faces anxiously, "how was the meeting with my uncle?"

Her father let out a weary sigh, settling heavily into his chair as though the weight of the morning pressed upon his shoulders.

"Just as expected," he admitted. "Magnus was outraged, furious that Olivia had dared to form an engagement in secret with a man who, in his words, was 'only a baron.' He shouted that she was promised to Lord Thatcher. Yet your cousin boldly told him the marquess had never intended to wed her."

Olivia's cheeks flushed, but she lifted her chin proudly at her uncle's words. Her father continued, his expression darkening.

"Magnus then demanded to know where Eleanor is. When we refused to tell him, he nearly struck out at both Olivia and Clara. Gordon and I had to step between them more than once."

Henry Huntington, who had been listening with his arms folded, shook his head grimly.

"When Olivia still refused to yield, Magnus lost what little composure he had left. He drew a pistol from his coat. Gordon had no choice but to knock him unconscious. We sent for the authorities at once and had him arrested."

Ellie's breath caught. "Will Aunt Clara leave him at last?"

Her mother's gaze softened. "I believe so, yes. We told Clara she may stay with us in Darlington. That way, she will be close to Olivia once she marries Lord Blackwood."

Ellie's heart constricted at the mention of Richard. She forced her face to remain composed, though a sharp pang twisted deep within her chest. With effort, she steadied her voice.

"And Eleanor? Where is she now?"

Olivia cleared her throat. "She is staying with the Duke of Devon."

Ellie gasped. "With the duke? But is that proper? Is not Lord Wallace also residing there? Two single men beneath the same roof as her? Surely that is highly irregular. Perhaps a governess or companion should be engaged at once."

Her mother's lips curved in a faint smile, touched with pride. In only a few short weeks away, her daughter had grown strikingly; her words carried the guarded wisdom of one already mindful of society's expectations and dangers. Yes, she would make a fine duchess indeed.

20

A Prince Rebuked

"She is not alone, my dear," her mother reassured her gently. "Her maids from the Ainsworth household accompanied her, and the Duke of Devon employs many respectable female servants who are tending to Eleanor now. She is being carefully looked after."

Ellie let out a quiet breath, some of the tension easing from her shoulders. Her grandfather spoke then, his tone grave yet softened with sympathy.

"The duke feels the weight of guilt, child. He regrets leaving Eleanor in his nephew's hands for so long, and he carries shame that he did not intervene sooner, even when whispers of Ainsworth's conduct toward his first wife reached him." He paused, his gaze thoughtful.

"This," he gestured faintly with one hand, "is his attempt at atonement. By sheltering Eleanor now, he hopes to make right what he once failed to prevent."

Ellie nodded slowly, her lips pressed together. It did make sense, and yet a faint unease lingered in her chest. The scars Eleanor carried, both seen and unseen, could not be erased so easily.

"I believe Clara intends to remain with Eleanor for some time before joining us in Darlington," her mother added gently. "Your father and Gordon will see to it that she reaches her daughter safely."

Ellie's gaze drifted toward the window, where sunlight filtered softly through the tall glass panes. She folded her hands in her lap, thoughtful. She had not realized how swiftly the web of their family's affairs had begun to unravel, nor how many lives were caught within its strands. What had begun as a desperate attempt to save her cousins had now drawn in dukes, princes, and entire households. Old secrets had surfaced, loyalties had been tested, and the future of more than one family now hung delicately in the balance.

And yet, beneath the weight of it all, one quiet truth remained. For the first time in many months, Eleanor was safe. Olivia was free. And though the road ahead was still uncertain, Ellie felt the faintest stirrings of hope that their long season of darkness might finally be nearing its end.

Two weeks after their arrival in London, the long-anticipated event finally drew near. Danielle's first ball. It was to be hosted by the Duke of Essex himself, who had resolved that this would be the evening his granddaughter was formally introduced into society. Preparations had been endless.

From early morning until late afternoon the townhouse bustled with activity. Seamstresses arrived with silks and lace, dressmakers knelt on the floor pinning hems, and jewelers came and went carrying velvet boxes filled with glittering ornaments. Footmen hurried through the corridors with crates of candles and polished silver, while the housekeeper oversaw the delivery of flowers destined to transform the ballroom into a garden of roses and white blossoms. Every corner of the house seemed alive with movement.

Yet beneath all the bustle, Ellie carried a quiet dread. For days she had endured a relentless stream of lessons. A dance master corrected the angle of her steps and the turn of her wrists. Her grandmother's former companion instructed her on the subtleties of conversation, how to greet a duchess, how to answer a prince, how to deflect impropriety with nothing more than a glance. Even the manner of her smile had been discussed at length. She had been taught how to stand, how to speak, how to walk, how to curtsy, and how to conceal any emotion that might betray uncertainty.

But no lesson could truly prepare her for stepping into that glittering world. Beyond the tall doors of her grandfather's ballroom waited the highest ranks of London society: nobles whose names carried centuries of influence, ladies whose judgments could shape reputations in a single evening, and men whose alliances determined fortunes and futures.

The thought of standing before them all, of being examined, measured, and whispered about, made her stomach tighten. Still, to the astonishment of those around her, Ellie revealed a natural elegance no tutor could claim to have taught. Grace and poise seemed to flow from her as naturally as breath. When she walked, there was quiet confidence in her step. When she spoke, her voice carried both warmth and dignity. Even her curtsy possessed a fluid ease that seasoned society ladies struggled to master. More than once, the instructors exchanged impressed glances.

What they had attempted to teach in careful instruction appeared to exist within her already. Her parents and grandfather had long suspected those qualities lay dormant, waiting only for their moment to bloom. Now, with the great night approaching, it seemed that moment had finally arrived.

Late one morning, however, Ellie's thoughts of gowns and dances were interrupted. A servant announced that she was wanted in the morning room. Expecting to find only her parents and grandfather, she stepped inside and froze. Baron Appleton stood before her.

Time had not been kind to him. His once-proud shoulders were stooped, his hair threaded with gray, and the deep lines etched across his face bore the unmistakable weight of regret. Ellie's heart stirred with pity. Before she could speak, he bowed low and began apologizing again and again, his voice thick with remorse.

"Please, My Lord," Ellie said gently, "there is nothing to forgive. You did nothing wrong."

He faltered, clearly overwhelmed by her mercy. She hesitated only a moment before asking softly, "What is your plan now?"

The baron exhaled heavily, his gaze dropping to the carpet.

"The Duke of Devon has been most generous in assisting me. My marriage to... her has been annulled. She has returned to her brother's house, where she must now live under his roof." His mouth tightened with quiet bitterness.

"She refuses to acknowledge her fall from grace. Refuses to believe she is now a woman without means or standing. But her brother will not indulge her. He is harsh, perhaps even cruel, yet… someone had to curb her destructive ways. He is the one man who could."

Ellie nodded slowly, sympathy softening her expression. "And… what of Felicity?"

At the mention of his daughter, the baron's face clouded.

"She is presently staying with relatives here in London. But the question cannot be delayed much longer. Her mother insists our daughter should live with her."

Ellie's chest tightened. *Poor Felicity.* The girl had been shaped by the worst of influences, a mother whose manipulations had poisoned nearly every thought and action. Ellie cleared her throat before speaking carefully.

"Perhaps… you should give Felicity another chance."

The words struck the room like the ringing of a bell. Her parents and grandfather turned sharply toward her, startled. The baron himself blinked, speechless. Ellie drew in a breath and lifted her chin.

"I know what you are all thinking. Felicity has not been kind. She has caused pain, especially among young ladies her own age, and it is tempting to believe she is beyond redemption." Her voice softened, though her conviction remained firm.

"But I believe her mother bears the greater share of blame. Felicity is still young, still impressionable. If she is guided firmly yet kindly, she may yet change."

The baron's eyes searched her face, a faint glimmer of hope flickering there.

"You truly believe she deserves another chance?"

"I do," Ellie replied without hesitation. "Of course, the decision rests with you, My Lord. But she may yet surprise us all." She paused before continuing more gently.

"The important thing is that she must understand this is no longer her mother's world. She must answer to you, and to you alone. For her own sake, she must be kept apart from Mrs. Appleton's influence. We all know too well the woman's manipulative nature." Her tone softened further.

"Make it clear to Felicity that this is a trial, a single chance to prove herself. If she fails, there may not be another. But if she chooses wisely... she could yet become a good and worthy woman."

The baron's composure wavered. For a moment Ellie thought he might break entirely. Shame and sorrow glistened in his eyes. She stepped forward, extending her hand, her voice low and kind.

"My Lord, what happened was never your fault. Do not let guilt consume you. You are a good man. Everyone in and around Darlington knows this. You could not have foreseen what sort of wife Mrs. Appleton would become. She deceived many, but perhaps her games are finally ended."

His lips trembled, as though unspoken words lingered there, but he mastered himself quickly.

With quiet reverence, he bowed over her hand.

"Thank you, Lady Danielle."

Ellie felt a weight lift in the room, and with it, a new one settle upon her own heart. Slowly, she turned to find her parents and grandfather watching her. Instinctively, her back straightened, bracing herself for correction. She had grown so accustomed to her mother's scolding. Yet when her eyes met theirs, she saw not censure, but warmth, pride, and approval. For the first time, Ellie allowed herself to wonder if perhaps she could impress others after all.

Ellie scarcely recognized the young woman gazing back at her from the tall gilt mirror. The gown her grandfather had insisted on shimmered in the candlelight, its pale silk embroidered with delicate silver threads that caught the light with every breath she drew. The bodice was fitted with exquisite precision, the skirts falling in graceful folds that seemed almost to float as she moved. Her hair had been swept into an elegant coiffure, each golden curl carefully arranged and threaded with pearls that glimmered like tiny stars. A single strand rested lightly at her throat, its soft luster echoing the quiet brilliance of the gown.

She looked breathtaking, every inch the young lady ready to be presented to society. And yet the reflection brought her no joy. A dull ache tugged at her chest as she studied the poised figure in the mirror. This was meant to be a night filled with anticipation and delight, the first true step into her future.

Instead, all she felt was the sting of loss. Her heart had not yet healed from Richard's absence.

Only weeks ago, she had imagined this very evening with him at her side, teasing away her nervousness with his familiar laughter, offering quiet reassurances when the weight of so many watchful eyes became overwhelming. Instead, he had eloped with Olivia shortly after their return to London.

Now they were settled in Darlington, far from the glittering ballrooms of the capital, leaving Ellie with an emptiness she could not banish. She had assured her grandfather there was no cause for concern, that she would find her own way, and that she would choose her husband when the time was right. But the truth was far less certain. The thought of marrying a man she did not love, of binding her life to a stranger out of duty or necessity, filled her with a quiet dread she could scarcely admit even to herself.

Her fingers tightened lightly against the edge of the dressing table. Tonight, she would stand on display before London's elite. Already she could imagine the curious gazes, the murmured speculation, the calculating interest of ambitious mothers and fortune-seeking gentlemen. The instant her grandfather made his proud introduction, the eyes of rakes and fortune hunters alike would turn toward her. All her fears seemed to gather around this single evening.

Yet as she lifted her chin and met her own gaze in the mirror, a faint spark of determination stirred beneath the sorrow. Whatever the night might bring, she would face it with dignity. She was a Huntington. And no matter how uncertain her heart might feel, she would not allow London to see her falter.

The summons came sooner than Ellie expected. A footman appeared at her chamber door, bowing respectfully as he delivered the message that the first guests had begun to arrive. Before she could fully gather her composure, she was being escorted down the wide staircase toward the great hall, where the evening's glittering spectacle had already begun. Candles blazed from tall sconces along the walls, their light dancing across polished marble and gilded frames. The hum of voices drifted upward from below, laughter, polite greetings, the rustle of silk gowns and the measured tread of polished boots.

At the foot of the stairs her grandfather waited, stately and imposing in his formal attire. He offered her his arm, his expression, one of quiet pride as he guided her toward the receiving line.

Ellie took her place beside him, her palms damp within her gloves. One by one the guests were announced. Footmen called out titles in ringing voices as each arrival stepped forward to bow or curtsy before the Duke of Essex, and before her.

"Lady Whitcombe and daughters."

"Lord and Lady Harrington."

"Sir Edmund Carlisle."

Ellie smiled politely, murmured the expected greetings, and inclined her head with careful grace. She answered each introduction as she had been taught, her voice steady and composed. Yet beneath that polished exterior her heart felt strangely hollow. With Richard and Olivia gone, the familiar warmth of companionship was absent. The easy laughter she had always relied upon to steady her nerves had vanished with them.

Perhaps Lord Beverton's grandsons would appear later in the evening, she told herself. But it would not be the same. Childishly, she had once imagined Richard leading her onto the floor for her very first dance, teasing her gently, whispering encouragement as the orchestra began to play.

That dream, like so many others, had slipped forever from her grasp.

Her thoughts wandered elsewhere, unbidden. *Would Lord Bennett attend tonight?* The notion startled her. Why should she think of him at all? True, he had shown her unexpected kindness in the end. He had defended her, stood before the entire ballroom and claimed her protection as though her honor were his to guard. But he could never be Richard. Never her dearest friend. And certainly not a man she could consider as a husband. She told herself she felt nothing for him but tolerance.

And yet the thought unsettled her more than she wished to admit. So lost was she in her musings that when a familiar voice sounded at her side, Ellie nearly leapt in alarm.

"Lady Danielle."

She turned quickly. Lord Bennett stood before her, bowing low, his smile warm and unguarded. "It is a pleasure to see you again."

Her cheeks flamed instantly. Her heart began to pound so furiously she was certain the entire hall must hear it.

What is wrong with me? she scolded herself.

He straightened slowly, his gaze resting upon her with a quiet intensity that made her pulse stumble. For a moment he simply looked at her, as though the crowded hall and the endless line of guests had vanished from his awareness.

"You look... extraordinary this evening," he added softly. The compliment, spoken with such sincerity, left her momentarily breathless. He extended his hand, and with practiced grace lifted hers to his lips.

The light brush of his mouth against her gloved fingers sent a surprising flutter through her chest, like a sudden rush of startled butterflies.

"Your Grace," she managed at last, dipping into a curtsy, praying she might vanish from sight altogether. But when she lifted her gaze to his, the world seemed to still. His eyes held hers, dark, steady, searching. For one dangerous, dazzling moment she was caught fast by that gaze, unable to look away. The crowded hall faded into a distant blur of candlelight and murmured voices. Even the music drifting faintly from the ballroom beyond seemed to dissolve into silence.

It felt as though the two of them stood alone in some hidden sphere, separated from the rest of the world by nothing more than the charged space between them. Her breath caught. His fingers lingered lightly around her hand, as though he too had forgotten the watching crowd.

Her grandfather's discreet throat-clearing shattered the spell. Ellie tore her eyes away, startled, only to find him watching them with an expression of amused patience, tempered by something warmer, almost understanding. With a subtle tilt of his head, he reminded her that a long line of guests still waited their turn. Ellie's stomach dropped.

Good heavens, had they all witnessed that? The heat in her cheeks surely betrayed every thought racing through her mind. Lord Bennett, however, merely smiled, an almost sheepish curve of his lips, as though he too had only just remembered where they were.

"Forgive me for delaying your other guests, Your Grace," he said smoothly to her grandfather.

Then his attention returned to Ellie. "And forgive me as well, Lady Danielle," he added quietly. "I had not meant to forget myself so completely." Something warm flickered in his eyes.

"But before I move along... may I be so bold as to claim the first two dances of the evening?"

The question lingered between them, heavy with expectation. Ellie suddenly felt the weight of every curious gaze in the hall upon her. Her cheeks burned hotter still. If only the floor would open and swallow her whole. Yet her training held firm. With great effort she managed a small nod, though her voice felt far too fragile to trust.

Lord Bennett's smile deepened, slow and unmistakably pleased. He released her hand at last and stepped aside, allowing the next guests to approach. But as Ellie turned back to the steady stream of introductions, she could not ignore the strange new awareness that lingered in her chest.

Nor the unsettling certainty that, somewhere across the room, Lord Bennett's eyes had not quite left her.

When a brief lull in the procession of guests left them momentarily alone, her grandfather leaned slightly closer, lowering his voice so that only she could hear.

"It seems the Duke of Somerset has caught your attention, Danielle," he murmured. "Do you suppose he is equally smitten?"

Ellie gasped, her head snapping toward him in alarm.

"Grandfather!" Her voice came out in a scandalized whisper, though the flush rising along her cheeks betrayed her all too clearly. "I am not smitten with him. In truth, when we first met, I could scarcely endure his company."

The old duke's eyes twinkled with undisguised amusement. His mouth curved into a slow, knowing smirk that made Ellie immediately suspicious he was enjoying this far too much.

"And yet..." he drawled thoughtfully, stroking his beard as though pondering a matter of great philosophical importance, "it appears you endure him rather well now."

Ellie straightened stiffly beside him, lifting her chin. "I merely tolerate him," she retorted. The words came out more sharply than she intended, too quick, too emphatic. The moment they left her lips, she knew she had betrayed herself. Her grandfather's brows lifted.

"Oh?" he said mildly. "That is a remarkable form of tolerance you possess, my dear. Most young ladies do not blush quite so charmingly while merely tolerating a gentleman."

Ellie shut her eyes in mortification. "Grandfather..."

He chuckled softly, clearly delighted. "I must say, it was quite the spectacle," he continued, leaning closer with conspiratorial cheer. "The way you two stared at one another just now. I feared the poor footmen might faint from the suspense."

Her eyes flew open. "We did no such thing!"

"No?" he asked innocently.

"No," she insisted, though her voice had dropped to a desperate whisper.

"Then I must have imagined the entire hall holding its breath while the Duke of Somerset kissed your hand as though he had forgotten there were two hundred people watching him."

Ellie pressed her lips together, determined not to give him further ammunition. Her grandfather studied her for a moment, clearly fighting the urge to laugh outright.

"Well," he said thoughtfully, "perhaps I misjudged the situation."

She exhaled in relief. "Yes," she said quickly. "You did."

"But if you are not smitten with him," he continued mildly, "then it would seem the poor fellow is entirely alone in his affliction."

Ellie blinked. "What?"

"The way he looks at you," her grandfather went on, perfectly calm, "one might suspect he is rather taken."

Ellie's heart gave a sudden, traitorous flutter. "That is absurd."

"Is it?" he said lightly.

"Yes."

"Mm."

She narrowed her eyes suspiciously. "You are teasing me."

"I?" he replied with great dignity. "Never." But the laughter dancing in his eyes betrayed him.

"I merely observe things as they are."

Ellie folded her arms, though the gesture was somewhat undermined by the continued warmth in her cheeks.

"You are imagining nonsense."

"Perhaps." He paused, then added thoughtfully: "Still, if a duke begins requesting the first two dances before the orchestra has even tuned their instruments, society tends to draw certain conclusions."

Her stomach flipped. "My word," she muttered under her breath. "Everyone must think—"

"Yes," her grandfather said cheerfully. "They probably do."

Ellie groaned softly and shut her eyes again. "I shall never survive this evening."

"Nonsense," he said, patting her gloved hand. "You are doing admirably." Then, with a grin that was far too pleased for her comfort, he added: "Besides... if you truly only tolerate him, the next two dances should be very educational."

Ellie shot him a look of pure exasperation. "Grandfather!"

Mercifully, another wave of guests swept toward them at that moment, interrupting whatever further mischief he might have unleashed. The duke straightened at once, his expression returning to its usual dignified composure as he welcomed the newcomers. Ellie followed suit, offering polite smiles and graceful curtsies. Yet even as she performed her well-practiced courtesies, she could not banish the echo of her grandfather's teasing words. Nor the memory of Lord Bennett's warm smile... and the unsettling way her heart had leapt when his lips brushed her glove.

After Lord Huntington officially declared the ball open, the musicians struck up a lively waltz. Couples eagerly swept onto the floor, silks swirling and jewels glittering beneath the golden chandeliers. Before anyone else could approach Ellie, Lord Bennett strode through the crowd with quiet determination, his gaze fixed solely on her. Without hesitation, and without granting a single rival the chance, he bowed and extended his hand.

"Lady Danielle."

His voice was warm, steady, and impossible to refuse. Her heart fluttered as she placed her gloved hand into his. A moment later, he led her onto the floor, and together they glided into the first measures of the waltz. She had known from their earlier meeting that he was an accomplished dancer, but tonight his focus seemed intent on more than merely guiding her steps. His eyes never left her face, and the intensity of his gaze stole her breath, making her heart falter before it found the rhythm again.

"Have you been enjoying London?" he asked quietly, his words meant for her alone. Ellie managed a small nod.

"I have seen some of it, though I confess I much prefer the country."

He looked as though he might respond, but before he could, a firm tap fell upon his shoulder.

Lord Bennett turned, his expression sharpening, and found himself face-to-face with Prince Carsten.

"Mind if I cut in?" the prince asked. His tone was not courteous but commanding, the demand of a man accustomed to immediate obedience. Bennett's jaw tightened. He glanced at Ellie, silently deferring to her choice. She shook her head, unwilling to yield.

"Actually, I do mind, Your Highness," Bennett replied evenly, unimpressed. The prince's eyes narrowed.

"The question was directed to the lady, not you."

Ellie straightened, her voice firm. "Thank you, Your Highness, but I promised the Duke of Somerset the first two dances."

A murmur rippled through the nearby couples. The music faltered, then ceased altogether as attention fixed upon them. Prince Carsten's voice rose, deliberate and cutting.

"Do you think it wise to refuse a prince who has singled you out?"

Her stomach twisted. Across the room she caught her mother's horrified face, while her father and grandfather looked ready to storm the floor. Yet neither dared risk open offense to a royal. She knew at once what Carsten intended, to corner her, to humiliate her before all of society. Ellie lifted her chin. Though her heart thundered, her voice rang clear.

"As I said, Your Highness, I promised the Duke of Somerset these dances, and I intend to honor that promise. It is never a mistake to keep one's word. What is a mistake, however, is to interrupt a couple mid-dance and demand your own way.

Courtesy, not coercion, governs the ballroom. I accept invitations, not commands. And no lady should be threatened for declining."

A ripple of astonishment swept the assembly, followed swiftly by murmurs of approval. The prince's face darkened.

"I am not accustomed to rejection, Lady Danielle. You would do well to show me the respect I deserve."

Lord Bennett's voice cut in, cool and biting. "Why persist, Your Highness? The lady spoke with perfect clarity. To press further is to insult her."

Before the prince could retort, Ellie stepped firmly between them, unwilling to let tempers ignite.

"Your Highness, not everything bends to your will. I have not refused you outright, only for now, as I am already engaged. Should you wish, you may ask me later."

Carsten sneered. "I do not chase after women. You should be honored I condescended to ask at all. In truth, you hardly deserve my notice, not after your disgraceful dealings with Lord Maughan."

The air froze. Silence descended like a blade. Every gaze in the ballroom fixed upon her. Though his cruelty struck deep, Ellie stood tall.

"I never sought your attention, nor do I desire it now. As for Lord Maughan, his name is not worth repeating. You may attempt to shame me, but I will not cower. Respect must be mutual, and you have shown none tonight." She turned to leave, but the prince seized her arm. "Unhand me at once!" she cried, fury flashing in her eyes.

He leaned close, venom in every word. "You are no lady. Do not forget, your father was disowned for marrying beneath him.

Without your grandfather's desperate bid to restore his heir, you would be nothing."

Gasps echoed through the hall. Though the words cut like knives, Ellie did not falter.

"If nobility means arrogance, cruelty, and prejudice such as yours," she declared, her voice ringing across the ballroom, "then I would rather be an outcast. Your conduct shames not me, but yourself." She wrenched free and swept toward the terrace, her gown whispering across the marble floor.

"Danielle Huntington!" the prince bellowed. "I am not finished with you!"

"That is enough, Prince Carsten." The commanding voice thundered across the ballroom like a crack of thunder. All heads turned. An elderly couple stood framed in the doorway, their presence like a storm breaking over the room. Recognition rippled through the crowd, followed instantly by a collective bow. The Grand Duke and Grand Duchess of England had arrived. Carsten paled.

"Uncle—Aunt—I—"

"You will hold your tongue," the Grand Duke snapped, striding forward, his face carved from stone. "Your behavior tonight is a disgrace to your station. To speak so to a young woman, to lay hands on her, to drag her family through the mud, shameful!"

The Grand Duchess's eyes blazed. "Is this how you wield your rank? A true prince defends ladies. He does not seek to humiliate them."

Carsten stammered, "Forgive me, I did not think—"

"... that anyone of royal blood would witness your cruelty?" his aunt cut in sharply. "We saw enough." Her gaze swept across the room before settling upon Ellie.

"Lady Danielle is not merely the granddaughter of a duke. She is the great-granddaughter of Grand Duke Constantine Huntington and Princess Isadora of Wales. You have insulted your own blood."

The prince flinched, his arrogance collapsing.

"You will leave at once," the Grand Duke commanded. "And you will offer Lady Danielle and her family a formal apology. We shall see to it personally."

"Go," the Grand Duchess added icily. Carsten bowed stiffly and withdrew, the shame of his dismissal clinging to him like a shroud. Turning to Lord Huntington, the Grand Duchess spoke gravely. "We are deeply sorry for our nephew's conduct. We heard mention of a viscount. Would you explain?"

"Of course, Your Graces," the Duke of Essex replied. "If you will allow me, we shall speak in my study." With a nod to his son to oversee the ball, he led the Grand Duke and Grand Duchess away, leaving behind a ballroom thick with whispers. And the unmistakable knowledge that society had just witnessed a battle of wills... and that Lady Danielle Huntington had not merely endured, she had prevailed.

Ellie lingered on the terrace only briefly before the swell of her emotions urged her deeper into the garden. The cool night air wrapped around her like a balm, yet her heart still pounded with the sting of the prince's cruel words. How could Prince Carsten have humiliated her so mercilessly before everyone? What had she ever done to deserve such scorn?

She walked slowly among the clipped hedges and blooming roses, their perfume drifting sweetly through the moonlit air. Gravel crunched softly beneath her slippers as she wandered farther from the glow of the ballroom windows.

At the far edge of the garden, the tall trees tempted her with the mischievous thought of climbing one, just as she had so often done in childhood. For a fleeting moment she almost laughed at herself. But she shook her head. No, that was no longer an option. She was no longer a little girl scrambling into branches to escape the world, but a young lady expected to carry herself with grace and composure before the entire ton.

Still, her spirit longed for release. She wandered until she found a stone bench tucked beneath a flowering arbor, its vines heavy with pale blossoms. Ellie sank onto it with a quiet sigh. Closing her eyes, she let the stillness wrap around her. Only the hum of crickets and the distant strains of music from the ballroom reached her ears. For the first time all evening, she could breathe.

Footsteps crunched softly along the gravel path. Ellie's eyes flew open. Her breath caught when she saw Lord Bennett approaching, his tall frame outlined in silver by the moonlight. Her heart leapt instantly into an unsteady rhythm.

"Your Grace," she whispered, her blue eyes widening as warmth crept across her cheeks. "What are you doing out here?"

He paused a few steps away, studying her with quiet concern before his expression softened into a warm, disarming smile.

"I came to see how you were, Lady Danielle." Then he extended his hand with gentle boldness.

"And," he added lightly, "to ask if we might continue our dance."

Her gaze flickered, torn between composure and the turmoil still churning inside her. She tried to mask her distress, but the softening of his eyes told her she had failed.

"Your Grace, I don't think—"

Before she could finish, he stepped closer and gently took her hand. The brush of his gloved fingers sent a flutter of butterflies tumbling through her stomach. His voice lowered, reassuring and calm.

"Prince Carsten is gone. He will not trouble you further. His aunt and uncle arrived just in time and rebuked him most severely. They sent him away."

She blinked. "His aunt and uncle?"

"Yes." Lord Bennett nodded, his thumb brushing lightly across her knuckles in an absent, soothing gesture. "The Grand Duke and Grand Duchess of England themselves."

Ellie stared at him in astonishment. For a heartbeat she remained silent. Then the corners of her lips twitched as she struggled, and failed, to suppress a smile.

"You are certain of this?" she asked, her tone turning teasing. "You did not, by chance, fight him yourself? Perhaps demand satisfaction and challenge him to a duel? That sounds far more in keeping with your character."

Lord Bennett gaped at her, momentarily speechless. Then he threw back his head and laughed.

"Lady Danielle, I am scandalized!" he declared with mock outrage. "And yet you clearly believe me capable of such reckless heroics."

Color warmed her cheeks, though a mischievous smirk tugged at her lips as she lowered her gaze.

"Well... you did challenge your cousin. A prince seems the next logical step if one is particularly fond of duels." She dared a quick glance at him from the corner of her eye. His grin widened into something roguish. Before she could retreat, he clasped her hand again and drew her slightly closer. She gasped softly as he bent nearer, his voice brushing her ear like velvet.

"I cannot decide which I find more enchanting at this moment," he murmured, "your beauty... or that charming, impish wit of yours."

Ellie's face burned as though the garden itself had caught fire. Her breath caught, and she instinctively stepped back, desperate to regain her composure. Yet even as she did, he straightened at once and offered his arm with effortless gallantry, as though nothing improper had passed between them.

"Shall we return, Lady Danielle?" His eyes held hers, steady, warm, leaving her both unsettled and inexplicably safe. With her heart still racing, Ellie placed her hand upon his arm. Together they turned toward the glowing terrace doors, both knowing that the moment they stepped back into the ballroom, the watchful eyes of London society would be waiting.

All eyes turned toward them as they reentered the ballroom. A hush of murmurs rippled through the crowd, trailing behind them like a wake. Ellie felt the weight of every curious gaze settle upon her shoulders as she crossed the threshold beside Lord Bennett. Had they seen Lord Bennett following her? Had they witnessed her distress before she left the ballroom, or were they simply watching now, waiting to see whether she would return triumphant or humiliated?

The question gnawed at her. Would this moment restore her reputation... or tarnish it forever?

Yet Lord Bennett seemed entirely undisturbed. His posture remained relaxed, his stride confident, as though the assembled nobility of London held no more importance than a passing breeze. More striking still, his attention never left her. His gaze remained fixed upon her face, steady, warm, unwavering, as though the entire ballroom had ceased to exist.

The realization sent an unexpected flutter through her chest. When Ellie finally dared to glance at him, she found him watching her with quiet intensity. The moment their eyes met, he rewarded her with a radiant smile that transformed his features, softening the usual sharpness of his expression. The warmth of it stole her breath. And despite herself, her lips curved in response.

Soon she was smiling too, her earlier distress dissolving beneath the thrill of the moment. Perhaps the whispers around them were not all scandal after all. Perhaps some of them were admiration.

The musicians struck up a lively country dance, the brisk rhythm filling the grand room with cheerful energy. The couples quickly arranged themselves into long lines as the set began. Lord Bennett guided her into place with easy confidence.

"Ready, Lady Danielle?" he asked softly. There was just enough teasing warmth in his voice to coax a reluctant spark of laughter from her. Ellie lifted her gaze to him, though a faint blush had already begun creeping into her cheeks.

"I believe so, Your Grace," she replied, smoothing an imaginary wrinkle from her skirt.

"Excellent," he murmured, offering his arm. "Because I should hate to discover the lady, I nearly fought a prince for is afraid of a simple dance."

Her eyes widened in astonishment, though a hint of amusement tugged at the corners of her mouth.

"You fought no one."

"Not yet," he replied lightly. Ellie arched a brow.

"And pray tell," she said, placing her hand in the crook of his arm, "how exactly would you have fought a royal and made him your victim?"

"That I cannot tell you," Lord Bennett replied smoothly. "A gentleman must be allowed certain secrets. Besides, I would have fought anyone who dared look at you twice."

She nearly stumbled. "That is absurd."

"Is it?" His voice lowered slightly as he guided her toward the floor. "A gentleman must defend his interests."

"Your interests?" she repeated, her tone sharp with disbelief, though her pulse had begun racing. Bennett's lips curved slowly, his gaze settling on her with unsettling intensity.

"Lady Danielle," he said quietly, "you cannot expect a man to remain perfectly civilized when such a lady appears before him."

Ellie felt heat rise in her cheeks again. "You exaggerate shamelessly, Your Grace."

"On the contrary," he replied. "I am exercising remarkable restraint."

They reached the edge of the dance floor as the musicians began the opening notes of the set. Bennett turned toward her and bowed with impeccable elegance before taking her hand.

As he drew her into the dance, he leaned just slightly closer, his voice barely more than a murmur meant only for her.

"Though," he added, a glimmer of mischief returning to his eyes, "should another prince appear tonight... I make no promises."

She laughed despite herself. The music swept them forward. His movements were strong, precise, and graceful. His hand at her back was steady without ever being possessive, guiding her through each turn and figure with quiet assurance. Soon Ellie found herself laughing as she spun through the lively steps, the earlier tension draining away with each pass down the line. Her cheeks glowed, not from embarrassment this time, but from exhilaration. The music lifted her spirits like a bright wind. And through it all, Lord Bennett's attention remained wholly upon her.

Whenever their paths crossed again within the dance, his eyes found hers instantly, as though the crowded ballroom contained no one else. A waltz followed swiftly after. As the couples paired off again, he stepped toward her without hesitation, drawing her smoothly into the sweeping rhythm of the music.

They glided across the polished floor, turning gracefully beneath the golden chandeliers. Even the Duke of Somerset, so often formal and reserved, seemed genuinely delighted. Laughter tugged openly at the corners of his mouth now, and the warmth in his eyes told her he was enjoying every moment.

Ellie felt lighter than she had in weeks. For the first time since Richard's departure, the ache in her chest loosened its grip. Not entirely. But enough. Enough that she could breathe again. Enough that she could laugh. Enough that when Lord Bennett's gaze lingered on her just a fraction too long, her heart no longer shrank away from the feeling.

Both dances ended far too quickly for Ellie's liking. The final notes faded, and the couples slowed reluctantly to a halt. For a fleeting instant, neither she nor Lord Bennett moved. Then reality returned. Etiquette, after all, demanded restraint. To dance more than two sets with the same gentleman would be considered highly improper, unless they were formally engaged.

21
A Proposal Without Love

Reluctantly, Lord Bennett led her back to where her parents waited. Ellie's heart whispered its disappointment. How she wished for just one more turn about the floor with him. The duke bowed and, with impeccable courtesy, withdrew.

The instant he was gone, Ellie felt her mother's arms encircle her. She braced herself for the reprimand she expected, but none came. Her mother simply held her tightly, the embrace both gentle and fierce.

"Mama..." Ellie began hesitantly, her voice low. "Please forgive me for my behavior earlier. I know how much you dislike it when I lose my temper. You are right, it is not ladylike. But I could not endure that prince's arrogance, nor the insults he cast upon you, Papa, and our family. I saw Papa and Grandfather about to intervene, and I feared what might happen if they angered him further. So, I thought it better if I spoke instead."

Her mother's hand rose tenderly to Ellie's cheek. "Oh, darling," she murmured, her eyes shining with unshed tears, "I am not upset with you. On the contrary, I am touched that you defended us so fiercely. I am not ashamed of where I came from, but it wounds me still when others sneer at it. To hear you speak with such conviction on our behalf…" Her voice broke softly. "It means more to me than you know."

Ellie blinked in astonishment. Her mother was rarely one for outward displays of emotion, and the sight of her misty eyes was both startling and deeply moving.

"You are not angry with me?" she whispered. Before her mother could answer, her father stepped forward and drew Ellie into a strong embrace.

"No, child. We are proud of you. You proved tonight that you have the heart and courage required to be the next Duchess of Essex. Yes, you possess a fiery spirit," he added with a warm chuckle, "but you tempered it with dignity. You stood your ground without lowering yourself to rudeness, and when the prince pressed too far, you chose to walk away. That, Danielle, is grace under fire."

A deep, resonant voice sounded from behind them. "You responded exactly as you should, young lady."

Ellie turned in surprise and found herself face-to-face with the Grand Duke and Grand Duchess. Her breath caught. How long had they been standing nearby? The Grand Duke's expression was firm, yet unmistakable approval shone in his eyes.

"Our nephew was utterly out of line. He is far too accustomed to cow others with his title. But you," he inclined his head with quiet admiration," reminded him that even a prince cannot trample another's dignity unchecked."

The Grand Duchess smiled warmly, her gaze softening as it fell upon Ellie.

"Indeed. Too many young ladies shrink before him, dazzled or frightened by his rank. It is refreshing to see a beautiful young woman with enough strength of character to defend herself and her family with both courage and composure. You did not allow him to diminish you, and that is rare."

Ellie's cheeks warmed beneath their praise. She dropped into a deep curtsy.

"Thank you, Your Graces," she said sincerely. Then, with a sudden sparkle in her eyes, the Grand Duchess turned toward her husband.

"Your Grace, I believe you should dance with Lady Danielle and show her that not all royals are rude and arrogant."

Before Ellie could protest, the duchess gently took her hand and drew her to her feet once more.

"There is no need for modesty, child," she whispered warmly. The orchestra began the opening strains of a waltz. The Grand Duke stepped forward, bowing with regal grace, though a glimmer of mischief danced in his eyes.

"Lady Danielle," he said solemnly, yet with unmistakable warmth, "would you do me the honor of this dance? I promise, unlike certain princes of my acquaintance, I know how to ask politely."

A ripple of laughter stirred among the nearest guests. Ellie's cheeks flushed again, though this time with relief rather than embarrassment. She curtsied gracefully, her lips curving into a soft smile.

"With great pleasure, Your Grace."

As he led her onto the floor, the Grand Duke bent slightly closer, his voice pitched for her ears alone.

"Do not let Carsten trouble you another moment, child. His bark is louder than his bite, and after tonight, he will think twice before daring to cross you again." His eyes twinkled. "Besides, if he gives you further offense, you have only to call upon me, and I will remind him that princes, too, can be put in their place."

Ellie felt a lightness spread through her chest. As she placed her hand in his and stepped into the dance, the lingering weight of the evening lifted at last. For the first time that night, she truly believed she had allies strong enough to shield her, yet wise enough to trust her to stand her ground.

The next few weeks slipped by in a whirlwind of engagements. Ellie's days filled quickly with invitations to balls, dinners, musicales, and an endless succession of social gatherings. She soon learned that London society possessed its own intricate language, one spoken not only in words, but in glances, gestures, and carefully measured smiles.

Before long, she could distinguish which young ladies greeted her with genuine warmth and the promise of friendship, and which regarded her with thinly veiled envy or suspicion. Some sought to draw close in hopes of sharing her rising influence; others watched her carefully, as though waiting for the slightest misstep that might topple her from favor.

Though the memory of her confrontation with Prince Carsten still lingered in whispered conversations, no apology was ever offered. The promised act of contrition never came. Instead, the Grand Duke and Grand Duchess graciously invited Ellie and her grandfather to dine privately with them on several occasions, a gesture that seemed less an attempt to smooth over scandal than a quiet declaration of support. The prince himself was conspicuously absent from every gathering.

Their Graces' displeasure was unmistakable, and though they were clearly angered by his conduct, their restrained reactions suggested this was hardly the first time their nephew had tested the limits of their patience.

If Prince Carsten remained something of a thorn in society's side, Lord Bennett proved quite the opposite. He called upon Ellie several times during those weeks, his attentions always polite, considerate, and unexpectedly charming. Gone was the vexing, arrogant young man she had once disliked so fiercely. In his place stood a gentleman of wit and easy confidence, one who seemed genuinely amused by the world around him and who, to Ellie's surprise, appeared to take great pleasure in her company. He never sought to overshadow her in conversation, nor did he display the overbearing pride she had once attributed to him.

Instead, he listened, truly listened, to what she said, answering her thoughts with a teasing intelligence that often left her laughing before she realized why. More than once, she caught herself recalling his smile long after he had departed. To her own astonishment, Ellie began to look forward to his visits with a quiet anticipation she dared not confess aloud.

During these shifting tides of society, the Viscount of Bromley extended an invitation of his own. He proposed a modest gathering, a picnic upon his estate just beyond the city. Unlike the glittering grandeur of London's assemblies, the event promised simplicity: fresh air, gardens, and informal company.

Yet the invitation carried a subtle complication. Bromley lacked both the wealth and the social connections required to host a truly fashionable affair. His gathering would be small, perhaps even awkwardly arranged by comparison with the opulent entertainments Ellie had recently attended. She hesitated. To accept might appear a step down in society's careful hierarchy. But to decline would be equally dangerous.

Such a refusal might easily be interpreted as a deliberate slight, an insult not only to the viscount himself but also to those who counted themselves among his allies. And in London society, perceived offenses often carried consequences far heavier than the offense itself. In a world where reputation could rise or fall on the smallest gesture, Ellie understood all too well the delicate balance she was expected to maintain.

It was a radiant summer afternoon when Ellie and her grandfather's carriage rolled up the long drive of the Maughan estate. Sunlight spilled across the sweeping lawns, and the grounds were already dotted with guests strolling leisurely through the gardens or gathered in cheerful clusters beneath the shade of broad, ancient oaks. Laughter drifted through the warm air, mingling with the distant notes of a small string ensemble stationed near the terrace.

As the driver helped Ellie down from the carriage, she smoothed the folds of her gown and lifted her gaze, only to catch sight of Lord Bennett dismounting his horse nearby. The moment his eyes found hers, he smiled. Not the polite, reserved smile of a gentleman greeting an acquaintance, but something far warmer, broad, genuine, and entirely unguarded. Ellie's heart leapt at once, stealing her breath for a fleeting instant.

The pleasant flutter did not last long. Among the ladies already assembled, none showed the slightest inclination toward friendship. They greeted her with impeccable courtesy whenever gentlemen were present, curtsying gracefully, offering polite compliments, and addressing her with careful civility. But the moment the gentlemen turned away, their expressions hardened. Some glanced at her with poorly concealed envy. Others regarded her with open disdain, their smiles tightening into thin, brittle lines. Whispers trailed in her wake.

More than once she heard a soft burst of laughter that carried an unmistakable edge of malice.

Ellie, however, refused to let it trouble her. If anything, their behavior confirmed precisely what she had already begun to suspect about certain corners of London society. She remained close to her grandfather as they made their way across the lawn, greeting the viscount with measured courtesy. Lord Bennett, ever attentive, appeared at her side before she had even crossed the garden.

"Lady Danielle," he greeted her warmly, inclining his head with familiar ease. "You look as though you might be in need of a loyal ally this afternoon."

Ellie's lips curved faintly. "You may be correct, Your Grace."

Several of the young women nearby cast sharp, jealous glances in their direction. One or two made an obvious attempt to draw the Duke of Somerset's attention, laughing too brightly, arranging themselves with calculated grace along the path, and offering smiles meant to entice him away from Ellie's side. Yet Lord Bennett seemed entirely impervious to their efforts. Not once did his attention wander. His gaze remained steadily upon Ellie, as though he saw through every false smile and simpering glance around them.

She nearly laughed at their transparent schemes. But instead, she composed her features into a calm and dignified expression, refusing to grant her rivals the satisfaction of seeing her amused.

They had scarcely chosen a place to sit when two figures approached. Lord Bennett stiffened at once, tension radiating through him. Ellie turned and nearly groaned aloud. Prince Carsten, wearing his familiar scowl, stood before them. She rose quickly, intending to excuse herself, but it was too late.

"Prince Carsten," she said, offering a brief nod and a curtsy that could scarcely be called more than perfunctory.

"Miss Huntington," he replied coldly, his disdain unmistakable. Her chin lifted a fraction.

"It is *Lady Danielle* to you," she returned, indignation heating her chest. His persistent disrespect cut more deeply than she cared to admit. Lord Bennett's voice cut through the moment like drawn steel.

"I believe you owe Lady Danielle an apology."

The prince merely scoffed, his lip curling with contempt. Ellie placed a light hand upon Lord Bennett's arm, silently urging him not to provoke the prince further. The tension between the two men was already thick enough to choke the air. At that moment, the second young man stepped forward, bowing with genuine grace.

"Perhaps I should introduce myself. I am Carsten's elder brother, Prince Edward." His smile was warm, an immediate and striking contrast to his brother's sneer. Ellie dipped into a deeper curtsy.

"It is a pleasure to make your acquaintance, Your Highness."

"How charming," Carsten spat, his voice dripping with contempt. Then, with sudden violence, he seized Ellie's arm and yanked her toward him. "You are kind and respectful to my brother," he sneered, "yet a wench to me."

"Release the lady at once," Lord Bennett snapped, his fists curling as though only seconds separated him from striking the prince. Edward moved swiftly between them, his tone sharp as a blade.

"That is enough, Brother. Leave now. Your manners are disgraceful." His gaze hardened. "I have heard of your dealings with Lady Danielle, and I do not blame her in the least for refusing you courtesy. Do you know why Father never permits you to travel abroad? Because you shame our parents at every turn with your temper and arrogance." He shoved Carsten back a pace. "Now go."

For one tense moment it seemed the younger prince might strike his brother. But after glancing at the gathering crowd, many of whom had paused to watch, he scoffed contemptuously and stalked back toward the house.

Ellie exhaled shakily, relief mingling with simmering anger. She turned to Lord Bennett with a small, grateful smile, silently thanking him for his restraint. Edward inclined his head apologetically.

"I beg your pardon, Lady Danielle, for my brother's behavior. He has ever been difficult, but of late his conduct has grown intolerable."

Ellie looked up at him earnestly. "Why does he despise me so? I have done nothing to him."

The prince shook his head. "I do not believe his anger is truly yours to bear. He cannot abide being put in his place, least of all by a lady of spirit. His hatred is nothing but wounded pride." He paused, then offered her his arm. "May I speak with you privately?"

Ellie glanced toward Lord Bennett. Though clearly reluctant, he gave a curt nod and stepped aside. Accepting Edward's arm, she allowed him to lead her along a shaded path toward the far edge of the estate, where a quiet lake shimmered beneath the afternoon sun. They walked in silence for several moments before the prince cleared his throat.

"You may wonder why I wished to speak with you," he began. "Upon our return, my parents and I were informed of the treatment you endured at my brother's hands, and of the demands Lord Maughan seeks to impose upon you."

Ellie's brows drew together.

"We appealed at once to Parliament," Edward continued, "but I fear my brother has already influenced them, bribery, no doubt. They remain firm in their decision: a woman must be married to assume land, estate, and title."

Ellie felt her stomach drop.

"With the Queen's intervention," he added, "we secured one concession. You need only be engaged, not yet married, by the viscount's one-and-twentieth birthday. But that," he finished quietly, "was all we could achieve."

Ellie gasped, her hands clenching at her sides. "How is that just? Only weeks ago, I scarcely knew of my inheritance, and now my grandfather must soon take up his duties as Grand Duke."

Edward's expression softened with sympathy. "It is not fair, Lady Danielle. I regret it deeply. I might petition for a delay in your grandfather's obligations at court, but it will not alter the core decree."

Her voice trembled with indignation. "Lord Maughan is no blood relation to my grandfather. He is kin only through my late grandmother. This is absurd."

"I understand your anger," Edward said gently, "but the council has spoken. You have but one week before the viscount comes of age." He paused. "You and Lord Bennett may wish to make your engagement official."

Ellie felt the ground sway beneath her. Heat rushed to her cheeks.

"Lord Bennett and I? But... we are not courting. There is no understanding between us."

Edward looked genuinely surprised. "I would not have guessed it. He is so protective of you. I would almost swear he harbors a deep affection."

Ellie hesitated. "We have only just learned to be friends," she said quietly. "Not long ago we could hardly bear each other. I cannot imagine he would ever consider—"

Edward's brows lifted thoughtfully. A long silence followed. Then he spoke, almost abruptly.

"Perhaps, then, you and I should marry."

Ellie stared at him as crimson flooded her cheeks. "Pardon me?"

He stopped walking and turned toward her. His hand lifted gently to brush a loose strand of hair from her temple.

"I know it is not your dream," he said softly, "and we are not in love. But such feelings might grow with time. You are beautiful, Lady Danielle, and I would treat you with honor."

His gaze remained steady. "With our marriage, the duchy would remain in your family, beyond Lord Maughan's grasp."

Ellie trembled faintly. His words were kind. His manner sincere. Yet her heart recoiled. Was this truly the choice before her? Duty... in place of love?

"You should not sacrifice yourself for me," she whispered. "We ought to marry for love."

Edward gave a faint smile. "Few of us in our station are granted that luxury. We must all sacrifice something." He spoke gently, but without hesitation.

"I offer companionship, respect, and perhaps, in time, affection. We need not marry immediately. But once our engagement is declared, it must end in marriage, or Maughan will inherit everything."

Ellie's thoughts spun. An unexpected memory rose in her mind, Lord Bennett's kiss from those earlier days when they had still despised one another. It had been reckless, infuriating... and yet it had left her breathless, her heart racing in ways she had never understood.

Edward leaned closer then and pressed a brief kiss to her lips. It was... nothing. No spark. No warmth. No flutter of breath or trembling pulse. Only emptiness. And yet he was a prince, handsome, honorable, promising kindness. Could she refuse such an offer when her family's future hung in balance? Sensing her turmoil, Edward gently lifted her chin until her eyes met his.

"I know it is much to ask. But think on it. We can keep the matter private for now." His voice softened. "At the viscount's birthday, we will make the announcement together." He studied her carefully. "Does this seem agreeable?"

Her breath trembled as she searched his earnest face. Slowly, reluctantly, she inclined her head.

"It is settled, then." Edward smiled, as though he had secured a victory. He pressed a light kiss to her forehead. Ellie forced a smile in return. But as they turned back toward the estate, her heart felt heavier than ever.

Prince Edward had only just begun to turn back toward the house when his eyes widened in sudden alarm. Before Ellie could even ask what he had seen, he reacted. Without a word, he seized her by the waist and dragged her with him as he hurled himself backward into the lake. A heartbeat later, the sharp crack of gunfire shattered the tranquil summer air. One, two, then several more shots rang out in rapid succession, the echoes rolling across the estate and scattering birds from the nearby trees.

The plunge stole Ellie's breath. Cold water closed over her head, choking and blinding her as the sudden shock of it sent her body into wild panic. Her skirts tangled around her legs, heavy and dragging as she fought to surface. When she finally broke through the water, sputtering and gasping, the world spun around her in a blur of sunlight and rippling waves. For a moment she heard nothing but the pounding of her own heart. Then she saw him. A dark figure was retreating quickly over the crest of a distant hill beyond Lord Maughan's property.

For the briefest instant, the sunlight struck the man's profile, just long enough for dread to coil tightly in her stomach before he turned and fled. She knew that face. She had seen it before. Her heart thundered violently. Frantically she searched the water around her.

"Your Highness!" she cried hoarsely. Edward surfaced only a few feet away, coughing violently as he struggled against the weight of his sodden coat. Water streamed down his face as he fought to regain his breath.

Panic surged through her. Stumbling through the shallows, she splashed toward him, the mud sucking at her shoes as she seized his hand and pulled him toward the bank. Together they struggled onto the muddy shore, soaked and breathless. Ellie dropped to her knees beside him at once, trembling violently. Her hands flew across his coat and chest in frantic haste, searching desperately for blood or wounds.

"Are you hurt?" she cried, her voice breaking. "Prince Edward, are you hurt?"

He rasped something she could not hear, her terror roaring too loudly in her ears. At last, he caught her wrists and gently but firmly stilled her hands. Then he lifted both palms to cradle her face, forcing her wide, panicked eyes to meet his.

"I am fine," he said steadily, despite the water streaming down his face. "None of the bullets struck me."

For a moment Ellie could only stare at him. Then relief crashed over her with overwhelming force. Her breath shuddered. Her vision blurred.

"Thank goodness..." she whispered faintly. The tension that had held her upright drained away all at once. The world tilted. And before she could stop it, darkness swept over her as she collapsed forward into unconsciousness.

22

The Ball of False Smiles

Edward lunged toward her, but he was a fraction too late. Another figure appeared, swift, sure, commanding. Lord Bennett. He reached her just as her knees buckled, catching Ellie in his arms before she could strike the ground. One strong arm swept around her back while the other steadied her shoulders, lifting her against his chest as though she weighed nothing at all. For a heartbeat he did not move. His jaw was set in grim determination, his eyes blazing with something far deeper than mere concern. Then he turned and strode back across the garden.

The guests scattered instinctively before him. Gasps and frightened whispers rippled through the gathering as people stepped aside, startled by the fierce urgency in his expression. He paid them no attention. All that seemed to exist in that moment was the woman in his arms.

"Fetch a doctor at once!" Edward's voice rang sharply across the lawns, cutting through the rising commotion. Servants scattered at a run. Ellie stirred faintly, her lashes fluttering. The world returned slowly, first as a blur of sunlight and shadows, then as shapes and voices that gradually settled into focus. The warmth of strong arms held her firmly, steady and unyielding.

When her vision cleared, she found herself gazing upward into the stern, striking features of the Duke of Somerset.

Her breath caught. Her heart stumbled over itself. For a moment she could not look away. His dark eyes, so often cool and composed, were filled now with unmistakable worry. The sharp lines of his face were drawn tight with tension as he searched her face, as though afraid of what he might find.

"What happened?" she whispered faintly. His answering smile was meant to reassure her. But she saw the truth beneath it. The fear. The unmistakable fear of a man who had come dangerously close to losing her.

"You fainted," he said quietly. His voice was softer than she had ever heard it before. Then his gaze dropped suddenly to her arm, and his expression hardened. "And I fear a shot grazed you."

Ellie followed his glance. A gasp escaped her lips. Her gown was torn at the sleeve, the delicate fabric stained dark with blood. For a moment she felt nothing but numb disbelief. Then the pain came. A searing burn flared across her arm, sharp and sudden enough to steal the breath from her lungs. She bit down hard on her lip, refusing to cry out before the many watching eyes gathered around them.

Lord Bennett noticed at once. His arms tightened instinctively around her, drawing her closer against him as though he could shield her from every danger that threatened. His jaw clenched.

"The physician will be here soon," he promised, his voice low but fierce with conviction. His hand shifted slightly, steadying her more securely against him. "You are safe now."

Ellie felt the steady strength of him beneath her cheek, the powerful rhythm of his heartbeat pulsing through his chest. *Safe.*

The word settled over her like a fragile shield. Exhaustion and shock washed over her in waves. Unable to resist the comfort, she let her head rest fully against his shoulder, her fingers curling weakly into the fabric of his coat.

Her pulse still raced with fear and confusion. Someone had tried to kill her. And deep in her heart, beneath the lingering warmth of Bennett's arms, a chilling certainty began to form. This would not be the last attempt.

Ellie stirred awake to the low murmur of the butler's voice in the hall, announcing her grandfather's arrival. She had not meant to fall asleep, but exhaustion and the shock of the afternoon had claimed her the moment her head touched the pillow.

As she shifted slightly beneath the covers, a sharp tug of pain shot through her arm. A ragged breath escaped her before she could stop it, the cry nearly breaking free before she bit it back. The wound still burned fiercely, as though the bullet had only just grazed her.

The door opened, and her grandfather filled the threshold. His tall frame seemed even more imposing than usual, yet the moment his eyes fell upon her, his expression softened. Worry lingered heavily in the lines of his face, though something darker simmered beneath it, anger carefully held in check.

"How are you feeling, Danielle?" he asked, his voice gentle despite the tension in it.

"It still burns," she admitted softly. Then, after a pause, her wide, searching eyes lifted to his. "Where were you?"

He exhaled slowly, the breath leaving him as though the question carried its own weight. Crossing the room, he moved to her bedside and lowered himself into the chair beside her.

"I was speaking with several men," he said quietly, "trying to learn why someone would take aim at you, and at Prince Edward."

Her heart skipped. "Has the man been arrested?" she asked quickly, hope trembling in her voice. Her grandfather shook his head.

"No."

The single word hung heavily in the air. His expression darkened as he continued.

"He vanished the moment the shots were fired. None of the guests caught a clear look at him. By the time the servants and footmen gave chase, he had already disappeared beyond the hills."

Ellie felt her pulse quicken. Carefully, despite the pain, she pushed herself higher against the pillows.

"I saw his face," she blurted, urgency sharpening her voice. "Only for an instant, but I did see him. He looked familiar. I know I've seen him before... I simply cannot remember where."

Her grandfather's eyes narrowed thoughtfully. He reached for her hand, resting his own firmly over it. His grip was steady and reassuring, grounding her racing thoughts.

"Then we shall find him together," he said with quiet certainty. "Your memory will return. And when it does, justice will follow."

Ellie leaned slightly into his touch, the tremor in her chest easing beneath the warmth of his presence. Yet even as her eyes drifted closed again, the image of that fleeting face on the hillside lingered in her mind, sharp, haunting, and maddeningly familiar. Somewhere in the depths of her memory, she knew the answer waited. And when it surfaced, it would change everything.

Ellie jolted awake with a gasp, as though torn from a nightmare. A sharp sting flared in her arm, and when she instinctively reached for it, her fingers came away wet with fresh blood. The bandages had loosened during her restless sleep, and the wound throbbed as if aflame. The pain pulsed through her arm in steady waves, sharp enough to make her breath hitch.

With trembling hands, she poured herself a glass of water from the bedside carafe. The cool liquid steadied her for only a moment. Then memory struck. Her eyes widened. The glass slipped in her grasp, sloshing water across the table as the realization crashed over her. She knew that face.

The man who had raised the pistol and fired at her and Prince Edward, she had seen him before. On the very night of her arrival, when she first stepped into Lord Ainsworth's house. He had been there. One of the visitors. One of the cruel men who had tormented Eleanor.

A shudder tore through her as the truth settled like ice in her chest. Tears pricked at the corners of her eyes. The nightmare of Lord Ainsworth was not finished. Though he now sat imprisoned, stripped of title and power, his shadow still reached for them. But why aim at Prince Edward? And why at her? Were both bullets meant for them, or only for one?

Her mind raced, chasing possibilities that made her stomach churn. Jonathan Ainsworth was disgraced and locked away. Yet somehow his influence still lingered beyond the prison walls.

Were there men still loyal enough to carry out his vengeance? What could they possibly hope to gain now, when everything had been taken from him?

Ellie pressed a shaking hand to her forehead, trying to quiet the sickening rush of fear. She did not even know the man's name. But Eleanor would. Eleanor had suffered under Ainsworth and his circle of companions. If this man had been among them, she would not have forgotten his face. The thought of disturbing her cousin, still fragile after all she had endured, filled Ellie with guilt.

Yet there was no choice. The danger was too great. They had to uncover who this man was if they hoped to stop him.

Ignoring the throbbing pain in her arm, she swung her legs over the side of the bed and stood. Her knees wavered slightly beneath her, but her resolve held firm. She rang sharply for her chambermaid. The girl entered at once, only to halt in alarm at the sight of her mistress, pale, shaken, and still clutching her wounded arm.

"My Lady—!"

"Wake one of the men," Ellie said breathlessly. "My grandfather must be told at once."

The maid curtsied quickly and hurried from the room. Within minutes the Duke entered, his expression taut with concern as he crossed the chamber in long strides.

"What is it, Danielle?" he asked, coming directly to her side. Ellie told him everything. How the memory had returned to her in a sudden flash. How the man with the pistol had been among Ainsworth's companions that first dreadful night. How certain she was that Eleanor would recognize him and know his name.

As she spoke, her grandfather's expression hardened. A muscle ticked along his jaw as anger tightened his features.

"Then we must act at once," he said firmly. Turning toward the servant who still hovered near the door, he gave a sharp command. "Send an express immediately to the Duke of Devon. Lady Ainsworth must be consulted without delay."

"Yes, Your Grace." The servant bowed and hurried off down the corridor. Silence settled heavily in the chamber once he was gone. Ellie sank slowly into a chair, her arm throbbing and her pulse still racing. Now there was nothing left to do but wait. Wait for Eleanor's answer. Wait for a name to be given to the face that haunted her. Until then, one chilling certainty remained. Whoever that man was, he was still out there.

Eleanor's letter arrived two days later, written in her familiar, delicate hand. Though her words were brief, they carried considerable weight. She named two gentlemen who had been present on that dreadful evening when Ellie first set foot in the Ainsworth estate, two men she remembered with painful clarity. Their identities gave shape to Ellie's fears and sharpened her sense of urgency.

Her grandfather wasted no time. Discreet inquiries were made, investigators quietly dispatched into the city to track both men. Within days, word returned. The first, Lord Darius Adams, Viscount of Rochester, had vanished. Neither his butler nor his steward could offer any explanation. Both swore they had not seen their master in weeks, their evasive answers leaving Ellie with the chilling impression that they either knew far more than they admitted… or that their employer had disappeared deliberately.

The second man, a baron of little renown, was still in residence. Her grandfather arranged a private meeting, and Ellie accompanied him. Yet the encounter proved disappointingly fruitless. The baron appeared genuinely bewildered by their questions and denied any knowledge of the shooting or of Ainsworth's continued schemes. Though courteous, he offered them nothing of value. Ellie left the interview with a hollow sense of futility.

The days that followed weighed heavily upon her. Each morning, she awoke with renewed hope that fresh news might arrive, and each evening she retired with her spirits a little lower than before. Restlessness gnawed at her until she felt she could scarcely breathe within the gilded walls of her grandfather's London townhouse.

Prince Edward called twice during those uneasy days. He was every inch the charming and attentive gentleman, and Ellie could not deny that she liked him well enough. His conversation was easy, his manners thoughtful, and his concern for her situation appeared entirely sincere. Yet whenever the thought of their possible marriage crossed her mind, her stomach twisted as though she had swallowed something bitter. Affection was not love. And the idea of pledging her future to a man out of convenience alone filled her with a dread so sharp she sometimes feared she might be ill.

She longed, desperately, achingly, for the quiet of Darlington: for the rolling hills and familiar air, for the freedom to wander among the trees without the constant scrutiny of London society. More than once she found herself wishing she could turn back time, return to the life she had known before titles, politics, and dangerous intrigue had swept her into their current. But even as the longing burned within her, Ellie knew such wishes were futile. Nothing would ever be the same again.

And then, like a shadow creeping slowly at the edge of her thoughts, another question began to trouble her. Why was Lord Maughan so determined to seize her grandfather's duchy? His own estate was far from modest. She had heard it praised often for its prosperity and order. His household appeared well managed, his staff loyal and efficient. What more could he possibly want? Was it merely the hunger for greater wealth? The pride of a higher title? The shallow ambition of hearing himself addressed as *duke* rather than *viscount*? Or was something darker hidden beneath it all, something she had yet to uncover?

The day of the last ball of the Season dawned bright, though Ellie scarcely noticed the sunlight streaming through her windows. She moved through the hours as if in a dream, quiet, subdued, scarcely touching her breakfast and answering conversation only when politeness demanded it. Her heart had been racing since the moment she woke, and a knot of dread sat so firmly in her stomach that even the thought of food made her queasy.

Her grandfather observed her with quiet concern. More than once his gaze lingered on her with a tenderness that only deepened her guilt, yet he pressed her on nothing. He made no mention of the looming prospect of her engagement, nor of the announcement everyone expected. Instead, he spoke of lighter things, humorous stories from his youth, memories of a long-ago hunting trip, gentle remarks about the weather and the guests they would likely encounter that evening. Ellie knew his choice of topics was deliberate, a kindness meant to ease her mind. And she was grateful for it.

The weight of her secret understanding with Prince Edward already consumed her thoughts. To speak of it aloud might have broken her resolve entirely. She could not tell her grandfather, not yet. He was clearly anticipating some revelation, perhaps even an announcement, but she clung to silence. To voice the truth would make it all too real.

At last, the time came to prepare. Her chambermaid and several of the household's female servants gathered eagerly, tending to her as though she were their own daughter or sister. They worked with devoted care, determined to make her shine for what might prove the most important evening of her young life.

When they had finished, Ellie could scarcely recognize the figure gazing back at her from the looking glass. The gown was a masterpiece of dark emerald silk, the bodice cut to flatter her slender figure, the rich fabric catching the light with every subtle movement. A pair of pristine white gloves reached nearly to her elbows, their simplicity lending the perfect note of elegance.

Her hair had been arranged with meticulous care, braided and pinned into an intricate knot at the back of her head, while two delicate curls framed her face, softening her features and drawing attention to the clear brilliance of her blue eyes.

23

Whispers in the Green House

When she descended the wide staircase, a hush fell instantly over the hall. Several of the male servants forgot themselves entirely. One footman stood frozen with the door half-open, another nearly dropped the silver tray he carried, and more than one pair of eyes widened in open admiration. Their composure returned only slowly, though the ripple of astonishment passing through the household could not be hidden.

Ellie felt heat rush to her cheeks and lowered her gaze at once, wishing she might vanish beneath the polished marble floor. Yet even so, she sensed the quiet awe that followed her as she moved down the final steps.

At the foot of the staircase stood her grandfather. He looked every inch the Grand Duke, distinguished and commanding, his evening attire lending him an air of quiet, unshakable authority. The silver at his temples caught the lamplight, and the set of his shoulders spoke of a man long accustomed to carrying responsibility without faltering. Yet when his eyes met hers, all that stately composure softened. A smile spread slowly across his face, warm and proud, almost fatherly.

For a moment he simply looked at her, as though seeing not merely the young lady before him but the girl she had been weeks ago. Then he bowed with courtly grace and extended his arm.

"My dear Danielle," he said softly, admiration threading his voice, "you are quite breathtaking tonight."

Ellie felt the compliment warm her far more deeply than the servants' astonished stares had done. With a shy smile, she slipped her gloved hand into the crook of his elbow. Her heart still hammered beneath the emerald silk. In that quiet moment, despite the heavy dread pressing upon her thoughts, gratitude swelled within her chest. Once, she had believed him distant, stern, perhaps even unkind. But now she knew him differently.

She knew him as a man capable of tenderness, loyalty, and remarkable strength in the face of scandal and danger. A man who had defended her without hesitation, who had stood beside her when others might have faltered. And tonight, as she prepared to step once more into the glittering lion's den of London society, Ellie realized she could not have asked for a steadier, or more steadfast, companion at her side.

When the carriage rolled to a halt before the castle where Prince Carsten and his family resided, Ellie braced herself for a cold reception. Yet to her surprise, their welcome was warm, almost overly so. Even Prince Carsten, whose disdain for her had been constant, stepped forward with a smile upon his lips and a show of enthusiasm that immediately stirred her suspicion. His sudden politeness did not reassure her. It unsettled her.

Prince Edward, gracious as ever, offered her his arm and escorted her into the grand ballroom. Chandeliers glittered overhead, casting warm golden light across the polished marble floors and illuminating gowns of every color imaginable. The room shimmered with elegance and expectation.

Yet Ellie scarcely noticed the splendor. Her gaze was drawn instantly to a familiar figure across the room. Lord Bennett. The moment their eyes met, heat rushed to her cheeks. His intent expression sent her heart skipping wildly, and she had to wrench her gaze away, sharply reminding herself of the man whose arm she rested upon. Prince Edward's steady presence calmed her outward composure, but it did nothing to quiet the restless flutter rising in her chest.

"Will you do me the honor of opening the ball with me?" Edward asked softly. His brother might have been the host, but everyone knew Carsten loathed dancing and rarely participated. Ellie curtsied gracefully and accepted.

The orchestra swelled into the opening waltz, and soon they were gliding across the floor. Edward was an elegant partner, composed, attentive, and perfectly practiced, and for a short time Ellie allowed herself to be carried along by the music. But the moment the dance ended, she found herself surrounded by eager young men, each vying for the next dance. Lord Maughan reached her first.

Suppressing a sigh, Ellie forced a polite smile as he led her into a lively country dance. To her surprise, he proved both skilled and enthusiastic. Against her will, laughter escaped her when he lifted her high during a swift turn of the set. For a fleeting moment she forgot her dread entirely, her smile lighting her face. When he lowered her safely back to the floor, his lips curved with quiet amusement.

"I believe that is the first time you have ever smiled at me, Lady Danielle."

Ellie's mirth vanished instantly. "It is not as though you have given me many reasons to, My Lord," she replied coolly. "From the moment we met, you have insulted and opposed me. You and Prince Carsten are pressuring me into a marriage I do not want, threatening my inheritance and my very future. Men inherit titles without question, yet I must fight for what is rightfully mine, only to be told it will vanish unless I wed. Tell me, where is the fairness in that?"

To her astonishment, Lord Maughan nodded gravely. "You are right," he said quietly. "It is not fair."

Ellie faltered, genuinely startled. Searching his face, she found no mockery, only something thoughtful, almost troubled, though a faint trace of amusement still lingered at the corner of his mouth.

"Why are you looking at me like that?" he asked with a half-grin.

"Because your sudden kindness unsettles me," she answered bluntly. "Prince Carsten greeted me with smiles as well this evening. It feels as though I am surrounded by snakes pretending not to strike." Her gaze flicked anxiously around the ballroom. "You did not hire another assassin, did you? Is someone here to kill me again?"

Lord Maughan looked genuinely horrified. "You think I would hire someone to kill you?" He reached out and gently lifted her chin so that she had no choice but to meet his eyes. His expression was not mocking but wounded, almost incredulous.

"I don't know who is responsible," Ellie whispered. "But I know Prince Carsten is involved. Prince Edward swore the assassin's aim was at me, not him. Why? Why am I such a threat? If I do not announce an engagement tonight, everything goes to you regardless. Why hunt me as though my very existence is intolerable?" Her voice wavered, and tears stung her eyes despite her effort to hold them back.

"I simply don't understand why I am so despised by you both. Have I wronged you somehow? I know I am blunt. I know I have a temper. But men claim to admire honesty, do they not? Or is this truly nothing more than ambition, titles and estates? Why is Prince Carsten so invested in my ruin?"

Before she could continue, Lord Maughan gently placed his hand over her mouth, his expression unexpectedly kind.

"You must allow me to answer," he said softly but firmly. "There is nothing wrong with your temper, nor with your outspokenness. You are a remarkable young woman, and your candor suits you."

"I wasn't fishing for compliments," she protested, muffled beneath his hand. He pressed it lightly again, a faint smile touching his lips as though he already knew her far too well.

"I know," he said quietly. "I see no vanity in you. I cannot speak for the prince, his motives are his own, but I swear to you, I have never desired your death. Nor would I ever take part in such an attempt." There was sincerity in his voice. Yet Ellie's heart still wrestled with distrust. She opened her mouth to question him further, but a clear, ringing voice cut across the ballroom.

"Ladies and gentlemen, dinner has been served. Please join us in the dining hall." Prince Carsten stood near the entrance, making the announcement with theatrical flourish as guests began drifting toward the great doors in a swirl of silk and lively conversation.

Ellie turned to following the others. But from the corner of her eye, she caught sight of Carsten slipping quietly through a side door. Every instinct warned her to let it pass. Instead, her pulse quickened. Something was wrong. Without hesitation, Ellie veered away from the crowd and followed him.

Prince Carsten moved swiftly through the corridor and out into the cool night air, his steps echoing faintly against the stone terrace. Ellie followed at a careful distance, her dance slippers making scarcely a sound as she slipped after him and into the gardens. The night was quiet, the distant music from the ballroom drifting faintly across the grounds. Moonlight pooled across the gravel paths and shimmered against the glass panes of the great greenhouses at the far edge of the estate.

Carsten headed directly toward them. Ellie slowed, keeping to the deeper shadows cast by the hedges and towering trees. Her pulse pounded so loudly in her ears that she feared it might betray her. At last, he stopped before the nearest greenhouse.

Ellie's breath caught when he turned suddenly, his sharp gaze sweeping the gardens as though he sensed he was not alone. Panic surged through her. She ducked behind a thick yew bush, pressing a trembling hand to her mouth to stifle even the faintest sound. For a dreadful moment she was certain his eyes had found her. But after a brief pause, he dismissed whatever suspicion had troubled him. With a curt movement he reached for the greenhouse door and pulled it open. The hinges creaked softly as he slipped inside.

Ellie remained frozen for several seconds, scarcely daring to breathe. Only when the door fell closed again did she slowly lift her head. Her heart was still hammering as she crept forward through the moonlit garden. But before she could reach the greenhouse, movement along the path to her left made her stop abruptly. A tall figure strode toward the building with determined steps. Lord Adams. His face looked grim in the pale light of the moon.

Ellie shrank deeper into the shadows, scarcely believing what she was seeing. He was not alone. Three other men followed behind him, strangers to her, their expressions dark and purposeful. Without hesitation they crossed the terrace, opened the greenhouse door, and vanished inside.

A cold shiver ran down Ellie's spine. Whatever this gathering was, it was no innocent meeting.

Her gaze darted around the garden as she searched desperately for some place from which she might observe them unnoticed. At last, she spotted a narrow window in the greenhouse wall, propped slightly ajar and half-hidden beneath a curtain of ivy. Fortune favored her further. A dense leafy shrub grew just beneath the window, its branches thick enough to conceal anyone crouching behind it. If she was careful, she might remain unseen.

Her pulse thundered violently in her chest as she slipped across the grass toward it, her breath shallow and uneven. Her skirts snagged briefly on the branches of a nearby bush, but she scarcely noticed. Dropping into a crouch beneath the shrub, she carefully pressed herself into the shelter of the leaves. Slowly, very slowly, she rose just enough to bring her ear level with the opening. Voices drifted out from within the greenhouse. At first, they were muffled, indistinct. Then one voice sharpened. To Ellie's astonishment, the men had gathered directly beside that very window. She gripped the branches with damp palms, forcing herself into absolute stillness. Every nerve strained as she listened.

"Packer, did you bring the materials?" Prince Carsten's tone was sharp, his eyes narrowing on the man across from him. Packer shifted uneasily before shaking his head.

"Harris took our money and ran. Left a note saying it was getting too dangerous, that he didn't want to be caught."

The prince gave a derisive scoff. "Too dangerous? He is a chemist, not a soldier. His role was minimal. He cannot simply vanish when it suits him."

Packer cleared his throat nervously. "I spoke to his apprentice. The boy said the Duke of Essex must have discovered something. His investigators are prowling London, questioning people, digging into every shadow. Apparently, Lord Huntington's granddaughter recognized the man who tried to shoot her and confided in her cousin. She gave them a name. And from what Harris told the lad, they've already searched your home, Lord Adams."

At that, Lord Adams stiffened, fury twisting his features.

"We need to silence her. That girl cannot be allowed to interfere again. From the very beginning she has been nothing but a thorn in our side, unraveling everything."

Prince Carsten folded his arms, unimpressed. "And what plans, precisely, has she ruined?"

"Everything, Your Highness. Everything." Lord Adams's voice was low and bitter. "Our work began long before Ainsworth's late father was hanged. He was the one who proposed using his brother's estate. The cellar already resembled a dungeon, and he had secretly constructed hidden rooms there. He knew that once his brother inherited the dukedom, he would abandon the house, too many ghosts lingered there after his wife's death. It was the perfect place for us to begin. But Ainsworth was careless. He was caught after murdering his sister-in-law, and the gallows claimed him." He spat the last words with venom.

Prince Carsten leaned forward slightly, his eyes glinting with cruel amusement.

"And so, the son took over where his father left off."

"Exactly," Adams growled. "Ainsworth Jr. stepped in quickly. He needed a wife, since the Duke of Devon made it clear his nephew could not take residence at the estate unmarried. So, he snatched Eleanor, and the cycle continued."

Ellie's eyes filled with tears as the words pierced her heart. Eleanor's suffering had been even greater than she had imagined.

"She was a charming creature," Carsten said with a dark laugh. "I enjoyed her company well enough myself." His tone dripped with wicked satisfaction. The sound of it was so vile that Ellie's stomach twisted. She nearly gagged. Carsten's voice lowered, thick with unholy pride.

"Having Eleanor in the house, with his first wife hidden away in the dungeon, sparked a new idea. Why not convert the cellar into a secret apothecary? A place where we could brew and store what we needed, sell the rest for profit, and—" his smile widened into something grotesque, "... keep a few women there as diversions for our amusement."

The men chuckled darkly.

Ellie clamped both hands over her mouth to smother the horrified gasp that surged up her throat. Her whole body shook with revulsion. *Demons*, that was what they were. Monsters draped in silk and titles. She bit her lip hard enough to taste blood, fighting the sobs that threatened to escape. Suddenly, scraps of conversation returned to her, words she had overheard one morning while standing in a dress shop queue.

Two widows had spoken in hushed, bitter voices of husbands lost to narcotic indulgence. The drugs had begun as remedies, easing pain and worry, but soon the men's bodies had craved more. The kind husbands they had once known twisted into cruel tyrants, violent when the effects wore off. Poverty had only sharpened the descent. When they could not afford their next dose, they stole. They raged. And at last, they died miserable deaths, leaving their families broken and destitute. The women had pleaded with the others in the shop.

"Warn your sons, warn your daughters. These poisons destroy not only the man, but everyone bound to him."

Ellie squeezed her eyes shut, her thoughts racing. She had read pamphlets warning of the same dangers, brave physicians and chemists urging caution. They had even written that mixing narcotic with strong drinks was a swift path to the grave. But too few listened. Too many dismissed it as nonsense.

Now she understood. This was the root of it all. The apothecary was not merely a business, it was their power, their corruption, their weapon. And if they succeeded, countless families would suffer the same fate as those poor widows had described.

"Our plans were moving in the right direction," Lord Adams hissed, his fists curling tightly at his sides. "For a time, everything unfolded exactly as we wished. But then Eleanor's cousin, Lady Danielle, came blundering into our affairs and unraveled everything. Ainsworth was arrested, the women freed, and the house reclaimed by the duke. All lost, because of her meddling."

"Why did she even visit her cousin?" one of the men demanded. Lord Adams gave a derisive snort.

"She claimed she was hiding from her grandfather, who was attempting to marry her off. But in hindsight, I would wager she discovered Eleanor was being mistreated by her husband. From what Ainsworth told me, Lady Danielle was protective of her cousin from the very beginning, ferociously so. She's not the sort who cowers. No, she is the kind who plants her feet and defends those who cannot defend themselves."

Prince Carsten's expression twisted, raw loathing etched into every line of his face.

"I can testify to that. The girl has no respect for men. She refuses to obey, refuses to hold her tongue. How her father allowed her such unladylike insolence, I cannot comprehend. I would be astonished if any man ever wished for so willful a wife."

"But aren't you the one helping Lord Maughan seize her grandfather's estate?" another man interjected. "All so she will be forced into a marriage?"

The prince's lips curled into a smug grin. "Precisely. Since she ruined our plans for the Ainsworth estate, we must secure another base. Somewhere discreet. Somewhere wives, future or otherwise, remain blind to our affairs. A perfect place for business," his voice dropped, dripping with malice, "and for pleasure." He dragged his tongue slowly across his lips, revolting, and the other men chuckled knowingly.

"Most women," Carsten went on, almost boastful, "are simple enough to manage. A stern word, a heavy hand, and they learn their place. And if they dare forget, it is our right, as men, to remind them through discipline."

Ellie's stomach churned, bile rising in her throat. She pressed both hands harder over her mouth to keep from crying out.

"But why," another man pressed, "do you still seem so consumed with Lady Danielle? If she is as impossible as you claim, surely, she will ruin herself in time."

Carsten's eyes narrowed, his jaw tightening. "Because she was meant to be ruined tonight. She was supposed to marry, an impossible task for a girl like her. No man alive would willingly take a wife with such arrogance, such defiance." His tone dripped with disdain as he leaned forward, lowering his voice.

"But when my parents and brother returned from their travels, my brother went crawling to Parliament. He convinced them to change the condition. Now, instead of a wedding, all she needs is an engagement announced this very evening."

"So, she could choose anyone?" the man asked in surprise.

"Yes," Carsten sneered. "But here lies the beauty of it, what she does not know. Engagements are binding in the eyes of court and society. She cannot simply announce one and then break it off once her title and estate are secured. If she does, she will be branded a fraud, her reputation destroyed. And when that happens, the inheritance will pass directly to Maughan."

A murmur of approval rippled through the group.

"But once Maughan has it," Lord Adams asked cautiously, "how do you intend to control the duchy yourselves? And what of the Duke of Essex? If he ascends to Grand Duke, he will wield even greater influence. What if he uncovers more of our dealings?"

Prince Carsten gave a careless shrug, though his grin turned wolfish.

"Maughan is already in my debt. Every coin he possesses has passed through my hands, and he is drowning. Once he inherits, he will have little strength to resist me. As for the old duke," his eyes gleamed with malice, "men of his age rarely require much of a push. An unfortunate fall, an unexpected illness, a quiet decline... accidents happen. Even nobles die of natural causes."

The men chuckled again, their laughter dark and cruel.

Ellie's entire body shook. Their words fell upon her like icy daggers, confirming every fear that had gnawed at her since arriving in London. This was no mere scheme of inheritance. It was corruption woven deep into the fabric of power. Murder disguised as inevitability. Greed cloaked as destiny. And she was standing on the very edge of it all, their next intended victim.

Ellie had heard enough. Her pulse hammered in her ears as she backed away from the greenhouse, every nerve straining for silence. She moved swiftly until she was far enough away that, should any of the men emerge, they would not see her. Her skirts brushed the grass as she hurried toward the castle, but her steps slowed when she passed a small pavilion nestled among the hedges. From within drifted muffled laughter and breathless giggles.

Frowning, Ellie crept closer. The pavilion lay shaded, its view obscured by thick bushes, but unease urged her forward. She peered inside and froze. Prince Edward. He stood with a young woman pressed tightly against him, his hands roaming as his lips claimed hers in a hungry, passionate kiss.

The sight struck Ellie like a blow to the chest. She gasped and stumbled back, but it was too late. The couple had noticed. They sprang apart in a guilty flurry, and Ellie fled, heat stinging her cheeks. She heard Edward murmur something hurried to the girl, followed by the sound of footsteps giving chase. A moment later his hand clamped down on her arm, spinning her around.

"Danielle, wait—"

"Why are you following me?" Ellie snapped, her eyes flashing. She wrenched against his hold. "Let me go at once."

He tightened his grip instead, his expression urgent. "We need to talk about this."

"No," she bit out. "We don't. I should have trusted my instincts. I should never have accepted your proposal. I knew it was wrong to let you sacrifice yourself for me." Her voice trembled with anger and hurt. "Tell me, are you courting her? Do you love her?"

Edward's shoulders sagged, a sigh escaping him. "It's... complicated."

Ellie laughed bitterly. "Complicated? Have you ever had a serious relationship, or are women merely toys to you? Something to play with until you tire of them?"

He blinked, startled, caught speechless by the accusation. Ellie drew a steady breath, forcing her tone calmer.

"If your heart belongs to her, then be with her. Do not chain yourself to me out of convenience or duty."

"I thought—" he faltered, his voice low, almost pleading. "I thought we could still marry."

Her eyes widened. For a long moment she simply stared at him, horror and disbelief mingling in her gaze.

"You mean to say... you would marry me, yet keep her?"

His silence, and the faint wince he could not disguise, was answer enough.

"I cannot believe you." Her voice rose with fury as she shoved him away. "You would make me your wife, yet keep a mistress on the side?"

Edward flushed crimson, his eyes darting nervously as though afraid others might hear.

"Many men do that," he muttered defensively, "and—"

He never finished. Ellie cut across him, her voice blazing.

"I will not share my husband!" she declared, fists clenched at her sides. "If a man cannot be faithful to one woman, then he is no man at all. Do you think women are so little? So disposable? Something to sate your pleasure and discard when you tire of us? Why even marry if you plan to keep another woman in your bed?" Her words struck like blows, sharp and unyielding.

"Are the women of your acquaintance so desperate that they would endure such humiliation?"

The prince stared at her, dumbfounded, utterly bereft of reply. Ellie's chest rose and fell with the force of her conviction, her voice trembling now but no less resolute.

"Marriage is sacred to me, Edward. A union of husband and wife under God's eye. No third person has any place in it. Scripture tells us Eve was given to Adam as a helpmeet, not as a slave, not as something to be replaced when his fancy shifted. Even kings who took concubines drew God's disfavor. Why is one woman not enough for you? Have you so little self-control that you must betray the vows you have not even spoken yet?"

Still, he said nothing. And in his silence, Ellie read the truth. He would not change. She drew herself up, her eyes shining with unshed tears.

"I am only glad I discovered this before any engagement was made public. As much as it grieves me to risk losing everything my family has worked for, I will not sacrifice my honor or my self-respect. Better to stand alone than bind myself to a man who cheapens the word *husband*."

Her voice cracked on the last word, but she pressed her lips together and turned away, nodding once in farewell before striding off into the garden. This time, Edward did not follow.

Ellie's steps carried her blindly away from the castle, down a different path than before. She scarcely noticed where she was going. Her thoughts tumbled over one another in a storm of anger, humiliation, and aching disappointment. She needed more air. Distance. Anything to escape the suffocating press of betrayal that seemed to close around her like iron bands.

The music drifting from the ballroom floated out across the gardens, bright and lively, a cruel contrast to the turmoil raging within her. Laughter rose now and then, mingling with the faint strains of violins. To anyone watching, the evening would appear perfect, glittering gowns, gallant gentlemen, and the graceful swirl of dancers beneath the chandeliers. But to Ellie, it suddenly felt like a gilded illusion.

She slowed near a stretch of hedges bordering the terrace, her breath uneven as she tried to steady herself. For a moment she considered slipping through a side entrance and leaving the estate altogether. She had no desire to face the glittering crowd again, not tonight. Then, almost against her will, her gaze drifted back toward the glowing windows of the ballroom. The sight that met her eyes stopped her cold.

Through the tall panes of glass, she saw the dancers moving in elegant circles across the polished floor, the candlelight reflecting off jewels and silk. And there, among them, was Lord Bennett. He looked every inch the gentleman, radiant in formal attire, his dark hair neatly arranged, his posture confident and composed. A warm smile lit his face as he guided his partner through the dance, his movements sure and graceful.

For a fleeting instant, something within Ellie lifted. Relief. Comfort. The quiet reassurance that at least one man she trusted remained exactly as she believed him to be. But the fragile moment shattered almost at once. Mid-turn, the woman in his arms leaned forward, her expression bright with playful boldness. Without hesitation, she pressed her full lips against his.

Ellie's breath caught sharply in her throat. The world seemed to tilt. Pain like a dagger carved straight through her chest. Only moments earlier she had stumbled upon the prince's betrayal, a wound sharp enough on its own. But this struck deeper. Far deeper.

Lord Bennett. The man who had spoken to her with such kindness. The man whose quiet strength had made her feel safe in a world that had suddenly grown treacherous. To see him now, smiling easily as another woman claimed his lips, felt like the final blow.

A sob rose hot and choking in her throat. Her vision blurred as tears filled her eyes, the ballroom lights smearing into indistinct gold and shadow. For a moment she simply stood there, rooted to the spot, her heart splintering under the weight of the evening's revelations.

How foolish she had been. Men spoke sweetly. They made promises. They smiled with warmth that felt genuine in the moment. And yet, when temptation appeared, they proved no different from one another. The laughter drifting from the ballroom struck her ears like mockery. Ellie pressed a trembling hand to her mouth, fighting the sobs threatening to break free. She could not bear the thought of anyone seeing her like this, shattered, humiliated, undone. Turning abruptly, she fled deeper into the garden's shadows, her skirts brushing the damp grass as she hurried along the winding path.

The lantern light from the terrace faded behind her, swallowed by the dark embrace of hedges and trees. Only the distant music followed her now, faint and haunting. She did not slow. All she wanted was darkness, some quiet corner of the gardens where she could hide her anguish from the world and gather the shattered pieces of her heart before anyone discovered how completely this night had broken her.

When she finally found another pavilion tucked at the far edge of the grounds, she sank onto the cool stone bench inside as though her strength had simply abandoned her. The structure stood half-hidden beneath climbing ivy, its wooden latticework casting soft shadows in the lantern light spilling faintly from the distant terrace. Here, the music from the ballroom reached her only as a muted echo, the lively strains of the orchestra drifting across the gardens like something from another world.

The night air clung damply to her skin, cool against the heat of her flushed cheeks. It carried the faint perfume of roses and freshly turned earth, mingling with the sweetness of blooming jasmine that trailed along the pavilion's pillars. Under any other circumstance, the quiet beauty of the garden might have soothed her. Tonight, it only made the loneliness sharper.

Ellie pressed her hands together tightly in her lap, her fingers twisting into the fabric of her gloves. Her chest rose and fell unevenly as she fought to steady her breathing. Her eyes burned. But she bit her lip hard, determined not to let the tears fall. She would not cry. She would not give anyone the satisfaction of seeing her broken. Not Prince Edward. Not the scheming men in the greenhouse. Not even herself.

Still, the ache inside her would not be stilled. Her thoughts drifted helplessly back to the ballroom windows, to the image that had seared itself into her memory.

Lord Bennett. The warmth of his smile. The ease with which he had moved across the dance floor. And then—

The woman leaning forward. The kiss. Ellie squeezed her eyes shut as though she might banish the image by force alone. *Why does it hurt so much?* she thought bitterly. Why did the sight of Lord Bennett kissing another woman feel like a blade driven straight into her chest? Her throat tightened painfully. It made no sense. They were not engaged. He had never promised her anything. No vow bound them. No understanding had been spoken between them. They did not belong to one another.

And yet the pain that gripped her now was sharper, deeper, more devastating than the betrayal she had witnessed from

Prince Edward only minutes before. Edward's conduct had angered her, disgusted her even, but it had not shattered her. This had. A soft, strangled laugh escaped her before she could stop it, the sound trembling in the stillness of the pavilion.

"How foolish you are," she whispered under her breath. *Of course, Lord Bennett could kiss another woman. He was free to court whomever he wished. Free to smile, dance, and offer his affections as he pleased.* Just as she was free to refuse Prince Edward. Just as she was free to walk away from every expectation placed upon her.

So why did it feel as though something precious had slipped through her fingers before she had even realized she was holding it? Ellie lowered her head, pressing her clasped hands against her lips as she struggled to master the storm of emotion swirling inside her. Perhaps the answer was painfully simple. Somewhere along the way, quietly, without her noticing, her heart had begun to hope. And now that fragile, unspoken hope lay shattered.

24

Defiance Beneath the Chandeliers

A low, mocking voice cut through the silence. "Pretty devastating, isn't it?" The sinister chuckle that followed curdled Ellie's blood. "You think your troubles are nearly over," the voice continued smoothly, "only to discover the man you placed your hopes upon was nothing but a liar."

Ellie stiffened. She did not need to turn to know who stood behind her.

"Leave me alone," she snapped, her voice tight with fury. Prince Carsten stepped from the shadows, the pale wash of moonlight catching the cruel curve of his smirk. He looked entirely at ease, as though he had stumbled upon nothing more significant than a bit of harmless entertainment.

"Ah, such fire, Lady Danielle." His tone carried a mocking warmth. "That temper of yours is both charming and dangerous." He clasped his hands behind his back, tilting his head slightly as if studying her distress with idle curiosity.

"You see, my brother... he truly is a good man at heart," Carsten continued in a tone of feigned sympathy. "But women have always been his weakness. He simply cannot help himself. It is his curse."

Ellie rose at once, her spine rigid, her fists clenched at her sides.

"Spare me your mockery, Your Highness."

Carsten laughed softly. The sound held no amusement, only the dark satisfaction of a predator savoring the helplessness of its prey.

"Since I pity you," he said smoothly, "I am prepared to offer a solution. An arrangement, shall we say, one that will benefit both you and Lord Maughan as well." Malice threaded every word. Ellie's lips parted. For the first time, unease flickered through her anger.

"What sort of arrangement?"

Carsten's smile widened. "You will see soon enough." Before she could react, his hand shot forward, seizing her wrist in a grip as hard as iron. Ellie gasped. "Come," he ordered coolly. "You will follow me."

"I will do no such thing!" she protested, wrenching against his hold. But Carsten only tightened his grip, ignoring her struggle entirely as he dragged her from the pavilion. The gravel path crunched beneath their hurried steps as he pulled her toward the castle. Ellie dug her heels into the ground, fighting for every inch, but his strength easily overpowered her resistance.

"Release me at once!" she demanded, her voice rising. He did not even glance at her. The glow from the castle windows grew brighter as they approached, golden light spilling across the terrace. The music from the ballroom swelled louder with every step, the lively rhythm grotesquely out of place against the dread tightening in Ellie's chest. Moments later they crossed the threshold.

Warm light flooded over them as they stepped once more into the brilliance of the ballroom.

Carsten did not release her hand until they stood at the very center of the room. Heads turned. The music faltered. Conversations stilled as curious gazes fixed upon the pair standing beneath the chandeliers. Then silence spread across the room like a ripple across water. Carsten's voice rose smoothly above the hush.

"My dear friends."

Every eye turned toward him. Near the dais, Ellie caught sight of her grandfather standing beside Prince Carsten's parents. His posture was rigid, his expression taut with unease as his gaze locked onto her with sharp apprehension. Carsten's smirk widened.

"It is my distinct honor to share joyous news with you all."

A few guests leaned closer, anticipation flickering across their faces.

"Lord Maughan and Lady Danielle are officially engaged," Carsten declared with theatrical satisfaction, "and shall be wed very soon."

Gasps rippled through the ballroom. Whispers ignited like dry tinder catching flame, spreading from group to group in a wave of astonishment. Ellie felt the blood drain from her face. Her knees weakened. For one terrible moment the world seemed to tilt, the glittering chandeliers above blurring as her vision swam. A dull ringing thundered in her ears. She forced herself to breathe. Once. Twice. Again. Slow, steady breaths until the dizziness receded and the room steadied around her. And then the truth settled into place with chilling clarity.

She knew exactly why Carsten had done it. Members of Parliament were present that evening. Nobles of influence. Witnesses whose words carried enormous weight within society. Such a public declaration could bind her as surely as chains. To deny the engagement outright could destroy her reputation. To accept it would cost her freedom. Either way, Carsten clearly believed he had cornered her. But he did not know her nearly as well as he imagined.

Something fierce and unyielding flared to life within Ellie's chest. If she were to fall, she would not fall silently. If she were to be dragged down, she would drag the prince with her. Her chin lifted slowly. Defiance blazed in her tear-bright eyes as she turned to face the sea of watching faces. She drew in a deep breath, steadying her voice for the storm she was about to unleash.

Before Lord Maughan could make matters worse, she lifted her chin, squared her shoulders, and forced herself to stand tall. Her heart pounded so hard she thought it might burst, but she knew she could not remain silent. She tried to speak, but her words were drowned in the tide of murmurs, gasps, and speculation rippling through the ballroom. The false announcement of her engagement had thrown the guests into a frenzy, and not a single head turned her way.

Desperation gripped her. She had only one option left. Drawing in a deep breath, Ellie slipped two fingers between her lips and gave a sharp, piercing whistle, the same whistle Richard had once taught her as a child to call the dogs from the fields. The shrill sound sliced through the chatter like a blade.

The room fell into stunned silence. Heads snapped toward her, some irritated, some scandalized, and a few of the younger gentlemen were clearly impressed by her audacity. Heat flared in her cheeks, but she met their stares unflinchingly. She had already broken every rule of decorum. One more hardly mattered now.

"Forgive me," Ellie began, her voice ringing strong though her knees trembled. "Forgive me for once again setting aside the rules of polite society. But I had no other way to command your attention, and what I must say cannot wait. Most of you scarcely know me, and you have little reason to trust me. Yet I beg you to hear me out. What you make of my words is yours to decide."

The silence deepened.

"I am not engaged to Lord Maughan," she declared, her gaze sweeping the assembly. "I never was, and I never will be. I do not love the man, and I will not marry for anything but love. Tonight's announcement was a fabrication, designed to trap me, and it came from none other than Prince Carsten himself."

Gasps broke across the hall, but Ellie pressed on.

"He wishes me to marry Lord Maughan for one reason only, so he may gain access to my grandfather's duchy." She fixed her eyes on the prince until he shifted uneasily. He opened his mouth to protest, but his father's stern glare silenced him.

"You may wonder why His Highness's temper is so unpredictable, at times charming, at times explosively cruel. There is a reason. Prince Carsten, together with Lord Adams and others, have fallen prey to narcotics. Their bodies crave them constantly, and when deprived, those cravings twist men into monsters. Rather than seek help, they chose to feed their addictions, and in their madness, they seek to build an empire upon it." Her voice rose, clear and defiant.

"I overheard their plans tonight. They intend to use my grandfather's estate as a secret apothecary to manufacture these vile substances, and worse, to turn it into a brothel where women would be held against their will, enslaved for their profit and their pleasure."

Cries of horror erupted throughout the hall. Ladies pressed kerchiefs to their lips. Gentlemen muttered in disbelief. Others looked toward Carsten with dawning disgust. The prince's face flushed crimson, his eyes blazing with rage.

"Footmen!" he thundered. "Seize her at once! Take that woman to the king! She shall answer for these lies, and for daring to slander a royal."

Several liveried men surged forward, but before they could lay a hand on Ellie, two figures broke through the throng. Lord Bennett and Lord Maughan planted themselves firmly at her side.

"Stay back," Lord Bennett commanded, his voice low and lethal. The footmen froze. "Lady Danielle has not lied. Though I confess we did not know until this moment that the prince himself was involved, we have long suspected darker dealings behind the Ainsworths. My uncle was arrested and hanged for murdering my family and that of the Duke of Devon. My cousin Jonathan mistreated his wife, imprisoned his first, and kidnapped his sister-in-law. For months we never understood why. Now we know, they were all pieces of this foul scheme."

Lord Maughan stepped forward, his tone calm but unyielding.

"Let me make this plain. I never sought to rob the Duke of Essex or Lady Danielle of their inheritance. I only pretended allegiance, playing a dangerous role to uncover the truth. My estate flourishes. I am not bankrupt. The money I fed into the scheme came from honorable men of standing, men determined to expose the corruption festering in our midst."

Ellie's breath caught. She had not expected this revelation. Carsten sneered.

"And who are these so-called men of honor? What fool would conspire against a prince of the realm? Is it your ambition to strip me of my title and seize it for yourselves?"

"No," came a deep, commanding voice from behind him. "That honor belongs to me."

A collective gasp shook the hall. Carsten spun around, his eyes widening. His father stood there, Prince Edward beside him.

"Father?" Carsten's voice cracked. "Surely you do not believe these lies. Why would you betray your own son?"

His mother's face was pale with fury, her lips trembling.

"Because we have watched you destroy everything good that once remained in you. You shame our family name. Do you think we do not hear the complaints? The servants you abused, the money that vanished, the church funds stolen from the mouths of the poor? Even your own footmen despise you. We turned a blind eye far too long."

His father's voice thundered like judgment. "We set men to watch you, to bring us word of your dealings. When I heard Lord Huntington intended to name his granddaughter his heiress, I knew it was the perfect chance to expose you. So, I went to the Duke of Essex and the Viscount of Bromley, and together we devised this plan. Lord Maughan agreed to play the spy. And tonight, your wickedness has been laid bare."

Carsten's face drained of color.

"You are guilty of theft, debauchery, and cruelty beyond measure," his father declared. "You preyed upon the weak, defiled the daughters of servants, and schemed to enslave women for profit. You are no son of mine. From this moment forward, you are stripped of title and rank. You and your companions will be imprisoned in Newgate, and the king shall decide whether you ever see freedom again."

The prince's knees buckled, but rage still burned in his eyes. He lunged for escape, only to be seized by a flood of footmen. He snarled and fought like a wild beast but was dragged from the hall with his accomplices in tow.

A heavy silence lingered in the wake of their departure. Guests stood pale and shaken, whispers of scandal and shock thick in the air. Ellie exhaled slowly, relief washing over her. But before anyone could stop her, she slipped quietly from the room. The crowd was too busy murmuring, too busy congratulating one another on the fall of corruption, to notice her departure. As she passed a window, she glanced back once.

Carsten's mother stood weeping silently, her hand pressed to her mouth. Ellie's heart ached. However vile the prince had been, the loss of a child, even to disgrace, was a wound no mother should ever bear.

25

A Duel of Hearts

Ellie hurried along the winding garden path, her slippers brushing softly against the gravel as she made her way toward the second greenhouse, the larger, more ornate one tucked behind the place where Prince Carsten and his vile companions had gathered earlier. Its tall glass panes glimmered faintly beneath the moonlight, reflecting silver across the surrounding hedges.

Inside, the air was warm and fragrant, the mingled perfume of roses and orchids drifting through the stillness. Exotic blooms thrived even in the chill of night, their colors glowing softly beneath the hanging lamps. A hush lingered within, broken only by the gentle trickle of water spilling into the pond at the center of the room.

Golden fish glided lazily beneath the surface, their scales catching the lamplight like scattered coins. Frogs perched along the stones, throats pulsing slowly as they rested in the warmth. Toward the back rose a grand aviary, its delicate wirework enclosing branches where rare birds slept with feathers fluffed and eyes closed, lulled by the quiet of the night. Ellie lowered herself onto a bench near the pond and closed her eyes. For the first time in hours, she allowed herself to breathe.

The evening's events pressed heavily upon her, Carsten's schemes laid bare, Lord Maughan revealed as a spy, and she herself standing at the very center of it all. Relief mingled with exhaustion, but uncertainty gnawed stubbornly at the edges of her thoughts.

Yes, Carsten was disgraced, and Lord Maughan no longer a threat. But what of her own future? Would Parliament release her from their impossible demand that she be engaged by night's end? Some of its members had witnessed Carsten's downfall with their own eyes. Surely that proved her honor.

And yet she knew too well how men of power often regarded women. Would they relent, or tighten their grip simply because she was female? Her gaze drifted to the sleeping birds in the aviary, their tiny forms puffed into feathery spheres. A faint smile touched her lips. They looked so peaceful. So untouched by human deceit.

Grateful for the calm, she lingered a moment longer before rising and crouching at the pond's edge. The fish darted like living jewels through the water, their graceful movements mesmerizing.

Then, suddenly, movement at her feet. A dark blur scuttled across her slipper. Ellie gasped and lurched upright. In her haste she stumbled, her arms flailing as the pond loomed dangerously close.

A strangled cry escaped her and was cut short as a firm hand caught hers. Strong fingers tightened around her wrist, yanking her backward. The next instant she collided with a solid chest, steadied by arms that wrapped securely around her. Her heart thundered as she looked up.

"Your Grace!" she breathed, half in relief, half in shock. "What are you doing here?"

He grinned, his arm still firm around her waist as though he had no intention of letting her go just yet.

"Rescuing you, apparently," he replied lightly. "You might consider thanking me. I saved you, and that beautiful gown, from a most unfortunate bath."

Her cheeks flamed. "Th–thank you, Your Grace," she murmured, breathless as her pulse continued to race. A mouse, she realized belatedly, had been the cause of her fright. But it was not the small creature that left her trembling. It was his nearness. The warmth of his hand at her waist. The strength of his arm around her. The unsettling flutter in her chest whenever his eyes settled upon hers.

"What brought you here?" she asked quickly, desperate to steady herself.

"Everyone was worried when you vanished," he said. "Your grandfather most of all. I came to find you."

"Oh!" Guilt pierced her. "I must see him at once. I only wished for a moment alone. I never meant to cause him alarm." She shifted to step away. But his arm tightened, drawing her closer. Her breath caught.

"What are you doing?"

His expression softened, the teasing light fading from his eyes as something deeper replaced it.

"We need to talk about us."

"Us?" The word slipped from her lips in a whisper as heat rushed into her cheeks.

"Danielle," he said quietly. Two fingers lifted her chin until her gaze met his. The touch sent a shiver racing down her spine.

"You cannot deny it," he murmured. "There is something between us."

"I… I don't know what you mean," she stammered, lowering her lashes in a futile attempt to shield herself from the intensity of his gaze. The air between them felt charged, dangerous. They had argued and sparred from the beginning. Their conversations were battles of wit and stubborn pride. Could all of that have hidden something else entirely? His lips curved faintly.

"I think you know exactly what I mean," he said softly. "Are you denying it, or are you simply too inexperienced with love to recognize it?"

The words struck like sparks against tinder. Ellie's indignation flared at once, her eyes blazing.

"Inexperienced? Because I am young?" she snapped. "Yes, I am young, but do not mistake hesitation for ignorance. My uncertainty comes from you, Your Grace. You mock me. You challenge me. You twist my words until I never know when you are sincere and when you are merely teasing. How can I believe in your feelings when I cannot even be sure of your heart?"

Her chest rose and fell with the force of her words. She drew a sharp breath, and in that instant, he closed the distance. His lips captured hers in a sudden, searing kiss. It was fierce yet threaded with a depth of longing that stole the breath from her lungs.

Ellie stiffened instinctively, her hands bracing against his chest as every instinct urged her to resist. But the strength of his arms… the warmth of his mouth… the unmistakable gentleness beneath the urgency—

Not demand. Desire. Heat flooded through her until her knees weakened. He must have felt the change in her, the moment her rigid resistance melted into trembling surrender. His embrace tightened, holding her as though she might vanish if he loosened his grip. Her heart thundered wildly as the world tilted beneath her feet.

When at last he drew back, breathless, Ellie's fingers clung instinctively to the front of his waistcoat. Before reason could intervene, she tugged him back. Their mouths met again. This time the kiss was hers. Not fierce now, but soft and aching, filled with wonder and something far more dangerous, something tender and terrifying all at once.

A quiet sound escaped her as he lifted her into his arms, drawing her closer as though the distance between them, even the smallest space, was suddenly unbearable. The world seemed to dissolve. No greenhouse. No pond. No whispering night. Only the wild pounding of her heart and the warmth of his lips against hers.

When at last they broke apart, both breathless, Ellie stared up at him with wide, dazed eyes. Her chest rose and fell rapidly, her lips tingling, her entire body trembling as though struck by lightning. Something inside her had shifted, something she could never quite return to what it had been before.

"Forgive me, Your Grace," she whispered, shame rushing over her in a sudden wave. "I do not know what possessed me. That was... wholly improper. I should never have returned your kiss." She tore her gaze away, her cheeks burning. What madness had overtaken her? She should have pushed him away. Instead, she had clung to him.

And then memory struck her like a blade. The ballroom. The woman leaning toward him. The careless kiss she had witnessed through the glass. A pang of hurt twisted sharply in her chest.

Shame, jealousy, confusion, every emotion tangled together until she could scarcely breathe. This was wrong. All of it was wrong. She had to escape before her heart betrayed her again.

"What are you doing to my granddaughter?" The voice boomed like a thunderclap through the greenhouse. Ellie whirled in shock, her pulse leaping straight into her throat.

"Grandfather, it isn't what you think—"

"You stay out of this, Danielle," he barked, his expression darker than she had ever seen. For the first time in her life, Ellie truly glimpsed her grandfather's fury, and it terrified her. His eyes, usually calm and thoughtful, now burned with righteous fire, and the rigid set of his shoulders made him appear every inch the formidable duke whose authority few dared challenge. His gaze shifted, hard as steel.

"Well, Bennett? What have you to say for yourself?"

"I am in love with Danielle." Lord Bennett's reply came without the slightest hesitation. His voice was steady. His posture unyielding. Not so much as a flicker of doubt crossed his features as he faced the duke's wrath.

"Stay away from her," her grandfather thundered. "I have other plans for her, and they do not include you."

Ellie's mouth fell open. *Plans?* He had never spoken so plainly before. Before she could gather her thoughts enough to protest, Lord Bennett stepped forward, his jaw tightening with unmistakable determination.

"I have no intention of staying away," he said firmly. "I must marry her, for I have compromised her honor this night. And it was not the first time."

Ellie's breath caught. Heat flooded her cheeks in a storm of mortification and disbelief. To speak so boldly, before her grandfather of all people. The duke's face blanched. Then it darkened, flushing crimson with outrage.

"You insolent scoundrel!" he roared. "You dare lay hands upon my granddaughter?" His finger jabbed toward Bennett like the thrust of a blade. "You will pay for this, Your Grace. Mark me, you shall never have her. Never!"

"If she desires me, there is nothing you can do," Bennett shot back, his eyes flashing with dangerous resolve. "We need no one's permission. We will elope, if that is what it takes."

"The hell you will!" Her grandfather's voice cracked like a whip. His entire body trembled with fury. "I challenge you to a duel, sir. Danielle will marry whom I deem worthy, and you are not among them."

"Grandfather, please—stop!" Ellie cried, rushing forward, her voice breaking. But neither man seemed to hear her. Their anger consumed them completely. Bennett's lips curved into a cold, defiant smile.

"If it is a duel you want, Lord Huntington, then a duel you shall have," he said evenly. "But know this, it will end with your death."

"No!" Ellie's scream tore from her throat, raw with desperation. But it was already too late. Both men turned away from her at once and stormed from the greenhouse into the open night. Ellie gathered her skirts and hurried after them, her steps stumbling as panic flooded through her veins.

They strode across the moonlit garden toward the broad lawn near the fountain, their long strides filled with furious purpose.

"Fetch the pistols!" someone shouted. Servants scattered. Moments later a pair of polished dueling pistols were brought forth, their barrels gleaming coldly beneath the moonlight. The stewards began pacing off the distance with solemn precision. One step. Two. Three. The sound of their measured footsteps echoed across the silent lawn like the tolling of a funeral bell. The commotion had already drawn others from the castle.

Guests poured out onto the terrace and down onto the grass, their voices rising in shocked whispers that rippled outward like a swelling tide. Among them Ellie saw Prince Edward and his parents, their faces pale with horror as they realized what was unfolding before them. A duel. Here.

Tonight.

Ellie pressed trembling hands to her mouth, her breath coming in ragged bursts. Terror clawed at her soul. This was illegal, utterly unthinkable. Why was Edward's father not intervening? As the highest-ranking member present, it was his duty to stop this madness. He should have put an end to it before it spiraled too far beyond control.

Her beloved grandfather, and the man who had just stolen her heart, stood facing one another across the measured distance. Both men rigid. Both men proud. Both willing to die. And all because of her.

Ellie's knees threatened to give way. Her vision swam as her grandfather and Bennett took their positions, pistols raised, the moonlight gleaming coldly on polished steel.

"No," she whispered. Then louder, "No!" With a surge of desperation, she gathered her skirts and ran. Gasps rippled through the crowd as she sprinted across the grass, heedless of scandal or propriety. Her slippers sank into the damp earth, her breath tore ragged from her chest, and she flung herself between the two men, arms outstretched as if her frail body could shield them both.

"Danielle, move at once!" her grandfather commanded, his voice like iron. She shook her head so fiercely her curls whipped about her face.

"No. I won't. Why must everything end in violence? Why do men cling to this endless need to duel over pride?"

"This is not your concern," he growled.

"Of course it is my concern," she shot back, her eyes blazing. "You promised me, Grandfather. You swore I could choose a man I deemed worthy, that I would never be forced into marriage unless, by my twenty-first birthday, I had found no one."

The duke's eyes narrowed, his expression unreadable. "So, you find Lord Bennett worthy to be your husband?"

Heat flooded her face. The flickering torchlight and silver moon seemed to betray every ounce of her turmoil.

"I think," she stammered, "we are getting a little ahead of ourselves."

"Why?" he countered. "Because he has not proposed yet?"

Her eyes flicked upward, irritation flashing through them. She pressed her lips together before giving a small, reluctant nod.

"Has he at least told you he loves you?"

Her heart lurched. She froze, caught neatly in the snare of his question. Slowly she turned her head toward Bennett and met his steady gaze. His eyes softened, and he inclined his head with the faintest smile, as though granting her permission. Swallowing hard, she gave another small nod.

"And how do you feel about him?" her grandfather pressed, the question sharp as a blade. Something inside her snapped.

"That is personal," she fired back, lifting her chin in defiance though her chest heaved with nerves. "I do not owe you, or anyone else here, an explanation of my heart. My feelings are mine alone, and I will not be paraded before society like a child to be interrogated."

Gasps rippled through the gathered crowd, but Ellie stood her ground.

"And while we are on the subject," she added sharply, "this ridiculous dueling ends now." Before her grandfather could react, she snatched the pistol from his hand. The weight of it startled her, almost as much as her own audacity. With trembling fingers, she opened the chamber. A gasp escaped her lips. It was empty. She stared at the weapon, then lifted her eyes slowly to her grandfather's face as realization crashed over her in a rush of fury.

"No... I do not believe it. This was all a charade?" Her voice trembled with anger. "You pretended outrage just to force me into admitting my feelings for Lord Bennett?" Her voice cracked, the hurt cutting deeper than the deception. Her eyes glistened as her whole body trembled.

"How could you, Grandfather? How dare you manipulate me like this?" Silence fell heavily over the lawn. Even the night air seemed to hold its breath. "I have had enough." Her voice was low but firm, carrying across the crowd like a final pronouncement.

With one last reproachful glance, she turned on her heel. The hem of her gown swept across the grass as she strode back toward the castle, her shoulders rigid and her head held high despite the tears threatening to spill. Inside, she found a footman and, with trembling urgency, ordered, "Fetch my carriage. At once."

She offered the hosts a curt word of thanks but refused to linger or explain. Moments later, the carriage rattled to the steps. Ellie climbed inside and slammed the door shut. For a long moment she sat frozen in the darkness, one hand pressed over her racing heart. Fury, hurt, and confusion warred within her. For the first time in her life, she felt utterly untethered, free, and trapped, all at once.

Ellie had barely given the driver instructions to take her home when the carriage door swung open. Lord Bennett vaulted inside with the bold decisiveness of a man who had no intention of letting her slip away. Ellie's eyes widened

"What are you doing?"

"You would leave without saying goodbye?" His tone was light, but the sharp arch of his brow betrayed unmistakable disapproval. Ellie's cheeks warmed, though she forced her expression into cool composure.

"I am quite upset with Grandfather," she replied crisply, her icy glance darting toward him. "And with you as well."

His lips quirked faintly, though his eyes searched hers with unsettling intensity.

"With me?" he asked mildly. "And what crime have I committed now?"

"You were part of this ridiculous scheme, were you not?"

He hesitated, just long enough for silence to condemn him, before inclining his head.

"Yes."

Ellie's shoulders stiffened. She turned away, staring out the window at the dimly lit streets as the carriage jolted into motion.

"Then you had best leave me now," she said coolly. "We should not be alone in a carriage together. People will talk."

"Perhaps I want people to talk," he countered smoothly. His gaze lingered on her profile, warm and intent. He leaned closer, his voice dropping low, almost intimate.

"Why don't you admit it, Danielle? You are in love with me. You kissed me back. You cannot deny what we both felt. Do not let your stubborn pride stand in the way of something real."

26

Hearts Restored

Ellie whipped her head toward him, indignation sparking like flint.

"My stubborn pride?" she shot back. "I think you would not enjoy hearing my present feelings, for I might not say anything to please you." Her words came sharp and quick, unsheathed like a blade.

"Do you even realize how vexing you are? How you twist me about? Every time I believe I understand your true nature, you confound me again. How can I trust that you are not merely playing with my heart?"

Her tirade broke off in a startled gasp. He had moved suddenly, closing the distance between them. One arm slipped around her waist, drawing her against him before she could retreat.

"What are you doing?" she demanded breathlessly, her pulse hammering wildly.

"I am proving that I care," he said simply. She wriggled back, her hands pressing against his chest.

"You will not kiss me again," she said firmly, her blue eyes flashing. He only smiled, infuriatingly amused.

"What if I asked permission first?" he murmured. "Would you grant me that?" His voice softened to a whisper, intimate and dangerous. Ellie's breath hitched. She dropped her gaze.

"We are not engaged, Your Grace."

"Andrew," he murmured gently. "Call me Andrew."

She shook her head at once. "That would not be proper. You are a duke, and I shall address you as such." Her gaze drifted stubbornly back toward the window. But his hand rose to her chin, tilting her face toward his until their eyes met again. His voice softened, losing all trace of teasing.

"I wish to become your husband, Danielle," he said quietly. "I want to marry you."

Her lips parted in stunned disbelief. Then anger flared anew.

"And what of the young lady you kissed earlier?" she demanded. "Do you intend to keep her nearby as well? Perhaps as a mistress when you grow weary of me?"

Andrew recoiled slightly, genuine shock flashing across his features before irritation followed.

"What?" he demanded. "Where would you get such an idea?"

Ellie's voice trembled with remembered hurt. "Prince Edward offered me a marriage of convenience. I believed him sincere until I found him kissing another woman. He told me we could still marry, but he would not give her up." Her cheeks flushed with anger, her eyes sparking.

Understanding dawned across Andrew's face, softening his expression. His hand closed gently but firmly over hers.

"Danielle... the woman you saw kissed me. I did not kiss her."

Ellie blinked.

"She is a marchioness from Wales," he continued calmly. "Already engaged to a baron. Her reputation is... infamous. She attempts to ensnare men of rank whenever she can. What you witnessed was her attempt to spin such a web."

Ellie's eyes widened. "And her betrothed tolerates this?"

Andrew's mouth tightened. "He is no better than she is. A rake and a fool. Their families push the match regardless, eager to rid themselves of the scandal." He lifted her hand slightly, his thumb brushing gently across her knuckles.

"But none of that matters," he said quietly. "What matters is you." His grip tightened with quiet intensity. "I swear to you, Danielle, there will never be anyone else. I want no mistress. No second love. Only you. Even when we were tormenting one another, I was already hopelessly smitten."

A small incredulous laugh escaped her. "We are still tormenting one another, Your Grace."

"Perhaps," he admitted. "But have you considered that I may need such torment? That I crave your stubbornness and your fire? You are not sweet and docile, and I thank heaven for that. You challenge me. You make me feel alive again."

Her throat tightened. "But what if you tire of me?" she whispered. "What if regret comes swiftly?"

He grinned boyishly. "Impossible. You will keep me on my toes for the rest of my life." Then his expression sobered. "Danielle... since the day my uncle murdered my family, joy has been rare for me. My sister and I survived only because we were in France at the time, but the loneliness nearly destroyed me. For years I wished death had taken me as well." His gaze softened as he looked at her. "And then I met you." He brushed his thumb lightly across the back of her hand.

"From the moment I saw you standing fierce and unyielding for your cousin, I admired you. You stirred my heart back to life. Even our quarrels, perhaps especially our quarrels, reminded me that I could still feel something again."

Tears blurred Ellie's vision, though she blinked them away. He leaned closer, his voice thick with emotion.

"I love you, Danielle. I want to spend my life with you, arguing, laughing, kissing you until you are breathless, and teasing you until you threaten my murder."

Her lips twitched despite herself.

"Danielle Marianne Huntington," he said softly, pressing her hand against his heart. "Will you marry me? Will you be my wife?"

Ellie's breath caught. She searched his face, the sincerity written plainly in every line, while her own heart thundered wildly in her chest. It was no longer merely attraction. It was love. Fierce. Terrifying. And utterly undeniable.

Her head dipped in a trembling nod. Andrew's smile broke wide and radiant. He pulled her into his arms, his lips claiming hers in a kiss both tender and triumphant. This time she did not resist. She kissed him back freely, her arms winding around him as though she might never let go.

When at last they parted, breathless, he rested his forehead against hers and brushed his thumb softly along her cheek.

"I love you, Danielle," he whispered. Her smile curved, impish, tender, and victorious.

"I love you too, Your Grace." Then, with a mischievous gleam, she added softly, "I love you too... Andrew."

"Let's announce our news."

"What?" Ellie blinked at him in astonishment, staring as though he had suddenly lost all sense.

"Most people are still at the ball," Andrew said easily, his eyes gleaming with a mixture of mischief and quiet determination. "Let us turn around and tell them."

"Andrew, wait!" She caught hold of his sleeve, but it was too late. He had already leaned halfway out of the carriage window, giving brisk instructions to the driver. The driver's muffled response floated back through the night air. The horses slowed, hooves scraping against the cobblestones as the carriage came about in a smooth arc. Moments later they were heading once more toward the castle.

When Andrew settled back against the seat, he looked entirely pleased with himself. Ellie could only stare at him in disbelief before shaking her head slowly, her heart hammering in her chest.

"We cannot simply walk back into the ballroom and make such an announcement," she protested, lowering her voice though urgency colored every word. "You have not even asked my grandfather or my father for their blessing."

To her astonishment, Andrew's grin only deepened, warm, confident, and utterly assured.

"Actually," he said mildly, "I have."

Ellie blinked.

"I spoke with your grandfather several days ago," he continued, as though this were the most ordinary thing in the world. "And I wrote to your father the very same evening I realized my intentions were serious. Both gave me their blessing."

For a moment she simply stared at him. Then her eyes narrowed with growing suspicion.

"So..." she said slowly, her tone sharpening. "It was exactly as I suspected."

Andrew lifted a brow.

"All that talk of duels today," she continued, folding her arms tightly across her chest, "was merely a ploy to force me into admitting my feelings for you."

His expression softened slightly, though the corner of his mouth still curved in that infuriatingly charming way.

"Yes," he admitted after a moment. "And no."

Ellie huffed softly in exasperation. "That is not an answer."

Andrew leaned forward slightly, his voice gentler now. "You know as well as I do that our history is not simple," he said. "Winning your heart was never going to be as easy as asking one polite question." His gaze held hers steadily.

"I could see the turmoil in you," he continued quietly. "The grief. The hesitation. The memories you were still carrying."

Ellie's breath slowed.

"I needed to know something first," he said. "I needed to be certain that your heart was truly free, that you were no longer mourning Lord Blackwood... and that there might be room in it for me."

The words settled over her like a soft, unexpected weight. Ellie's lips parted, ready with some sharp retort, but none came. Instead, understanding slowly unfolded within her. Her gaze dropped to her hands folded in her lap. That... did make sense. And, she realized with a reluctant warmth stirring in her chest, that it sounded very much like him.

Andrew wasted no time. The moment they re-entered the ballroom, his presence seemed to command the entire chamber. Conversation faltered as guests noticed their return, heads turning one after another like ripples spreading across water. Still holding Ellie's hand, Andrew guided her forward through the glittering crowd. Her cheeks burned beneath the curious gazes, and her heart pounded so fiercely she feared everyone must surely hear it.

The music faltered as the musicians, sensing something important unfolding, gradually lowered their instruments. Andrew led her straight to the center of the floor. The chandeliers blazed overhead, casting golden light across polished marble and shimmering gowns. The entire room seemed to draw breath at once. Ellie's fingers tightened instinctively around his arm. Her pulse raced wildly between dread and exhilaration. Andrew stopped, his posture tall and confident. Then he raised his voice.

"Ladies and gentlemen." The words rang clear through the gilded chamber. Conversations died instantly. All eyes turned toward them. Andrew's gaze swept calmly across the assembled guests before he continued.

"I have the honor of announcing that Lady Danielle Huntington has accepted me as her future husband."

Gasps rippled through the ballroom. A wave of murmurs followed, spreading from group to group like the rustle of wind through silk and lace. Ellie clutched Andrew's arm more tightly, her heart hammering in her chest. For one terrifying instant she braced herself for scandal, raised brows, whispers of impropriety, perhaps even outrage. But what she saw instead left her blinking in astonishment. Smiles. Warm, knowing smiles.

Her grandfather stood near the dais, arms folded, watching them with unmistakable satisfaction. Nearby, Prince Edward gave Andrew an approving nod, while the princess dabbed delicately at her eyes with a lace handkerchief as though the announcement had delighted her beyond measure. Around the room, familiar faces exchanged amused glances. Whispers floated softly through the crowd.

"Of course."

"At last."

"I wondered how long it would take."

Ellie's breath caught. Very few people looked surprised at all. It was as though the entire ballroom had been waiting for this moment, patiently observing the sparks between them long before she herself had dared to acknowledge them. As if everyone present had seen the truth plainly... and had simply been waiting for her to discover it for herself.

It was long past midnight when Ellie and her grandfather returned home. The house lay hushed, as though even the walls slept, yet neither felt ready to retreat to their chambers. At Lord Huntington's request, a maid soon appeared with a tray bearing a pot of steaming tea. The delicate china rattled softly as she set it upon the low parlor table.

Only after the servant had bowed and withdrawn did grandfather and granddaughter settle opposite one another. The silence between them felt heavy, weighted with all that had gone unsaid.

Ellie's fingers traced the rim of her cup, her blue eyes lingering on the amber liquid before she finally cleared her throat.

"So," she began, her voice unsteady, "you have been lying to me this entire time about Lord Maughan. He was never truly after the duchy, but working with you... to bring down Prince Carsten?"

Her grandfather's expression grew grave, though no denial flickered in his eyes. After a moment he gave a slow nod.

"Yes. I took no pleasure in deceiving you, but it was necessary. After Prince Edward and his father approached Lord Maughan and me, we devised the plan, to feign enmity, to make it appear as though he coveted Colchester and your inheritance. It was the only way to draw Carsten into the open." He paused, his gaze steady.

"At no time was Maughan truly a threat to you, not until Carsten dragged Parliament into the matter. That was never part of the design."

Ellie's brows knit together. "But why was I not told?" she asked quietly. "Why keep me in the dark?"

"Because your reaction needed to be genuine." His voice softened as he leaned forward, folding his large hand gently over hers. "If you truly believed everything our family had built was at risk, you would fight for it with every ounce of spirit within you. And that, Danielle, was precisely what made the ruse believable."

She stared at him in astonishment, her voice catching. "But you hardly knew me, Grandfather. How could you be so certain how I would react?"

A shadow of a smile touched his mouth. "Because I had already seen you in action. The way you stood for your cousin, the ferocity with which you defended Eleanor when others might have yielded, that told me all I needed to know. You possessed the strength we required." His eyes softened further. "And," he added gently, "I recognized something else in you."

Curiosity stirred despite herself. "And what was that?"

His gaze grew distant, almost reverent. "Your great-great-grandmother's spirit. I told you before, she was fierce, determined, utterly unyielding when it came to protecting her family. I saw that same fire in your father when he was a young man. And now I see it burning just as brightly in you."

Ellie's throat tightened. She lifted her teacup and took a slow sip to steady herself before asking, more quietly still, "Did you think what happened with my cousins was connected to all this?"

He shook his head gravely. "No. I had no idea Lord Ainsworth was entangled in the same web of evil. But both Lord Bennett and Lord Wallace confirmed tonight that they recognized some of the men arrested, men they had previously seen in Ainsworth's company."

Silence settled again, broken only by the faint crackle of the fire. After a moment, Lord Huntington tilted his head, studying her closely.

"Tell me something, Danielle. How is it that you know how to load a pistol? You handled it like someone well practiced."

Ellie flushed, though she lifted her chin with quiet pride. "Papa taught me, two years ago. I pestered him for weeks. He insisted that such things were not meant for a lady, but I refused to relent. In the end he gave in." A faint, mischievous smile curved her lips. "He even showed me how to fire it. And I must confess... I am a fairly decent shot."

A bark of laughter escaped him, warm and unmistakably proud.

"I believe that with all my heart." His eyes twinkled as she lowered her gaze, her cheeks faintly pink. "By the way," he added, "I could not be more delighted about you and Lord Bennett. You make a handsome couple, and I daresay a formidable pair. Happiness, I think, is quite certain for the two of you."

Ellie's smile faltered slightly, worry clouding her expression. "Do you think my parents will approve of him as well?"

"Approve?" her grandfather scoffed gently, waving a dismissive hand. "Child, they already have. Bennett sought not only your father's permission but his blessing. Your father was quite taken with him when they met after Eleanor and Olivia were rescued." He leaned back comfortably.

"But even if they had harbored doubts, they would never deny you happiness. Their only wish is to see you well and content."

Ellie released a long breath, as though a weight had slipped from her chest.

"And what of the duchy?" she asked softly. "Of his own estate?"

"Bennett is more than willing to move to Colchester. The Wellington duchy remains in ruins since his uncle ordered it burned. Rebuilding has begun, but it is Lord Wallace who will inherit it, joining it with Plymouth." His expression darkened briefly.

"As for the house where Eleanor lived with Ainsworth... I expect it will be repurposed into a barony or something of the sort. Too much wickedness clings to those walls. Neither His Grace nor his nephews wish to dwell there."

"I cannot blame them," Ellie murmured. "For the Duke of Devon to return only to find his estate so defiled... it must have been dreadful."

Her grandfather nodded solemnly, then brushed the gloom aside with brisk practicality.

"Enough of dark matters. Let us speak of happier things. You are to be a bride, and soon." He rubbed his hands together thoughtfully.

"I propose we arrange the wedding before autumn steals the season from us. That gives us only a handful of weeks. I shall have the Colchester estate prepared for you and your husband, while I remain here in London. My obligations will keep me here, and it will be good for your tenants to meet their new mistress and master without me hovering at their side."

A flicker of doubt clouded Ellie's eyes. "Let us hope they will accept me, Grandfather. I am rather young to take on such a role."

Without a word, Lord Huntington rose and crossed the room. Taking her hand, he gently drew her to her feet and wrapped her in a firm, steady embrace.

"They will love you, Danielle," he said softly, his voice rumbling reassuringly above her head. "I have already instructed my steward to prepare them for your arrival. And in time they will not merely accept you, they will revere you." He gave her shoulders a gentle squeeze. "For you are every inch your great-great-grandmother's great-great-granddaughter."

Ellie closed her eyes, comforted by his words, and allowed herself to lean into the warmth of his promise.

Wedding preparations consumed the household in the weeks that followed. Every corridor seemed alive with movement, servants hurrying from chamber to chamber, hushed conversations drifting through open doorways, and the constant rustle of fabrics being carried from seamstress to fitting room and back again. The great house, once dignified and serene, now thrummed with cheerful chaos.

Florists arrived each morning bearing armfuls of fragrant blooms, roses, lilies, and delicate sprays of baby's breath that filled the air with sweetness. Vases were arranged, rearranged, and debated over with near-military seriousness. Meanwhile, the cooks in the kitchens tested menus with anxious precision, sending trays of pastries, soups, and roasted delicacies upstairs for approval.

Footmen hurried endlessly through the halls beneath the weight of deliveries, crates of fine wines, boxes of lace gloves, ribbons, candles, and countless other necessities no one had thought of until the very last moment. Excitement lingered everywhere, almost tangible in the air, mingling with Ellie's own mounting nerves.

Her family arrived a week before the ceremony, their presence transforming the house even further. Laughter echoed through the drawing rooms, conversations spilled into the corridors, and familiar voices rose in affectionate teasing that warmed Ellie's heart in ways she had long missed.

For the first time in many months, the house felt truly alive with family.

Yet beneath her bright smiles and eager participation in the endless preparations, Ellie's heart fluttered constantly with a restless mixture of joy and trepidation. The nearer the special day drew, the more she felt herself suspended between anxious anticipation and a happiness so sharp it almost frightened her. She was about to marry the man who had stolen her heart. *Andrew.*

The very thought of him made warmth bloom inside her chest. His steady gaze had become a source of comfort she found herself seeking again and again. His strong arms, once so teasingly confident, had become her safe harbor in moments when the future felt overwhelming. He visited whenever propriety allowed, sometimes under the polite supervision of chaperones, sometimes merely to exchange a few hurried words before being ushered away again.

At times he offered little more than a quiet word of encouragement, spoken softly so that only she could hear. At others he would steal a moment to clasp her hands or brush his fingers lightly along her sleeve, small gestures that sent her pulse tumbling wildly.

Once or twice, he had even dared to pull her into a brief, unannounced embrace when no one was looking, an action that left her cheeks flaming and her heart racing for hours afterward. But always his eyes held the same warmth. The same unwavering certainty. And with every moment spent in his presence, Ellie understood more clearly what had once frightened her to admit. She loved him. Without condition. Without hesitation. Without end.

Two days before the wedding, a maid informed Ellie that she was wanted in the drawing room. Expecting a cheerful tea with her parents and sisters, she entered with light steps, only to stop short in surprise. Sitting primly on the edge of a chair, her hands folded nervously in her lap, was Felicity Appleton. Ellie's breath caught. She had not seen Felicity since the dreadful ball at Ainsworth's estate, and the sight of her now, without her mother's domineering presence, was startling.

Felicity appeared subdued, almost timid, so unlike the haughty young woman Ellie remembered. Recovering quickly, Ellie crossed the room and gestured politely toward another seat.

"What can I do for you, Felicity?"

The young woman rose to curtsy before sitting again, her composure clearly strained. Ellie noticed how her fingers twisted in her lap, her eyes darting everywhere except directly at her.

To ease the tension, Ellie cleared her throat and asked gently, "Is your father here with you?"

Felicity shook her head. "He arrives tomorrow. I have been staying with relatives in the meantime."

An awkward silence followed, heavy enough to press upon Ellie's chest. Before she could think of another polite question, Felicity drew in a breath and spoke.

"I have wanted to apologize to you for a long time, Lady Danielle." Her voice trembled, though she steadied it with effort. "After Lord Ainsworth was arrested, and my mother and I were placed under house arrest, I believed my life was over, that I would be sent away to live with my mother's family. But then my father told me he had spoken to you... and that you had suggested he give me another chance."

"That is correct," Ellie replied softly.

"Why?" Felicity asked, lifting her eyes at last. Confusion shone plainly in them. "Why would you do that? I treated you horribly, just as my mother did. I was cruel to other women as well. I gave you no reason to show me mercy."

Ellie sighed quietly, her expression gentling. "Because I pitied you, Felicity. I could not bear to see your entire life ruined because of the example your mother set. Yes, you are responsible for your own choices now, but anyone could see how heavily her influence weighed upon you." She paused before continuing more gently.

"I believed that once you were free from her grasp, you might change. And I trusted your father's good sense to guide you more kindly than she ever did."

Tears shimmered in Felicity's eyes. "Thank you."

"There is no need to thank me," Ellie said firmly. "Simply prove that you are more than her shadow. Show us that you carry more of your father's goodness than your mother's cruelty."

Felicity nodded tentatively. "I will try. My aunt and uncle here in London have shown me kindness, but they have also been... firm. They do not allow me to excuse myself as I once did. Their lessons have been difficult, yet I see now how blind I was to my mother's faults."

Ellie tilted her head thoughtfully. "That cannot have been easy to accept. But surely, even while your mother controlled everything, you must have resented her interference. Were there not young men you found interesting, only for her to drive them away in hopes of securing a more advantageous match?"

A reluctant smile flickered across Felicity's lips before fading.

"Yes... there were such moments. And once... a young man told me outright that no one would ever marry me if I continued to behave like a spoiled brat." Her voice caught, tears gathering again at the corners of her eyes.

"It cut deeply," she admitted quietly, "though I knew he spoke the truth."

"The truth often wounds," Ellie said softly. "But it also teaches. If we allow it to, it can set us upon a better path."

For a moment Felicity sat silently, dabbing at the corner of her eye. Then she said quietly, "Father does not allow me to see my mother. At first, I was devastated… but also relieved. She will never change, and her letters prove it." She hesitated before continuing.

"I am permitted to write to her, but only under my aunt's supervision. She reads every word I send, and every letter my mother writes in return."

Ellie felt a tightness in her chest. It must feel suffocating, and yet she understood why it was necessary.

"At first I hated it," Felicity admitted. "I thought it a terrible invasion. But soon I realized my aunt was protecting me. My mother's words are vicious, always grasping, always trying to reassert control. My aunt answers with sharp rebukes, refusing to allow her poisonous influence to pass unchecked."

"I suppose that means your mother still refuses to accept any blame for what she has done?"

Felicity's mouth twisted bitterly. "Yes. She will never accept it. Father says only a miracle could make her admit fault. He also tells me my uncle, her brother, is harsh with her. Ruthless, even. But he insists it is the only way to contain her. If he shows the slightest softness, she will seize upon it and rule over him as she has tried to rule over everyone else."

Ellie's eyes narrowed thoughtfully. "Do you think she still parades herself as a baroness?"

Felicity gave a short, bitter laugh. "Yes. She still clings to her title, though no one acknowledges it. Father said she attempted to maintain her old friendships among the ton, but they have all turned their backs on her. Now she is ignored, shunned." She paused before adding quietly, "She even threatened to refuse signing the divorce papers, but my uncle forced her hand."

"Will he keep her in his household?" Ellie asked. Felicity shook her head.

"No. Father has purchased a small cottage near my uncle's farm and gifted it to him. They are determined she will work for her bread, though they will ensure she does not starve. She must learn, at last, that her days of indulgence and vanity are over."

Ellie leaned back slightly in her chair, watching Felicity with a mixture of sympathy and caution. Beneath the wounded pride and lingering bitterness, there was indeed something new in the young woman's expression. A fragile, uncertain beginning.

Perhaps, Ellie thought, *the faintest chance of change.*

The household buzzed like a hive on that bright morning. Servants hurried through the corridors carrying ribbons, bouquets, and freshly polished shoes. Laughter and cheerful chatter floated through the air as relatives gathered, preparing to leave for the church. The grand day had finally arrived. Ellie's wedding day.

Her mother was in a flurry of tears and tissues, alternating between issuing brisk instructions to the maids and dabbing her eyes with delicate lace handkerchiefs. Guests arrived steadily, filling the halls with cheerful voices and the soft rustle of silks and satin. And in the midst of it all stood Danielle, radiant in her wedding gown, her nerves thrumming like a taut violin string. She clasped her hands together, willing her breath to steady, when the door opened and a familiar figure stepped inside.

"Eleanor!" Ellie gasped, joy lighting her face. Without hesitation she crossed the room, and the cousins folded into each other's arms, holding on as though neither wished to let go. Tears glistened in both their eyes, mingling with smiles too full to contain.

"I never had the chance to thank you properly," Eleanor whispered, her voice breaking with emotion. "For everything you did, for all the risks you took for me. My heart cannot begin to express how much it means. I shall be in your debt all my life."

Ellie drew back just enough to meet her gaze, her hands still resting gently on her cousin's shoulders.

"Nonsense," she said warmly. "There is no debt between us. You are my family, my friend, my sister in every way that matters. No matter the danger, I would do it all again, for you, or for anyone I love."

Eleanor's lip trembled, and she pressed her forehead briefly to Ellie's before drawing back. Ellie's expression softened into a radiant smile.

"And tell me," she asked gently, "have you begun to heal? Not only from your injuries, but from that dreadful marriage?"

This time Eleanor's eyes shone with something brighter than tears, happiness.

"Yes. Lord Ainsworth has done everything in his power to restore me. He insists on spoiling me, showering me with comforts and reassurances I hardly deserve. I keep telling him he owes me nothing, that none of this was his fault, but still he persists." Her smile deepened with quiet affection.

"He is the kindest, most generous of men, and I am grateful that he is still in my life. If there was one good thing to come from that terrible union with his nephew, it is that it led me to his care and friendship."

Ellie smiled knowingly. "And what of Lord Wallace? Has he remained with his grandfather all this while?"

At the mention of his name, a rosy blush crept across Eleanor's cheeks. She lowered her eyes, though the warmth of her expression betrayed her. Ellie's grin widened.

"Yes," Eleanor admitted softly. "He has been most attentive, always thoughtful. And he has become a dear friend."

"A dear friend?" Ellie teased, arching a brow. "Are you quite certain it is only friendship, Eleanor?"

Eleanor's blush deepened as she shook her head slightly.

"Oh, Ellie, you must not tease me so. He has shown no interest beyond kindness, and I would not expect it. After what I endured... after what my husband made of me, I fear I can never again be a woman of worth in any man's eyes."

Ellie's heart clenched at the quiet despair in her cousin's voice. She clasped Eleanor's hands firmly, her own voice fierce with conviction.

"You are wrong, Eleanor. So very wrong. Nothing your husband did, no cruelty, no degradation, has the power to strip away your beauty, your dignity, or your worth. Those belong to you, and no man, least of all that wretch, can take them." Her grip tightened gently.

"You are still the Eleanor I have always loved: gracious, charming, and strong. And any man with sense will see it too. Do not allow the ghost of your husband to linger in your mind. Do not let him hold power over you even now." She smiled softly.

"Cast him off, and make room for men with honorable, tender hearts, men who will treat you as you have always deserved to be treated."

Eleanor's eyes shimmered with fresh tears, though this time they sprang from hope rather than pain. She squeezed Ellie's hands tightly and whispered, "You always know just what to say."

Ellie smiled, her nerves for the ceremony momentarily forgotten as love and strength flowed between them. For that moment, it felt less like a wedding morning and more like a renewal of family bonds, of hearts mended and futures reclaimed.

Before long, Ellie found herself standing beside Andrew at the altar, her hand trembling only slightly in his as the minister spoke the final words of the ceremony. The church seemed to glow with soft afternoon light streaming through the tall stained glass windows. Friends and family filled the pews, their faces bright with anticipation, yet Ellie scarcely noticed any of them. Her world had narrowed to the warmth of Andrew's hand wrapped firmly around hers. His thumb brushed gently over her knuckles, a quiet reassurance that steadied the fluttering storm inside her chest.

The solemn vows and promises, spoken before God and those they loved, passed like a dream. Ellie heard her own voice answer, heard Andrew's low, steady reply, but the words themselves seemed to blur into the overwhelming certainty of the moment. At last, the minister's voice rang clearly through the chapel.

"By the authority vested in me, I now pronounce you husband and wife."

A hush fell. Andrew turned toward her. His eyes glowed with unmistakable warmth, the fierce tenderness in his gaze stealing the breath from her lungs. For one suspended heartbeat, neither of them moved. Then his hand rose gently to cradle her cheek. Ellie barely had time to draw a breath before his lips claimed hers. The kiss was deep and reverent, yet filled with unmistakable passion, a promise sealed not only with duty, but with love.

A delighted cheer rose from the congregation. For a brief, shining moment the world disappeared entirely. There was only the warmth of his arms around her, the steady strength of his embrace, and the lingering sweetness of his kiss. When they finally parted, laughter and applause erupted around them. They were immediately surrounded, embraced by jubilant relatives, clasped by friends, and showered with congratulations from every direction.

27

The Price of Love

Hand in hand, smiling and radiant, the newlyweds were guided outside into the golden warmth of the afternoon. Church bells began to toll joyfully. The waiting crowd erupted into cheers. Rice rained down in playful showers, scattering into Ellie's hair and across the stone steps as she ducked against Andrew's shoulder, laughing as the grains bounced harmlessly from her gown. Andrew only laughed with her, his arm instinctively tightening around her waist. With a flourish, he guided his bride toward the waiting carriage.

Before climbing inside, he turned and signaled to his steward and first footman, who stepped forward carrying small leather pouches. Grinning broadly, Andrew scooped up handfuls of shining coins and scattered them into the gathered crowd. A fresh roar of cheers erupted as men and women bent eagerly to gather the glittering gifts, voices rising in delighted blessings for the generous new husband. Ellie laughed at the spectacle.

Not to be outdone, she reached into the small basket she carried and began handing out sweets, sugar-dusted candies and little wrapped chocolates. Children rushed forward at once, their bright eyes shining with excitement as they jostled one another to reach her.

Ellie's heart swelled at the sight. She leaned down with a warm smile, pressing a chocolate into the eager palm of a wide-eyed little girl whose delighted grin could have melted stone. At last, the basket stood empty and the final coins were gathered. Andrew turned back to her, his eyes warm with unmistakable pride. With exaggerated courtliness, he bowed and offered his hand.

"Your carriage awaits, My Lady."

Ellie laughed softly and placed her hand in his. His grip was steady at her waist as he helped her into the carriage. The door closed behind them with a solid click. Outside, the coachman cracked the reins. The horses surged forward, and the wheels began their steady rhythm across the cobbled street as the cheering crowd slowly faded behind them.

For a moment they simply looked at one another. Then Andrew moved. With one swift motion he drew his bride into his arms, tilting her face upward toward his. This time there were no watchful relatives, no eager guests. Only the quiet privacy of the carriage. Their lips met again, freely now, without restraint, the kiss deepened by the thrill of belonging wholly to one another.

Ellie melted against him, her hands curling instinctively into the fabric of his coat as the carriage rattled through the streets. His arm tightened around her, holding her close as though reluctant to ever release her again. Outside, the city continued on as it always had. But inside the carriage, Ellie felt the world shift beneath her feet. The life she had known was behind her. And ahead of them, waiting just beyond the next turn of the road, was the first chapter of their new life together.

Relatives and friends of the bride and groom gathered that afternoon at the London country estate of the Duke of Huntington, eager to prolong the joyful celebration. The gardens, alive with the scent of roses and the gentle hum of bees, provided a perfect backdrop for laughter and cheerful conversation.

Children darted along the gravel paths while musicians strummed light, cheerful tunes beneath a nearby pavilion. Servants circulated among the guests with trays of sparkling punch, delicate pastries, and savory meats, ensuring that every visitor was well attended.

Eleanor stood quietly at her sister's side as she conversed with their aunt and uncle. Though still reserved in large company, she allowed herself a small smile when Lord Wallace approached, his manner warm and reassuring. Her mother trailed close behind him, ever watchful, as though determined not to let her daughter stray beyond her protection.

The festivities carried on in easy cheer until a sudden, sharp gasp tore through the merriment. Ellie's mother clutched her husband's arm, her eyes wide with horror. Instantly, a hush fell over the gathering. Every face turned toward the sound. Conversations died as gazes swept toward a cluster of thick bushes at the far end of the lawn.

At first, nothing stirred, only the rustle of green leaves shifting in the warm summer breeze. Then, as if conjured from the shadows themselves, a man stepped out. His clothing was disheveled, his hair matted, and in his hand gleamed the unmistakable barrel of a pistol, already raised and steady.

Murmurs rippled through the crowd before fading into terrified silence.

"Magnus." Ellie's father's voice rang with fury as he moved swiftly to shield his wife and daughters with his own body. The color had drained from his face, yet his eyes burned with controlled wrath. "What are you doing here? How did you escape prison?"

His brother-in-law's lips twisted into a sneer. A low, devilish laugh slipped from him, sending several ladies gasping and shrinking back.

"Ah, dear Benedict," Magnus drawled mockingly, "you always did underestimate me. Someone owed me a favor, and a prison guard proved quite easy to persuade, with the proper bribe."

"You are not welcome here," Benedict barked, his voice sharp as steel. He shifted his stance, keeping his family firmly behind him. "Leave at once before worse befalls you."

"Drop the weapon, sir, or you will not leave here alive." Gordon's voice thundered from across the lawn. The duke's steward had also taken position, his pistol drawn and aimed with deadly precision. Several of the duke's footmen emerged from the hedges at the same moment, flanking Magnus in a tightening semicircle. Each man held a weapon trained upon him. Their expressions were grim and unyielding.

For a moment, Magnus merely laughed, a harsh, broken sound that cut through the thick tension like a blade. Then, without warning, he swung his pistol toward his wife. Gasps and cries erupted. Ladies clutched their pearls while children were hastily gathered into their mothers' arms.

Before anyone could react, Magnus shifted his aim again, his eyes gleaming with cold malice as he fixed them upon his daughter. Eleanor's breath caught. Her hand flew to her chest, yet she stood frozen where she was, unable to move. Two deafening shots split the summer air.

As soon as Danielle and Andrew arrived at the Colchester estate, a small group of servants hurried forward to greet them, their faces bright with warm smiles and respectful bows. The butler stepped forward first, dignified and welcoming, while the housekeeper followed close behind. Together they guided the young couple through the grand halls, their footsteps echoing softly beneath the high ceilings as they led them toward the master bedchamber prepared for their arrival.

The estate seemed to glow in quiet anticipation. Lamps burned warmly along the corridor, their golden light reflecting off polished wood and framed portraits that lined the walls. When the doors to the bedchamber opened, the care taken for their comfort was immediately evident. A fire crackled gently in the hearth, casting soft flickers of amber light across the room. The bed stood ready with freshly turned linens and embroidered pillows, the coverlet smoothed with meticulous care. Nearby, a small table held a tray prepared for them, warm bread, roasted meats, fruit, and a decanter of wine accompanied by two crystal glasses.

Everything had been arranged to welcome the new lord and lady of Colchester. The servants bowed once more before quietly withdrawing. When the door closed behind them, a deep hush settled over the chamber, broken only by the soft crackle of the fire and the faint rustle of Danielle's gown as she turned. Andrew was watching her. The warmth in his gaze stole her breath.

For a moment neither of them spoke. The long journey, the wedding, the endless congratulations, all of it seemed to fade away until there were only the two of them standing together in the quiet glow of the firelight.

Andrew stepped toward her slowly. His expression softened, though the intensity in his eyes burned brighter with every step. Without hesitation, he gathered her in his arms. His lips found hers in a kiss that was at once tender and fiercely possessive, the kind of kiss that seemed to hold every unspoken promise between them.

Danielle clung to him instinctively, her heart racing wildly as warmth rushed through her. The world seemed to tilt beneath her feet as she lost herself in the strength of his embrace and the steady certainty of his touch. His hand slid gently along her back, drawing her closer still. Before she could catch her breath, Andrew lifted her into his arms as though she weighed nothing at all.

A soft laugh escaped her in surprise, though it quickly melted into another kiss as his mouth returned to hers. The kiss deepened, slow and lingering, filled with the quiet urgency of two hearts that had waited far too long to belong to one another. He carried her across the chamber toward the hearth, where the dancing firelight wrapped around them in warm shades of gold. There he set her gently upon her feet.

For a moment he simply looked at her. The flickering glow of the flames shimmered along the ivory folds of her gown, catching in the delicate embroidery and turning her veil to a soft halo of light. Andrew lifted his hands to her face, cupping her cheeks with reverent care. His thumb brushed tenderly along her skin as though committing every detail of her to memory.

"You are mine now, Danielle," he murmured, his voice thick with emotion. His forehead rested briefly against hers. "And I am forever yours."

Danielle's breath trembled as she looked up at him, her heart overflowing with the quiet certainty she had once feared to trust. She slid her hands into his, her fingers threading through his with gentle strength.

"Then we shall belong to one another," she whispered softly, her eyes shining in the firelight, "for all our days."

Andrew's answering smile held both tenderness and fierce devotion. And as the firelight flickered around them, the quiet room bore witness to the beginning of their life together.

The morning sun pushed stubbornly through the heavy curtains, spilling warm golden light across the chamber. Ellie stirred slowly, blinking as consciousness returned. For a moment she lay perfectly still, unsure why she felt so warm, so wonderfully secure. Then she realized. She was still nestled comfortably within her husband's arms.

A soft smile curved her lips as she listened to the steady rhythm of Andrew's breathing against her hair. One of his arms was draped protectively around her waist, holding her close even in sleep, as though some instinct within him refused to let her drift too far away. For a blissful moment she lingered there, content and safe. The previous day returned to her in gentle fragments, the vows, the cheers, the carriage ride, the quiet warmth of the firelight in their chamber.

Her cheeks warmed. Very carefully, she tilted her head upward. Her breath caught. Andrew's bare chest rose and fell slowly with each breath, the broad strength of his shoulders half-covered by the rumpled sheets. In the clear light of morning, she became suddenly aware of just how close she was, how very *married* she now was.

Her cheeks went wildfire. Perhaps she could slip away quietly before he woke. Slowly, very slowly, she attempted to ease herself from his hold. The movement was slight. Unfortunately, it was also enough. Andrew shifted, his arm tightening instinctively around her waist before his eyes opened. A lazy, thoroughly amused smile appeared the moment he caught sight of her blush.

"Do you have somewhere urgent to be?" he asked. His voice was deep and rough with sleep, the sound of it sending a curious little shiver down her spine. Ellie nearly jumped.

"We... we should probably get up," she whispered, her voice betraying far more shyness than she intended. Andrew glanced toward the bright sliver of sunlight creeping across the bed before returning his gaze to her.

"I see no compelling reason," he replied dryly. "In fact, I believe we are entirely entitled to remain here all day." His smile widened slightly. "After all, we are newlyweds."

Ellie turned her face away at once, though the smile tugging at her lips betrayed her. But Andrew had no intention of letting her escape so easily. His fingers slid gently beneath her chin, turning her face back toward him. Before she could protest, his lips brushed hers.

The kiss was slow and unhurried, warm, familiar, and entirely irresistible. Ellie melted against him before she could remember any of the sensible arguments she had prepared. His arms tightened around her, drawing her closer as though he intended to prove precisely why remaining in bed was such an excellent idea. Just as the moment deepened—

Knock. Knock. The sound shattered the quiet intimacy like a stone through glass. Andrew broke the kiss with a long-suffering sigh before pressing one last lingering kiss to her forehead.

"I shall have to demand considerably more privacy from the staff," he murmured. He slipped from the bed in one smooth motion. Ellie immediately grabbed her dressing gown, wrapping it hastily around herself while her cheeks continued to burn.

"You might wish to put on a shirt, Your Grace," she said hurriedly. "The staff should not see you like this."

Andrew paused mid-step. Slowly, he turned back toward her with a wicked grin.

"Is that so?" he asked lightly. "And why, pray tell, should I put on a shirt?"

Ellie's blush deepened, though she lifted her chin bravely. "Because it is not proper," she said firmly. Then, after a moment, she added with shy determination, "Besides... you are married now. Which means only *I* am allowed to see your manly chest."

Andrew stared at her for half a second. Then he threw back his head and laughed, a rich, delighted laugh that filled the room.

"Noted, My Lady," he said, still grinning. He disappeared behind the room divider to dress. Ellie was still attempting to regain her composure when she finally opened the door. The butler stood waiting in the corridor. He bowed deeply.

"Forgive the intrusion, Your Grace," he said gravely. "But an express has just arrived from Lord Huntington." He handed her a sealed letter before withdrawing quietly. Ellie's fingers trembled slightly as she broke the seal. Andrew stepped beside her a moment later, slipping an arm gently around her waist as she unfolded the letter.

Her lips moved silently as she read. Then the words reached her.

Danielle,

I am sorry to disturb you and your husband so soon, but tragedy has befallen us. Your uncle has escaped from prison. He came to the reception after you departed and opened fire. Your aunt was struck, and though Eleanor was nearly hit, Lord Wallace threw himself in her path and received the bullet instead.

I grieve to tell you that your aunt passed away from her wound. Lord Wallace yet lives, but his condition is grave and uncertain. Your mother, sisters, and cousins are overwhelmed with grief, and I have promised your mother that I would send for you at once.

I know this is not what one hopes for newlyweds, but your family needs you now. Your uncle was killed, but the shadow he cast still lingers. I fear I can offer your mother and sisters little comfort until you arrive.

Lord Henry Benedict Huntington

A broken sob escaped her throat. The letter slipped from her trembling fingers as tears spilled down her cheeks. Andrew caught her instantly, pulling her tightly into his arms.

“Hush, my love,” he murmured, pressing gentle kisses against her damp cheeks. “What is it?”

He picked up the fallen letter and quickly scanned the contents. His expression hardened. Without hesitation he rang for the butler.

“We leave at once,” he said firmly when the man appeared. “Have the carriage prepared immediately. Our trunks are to be packed within the hour.”

Servants flew into motion at once, their hurried footsteps echoing through the corridors. Ellie clung to Andrew as her sobs softened into quiet tears. After a moment he gently lifted her chin so their eyes met.

“We leave as soon as the carriage is ready,” he promised softly. His jaw tightened, a storm gathering behind the calm in his gaze. “And if God wills, Wallace will survive this attack.” His voice grew colder.

“But hear me also, Danielle, whoever aided your uncle’s escape will face justice. He knew what your uncle intended, and he will answer for it.” His arm tightened protectively around her shoulders. “None who conspire to spill innocent blood shall go unpunished.” He drew her close again, pressing her head against his chest. And at that moment Ellie realized something that steadied her heart. The grief waiting for her in London would be heavy. But she would not face it alone.

-To be continued-

Did you love *Duchess in Waiting*? Then you should read *A Duke For Eleanor*[1] by Rebecca Lange!

[2]

A shattered life. A fearless cousin. A chance to begin again."

Eleanor Huntington has lost everything—her parents, her home, even her title. Scarred by a cruel marriage and trapped by society's scorn, the only light in her dark world is Lord Joshua Wallace, the man who once saved her. But with his family determined to keep them apart, Eleanor fears she will never escape her past.

Her cousin Danielle, a fiery young duchess, refuses to let the ton dictate Eleanor's fate. Defying hypocrisy and scandal,

1. https://books2read.com/u/496Br0
2. https://books2read.com/u/496Br0

she shields her cousin and uncovers secrets powerful enough to change everything.

As Eleanor struggles to believe she deserves love and happiness, the truth that Danielle unearths may give her the courage to claim both—if society doesn't silence her first.

About the Author

Rebecca Lange is a devoted romantic at heart. Though she has explored a variety of genres throughout her writing journey, her deepest passion lies in historical fiction—particularly stories set in the 1800s American West and the Regency era.

A passionate advocate, Rebecca uses her stories to raise awareness of abuse, human trafficking, and the devastating impact of drug and alcohol addiction. These themes are not woven in for suspense alone, but as a reminder that such struggles are tragically real—and that victims are never to blame.

She is also a firm believer in women's rights, inspired by the courageous women of the 1800s who fought to prove they were not the property of their husbands but their partners and equals. Rebecca upholds the conviction that violence has no place in relationships or marriage.

Originally from Germany, she was born and raised there before moving abroad in 2002 to serve a mission for her church in Scotland. A member of The Church of Jesus Christ of Latter-day Saints, she now lives in Utah with her husband, their two sons (ages 18 and 20), and two lively Yorkie puppies.

Her writing motto is: *Never Smut, Always Sizzling Kisses, Consistently Closed Door.* Rebecca delights in weaving passion and tenderness into her stories, offering what she calls "sweet and diet spice" romance. Diet spice—what is that, you ask? It's the thrill of longing gazes, passionate kisses, and close embraces that build anticipation without ever crossing into explicit territory. For her, the most powerful love stories are those that remain tasteful and teasing, proving that romance can be both heart-stirring and wholesome.

Read more at https://authorrebeccalange.wixsite.com/bookstolove.

www.ingramcontent.com/pod-product-compliance
Lightning Source LLC
LaVergne TN
LVHW020649110826
845149LV00012B/1954

* 9 7 8 1 9 5 7 0 8 9 3 3 1 *